The Ch

Janson Mancheski

Table of Contents

Also by Janson Mancheski:
The Chemist
Trail of Evil
Mask of Bone
Shoot For the Stars
The Scrub
Drowning a Ghost

The Greatest Hits—Best of The Chemist Series
In memory of my brother-in-law, the late Norbert "Nubs" DeCleene, a gallant marine, a good cop, and a rarity today: an honest politician. Now patrolling the skies as a guardian angel.

1. http://jansonmancheski.com/

2. http://jansonmancheski.com/

The Chemist

The Chemist Series – Book One

Original Copyright © 2011 Janson Mancheski

THE CHEMIST

Library of Congress Control Number: 2011914807

Printed in the United States of America

Fearless Publishing House rev. Dates: 12/23/2019

3rd Revised Edition

TABLE OF CONTENTS

PROLOGUE

Jagged clouds scudded across the starless June night sky. A dark SUV bounced along the gravel access road, the countryside vegetation thick on each side and covered by tall trees. The foliage thinned near a small boat landing where fresh lake waters lapped at the rocky shoreline.

The SUV eased to a halt—three men with skin as dark as the surroundings emerged, closing the doors. The night was serene, the humid air thrumming with insects abuzz in the unkempt patches of sawgrass.

One of the men popped the vehicle's rear latch and opened the backdoor. They lifted an unconscious woman with modest effort—naked and gagged, wrists and ankles bound with plastic zip-ties—from inside.

Barrel-chested and pock-faced, the team leader was an African in a dark sports jacket. Sleeves pushed up to his elbows. He led the silent procession, his underlings carrying the woman up the narrow dock toward a small skiff rocking gently in the water. Minutes later, they headed across Lake Michigan, the sky heavy above them like a black coverlet.

The skiff's engine was cut a quarter mile out, and the craft bobbed in deep water. One of the men used a knife to slice the plastic ties that bound the woman's hands and feet. He removed the gag from her mouth. They raised their silent victim to a kneeling position on the boat's port side. Behind her, the bulky African withdrew a ceremonial sword from a case of polished teakwood.

"Keep her head up," he ordered, speaking his native tongue.

One underling grabbed a fistful of the woman's blonde hair, holding his arm straight. He leaned aside, mindful of the blade's impending arc.

The woman moaned, coming around from her stupor. She sensed the danger on some limbic level.

The African swung the blade through the still night air. A wave slapped against the skiff's port side, making a sound like halving a watermelon. The men then pitched the woman's headless body into the black water with the ghost of a splash. The lake's giant mouth had swallowed a new victim.

"The head, too?" The man still held the dripping, stark-eyed object by the hair like a pumpkin by its stem.

8

The larger African wiped his blade clean with a soft cloth and placed it inside the ornate wooden case. "Double–bag it into the container. No bloodstains on the boat."

The skiff headed back toward the silhouetted shoreline, almost invisible against the starless sky.

"What you want the head for?" the holder asked, uneasy.

The pock–faced African's smirk was invisible in the darkness. "Make a good paperweight."

The massive cargo freighter *Kwensana* sat perched in high water at the North Shore docks in the port of Chicago. The city's famous skyline stood guard in the background, stretching high enough to graze the low ceiling of the bruise-colored clouds. It was a windy, gloom-filled night, but the ship was too large to be affected by the breeze rocking her imperceptibly against the thick-roped moorings.

The bulky African lumbered along the freighter's deck in a dark business suit, phone in hand. Behind him in dark coveralls, his two partners carried a heavy canvas sack. The parade went to the hatchway and disappeared inside out of the wind.

Deep in the *Kwensana's* cargo hold, three oversized crates stood empty in a private storage area. The crates, upright, were warning labeled: DANGER. EXOTIC ANIMALS. DO NOT TOUCH. Each crate bore a series of perforations near its base and upper lid, allowing air circulation inside. Large skull-and-cross bones were stamped in black ink on all sides—warnings to inquisitive workers.

The men set their sacks down on the cool floor. The giant African muttered something, and the men unfastened the canvas bags and unveiled a pair of unconscious females. The women were garbed in loose-fitting hospital scrubs, shoeless. Their mouths were gagged with cloth and hands bound behind their backs.

"The third box?" one worker asked.

"Maybe just your size?" The African leader let out a throaty laugh. His partners joined nervously, not sure if he was kidding.

The workers tipped one of the boxes sideways, lowering it to the floor. They unfastened the lid and eased one of the women inside. Feet first, they pushed, pressed, and slid her into the coffin-like crate. They secured the top and raised it back upright.

Then they moved to the second crate.

PART ONE
CHASING A GHOST

CHAPTER 1

On a Friday morning in spring, a blue windowless panel van sat as patient as a hearse parked outside a church. Puddles spotted the grocery store's parking lot, the final traces of winter snowmelt. The chemist had taken less than thirty minutes to spot his victim. A slender, determined young woman—age twenty-two, twenty-three—exited her green Honda Civic and walked toward the store's entrance. She was blond and dressed in workout leggings and an oversized sweatshirt. Judging from her gait and demeanor, he calculated she would not be inside for long.

A worn leather medical bag sat on the van's passenger seat. He opened the wings and withdrew a plastic squeeze bottle filled with clear liquid. The wording on the bottle read "Compact Disc Cleaning Fluid."

Gazing out the van's front windows and checking all directions, the chemist exited the vehicle. He was a picture of calm as he strolled around his van under the pretense of checking tire pressures. He wore black jeans and a dark navy peacoat with the collar up. His ballcap was low to hamper the CCTV. He also wore thin lambskin gloves.

No actor in Hollywood could have feigned interest in Goodyear Polytreads with greater aplomb. From the corner of his eye, he watched a handful of people move toward the store's front entrance. As far as they were concerned, he might as well be invisible.

Wandering from the van, he slipped between the rows of parked cars. He sidestepped a bumper, then a wayward shopping cart. Withdrawing the plastic bottle from his coat pocket, he doused the driver's-door handle with a clear, slightly viscous fluid.

Back inside his van, he fought to keep his heart from galloping. His forehead felt damp near the hairline, and his shirt clammy at his lower back. The trap was set. It was time now to sit and wait.

Rain clouds above were threatening, and any chance of precipitation concerned the chemist. Dilution might affect the solution's effectiveness. He stared out the window and watched the store's automatic doors open and close. Dark tortoise-shell glasses framed the eyes of a predator. Patience, he reminded himself. Wait for the trap to be sprung.

While he waited, he eyed the medical bag sitting on the seat beside him. The liquid concoction inside was his most pleasing discovery. It had transformed him. Set him on his course of liberation? Yes, it was accurate. Thanks to his invention, he had never felt so free. The simple chemical compound had turned him from a casual dreamer into a catcher of dreams.

"Dream catcher," he said aloud. The chemist smiled. He liked the way it sounded.

The doors to the store slid open again, and the girl in the workout leggings and sweatshirt appeared and moved in the direction of her car.

His gloved hands gripped the steering wheel. He could discern the narrow lines of her body as she walked, dodging muddy puddles in her white cross-trainers. Perfect balance. Lean and graceful as a dancer.

Lost in thought, she paid little attention to the meandering people who moved around her. And even less to the blue van parked three slots down from her car.

The chemist turned the ignition key.

Cindy Hulbreth tucked the grocery bag under one arm and fished in her sweatshirt pocket for her keys. She popped the door locks of her Civic with the remote, grabbed the door handle, and opened the door. The handle was slick with what she decided was mist. She stared at her hand, rubbed her fingertips together, and sniffed them. It felt weird, but no odor existed. She smoothed the dampness off on her leggings, deciding it shouldn't stain.

Cindy placed her groceries in the tiny backseat. She slipped inside, pulling the door closed. As she fumbled with her keys, she glanced in her rearview mirror. Some idiot in a blue van had pulled in behind her, blocking the way. She exhaled, sliding the key into the ignition but not turning it. Another glance in the rearview showed the van still there.

Turning in her seat, staring out the back window, Cindy wondered what the hold-up was. The van remained in place as if waiting for someone up ahead. Some other car? An elderly pedestrian with a shopping cart?

She considered leaning on her horn. She didn't want to be rude, but her clothes were gamey from her workout, and a hot shower awaited her at home.

Cindy ran her tongue over her teeth. Her mouth felt cottony. She licked her lips for moisture and rummaged through her pocketbook for a piece of gum. She crumpled the wrapper in the ashtray and glanced again out the back window.

One-forty-six. One-forty-five, one-forty-four...

The chemist glanced at his wristwatch above the edge of his glove. The silent countdown in his head matched the precise time on the onyx dial.

Becoming vexed, her forehead growing warm, and her neck flushed, Cindy watched the van sitting behind her like a lump.

"Get a move on!" she shouted. "Move your fat blue butt!"

She blinked, staring out the front windshield at nothing through widened eyes—cars, the parking lot, the gray April sky. Small auburn blotches, web-like, bloomed at the periphery of her vision. Shaking her head, the blotches failed to dissolve. Should she be amused? she wondered. Brown kaleidoscopic patches were now spreading across her visual field. Sparkles shot off at the distant edges. My God! Watching this would be entertaining if she didn't feel so rotten. Fireworks were going off inside her eyeballs.

Thirty. Twenty-nine, twenty-eight...

Cindy's chin drooped against her chest like of prizefighter between rounds. Rubber Leg Street, she remembered her dad calling it once while watching a boxing match. She remembered laughing at the term. She'd been ten or eleven at the time. This moment was far less humorous. Her head was as heavy as a concrete block.

A rush of panic made her cry out. A rasping sound escaped her lips.

The chemist watched the girl inside the car keel sideways, restrained by her seat belt like a pilot who'd crashed.

Checking his mirrors, front and behind, he eased the van forward and pulled into an open slot up the row. Exiting, his hands inside his peacoat, he moved forward. Exposed now, he walked between the cars with his head down.

He opened the Civic's passenger door and leaned inside. Three times previously, a year ago, he had learned that the passenger-side door provided the best access to the seat belt clasp. It was easier to pull an unconscious person toward you than push one away.

He unlatched the buckle, and the girl toppled toward him onto the passenger side. He pulled her into the vacant seat, grasping her beneath one arm and the opposite shoulder.

Seconds ticked in his head. The chemist closed her car door and edged around to the driver's side. Employing the hem of his dark coat, he cleaned the door handle of residue. He opened it and slipped inside.

Silence.

Save for the roar of pulse in his ears. His heart was tom-tomming against his sternum, but *wow,* if he didn't feel *alive.* With a gloved finger, he touched the girl's neck. Her pulse, unlike his own, seemed steady. Her heart-shaped face was pretty, even without makeup. After a workout, rained upon, and her face slackened from her stupor, he doubted she'd consider herself attractive. How wrong she was.

In the distance, a dozen people strode in different directions, moving with apparent purpose and bored looks.

Key already in the ignition, the chemist started the car and eased from the parking spot, mindful of any traffic. After pulling free, he looked at the sleeping beauty beside him and finally relaxed.

Moments later, the small green car exited the parking lot and accelerated away from the scene.

CHAPTER 2

Late Friday morning, the green Civic rolled up the driveway and disappeared into the maw of the shadowed double-stall garage. The door closed behind him, and the chemist sat silently, listening to the sounds of the automobile's pinging engine.

"Son of a—" he cursed out loud. He pounded his gloved hand on the steering wheel.

This was not his fault. Who would have guessed the stupid cow would've allowed her gas tank to run down to fumes? "*Bloody* son of a prick!" he repeated.

The echo of his outburst hung in the stale air of the compact car. He forced himself to calm down. He cricked his neck to one side, then the other. and worked his jaw—exhaled and pictured azure skies and a caressing mountain breeze.

Despite these efforts, the chemist could not stop his insides from tightening. Adrenaline revved him up, causing his neck to warm and pupils to dilate. The fear of getting caught, whatever its genesis, held him in a python grip.

Unwilling to run out of gas—how monumental a screw-up would it be?—he'd been forced to stop for five dollars' worth. There had been no alternative short of abandoning the abduction, which would have put him at even greater risk. It would have meant wheeling the car and parking in the store lot. Exiting. Hoofing it back to his van.

Increased exposure.

Instead, he'd pulled into the nearest filling station and pumped enough gas to get him home. Eyes lowered, he'd paid the youthful attendant without uttering a word. Then he was gone, quiet as the wind. Invisible.

Or so he'd hoped.

The capture had been clean. The escape, however, had been compromised to an amateurish level.

Not my fault, he told himself.

He glanced at the girl still slumped in the passenger seat. She had moved no more than inches during the entire fifteen-minute drive. The chemist reached over and felt her neck for a pulse. She moaned, and her leg twitched. He still had plenty of time.

Five minutes later, he plopped his victim atop the unmade, coverless bed in the house's basement. It was a decent-sized bedroom without windows.

The house was an isolated ranch at the far end of a cul-de-sac in a secluded, almost rural section of outer suburbia. "Modest landscaping made cozy by many mature trees" (so described in the real estate spec sheet) and a generous backyard. A new two-story Cape Cod was listed for sale next door, then three neighboring houses after it. A five-acre stretch of thick woods spanned behind the back of all the property lines. Beyond the woods stretched multi-acres of flat cornfields. Then another copse of trees appeared near an isolated older farmhouse.

The uninhabited, two-story Cape Cod sported an attached double-door garage. The unoccupied home remained vacant since the chemist had moved in over a year ago. A For Sale sign was planted in the front yard, not far from the open-fence porch railing, which ran the length of the front-facing. With the economy stagnant and the housing market at a standstill, he envisioned no new neighbors residing there anytime soon.

The girl remained unconscious on the bed. The basement bedroom had a small adjacent bathroom with a full tub and shower. The small upper window was boarded from the outside, with no secondary fire exit.

No escape.

He watched as a string of drool slipped from her lips. Her leg twitched again, and the unwrinkled forehead displayed delicate frown lines.

She didn't awaken, however, and quickly descended back into dreamland.

Let her sleep it off. It would be at least another few hours before she became conscious enough to figure out she wasn't where she was supposed to be.

This thought amused the chemist. But he maintained his focus while withdrawing a pair of heavy-duty leather bands from the nightstand drawer. He fastened them around the girl's slender wrists. The items had been purchased via the Internet from an S&M porn site. He'd used a stolen credit card and had the items shipped to an anonymous PO Box, which he'd paid for in cash. Untraceable.

Each leather band had a silver metal hoop, and he'd inserted a nylon cord into these. He fastened the free ends to the sturdy bed-legs at the base of the headboard.

Face down, spread-eagle, he removed the young woman's cross-trainers, leaving on her ankle socks. He yanked down her leggings and left her stretch briefs in place. He similarly secured her ankles. Then he applied a strip of silver electrical tape across her mouth.

Only then did he allow his fingertips to trail down the back of her bare leg. He sighed. Rising, he covered her with a blue-and-white comforter. Stepping back, the chemist studied his prize in the dim light of the basement bedroom. She was peaceful, breathing at an acceptable rate.

For the first time since the capture, he allowed himself a smile.

Climbing the basement stairs, he removed his peacoat and hung it in the hall closet, trading it for a distressed, gray-leather bomber jacket. The chemist put the lambskin gloves back on. They proved excellent for driving the motorcycle.

Inside the garage, he located his dark helmet. Its tinted visor blocked the light. He wheeled the Suzuki toward the doors and started the bike inside the garage, allowing the sound to equilibrate. The wide door lifted open, and daylight appeared once again.

Using the tips of his boots, he rolled down the driveway while ensuring the garage door had fully closed. Then he accelerated off into the overcast gray morning.

The motorbike wove its way across the grocery store parking lot. The chemist pulled behind the blue van still parked where he'd left it.

He cut the engine. It was almost noon.

The parking lot crowd was denser than earlier. Customers were filtering into the store, intent on grabbing a few items over lunch. No one paid the slightest attention to a lone man on a motorbike.

The chemist unlocked the van's back doors and pulled down a narrow ramp he'd had custom installed. With a modest effort, he rolled the bike up the ramp and into the back of the van.

He laid the motorcycle on its side. It was heavy enough not to slide or slip on abrupt turns, which he would try to avoid. He hopped out the back and slid the ramp beneath the van's undercarriage. Once he'd closed the double-panel rear doors, he glanced at his watch. He had put away the bike in under sixty seconds. Excellent.

Inside the van, soft jazz music filled the air. The chemist removed his helmet and set it on the passenger seat. The dark medical bag remained on the floor below the glove box where he'd left it.

He backed from the parking spot, double-checking his side mirrors, alert for cars pulling out or scampering kids as he drove away down the lane.

No more mess-ups this morning.

Moments later, he merged into the street's traffic flow. Safe, steady, staying in his lane, he plucked his phone from the medical bag and pressed the speed-dial number for his wife.

CHAPTER 3

There had always been a brunette in his life, or so it seemed to Cale Van Waring. His mother and sister both had dark hair, as had a parade of other girlfriends who'd marched him along for his thirty-seven years.

The one time he had fallen in love with a blonde, it had ended in disaster.

This time, the brunette's name was Maggie Jeffers. She worked as an attorney with the public defender's office. What mattered more to Cale than her dimpled smile and lithe figure was how she could turn a clever quip faster than anyone he'd ever known. And as a homicide detective seventeen years in, he had run across his fair share of savvy quipsters.

They'd been living together for fourteen months, and their friends, family, and coworkers—almost everyone they knew—referred to them as the "perfect couple." In Cale's opinion, at the risk of being pessimistic, the endorsement might as well be called the "Kiss of Death."

How could he, they, or anyone else, live up to the billing?

The fact was, they couldn't. It was the underlying reason Maggie was walking out of his life—if it's what she chose—on the upcoming July Fourth weekend, as she had somewhat arbitrarily announced—three months from now.

Unless things improved between them.

These were the grim thoughts niggling at him as he pushed and pulled at the oars. The scull swept through the steel-gray water, skimming across the flat surface. Gulls called, soaring overhead.

The high-pitched squeal of a red-crested thrush broke his mental imagery, yanking him back to the present.

Cale let the oars go slack and leaned back, panting from the exertion. Twenty-two minutes steady, and now sixty seconds recovery. Cheeks flushed, chest heaving, he listened to the waves slurp against the narrow hull.

Rising from the rowing machine, he flicked off the giant flat-screen television. The majestic woods and pristine lake vanished.

Standing in the middle of the den, the thrush's trill was transformed into the squeal of the distant teapot on the kitchen stove. Maggie, he knew, was up and about.

Cale spotted the plump gray-and-white tabby staring up at him beside the couch. Reaching, he ruffled the cat's fuzz-ball head. "Sorry, Hankster," he said. "No birdies for breakfast today."

Cale strode out of the den and across the open dining room, entering the high-ceilinged kitchen. He removed the whistling kettle from the electric burner.

"Why not use the microwave?" he called out, his voice echoing through the house. He opened the refrigerator and withdrew a water bottle. Out the window, the sky appeared pale, a hint of breeze swaying the uppermost tree branches. These separated the yard from the rest of the metal and concrete world—their private paradise.

Maggie emerged from the basement stairs in navy-colored sweats, her dark hair pinned up with clips. She held a pair of folded black slacks across one arm.

"It's my mom's kettle. Besides, microwaving water seems, I don't know, impersonal," she said with a shrug.

Cale leaned on the counter. "Strong word, 'impersonal.'"

"Strong woman." She flashed him a dentist's dream of a smile.

Cale had a white towel wrapped around his neck. His red Wisconsin Badgers T-shirt was moist across his chest and back. Hank leaped onto the counter and waited to be noticed. Cale rubbed the cat's neck, and he purred.

Maggie said, "We were watching you row. You didn't seem to notice."

"My first ever cheering section?" His half-grinned. "How'd I look from the stands?"

She poured water from the teakettle and plunked a single bag into a cup. "Like usual. A thousand miles away."

"I was pondering world starvation. War with North Korea. Global warming."

Maggie's arms were crossed, waiting for her tea to cool. The kitchen smelled like raspberries. "Solved them all, did you?"

"You bet. Let the secretary-general know when he calls."

From the countertop, Hank flopped onto his side. Maggie said, "Missed you in bed last night."

Cale had always been a baseball nut and stayed awake late watching the Milwaukee Brewer's opening road game. At the moment, though, he doubted she was asking about baseball. After living together for over a year, her innocent question rendered him uneasy.

"Tavarez got hit in the head with a fastball," Cale said. "They carted him off the field in a neck brace."

He could sense the gulf between them grow as each day passed. Maybe his imagination? He doubted it.

"Why didn't he duck?" Maggie asked.

Typical Maggie. Her lawyerly logic often unnerved him. "Took one for the team. One of baseball's unwritten rules."

Hank stuck one paw straight up, and Cale rubbed his belly.

"You're a traitor, Hank," Maggie said. To Cale, she added, "He's up to fifteen pounds from all the treats you give him."

Hank perked an ear at the magic word.

"Besides," she continued, "your 'unwritten rule' sounds lame. Who will remember poor Tavarez when he's sixty years old with dementia, drooling like a fool?"

Cale pondered her point. These days, every topic they discussed seemed spoken in some code. He glanced from the window's gray color back at her.

"You're mad at me for making the cat fat? Is that what you're saying?"

"Not mad at anything." She sipped her tea and glanced at the stove clock. "Uh-oh—some of us are running late."

On cue, Hank jumped down from the countertop.

Maggie faded down the hallway, her stocking feet silent on the tiled floor.

Cale considered rushing after her. He thought about grabbing her hard and spinning her at the base of the stairs—perhaps like Humphrey Bogart—sweeping her into his arms and kissing her madly. Instead, he listened to her footsteps climb the steps.

Maggie's voice called from the landing. "You know the saddest part about dementia, don't you?"

"What?"

"You're always the last to know."

Cale turned from the bedroom mirror. He holstered his 9mm Glock beneath his left arm and clipped his gold shield to his belt. Another routine Tuesday morning.

"Remember," Maggie called from the bathroom. "We're having dinner with Chloe and Ed tonight. In case you forgot." She wore a navy pantsuit with a white blouse and low-heeled pumps—ready for court.

Cale grimaced. Another dinner with Madam Zola and Bozo T. Clown was challenging. However, considering the eggshells they tiptoed over these days, he kept his private thoughts to himself. "Seriously?"

"Can't choose our relatives, can we?"

Maggie's older sister by two years, Chloe fancied herself a psychic and tarot card reader, blessed even further with the occasional "vision." In Cale's opinion, any seer worth her salt would be living in a mansion and banned from every casino in Las Vegas.

Instead, Chloe was a hairstylist. She inhaled perm fumes down at the Mood Indigo Beauty Emporium. Maybe that was her problem? Cale theorized. Perhaps her brain cells were clumping together like some glue huffer?

"You're in court," he said, hopefully, as he watched her step from the bathroom. "You might run late for dinner."

"You'll have to dazzle them with your wit and charm. At least until I get there."

"Card tricks?"

"That'd be nice. Except you don't know any."

Cale smirked and stepped closer to her, but she checked his advance with narrow eyes.

"I was hoping we could spend the night alone," he said, giving the Bogey act some line. "You know? Relax? Have a few six-packs together?"

"Such a smooth talker when you want to be, Van Waring." Her nip of a laugh betrayed her. "But you're not worming out of dinner with my sister tonight."

Hank stared at them from the unmade bed. "When we get home, you can have as many beers as you like. How's that for compromise?"

To Hank, Cale said, "Think I'm being blackmailed here?"

"My, you *are* a detective."

Cale's phone chirped, interrupting them. The readout revealed: Detective Anton Staszak.

"Yeah," Cale answered.

"We might have something," Staszak stated calmly, "related to the kidnapping case." He paused. "Hope I'm not interrupting your Egg McMuffin." Staszak was a former homicide detective nearing retirement who headed up the department's Missing Persons Unit.

Cale shot Maggie a glance. "My McMuffin's fine."

Across the room, she rolled her eyes.

"We got an MP call yesterday afternoon," Staszak said. "Girl's missing since last Friday. Age twenty-two. Same MO as the others."

"The ones from last spring?"

"We might have a witness," Staszak said. "Gas station kid thinks he spotted our MP's vehicle."

Cale knew the case well. He was the lead investigator. Last spring, three young women had gone missing and were presumed kidnapped, though nothing had ever been proven. There were no clues, no evidence, and no suspects. Then last November, the headless body of Kimberly Vanderkellen (one of the missing females) was found floating in Lake Michigan. However, with zero clues or evidence, the case had turned as cold as the frozen ground over the winter months.

Cale glanced at his watch. "Be there in fifteen," he said and ended the call.

Across the room, Maggie studied him. Being around cops and attorneys most of her days, she understood how a room's atmosphere shifted with a new discovery. "Are you going to make me guess?" she asked.

"Something—maybe—in the missing girl case. The one from last year."

Maggie recalled how Cale had awakened with nightmares for almost two months after the girl's remains had been fished from the ice-cold lake.

"The girl they found floating? The one without the—"

"Head." He finished it for her. "If I get caught up, I might not make dinner tonight."

"Meaning late, right?"

"Meaning, who knows?"

They understood that solving a murder case trumped dinner with your girlfriend's sister. Maggie's sigh summed things up. Whatever happened would happen, and neither could do much about it.

From the bed, Hank yawned and closed his eyes.

CHAPTER 4

The sun punched a bright hole in the cloud-stippled Tuesday morning sky. Gone was the harsh metallic scent of winter. The spring air smelled pungent with the aroma of awakening flowers and mowed grass.

Cale parked his silver Bronco in the station's back lot and strode to the rear doors. He swiped his security pass through the familiar slot and entered.

James "Slink" Dooley performed bench presses on a fancy Nautilus machine in the basement gym. "You talk to Staszak?" Cale asked as he approached his partner.

"Fifteen, sixteen"—Slink grunted—"seventeen...." Arms wavering, he let the weights fall with a clang and gave Cale a narrow look. "I was about to set my record."

Cale took note of popping veins in his partner's sinewy forearms. "Benching sixty pounds, some record."

"I'm in rehab. Remember?"

The department physician had suggested Detective Dooley take a week's rehab for a pinched nerve in his neck. He had slipped on an ice patch chasing a narcotic informant over a month ago, and Slink—not surprising to Cale—had ignored the medical advice.

"Last week, I could barely manage eight reps."

"Too much..." He made a sliding gesture with one hand.

"Says the voice of experience."

A pair of off-duty cops nearby chortled. Ignoring them, Cale said, "Upstairs. Staszak's desk in ten."

The open-concept investigations area was filled with a neat array of desks. It looked more like a college classroom than a detectives' workstation. The computer equipment was top-grade. The various investigative units were separated by four-foot-high partitions, a nuisance because, half the time, their cases overlapped. The whole place sometimes felt to Cale like they were working at IBM. With one-tenth the pay.

He flicked on his desk computer. Yellow stick-em notes cluttered the screen. He pulled them off, chucking most of them.

Cale headed the Special Crimes Unit when he wasn't working regular Homicide. These were cases falling outside any standard mold, or as he'd once explained to Maggie: "The crazy stuff nobody else wants."

Fortunately, not many cases fit the mold of Special Crimes. On the other hand, those that did proved extra challenging.

Four desks down from Cale sat Detective Anton Staszak. A human tree trunk, Staszak owned one sport coat the color of a brown paper bag and two clip-on neckties, one gray, one green. Each ended inches north of his navel. Today he had on drab trousers and brown loafers. Despite his need for a fashion makeover, "Stasz" was a tough-as-nails street cop, hardened by decades in Robbery-Homicide.

Staszak had taken over Missing Persons three years ago. The job consisted of hours of phone and computer searches and less actual street duty. This suited Staszak fine, saving wear and tear on his gimpy knees before the trumpets of retirement blared.

"Can you see anything without your reading glasses?" Cale asked, sliding closer to Staszak's workstation. The hefty detective slid his computer mouse back and forth, jacket off, revealing a coffee-stained blue shirt.

"If I squint hard enough."

"He's Detective Magoo!" Slink's playful voice approached.

Scowling, Staszak flipped him the finger.

"As I said," Slink crowed, winking at Cale. "Eyes like that, he should've been a mortician."

Slink wore a spiffier variation of the detectives' dress code: gray slacks, a leather sports jacket, and no tie. His thinning hair was swept back and still damp from the shower.

Cale accepted the good-natured horseplay. Real cops, he understood, were serious when they had to be. Staszak and Slink were proven investigators, guys he'd go to battle with any day. It was respect forged from coming up through the ranks together.

"Plunk your arses down." Staszak nodded at his screen. "I'll show you what we've got."

Slink rubbed his hands together like a seventh-grader. "I'll grab the popcorn."

Staszak frowned and fantasized about his retirement.

Staszak reminded them the case had begun a year ago in the spring:

Leslie Dowd: Victim Number One. Gone missing in mid-April. The twenty-three-year-old hairdresser had locked up her nail polishing job around nine p.m. on a Thursday night. She'd been alone, as far as anyone could tell.

She never returned home from work.

The following afternoon, her aunt notified the police after the shop called, saying Leslie had a pair of clients waiting and no one had heard from her.

Standard procedure dictated the police wait forty-eight hours before filing a report on a missing adult. Although no suspicions of foul play were clear, Anton Staszak had dispatched a unit to examine the girl's apartment. Her aunt had met the uniformed officers and allowed them entry with her spare key. Nothing appeared amiss.

And no signs of the missing young woman.

With the absence of a suicide note, no packed bags, no missing toothbrush, and no indications of criminal activity, there was little else the police could do.

The next day an MP report was filed. Staszak had run down all the usual angles. He'd checked her laptop, phone records, and credit cards. He interviewed her friends and coworkers and talked to her boyfriend. Social media accounts were all checked. No medical problems were unveiled, no pregnancy issues, and no indicators of clinical depression.

Nothing. Zilch.

Leslie Dowd, along with her vehicle, had vanished into the ether.

The disappearance seemed headed toward the cold case drawer, with regular cases increasing daily. And yet, the image of the missing twenty-three-year-old kept Anton Staszak wide awake for many nights.

Staszak had a pair of teenage daughters. He understood the devastation if one of them, for no apparent reason, vanished off the face of the earth. What if this was one of his little girls?

April had progressed into June. Two cases of similar nature followed on the heels of the Dowd disappearance. In May—one Mary Jane Moore, age twenty-four—disappeared similarly without a trace. The third victim, gone missing in mid-June, was named Kimberly Vanderkellen—age twenty-three.

The Missing Person's detectives ran the routine. They worked around the clock for weeks, performing the usual interviews and legwork. Friends, neighbors, and family hung flyers on store walls and utility poles. Group field searches were conducted. Good Samaritans and others pitched in. Sniffer dogs scoured large areas of tree glens and abandoned spots, assisted by police choppers.

All to no avail.

The poster faces of the victims stared blankly at citizens and cops alike as if mocking their inability to locate them.

To Staszak's way of thinking, the similarities of the disappearances prevented their dismissal as random. The age and physical characteristics of the victims were similar. However, the lack of clues and the nature of the abductions—if indeed they even *were* abductions—connected them. The modus operandi was identical: no girls, cars, or clues. Three young women had evaporated into thin air.

In Staszak's opinion, the odds predicted that one sick perpetrator had carried out the abductions.

Stasz had tapped Cale's brain for ideas on the baffling case as the months passed. Theories abounded—everything from cults to witchcraft covens, from serial kidnappings to random relocation from the area.

As the months passed, the question remained: How could three healthy, drug-free young women, along with their automobiles, vanish without a trace?

Staszak had accepted the missing person's position to save some grind on his spongy knees. Now he lumbered home most nights with a migraine headache and acid stomach. Not the trade-off for which he'd hoped.

The how and why of it compounded the mystery. Did the female victims, separately, run off with some acquaintance? A random Cassanova they'd met in a tavern or restaurant? Or some pervert on the Internet? Nothing was ruled out—even organized drug gang snatch-and-grabs.

Why? The question plagued Anton Staszak, burning in his gut like hot lead each night.

"Maybe a pair of them?" Cale had theorized one afternoon, leaning back with his coffee cup. "A tandem, like Henry Lee Lucas and his partner? The stupid one?"

"Ottis Toole." Slink had recently returned from a three-day conference on serial profiling.

"The cannibal," Staszak said humorlessly. He'd popped a pair of Maalox tabs, his recent favorite snack. "And don't tell me our victims have been eaten."

If only they had a witness or any suspicious vehicles to investigate. Or even—sick as it sounded—another body.

All of this had transpired in the spring and summer before the weather had turned cool. Then had arrived the witch-fingered winds of November.

"Be careful what you wish for," a dark voice in Staszak's head had warned.

The voice turned out to be prophetic.

CHAPTER 5

It had been a little after a hesitant sunrise the week before Thanksgiving, and the wind whipped the choppy gray waters along the Lake Michigan shoreline. Soppy weeds clung to the officers' clothes in the gray, freezing water as they guided the bloated human body to shore.

"Aw, Jesus H..." a young deputy groaned.

The pair of mottled bare ankles slipped from his hands as he'd turned and expelled the contents of his breakfast onto the brown rocks.

"For God's sake, Jepson!" the sheriff had barked. His hands stung from the near-icy lake water, and he could feel his shirt cling clammily to his lower back.

A second deputy, waist-deep in the water, had called out. "Hurry up, would you? I'm dropping her."

A third officer sloshed into the weed-filled lake yards from the shore. He'd grabbed the slippery bare ankles. "My God!" he whispered, turning to the others with a horrified look. "She doesn't have a head!"

"We can see that, dumbass," the sheriff had growled. "Just get her out of the water!"

Having been discovered on the Wisconsin side of the chilly Lake Michigan waters, Manitowoc County held jurisdiction over the body. Knowing that Green Bay had a string of missing females under investigation, Manitowoc's district attorney called Green Bay PD and arranged to turn it over.

By midmorning, Cale was staring at the flickering lights of half a dozen police cruisers. The County Sheriff's Department and the Wisconsin State Patrol were on the scene. Their lights lit up the rock-infested shoreline, casting eerie shadows between the thinning November trees.

The weather had turned cold, and a pair of salmon fishers spotted the floating body drifting closer to shore. A deputy coroner ruled out a boating accident. Propellers didn't hack swimmers' heads off.

Cale understood they were staring at a homicide.

The following day's autopsy was performed at the Brown County morgue. Despite the number of bodies he'd viewed over the years, Cale had to fight off heebie-jeebies. The mutilated, cyanotic corpse became etched in his mind.

Dr. Heinz Mocarek, the medical examiner, had concluded his autopsy. The investigators were inside the room, asking their questions.

The ME spoke in a toneless voice, "No water in the lungs. Until we get lab work, I'm recording COD as 'beheading.'"

"No kidding," Anton Staszak had said. He stood behind Cale and leaned against a countertop.

"Water degrades the forensics. But the vessels appear to have been cleanly severed." The ME arched an eyebrow." Maybe a machete?"

Machete? Cale had thought, his brain summoning zombie voodoo movies he'd watched as a boy.

The doctor peered through a high-mag loupe, studying the neck. "Very sharp. Likely one blow."

"Before or after she died?" Cale asked.

The ME said he couldn't tell.

"Are the ligature marks postmortem?" Cale had asked. "Maybe the body weighted before tossing it in the water?"

Cale reasoned that people didn't usually allow their heads to be lopped off without a struggle. So she'd been tied, beheaded, then dumped in the vast lake. But if so, why were the wrists now untied? No one could answer his question.

"Two or three months in the water." The ME had set aside his magnifier. "Cold water might help ID her."

"Some sick scumbags out there," Staszak said as they left.

The day after the headless Jane Doe had been autopsied, Howard Vanderkellen—father of the third missing victim—had visited the morgue to view the remains. His wife, on Cale's insistence, remained in the waiting area.

An appendectomy scar. A small tattoo of an angel on the left shoulder. Mr. Vanderkellen, shaken, had shown them a photograph of his daughter taken two summers prior at the family cottage. Three moles on the small of her back matched the incomplete corpse lying in the stainless-steel body drawer. They all helped in ID-ing the victim.

Jane Doe, at least, now had a name.

Kimberly Marie Vanderkellen. She went by "Kimmy" to her friends and coworkers. Victim Number Three. She had vanished without a trace along with her car—the same MO as the first pair of missing young women. But unlike the other two, Kimmy's body had floated up in the November waters of Lake Michigan.

Where her head might be was anyone's guess. A sick trophy? The same way Jeffrey Dahmer had collected body parts? Storing them in his refrigerator, his freezer, or a giant steel drum.

The thought made Cale's stomach clench.

He had watched the numb and tortured face of Howard Vanderkellen as the man broke the news to his wife. He watched them clutch one another, the father's rough hand patting her hair until her wails of grief subsided to breathless gasps.

One family, at least, could begin the task of making burial arrangements—one family out of three.

Staszak had been right. Sometimes it was a sick business they were in. This was one of those times.

CHAPTER 6

"Can't be a homicide without a body." Slink proclaimed this now with a headshake.

He and Cale had dragged chairs closer to Staszak's desk computer screen like biology lab students. They were ready to review their latest apparent abduction—victim Number Four.

"We didn't have a body before Vanderkellen," Staszak said gloomily. The oversized detective indicated his screen. "Same MO as the other three. Her name's Cynthia Hulbreth. I met with her mother and filled out the MP report."

Cale asked, "She's been gone four days now?"

"What her mom thinks. Assuming she was snatched last Friday." It was Tuesday morning now,

Slink looked their way. "We're thinking the same perp from last spring?"

"Picking up where he left off," Cale nodded grimly.

Five chilly, damp, snow-frosted months had flown past since they'd identified the headless body of Kimmy Vanderkellen. The Green Bay PD had handled forty-seven other missing person cases since. Most of them were runaway teens or disgruntled spouses acting out.

The toxicology report on the Vanderkellen girl had come back from the state crime lab three weeks after the autopsy. Positive for Rohypnol, GHB, and the opioid fentanyl.

"Enough to knock a bull on its butt," Dr. Mocarek had told Cale in a phone conversation. "The fentanyl alone."

"It confirms how he's snatching them without struggle," Slink had agreed.

It was springtime, a year since the first abduction, and they had a new missing victim. Number two or maybe four? Perhaps a full dozen? They had no way of actually knowing. Or was Cynthia Hulbreth's disappearance part of a different case?

Staszak shook his head. "Fits last year's MO. I can see the headlines: 'Date Rape Killer Strikes Again.'" His humor failed to elevate their spirits. He added, "Claimed she was spending the weekend with her boyfriend,"

"But she failed to show, right?" Cale asked Staszak.

The large detective nodded. "I put the vehicular alert out after we got a hit on the car this morning."

"Our kid from the gas station?"

"Lukewarm," Slink said, "but we better check it."

Cale and Slink rose in unison. They left Staszak in place, massaging his lumpy knees. A uniformed officer waved at Cale. "Nothing urgent, Lieutenant." The heavyset cop's name was Sgt. Burke. "Message for Stasz."

They looked at the officer together.

"A lady flagged our cruiser behind the Dairy Queen," Burke said. "She claims her *other* daughter's missing now—the youngest one."

"What?" Staszak looked incredulous.

"Her name's Agnes Hulbreth," Burke reported. "Says she filed a report with you yesterday on her missing daughter?"

Cale said, "Our newest MP, right?"

"Youngest daughter's name is Angela," Burke continued. "Seventeen. In high school."

"Likely at the mall with her friends." Slink offered. "Kids her age pull this stuff for attention."

"Sure, they do." Staszak's voice sounded withered. "And I'm booked on the next shuttle to Jupiter."

Cale drove the pewter-colored unmarked Ford Taurus, their usual ride, past a small park on the city's east side. He could imagine early spring buds rising from the softening soil like tentative doughboys peeking out from a trench.

In the passenger seat, Slink fiddled with the phone in his lap. Slink was also a baseball nut, and talking about sports made their travels seem less tedious.

"Red Sox or Royals?" Slink asked pointedly. "Opening day at Fenway?"

"I don't bet anymore. Remember?"

"It's a guess."

"Let's go with the home team."

"That's what I love," Slink said. "A man with a system."

Five minutes later, Cale spun the Taurus into the parking lot of a Speedway station. 11 a.m. The place was quiet, with only a solitary beat-up station wagon at one pump.

The attendant was a college-age kid with a Moe Howard haircut. He sat on a stool behind the counter studying a *Maxim* magazine and didn't bother glancing up.

"You Teddy Brickner?" asked Cale, approaching the counter. They flashed IDs.

The kid set aside the magazine.

"You spoke with Detective Staszak earlier," Slink said. "About a green Honda Civic? Last Friday morning?"

Brickner nodded, setting aside the magazine. "I saw the flier this morning when I came in. I might've seen the car."

Fifteen minutes later, they were back in the Taurus with frustration etched on their faces. They had learned the young man had failed to get a look at the suspect who had driven the Civic. Even worse, the gas station's surveillance unit was broken, meaning no recording of the stop. Even crazier to the detectives, the station's owner—Ray Tolver—had perished over the weekend of a heart attack.

Cale ground his teeth, recalling the attendant's meager description of the Civic's driver:

"Ballcap dude is all I remember," Brickner had informed. "Sunglasses. Dark jacket. I never got a decent look. Set a fiver on the counter and split. I was with another customer."

Back in the Taurus, Slink cursed. "Narrows it down to about ten thousand guys."

Cale understood they'd have to check into the station owner's untimely demise. This meant greater legwork and wasted time, knowing the clock was ticking on the abducted female.

The Taurus wheeled from the Speedway lot.

"There's a chance he lives close by. Like a neighborhood guy?" Slink arched an eyebrow.

Cale considered it. Five bucks of gas still got you forty miles in any direction, especially in a Honda Civic. It created too wide a geographical range to formulate a workable net.

Merging into noonday traffic, Cale replayed what they'd learned from Teddy Brickner. "Maybe we're giving our guy too much credit?"

"How so?"

Last year, the detectives had decided their abductor was more intelligent than average, cleverer than the usual snatch-and-grabber.

"A five-dollar gas guy? It sandbags our prior profile."

Slink nodded. "I counted four cameras watching."

Cale slid the Taurus through a right turn. "Runs out of gas during an abduction—not the Einstein we suspected, is it?"

Slink was thumbing through his texts without looking up. He stated: "Cross out Professor Moriarty. Say hello to Colonel Dumb-F."

"Something like that."

After a minute, Slink asked, "How about he's Mr. Lucky?

Remember the old gambler's motto?"

He nodded. "Better to be lucky than good."

CHAPTER 7

"The eye of the beholder, gentlemen." Captain Leo McBride puffed out his chest. "It's the wonder of art."

Cale and Slink stood inside the captain's office. They were staring at a particularly amateurish rendition of a sailboat in a chalk-colored harbor, which hung on one wall.

"Never seen a green sky before," Slink admitted.

"Reflection off the grass," the captain said. "Look at those brush strokes on the boat hull. This painting speaks to me."

Cale also decided it spoke to him, screaming, "Sprint away fast! Before some huckster tries pawning me off as real art." He kept quiet and sat down on a chair.

Slink stood peering at the captain's precious wall pieces with renewed interest.

Cale watched them from across the room. The captain was a chesty and balding black guy, and he imagined the closest Leo McBride had ever come to sailing was with a toy schooner in his childhood bathtub.

McBride returned and sat behind his cluttered desk. The wall behind him was peppered with commendations, framed photos, and award plaques. Before his promotion up the chain, the captain had been a decorated street cop.

"Thanks for showing us the art, Cap," Slink said. "One day, you'll find one of those gems."

McBride smiled knowingly, and Cale rolled his eyes.

Two years ago, the McBride family had taken up collecting amateur art—a kind description of what currently graced the captain's walls. His wife had read a story about an Illinois couple who'd purchased a "garage sale" piece that turned out to be a genuine Johann Vermeer. Worth too much to count. These days, the McBride family's passion lay in scouring two-bit garage and warehouse sales on weekends, searching for treasures the way most couples seek out a favorite pizza parlor.

Anton Staszak now rapped and entered, grabbing the final empty chair.

McBride said, "We have anything on this Hulbreth thing?"

Did he mean the first missing sister or the latest one? Cale wondered. He eyed Staszak. Nothing was official yet, and they were still confirming facts.

"Similar MO to last spring." Cale closed the silence. "Could be our same guy. And we've got a witness who claims he saw her car—and maybe even the perp. We're sending over our sketch artist."

McBride nodded at the positive news. "If it's true, we've got four victims now?"

Cale wasn't going to reveal the younger sister yet.

McBride stared at them all. "Chief Harris wants Special Crimes officially on this as a *priority*. Any missing females who fit the profile."

With a nod, the detectives made for the door.

"And get your act together," McBride added for effect.

"One question, Cap." Cale turned at the door. "How are we handling the press?"

"Tap dancing as long as possible."

The Chemist.

The basement bedroom is encased in shadows. The girl lies face down on the bed, gagged, spread eagle. Straps bind her wrists and ankles, extending toward the mattress's corners.

Da Vinci's Vitruvian Man in reverse.

You are positioned just inside the doorway. You watch with clinical fascination and detachment—like a researcher monitoring the human response to abject terror.

Enter the room and strike a match; light the three-candle candelabra on the rustic walnut bureau. Press "Play" on the portable CD player, and the room swells with music.

The girl, stretched out on the bed, thrashing and mumbling incoherent protests around her gag. The blindfold is in place, and she can do little other than squirm against her bindings and moan.

How delightful.

A bottle-cork pops. You fill a pair of tall flutes, asking yourself: What good is a new date without champagne? After sipping from one, you set the glasses on the bedside table. The prize positioned before you is a treasure, a trophy won. She won't enjoy this romantic interlude as much as you will.

With tantalizing deliberation, you begin unbuttoning your shirt.

Cindy Hulbreth had no way of knowing the time. Not the hour, day, or minute. Was it light or dark outside? Sunny? Drizzling?

From her windowless basement dungeon, she had no clue.

She had passed out, thank God. Then as if abandoned by Him, she regained consciousness somewhere toward the end of her assault. Her assailant remained pressed lewdly against her numb and cringing flesh.

A bland cottony gag stuffed her mouth. To her dismay, Cindy's attempt at thrashing and bucking him off had only excited him further. Beneath the blindfold, salty tears stung her eyes. She feared to imagine what violations against her body and spirit were yet to come.

Not that this wasn't bad enough.

She was disoriented and shell-shocked, and her stabbing headache failed to subside even after her sick assault had ended. Cindy felt dirty and disgusted, inside and out. Though terrified beyond measure, what frightened her more was what he *hadn't* done. When would he kill her? And how long would she last before she welcomed it?

CHAPTER 8

"Oh, to be seventeen again."

Slink stared at a trio of adolescent girls standing on the street corner. They stood energized, wearing skinny jeans, leggings, and jacket sleeves tied around their waists. Spring was officially here.

"Seventeen was rough for you if I remember," Cale said. They had parked the Taurus curbside and walked up the sidewalk to a modest house in an older neighborhood.

"Had acne and a crush on my geometry teacher."

"That's right," Cale recalled. "What was his name again?"

Slink smirked. "You missed your calling, Dave Chapelle."

They rang the doorbell. The afternoon sunlight reflected off the quarter-paned windows as Cale noticed a slight quiver in the curtains.

The house stood in a blue-collar section of the city with abundant trees. It showed a double-stall garage, aluminum siding, updated roof. The pine shrubs in front appeared well-tended.

A forty-something lady wearing dark sweatpants and a *"Marquette"* sweatshirt answered. Agnes Hulbreth might have been a beauty once, but her hair was grayer now than brown, and her skin showed the weathered look of excessive sun exposure in her youth.

She ushered the detectives inside, where a sawed-off grandfather clock ticked in the front hallway. It added a funeral-like stillness Cale imagined went along with missing children.

"I shouldn't have approached those officers," Agnes said, "but I drove around the neighborhood looking for Angela." Her eyes were watery. "It's just, first Cindy, you know? Now Angie?"

"You did the right thing," Cale said.

The detectives sat on a living room sofa. Agnes perched herself on a recliner Cale pictured as her husband's favorite. The flat-screen HD stood twelve feet away, dead on.

They asked the usual questions, even though it was more than unusual for two sisters to go separately missing.

Agnes could not disguise her distress, "I've called her phone all morning and got nothing." She paused. "Angie's a headstrong girl. With Cindy missing, I'm afraid of what's happening inside there." She pointed to her head.

"Any indicators she ran away? Like left a note, maybe?"

Agnes shook her head. The hallway clock ticked.

Cale couldn't accept both sisters being kidnapped. What were the odds? Still, they couldn't rule anything out.

Agnes continued with her story. "When Cindy didn't arrive at the cottage Saturday, we called and called. But by Sunday afternoon, well, you know the rest."

Her voice faded like a song's end.

Slink wrote in his notebook. "Cindy's boyfriend?" he asked. "Could he be involved somehow?"

A well-established statistic: Percentage-wise, most victims knew their kidnappers.

"It's Angie's theory. That Ronnie—" She meant Ronnie Dereene, the boyfriend. "—they were having problems. At least what Angie says."

Cale's phone buzzed. He stepped into a hallway while Slink continued asking the customary mundane questions. The boyfriend's job, demeanor, and the kind of guy he was.

Cale re-entered. "Good news," he announced. "Angela's all right. A minor disturbance was reported at the home of Ronnie Dereene."

"And Cindy?" Agnes asked breathlessly.

Cale didn't want to give too much away. "We're heading there now. A cruiser will bring Angie home in a few minutes." He added, "There's been some apparent property damage. Mr. Dereene might seek restitution."

Agnes swiped her eyes as she escorted them out.

Inside the Taurus, Cale glanced back and saw the curtains ruffle. The mother's owlish eyes stared back at them.

"Jesus. She's going through a lot." Slink's voice was sober. "A dipshit for a husband can't make it any easier."

Cale turned to him.

Slink added, "He's working his normal shift? Me? If it's my little girl, I'm at the boyfriend's place with a forty-five."

Cale side-eyed his partner. "You missed your calling, Wyatt Earp."

CHAPTER 9

They parked a short distance from a red Subaru at the curb and walked to the condominium's front door.

"Injured guy's in there, Lieutenant," said a uniformed officer at the door. "Got whacked in the shoulder with a golf club."

The detectives entered the condo. "What number?" Cale asked over his shoulder.

"Seven iron, I think."

"He means the apartment," Slink rolled his eyes at the young officer, whose face flushed.

The investigators moved into Ronnie Dereene's condo and surveyed the damage. The interior was frat-house beige. The carpet was thin, with three matchless chairs around an oak table, all trapped inside a diminutive dining room. A fourth smashed chair was overturned.

The living room couch was a folded black futon with half the stuffing ripped out. The room was highlighted by a fifty-inch flat-screen. The stereo system likewise appeared top-notch. Cale recalled being twenty-five, out of the Academy for two years, and working street patrol. He imagined they'd find more beer in the refrigerator than food.

They greeted Sergeant Howie Rottier in the kitchen. He'd been first on the scene. "Staszak told us you'd be stopping."

Sunlight seeped down through a central skylight. It cast a beatific glow on the young man, who sat holding an ice bag against his shoulder.

"What reeks in here?"

Sgt. Rottier shrugged. "Young girl tracked in dog crap."

"Neighbor's mutt," Dereene reported with a whine.

Staszak had given them the Cliffs Notes version during their drive across town. Angela Hulbreth, the younger sister, had entered the condominium's backdoor via a key hidden under a flowerbed rock. Catching the guy by surprise, she attacked him with a club from his bag in the back hallway.

Cale stared at Dereene. He felt empathy for citizens who were victims of violence in their homes. The guy had a legitimate gripe—you return to your empty condo only to get whacked with a seven iron.

"When's the last time you talked to Cynthia?" Cale asked. Dereene had wavy auburn hair and wore a short-sleeve avocado shirt and tie combo.

The young man frowned. "Why?"

"Don't be a dickhead." Slink leaned against the kitchen counter.

"Last Thursday night on the phone." Dereene's eyes swept the room. "I wanted to join her at her cottage this weekend."

"And?"

"She said no." He exhaled. "She said we were breaking up."

Cale's look was tight. "And now your girlfriend's missing, and her sister's here attacking you with seven iron?" His forehead crinkled. "That's your story?"

"Go to hell."

Cale ordered Sergeant Rottier to ensure the medics cleared the man when they arrived. Rottier would drive him to the downtown station, and Det. Staszak would record his statement and timeline the guy's movements from Thursday evening onward. Also, grab all his phone, social media, and email records.

After exiting the kitchen, the detectives toured the remaining destruction of the condo. Slink asked, "Young lady did all this with a short iron?" He seemed impressed by the carnage: broken mirrors, the smashed and gouged end tables, the chipped fireplace mantle.

They worked their way downstairs to the basement—a typical washer, dryer, and water heater in a corner opposite two storage bins. The workout equipment appeared unused. They discovered one cubby-hole with a curtain drawn, and Cale found cleaning supplies, insect repellent, a bottle of acetone, and rubber tubing.

Slink whistled softly. "Rat poison? One step away from cyanide."

Cale let the curtain fall back, and they stepped beneath the 70-watt ceiling bulb in the basement's center. Eerie shadows danced at the periphery.

"What are the odds?" Slink picked up a wooden croquet mallet. "The boyfriend's angry with a shelf of chemicals in his basement?" He tapped the mallet's head against the dense concrete floor.

"He doesn't seem the head-chopper type." Cale's tone was dismissive.

"Same thing they said about John Wayne Gacy."

"I tell you what. You can dig up this entire basement if we find a clown suit in his closet."

CHAPTER 10

The Chemist

You study the unmoving naked girl on the mattress. Is she sleeping or faking it? It matters little as long as she's alive and breathing and her heart thumps merrily. This is your primary concern. You cannot stomach another "dead body" incident like a year ago when you had to phone Tazeki Mabutu with a panicky plea for help.

Kimberly Vanderkellen. Yes, it was the psychotic girl's name. You feel the dark twist in your stomach, recalling the insanity of what had happened. As science always teaches, a lesson learned by trial and by error.

Standing bedside here in the faint, muted light, you touch the girl's slender neck. Search for a pulse. And there it is, steady, rhythmic, yes.

The solid beat makes you smile.

The man calling himself the "Chemist" rewarded his actual self with a hot shower in the first-floor bathroom of the cul-de-sac house. He dried off with a terry bath towel and combed his dark hair straight back. He again put his designer eyeglasses on and padded barefoot into the living room with the towel around his waist. He sat on the rust-colored couch he'd bought to make the place feel more livable. The cushions were stiff beneath his bare thighs. Little surprise. He hadn't been to the house much during the winter, only to ensure the furnace pilot hadn't cut out.

The chemist punched at his phone. His young daughter answered. "Hey, honey boo. Why are you home so early?"

"We're off school today, Daddy. Teacher's conference. Miss Pelsky told Mom I'm getting straight A's."

"Wonderful, sweetie. You're my little brainiac."

She giggled. "You're funny, Daddy."

He pictured her standing with her blond hair braided and braces on her teeth. "Is Mommy home now?"

"She went to the store."

Mrs. Beckwell, the housekeeper, would be watching the kids. He was calling to see if his wife needed him to pick up anything on his drive home. Splendid. This saved him a trip. He had a flash of returning to the same supermarket where he'd abducted the newest girl. What would it be, five days ago already?

Stay away, a voice in his head cautioned. We do not revisit a crime scene.

The chemist pulled his attention back. "Tell Mom I'll be home in time for dinner. Okay?"

With a smoochy goodbye, he ended the call. He grinned at the image of his daughter acting so grown up. Straight A's? Not bad. Perhaps she'd qualify for a chemistry scholarship as he had way back in the day, like father like daughter. Well, perhaps not, he thought darkly.

The blue windowless panel-van backed out of the garage and onto the driveway a short while later. The afternoon sun was hazy, scattering warmth across budding tree branches. A pair of jays flitted above the stretching elm trees behind the house—their home base.

He spotted the Suzuki against the side wall as the garage door lowered. Beside it, the canvas cover hid the Honda Civic. Five dollars of gas. My God! It was almost a monumental disaster. An amateurish screw-up. Good thing he'd acted swiftly to eradicate the problem.

His mind flashed back to last Saturday afternoon when he'd hovered over the dazed and disoriented man who lay crumpled on the floor of his home's basement.

"Machine broke... recorder... don't work...."

The gas station owner had gasped out the words, barely conscious with the drug mixture charging through his veins. Through dilated pupils, his desperate look remained fresh in the chemist's mind.

Afterward, he had prepped the killing zone like the set of a Broadway play. Hid drug paraphernalia in the laundry sink; planted hoses, vials, and glass beakers laced with meth residue. Old acetone bottles and a Bunsen burner. He even hid a sack of twenty-dollar bills in a panel behind the washer. Three grand. A small price to pay.

The chemist had done all this while ensuring no trace remained of his presence. He must stay the invisible ghost. Nor could he allow any video of his emergency gas station to exist.

It hadn't mattered that the surveillance recording of his gas stop had never happened. The devil lay in the details. The trivial things always tripped up amateurs in their panicky haste. Some overlooked unforced errors.

When the police discovered the station owner's body—cold, stiff, drug OD'd—they would assume the fatality to be an "accidental" overdose. The poor man's heart had exploded from a meth and fentanyl combination strong enough to fell Secretariat.

Backing the blue van from the driveway, the chemist realized his hands were choking the steering wheel. Relaxing, he rolled his shoulders and allowed his tension to seep away. He would attend to the Civic once the risk of moving it had diminished. Make it disappear like the other vehicles had vanished—traceless. The green Civic tied him to the girl's abduction. It could not remain in the garage for any length of time.

He stared across the lawn at the vacant house next door. The For Sale sign made it appear desolate. He doubted any uninvited guests would venture into such a discrete, five-home cul-de-sac neighborhood. It's why he'd been so careful in choosing this house in the first place.

The details again.

The garage door closed like a castle portcullis, concealing its secrets, and the chemist drove away as soundlessly as possible. Seconds later, he turned the corner and drove south down another drowsy street.

The rental garage storage facility stood on the city's far North Side. Rarely utilized, it was perfect for his needs. The chemist had leased two oversized sided-by-side garage units. He'd paid for them six months in advance—anonymous—with a large manila envelope filled with Ben Franklins.

No one questioned anything when you paid in cash and required no receipt. Just ask the Mafia.

He steered the blue van inside after raising the storage garage door. Securing the bulky vehicle, he closed and locked the corrugated aluminum barrier. He had chosen the place because of the sparse security. The upper yard lights worked, of course, but he'd disabled both surveillance cameras aimed at his double-storage units and altered their angles enough to disguise his comings and goings, having performed the tasks himself in the dead of night.

Opening the second garage revealed the red BMW sports car registered to his private company. Backing out with the engine purring, the chemist hopped athletically from the vehicle. He closed and locked the second garage door behind him.

He stuffed the keyring back inside the sports car glove box. A Springsteen CD filled the Beamer with music. He sang along with the lyrics about being born in the USA.

His fingers tapped the leather steering wheel as he exited the open gates of the storage facility. Driving down the tree-lined street four blocks from the highway, he intended to enjoy the rest of the pleasant afternoon.

CHAPTER 11

The Chemist.

You remember those tantalizing early experiments like they were yesterday.

Select the proper concentrations, combine the drugs, and titrate the mixture in your private lab above the boathouse. The critical discovery point was the "accelerant." The agent allowed for multiple times the rapidity of standard dermal penetration. Through the skin in less than ten seconds and immediately into the bloodstream. A breakthrough, beyond any doubt.

The practice trial with the dog, of course, was unfortunate. Too strong a dose for the body weight. But there's science for you, the continual trial and error—especially employing the opioid fentanyl, where a few micrograms can be lethal. After said canine post-mortem, you decided to switch to more controllable opioids and surgical sedatives. But they were far more expensive than the so-called "Apache" street fentanyl and harder to obtain.

Nevertheless, a damned shame about the dog: the kids loved her so much.

Afterward, the time arrived for your first human subject. Marla had harbored no suspicions, of course. She'd been cast in the unflattering role of a "lab rat," blissfully unaware of anything amiss.

Peeking out from inside the bedroom closet, you observed her trial with cold fascination, akin to how a hawk on a high branch studies a morning dove. The exposure, followed by the onset of dizziness and her toppling to the carpeted floor a minute later, proved successful. She'd become dazed and then disabled, followed by rapid loss of consciousness.

As far as experiments go, an excellent result.

Now the mission advances full throttle. Though far too soon for accolades, it has met with satisfying success to date: no witnesses, evidence, or clues. And the police continue to remain baffled.

By how it is defined, you have accomplished the legendary "perfect crime."

Slink Dooley's maroon Mustang pulled into the driveway, and Y-turned on the concrete apron bordering the garages. Cale emerged from the backdoor. He held a map of the city and a bunch of Missing Person fliers he'd grabbed off Staszak's desk. Opening the passenger door, Cale slipped inside. Before he could speak, Slink handed him a copy of the *Green Bay Press-Gazette*. His partner had highlighted the headline.

GIRL MISSING ON EAST SIDE

Police Suspect Possible Abduction

The article read: *A Missing Person's report has been filed for Green Bay resident Cynthia Hulbreth, age 23. She was last seen Friday morning at the GNC Fitness Center on the city's east side. The disappearance marks the fourth female victim in little over a year, all in their early 20s. Authorities report no witnesses or suspects and describe the vanishings as "suspicious."*

The body of one previously alleged local victim, Kimberly Vanderkellen, 23, was discovered floating in Lake Michigan last November. Of the latest disappearance, Captain Leo McBride, Green Bay PD, said, "It fits the pattern of a string of previous missing females."

An employee at a local Citgo gas station may have spotted Hulbreth's green Honda Civic hatchback. However, McBride quickly dispelled this rumor as "Unsubstantiated."

Police have asked residents inside a ten-block radius of the Main Street Speedway Station to check their basements, garages, and yards. Residents are asked to report anything unusual they may have witnessed by contacting the Green Bay Police tips hotline.

According to our sources, the FBI has been notified and is monitoring the disappearances with the assistance of local law enforcement agencies, who remain in charge. Special Agent Eddie Redtail, the Wisconsin FBI Agent in Charge, has confirmed today: "Conversations are ongoing with the Green Bay Metro PD. We're keeping an active eye on the situation."

Cale tossed the newspaper into the Mustang's backseat. "At least they don't know any more than we do."

"For a change."

A parade of homes swept past, the budding trees along the street dappled with thin shafts of afternoon sunlight. Cale noticed Slink had also changed clothes, clad now in a pair of slacks, a light leather jacket, and wrap-around sunglasses. His hair was slicked back from the shower. He decided Slink could pass for an Italian detective in a Grade-B thriller. Dangle a thin cigarette from his lips, and he'd be the apple of some casting director's eye.

Slink accelerated the Mustang through an intersection. "We got a game plan here?"

"I confirmed what the gas station kid—Brickner—told us. His boss perished from a meth OD." Cale glanced his way. "Over the weekend, believe it or not."

Slink's eyes remained hidden behind his shades.

"Harry Blum caught the case," Cale continued. "The drug overdose roused suspicions. They've assigned it to Homicide until proven otherwise."

As they drove, Cale described Detective Blum's relaying the usual cooking paraphernalia discovered in the victim's basement. His prints were everywhere. Plus, they found a stash of cash hidden behind a clothes dryer—twenty G's. The guy was into manufacturing methamphetamines and likely dealing on the side.

Slink allowed an SUV to pass on their right. "What aren't you telling me?"

"It looked too neat, Blum says. Tolver's got no street history with narcotics. So they're thinking—"

"A set-up." Slink finished it for him. "Maybe staged for our benefit?"

"Blum says he'll keep us in the loop."

Autopsies were required by law in drug-related deaths. The body's condition would reveal if the victim were a long-term user. Until then, theories were guesswork.

Cale rolled the idea of a staged murder scene against their known facts. Now into the second year, they had a string of vanished females, one deceased. Add in another missing female who had threatened to leave her boyfriend; then add a seemingly illogical pit stop for gas by one missing victim's Honda Civic. A potential homicide victim (Ray Tolver) was outside a typical narcotics dealer's profile. Could he have been murdered to obtain a surveillance video of the kidnapping? Was his death set up as a drug OD to conceal the abductor's identity?

Did any of it make sense?

Cale recalled their initial feeling of the perpetrator being luckier than he was brilliant. A different vibe seemed evident now. The kidnapper couldn't simply be some lucky amateur, could he? Not if he were clever enough to disguise a murder scene.

Cale concluded that too many essential puzzle parts were absent, making the mystery almost unsolvable without their revelation. Time, he supposed, would tell. At least, he hoped so.

The Mustang pulled into the same Speedway station they had visited earlier. Three city police cruisers and Detective Blum's unmarked Dodge were already present.

"It looks like the party's already started without us," Slink said, cutting the engine.

"Wouldn't be the first time."

CHAPTER 12

Cindy Hulbreth awoke to an unfamiliar shadow world. Her mouth was taped shut, hands locked behind and secured to something long and hard like rubber, she guessed, which stretched across her back.

She turned her head and breathed through her nose. Her eyes, Cindy knew, were wide with fear. She might vomit any second, but she feared choking to death if it happened.

Drugged. What other explanation could there be? But how? By whom? Nothing made sense, and her brain felt confused and unable to remember simple thoughts from ten seconds ago.

The countless boring lectures she'd heard back in school rushed back now. Date rape drugs. Or substances creating mental confusion and memory loss. Cindy recalled lapping from a bowl of tepid water like an animal and had memories of shuffling across a room the way prisoners did. Why did it all feel like a childhood dream?

Another image came—even more frightening—of a dark figure advancing toward her from a vampire mist.

Shadowman.

He seemed formed more of vapor than substance. Had she indeed seen him? Or was her mind fashioning bogeymen to torment her?

No. Cindy hadn't imagined it—someone real had groped her, and his visits summoned images of glowing candles and sticky, saccharine melodies.

This man raped her. She remembered it now.

Her heart thudded, and painful tears saturated her eyes. How many times had he come for her? How long had she been tied here like a plaything, protesting, crying, screaming through her veil of tears? One gut-clenching fact now grabbed Cindy by the throat: the Shadowman would return.

And this, she realized, was her most terrifying thought of all.

Cale stared out the dining room window of their house as the twilight shadowed the yard like a purple canvas.

Maggie was upstairs, changing from her lawyer clothes. With Hank staring at him from his usual chair—plopped on his side like a laconic centerfold—Cale phoned Staszak.

"One down, one to go." Staszak sounded exhausted.

"Meaning?"

"The younger sister—Angela. Her parents agreed to pay property damage to Dereene's condo."

"Cute kid, I'm sure."

"Aren't all seventeen-year-olds?" Staszak pictured his own two teenage daughters. "At least it gets McBride off our case." He paused. "Any progress on the gas station lead?"

Cale stared out his window at the stand of trees bordering their property's back edge. They were the same trees he had played in as a child. Back then, he'd pictured them being a forest.

"Blum agrees with us. He thinks Ray Tolver's death wasn't an accidental OD. Says it reeks of a homicide."

"You think it's connected to the kidnappings?" Staszak asked.

"It's what they pay us to find out."

Staszak shifted topics. "You catch the evening news? The Hulbreth family's organizing a search party for tomorrow."

It came as no surprise to Cale. The families of the earlier victims had done similar searches, trying everything in their power to locate their missing loved ones. Especially when the police—in their opinion—appeared frustratingly inept.

"Are we involved in the search?"

"Sheriff's deputies are overseeing it all." Staszak sighed his frustration with the confounding case.

Cale couldn't blame the families for trying whatever they could. "Who knows? Maybe they'll find some clue?"

"Better lucky than good. Like you're always preaching."

"Ninety times out of a hundred."

They finished the call, and Cale left his phone on the table. Maggie's soft footsteps descended the stairs, and she spotted him sitting alone. She slipped into her shoes. Late-afternoon shadows filled the room.

"You doing all right?" she asked. She opened the hallway closet door, pulling out a light jacket.

Cale gave a half-smile.

"Just perfect." He moved across the room to the backdoor, opened it, and stood like a doorman on duty.

"I'll leave that one alone." She added, "Let's try and have fun tonight. Okay?" She kissed his cheek and brushed past him into the light of early evening. Blocks away, the church bells began to toll.

"Don't we always?"

The Hinterland Brewery and Restaurant are on the city's west side, nestled in the famous shadows of Lambeau Field. The popular restaurant is known for its friendly atmosphere, pub-style décor, tall, beveled windows, and superb menu. Add in the brass bar rails, teakwood floors, and homestyle draughts as reasons for its popularity.

On Tuesday night off-season, the raucous football crowds were nowhere to be found. The same went for the Packers' most recent Hall of Famer, Brett Favre—whose football career had ended a decade ago. The Old Gunslinger was reputed to stop by when visiting his old stomping grounds. The local team's legend was nowhere to be seen on this night. Cale hoped Slink—a notoriously avid Favre fan—wasn't too disappointed about not procuring an autograph.

Their party of six seated themselves at an oversized table across from the mirrored bar. Chloe's pharmacist husband, Ed, and Slink's lovely wife, Janet, rounded out their team. Attendance at the bar was sparse on a weeknight, and they were thankful for the extra elbow room. Across from Cale, Maggie sipped her pint of dark homebrew. Knowing she was due in court tomorrow morning, he wasn't concerned about her consumption.

Cale noted her amusement as he angled away from Chloe, seated beside him. Maggie's sister had dressed in one of her usual get-ups as if she might be called on stage. A glittery red satin pantsuit and a half-dozen (Cale counted them) arm bracelets, these set off by gaudy rings. Madam Zola, he reminded himself, and he often wondered if Chloe possessed even an ounce of psychic ability.

It might have been the beers. Or the cozy atmosphere. Or Cale's frustration with the recent kidnapping case. Or it might simply be the stress of it all. Whatever the reason, he decided tonight was a good night to test Maggie's sister's reputed psychic acumen.

Dinner moved along briskly, with discussions of current events leading to the detectives' progress in the "missing girl's" case. As adept as they were at dodging reporters' queries, Cale and Slink fielded the group's questions like a pair of seasoned infielders.

Midway through the meal, however, Cale turned to Maggie's sister during a lull in the conversation. No, he couldn't blame the beer. He was only on his third pint of amber ale.

"So, Chloe," he said casually. "With these visions of yours? Have you ever helped solve a murder case?"

Silence covered the table like a shroud, and Slink offered him an owlish stare. Cale added, "Just asking?" It was an innocent enough question, yet he could feel Maggie's eyes boring into him from across the table.

Chloe barely flinched. She replied as if repeating a line from a Noel Coward play, "Certainly, Detective." Her ruby lips pursed, and she turned his way. "Why on earth do you ask?"

"Blindsided?"

"You know what I'm talking about," Maggie said fervently from the passenger seat.

Cale spun the Bronco through a right-hand turn. "Sounds like an indictment, if you ask me." He enjoyed tossing legal terms her way at times. Especially after a few brews under his belt.

"If the shoe fits," Maggie countered.

He sighed, taking it down a notch. "Asking your psychic sister about her ability isn't *blindsiding*. I think it's a little harsh."

"It's a sensitive subject to her. How would you feel?"

How would he feel? "I'm not the one who's a psychic!" He gave her a sidelong glance while watching the Bronco's twin beams turn onto a shortcut they always took home.

Maggie's jaw was firm. Cale had seen this look many times in recent weeks. The identical way she'd faced him when announcing she was considering moving from the house if their level of communication didn't improve.

"Look, Mags—" He half-turned in the shadows. "No offense, but Chloe dresses like a storefront palm reader. I'm only wondering if it's for real?"

"People who are *different*." Her voice trailed off, and she looked out her window in frustration. "Why am I wasting time explaining this to you?"

Wonderful, Cale thought wearily. Now they had another thing to quarrel about.

They drove another five minutes in stubborn silence. Maggie sat with her arms crossed, eyes locked on the dark, tree-lined road ahead. She noted how Cale barely glanced her way, maintaining the quiet even as they navigated past a local cemetery. Her thoughts had darkened into a spider's web, and he seemed hesitant to aggravate things with more comments.

Maggie examined the shadowy cemetery closer as they passed. If she witnessed a troop of merry ghosts waltzing around a tombstone, she doubted Cale would believe her. Even if she shouted, pointing at them, and he spotted the identical vision himself, she guessed he'd pigheadedly deny what he saw.

Such a skeptic, Maggie told herself. And her with a psychic for a sister, no less. She wondered how she'd fallen in love with a naysaying, scoffing, nonbelieving Doubting Thomas.

Staring at her blurry reflection in the passenger window, Maggie reminded herself for the twentieth time in the past month: *No wonder I'm moving out.*

CHAPTER 13

Wednesday morning arrived overcast and drizzling together. Rising, Cale was thankful he'd limited his beer consumption last evening. Dinner with their friends had been amusing, despite the debate on the drive home over Chloe's "psychic" talents. It hadn't mattered that Maggie had been chilly in bed after they'd retired. She had a court case this morning.

After dating for their first two months, they had agreed on a rule: They would never go to sleep with an argument dividing them. Nonetheless, Cale hadn't considered last evening's debate any actual disagreement. He had merely questioned Chloe on her favorite topic: being a psychic. Maggie certainly understood his point about asking her sister if "seers" could assist law enforcement in resolving puzzling crimes, didn't she?

He hadn't even directed his query at Chloe, per se. He'd kept it vague. Still, he chided himself because Maggie had misread his questions as if he'd challenged her sister's core beliefs.

Thirty minutes later, fresh from the rowing routine—Hank enthralled by the chirps and chittering of animals on the giant screen—Cale moved into the kitchen. Maggie eyed him from near the stove.

"Want some tea?" She wore dark slacks and a matching blazer, ready to take on the day.

He tugged on the towel wrapped around his neck and sat on the counter stool. Declining the offer, Cale instead took a swig from his water bottle. "Somebody looks ready for battle." He kept the tone light—no point in rehashing last evening.

Maggie stirred her tea and opened a can of cat food. "Ready as I'll ever be, I suppose."

Cale understood the morning court case was essential to her confidence. As a public defense attorney, the last pair of juvenile gang members Maggie had represented were found guilty of aggravated assault. Deservedly so. They had beaten—almost murdered—an elderly grocery store owner. Despite Maggie's efforts at mounting a plausible defense, both youths were shipped away to the state juvenile correction facility. The case left her shut out defending gangbangers.

"The lad's going to need a sound defense today, Maggie May." He frowned as if troubled. "Not good if he finds out his attorney was out boozing the night before his trial."

Maggie set Hank's food dish down on the floor. He came running, a stiff-legged trot. She reached for her teacup on the counter and sipped. "It's an arraignment hearing."

"Not much diff—"

"And I wasn't out 'boozing,' as you so eloquently put it." Maggie gave him a dimpled grin.

Cale was pleased he could still make her laugh. It had to be worth something.

She slipped across the room and gave his shoulder a playful slug. He yelped while she strode down the hallway, climbing the stairs in her stocking feet.

"If you lose," he called out, "you'll be on their *No Mas* list!"

"I'm getting Sanchez off!" Her voice echoed off the walls of the hallway. "You can bet on it."

"I don't bet anymore. Remember?"

The high walls of the stairway swallowed her answer. Cale grinned in the morning light. He knew better than to ask her to repeat it.

The station house was filled with cops changing shifts. Cale had chosen to wear a gray shirt and no tie beneath his light jacket. He prayed his colorless tones weren't indicative of the day in-store, like the fashion equivalent of a mood ring.

At his desk, coffee in hand, he watched Slink stride in fresh from the workout room. His hair was slicked back as he approached Cale's desk. He leaned his knuckles on the paper-strewn surface.

Cale asked, "Fun last night?"

Slink rubbed his forehead. "Aside from the throbber I had waking up."

"Talking about your headache, I hope."

Slink shook his head and shifted the subject. "Chloe's husband's not a bad guy. He suggested I try a special nasal spray for my allergies."

"Seems to know his drugs, all right."

"He's a pharmacist. It's what they do." Slink's expression turned thoughtful. "By the way, since Chloe's our locally known psychic?"

Cale shot him a dangerous look.

Slink held up both hands. "Did she comment to Maggie? About you throwing it out there?"

"Sensitive subject."

"Couldn't hurt, could it? Her helping us out?"

Cale turned sarcastic. "Let's see, an amateur psychic, not to mention she's the sister of the lead detective's girlfriend. Yeah. I'm sure the press will give us an easy pass. Be real understanding of our position."

Slink sipped from his bottle of Gatorade.

Anton Staszak ended the discussion, approaching them with his bowlegged gait, like the steady lumber of a Kodiak bear. Reading glasses perched on the end of his nose, he held a manila case folder in one oversized paw.

"Been going over the profile on the three MPs. From last spring," Staszak said. He sat at his desk across the aisle and two up from Cale. "You think the Hulbreth disappearance adds anything new?"

Cale's brain spasmed. The perpetrator's stop for gas was still giving him heartburn. He'd been wrestling for the past twenty hours with what it meant to the profile on their abductor.

"My gut tells me it's relevant," Cale kept his tone even. "But we're still missing something."

After the autopsy last November—the headless body of Kimberly Vanderkellen—Cale had called Milwaukee and spoke with an FBI profiler—Special Agent Eddie Redtail. Despite the dearth of physical evidence in the case, Redtail had put together a physical description and a personality composite of their unknown subject.

Though criminal profiling often seemed more art than science, Agent Redtail possessed a true talent. Over the winter months, with their perpetrator having gone "inactive," the investigators realized their case had hit a solid wall. Yet Eddie Redtail's profile had remained unchanged.

Until now, Cale decided grimly.

The sloppy method of escape and five-dollar stop for fuel bothered him. Not to mention a potential eyewitness and the presence of security cameras. Their image of a clever criminal was dissolving like smoke.

His analytical mind, however, kept reeling him back to a simple assessment—the guy was luckier than he was bright.

"Our guy's stop for gas?" Cale said, arching an eyebrow at Staszak. "His victim might've even been in the car. You don't think it changes his profile?"

"Plus the murder of the station owner," Slink added. "Very sketchy timing there."

"If they're related," Staszak grumbled. "Still a huge if."

"They're related."

"Different MO." Staszak countered. "The Vanderkellen girl was beheaded. Tolver's a drug OD. Doesn't sound like the same guy to me."

"A perp can't change his MO?" Slink's voice climbed an octave. "You take a new criminology class or something?"

Staszak shook his head. "A stop for gas. So what?"

Cale pinched the bridge of his nose. "Last spring, didn't we decide our guy was tightly wound, like a control freak? A perfectionist?"

"Even perfectionist's cars need fuel." Staszak slapped the manila folder on his desk. "Don't run on helium, the last I checked."

"He lost control of his situation." Cale laced his fingers behind his neck. "He panicked."

"We still should've had the prick on CCTV." Slink couldn't let it go. With the perp's identity recorded, they'd have the case closed in a week.

"By my book," Staszak said, "he knew what he was doing."

"Runs out of gas during a kidnapping?"

"Maybe no genius—granted. It doesn't change how he's still three steps ahead of the Einsteins trying to catch him."

Silence formed around them.

Cale flicked on his desk PC and typed in a file number. The case's frustrations had them all on short fuses—the lack of evidence fraying at your nerve endings. Regardless of the profile, the facts didn't change. There were still missing victims out there, and time was evaporating.

Slink joined Cale at his desk. "The boyfriend? Dereene? Is he still a person of interest?"

Cale said, tapping the keyboard, "A juvie offense for public indecency. Ten years ago. Does he sound like a plausible threat?"

"A lot of serial killers get started by killing neighborhood pets. They've got to start somewhere."

Staszak called over his shoulder. "He didn't seem the type. Not from my interview with him."

"Same thing they said about Jeffrey Dahmer."

Cale leaned back in his chair, staring at his computer screen. "Okay. Kimberly Vanderkellen. She goes missing in June of last year. Last known whereabouts the East Side. Her apartment."

Slink hovered at his shoulder, leaning in. "Opposite side of town from the Hulbreth girl."

"We aren't living in frigging Manhattan," Staszak groused.

Their previous attempts at a geographic profile had failed, further complicated by their inability to have located the victims' missing vehicles.

"Hulbreth has blond hair," Cale stated. "They all did. Weight between one-ten and one-thirty. Each driving alone in their own cars."

Staszak rotated in his chair. "Why's the weight important again?"

"The sedatives he's using. Confirmed by the Vanderkellen autopsy. Maybe something to do with the correct dosage would be my guess."

"Or he just likes blondes," Slink stated. "His fixation; his paraphilia."

They mulled this in silence. Cale studied his screen. "The key has to be the cars."

They had run the makes and models through the FBI's national registry three times. No registrations had popped on vehicular resale rosters or in any known chop-shop listings.

"My guess is he's picking his victims on the fly. At random."

"If we're even talking about the same perp." Staszak's tone was cautionary.

"It's the same guy—I can feel it in my bones."

"Why does he take five months off?" Staszak asked. "Three vics last spring—bing, bing, bing. One dead body floats up. Then what? He goes on a European holiday?"

"BTK. In Kansas." Slink toyed with a pen. "Guy took several years off between victims."

Around them, uniforms and secretaries bustled, phones trilled. The station was a beehive of activity. The detective trio sat silently through it all, contemplating the many holes in their investigation, their frustrations compounding.

Cale decided they must look like three impotent men sitting in the waiting room of a fertility clinic.

CHAPTER 14

"How do the cars disappear?" Cale pointed at his screen with a ballpoint pen. "How's he ditch them afterward?"

Automobiles, he reasoned, didn't just vanish into thin air. Furthermore, why had there been no reported sightings of the perpetrator's car? No lingering, vacated, or abandoned vehicles had been noted by officers, citizens, or security personnel at any of the various potential abduction points.

At his desk, Staszak sipped from a Styrofoam cup. "We don't even know where these snatchings took place."

"Maybe he arrives on foot?" Slink sat perched on the corner of an open desk. "A guy dressed as a jogger would seem innocent enough. To most strangers, anyway."

Their silence matched the dreary weather outside. Cale could see a sky filled with brooding clouds through the nearby window. Rain was dotting the glass, and across the investigations area, phones buzzed, and fellow investigators shuffled about.

Cale flicked off his PC and kicked his chair back. How was their perpetrator choosing his victims? From movie theaters? Shopping malls? Grocery stores or restaurants? Health clubs? Vacant parking lots?

The list of possibilities seemed endless.

"Plus the date rape drugs," Slink said. "How's he getting his victims to ingest them?"

"Coffee? Soda?" Staszak offered. "Bottled water?"

These were healthy, aware young women, Cale reminded them. Without their suspicions aroused, they'd hardly accept unsolicited food or drink from a stranger.

"He jimmies their cars," Slink offered, "A backseat Dexter. Uses chloroform or whatever—knocks them into la-la land."

"Only in the movies." Cale was dismissive. "Women know enough to check their backseats. Hell, Maggie does it every time we drive half a block."

"Lawyers are suspicious by nature."

Cale shook his head. "Not a chance. We'd have a witness. Somebody would've seen something."

"So no chloroform. No Taser gun. What have we got left?"

"Zilch." Staszak's tone was glum. "We're right back where we started."

"Well, we can't just sit here." Slink studied them.

"We need the assistance of an actual professional psychic," Staszak commented with a groan.

When Cale glanced at Slink, he wasn't surprised to see his partner's sardonic smirk. Cale asked his partners: "Okay, hypothetical, then...how do you get an attractive, twenty-something female to let you into her car?"

He quickly added, "Without witnesses? Without drawing any attention?"

"And in broad daylight," Cale said, his eyes shifting between them. "Not just strolling up and sticking a gun or Taser in their ribs."

Cale steepled his fingertips, sitting back in his chair. At the water cooler in the near distance, he could hear a pair of narcotics detectives sharing an off-color joke.

"And we're sure this isn't a woman?" Staszak arched his eyebrows. "Or maybe he's got a woman accomplice?"

"Let's assume not. For the sake of argument."

Slink had moved a few paces away. When he turned, Cale noted his coy expression. "How about our abductor's not a stranger?" he asked. "What if he's somebody well-known? A local celebrity, say? Someone our vics might recognize?"

Staszak huffed at the suggestion. "We're not living in Tinsel Town, are we? No guys named Gosling or Reeves have moved next door to me lately." He removed his reading glasses and massaged his potato nose.

"TV news anchors." Cale threw it out there. "Weathermen. Talking heads. Faces people would recognize from TV ads."

"Local politicians."

"Priests and doctors. Even cops."

They were silent, giving the idea some legs. Cale noted the snark on Slink's face. "You don't think cops are above the law?"

Slink shook his head. "You're both Inspector Clouseau's." At their perplexed looks, he added, "Hello? Celebrities? How about the two-ton elephant in the room?"

Staszak cast eyes around the investigation's room.

Cale now heard the alarm bells in his head. Slink's idea was so far-fetched his heart began to gallop.

Staszak cracked his knuckles. He said to Slink, "You're not about to suggest—"

"Why not—"

"Because it's sick."

Slink opened his palms like a preacher. "All I'm saying is it's an angle. We're talking celebrities here, aren't we?"

Cale sensed the room narrowing as he calculated the odds of Slink's suggestion, including the dangerous political fallout. He gave Slink credit, though. It was an angle they should at least consider.

Cale pictured famous athletes in the national spotlight. Ballplayers in handcuffs doing perp walks or reading press statements, sharp-suited lawyers at their sides, proclaiming their clients' innocence.

He glanced at Staszak and saw the detective's shoulders were slumped in defeat. He lifted his head and stared at Cale.

"You guys aren't serious, are you?" Stasz asked.

"*Proud to Serve and Protect?*" Slink said, "Our motto?"

Staszak shook his head, but Cale rose and grabbed his jacket. A glance out the window showed the misting, overcast skies. "Our new motto is *No Stone Left Unturned.*"

"You can't change the motto," Staszak protested.

"I think he just did."

"Total BS."

Cale exited the bullpen, and they watched him disappear around the far corner.

Staszak glanced at Slink. "Where do you think he's going?"

"Where else?"

"Geez, Louise." Staszak's voice was as gloomy as the chilly wind against the window.

CHAPTER 15

Maggie wove her Mazda four-door through the morning traffic. She was trapped in the right-hand lane behind a city bus and took several calming breaths. Her phone chirped. She grabbed it off her passenger seat.

"About last night?" Chloe said, skipping formality. "Why was Cale asking about the psychic stuff?"

Maggie understood how Cale failed at taking anything paranormal seriously. It was doubtful he ever would.

"Just making small talk." Maggie decided to slough it off. "You know? Being sociable?"

"Do you think the police might want my help?"

Maggie's pulse quickened. She'd be in court in fifteen minutes. "Don't sweat it, Chlo. If they do, they'll let you know."

"I'd like to help, Mags, but I don't know if I can."

"They're stuck in a case. Grasping at straws."

"But it's a murder case. It's not some cat up a tree." Chloe sighed. "I didn't mean—I'm not brushing it off."

Maggie flipped her blinker on and bounce-turned into the courthouse's parking lot. She usually felt tense appearing in court. Still, wasn't there something hidden in her sister's voice? "Chloe? You sound strange. Is everything all right?"

Silence lingered between them. "Mags. I'm not sure if I should tell you—"

"Tell me what?"

Chloe exhaled dramatically. "I haven't had a true vision in quite some time."

With her hair pinned up, Maggie had dressed conservatively in a charcoal-gray pantsuit, cream-colored blouse, and low pumps. She sat at the defense table in the municipal court building, reviewing her notes, oblivious to the hushed voices and shuffling footsteps behind her.

A nearby cough caught her attention. ADA John Zackary stood beside his chair at the prosecution table and smiled when she turned. "Ready for another round?"

Maggie half-smiled. "Not much choice, do we?"

"I suppose not."

The ADA was in his mid-thirties with a reputation for being tough on juvenile gang crime. He had put away the last two gang members Maggie had defended.

Maggie, in truth, wanted little part in defending another gangbanger. She believed in defending the downtrodden, the weak, the defenseless, and those in genuine need. This did not include violent young street punks out for easy cash by ripping people off or dealing drugs to school kids.

Maggie had little passion for defending violent thugs. She wondered if, at times, it showed.

Today, her client was Juan-Julio Sanchez, another Latin King. Though only seventeen, he was a juvenile gang lieutenant who ran his own crew. Sanchez had been charged as an accomplice in a drive-by shooting—felony use of a deadly weapon (9mm Glock), having fired (allegedly) from a vehicle ('07 Camaro) at a group of teenage boys (East Side Ghouls) who'd been perched on the front porch steps of a ramshackle house (drug drop).

That the lads on the steps had responded with a barrage of return fire seemed of little relevance to the prosecution. The DA's office had been unwilling to reduce charges to unlawful possession, a misdemeanor. Instead, they wanted to make an example of Juan-Julio Sanchez.

"He claims he's innocent," Maggie said.

"There's a news flash."

Maggie ignored Zackary's sarcasm, glancing instead at her notes. "Says he was simply the driver."

"And Hannibal Lecter just drinks beer with brats."

The comment caused Maggie to smile.

They were in court for the arraignment hearing. An actual trial date would be set based on the defendant's plea, with Maggie then confirmed as his judge-appointed attorney.

Behind them, the courtroom had filled with friends and supporters of the accused.

Maggie shifted her attention to the front. A tan-shirted sheriff's deputy escorted in her client. Juan-Julio Sanchez had jet-black hair with blond highlights, shaved at the sides, and a pencil-thin mustache. One tattoo depicted a twisting crucifix on his wrist. More ink—four tiny red blood droplets on his neck. He wore a baby-blue jumpsuit, his wrists shackled in front.

He was already more of a man than an adolescent. His demeanor proclaimed the typical indifference of gangsters.

Maggie had wondered if many of them had a "violence gene" imprinted in their DNA. She recalled Cale's rebuttal: "They're in it for the bling, Maggie May. No more, no less."

Probably so, she admitted.

Two prior meetings occurred between her and Sanchez in his detention cell. It had been a game of cat and mouse. He played hardass on the initial visit, proclaiming his innocence. The whole thing felt like a set-up.

At their second meeting, the youth had challenged her—barely disguising the sexual innuendo in his voice—how it was Maggie's responsibility to "get him off."

After the second visit, she requested a case transfer. The juvenile offender had threatened her, Maggie inferred. She offered little in the way of proof to support her claim. In her mind, however, the implication had been apparent.

With the number of cases the public defender's office had on the books, Maggie's request had been denied. Like it or not, she was stuck defending Juan-Julio Sanchez. Watching her client enter the courtroom now, she wished she hadn't made her boastful earlier claim to Cale morning: "I'm getting Sanchez off." She had a feeling the declaration might come back to haunt her.

Throwing off attitude, Juan-Julio arrived at the defense table and half-slumped on the wooden chair beside her. He acknowledged her with a tight smirk, intimating he held little confidence in her ability to win him his freedom.

Behind them, the crowd buzzed. Sanchez swung his head around, mugging, raising his cuffed fists, and thumbs-upped his gallery of supporters.

"All rise!" the bailiff called. The thirty-odd citizens lifted from the butt-numbing benches like Born Agains from their pews.

Judge Ambrose Hoskins, a dour-faced man with saggy jowls, strode into the courtroom, robe flapping, and took his place behind the bench. The bailiff handed him the docket, and the spectators flopped back in their seats like it might be their most taxing accomplishment of the week.

"Let us proceed." Judge Hoskins focused on the defense table. "Ms. Jeffers, we are all familiar with the charges. You have now been assigned officially as the defendant. Would your client like to enter a plea at this time?"

Maggie rose. In a firm voice, she said, "Mr. Sanchez pleads not guilty, Your Honor."

Cheers erupted in the courtroom.

CHAPTER 16

Judge Hoskins peered down at Maggie over his spectacles. He nodded at the bailiff. "Duly noted, Ms. Jeffers. I'm setting the trial date for—" He studied his calendar. "—July seventh. Nine a.m."

The parties were busy noting the date when a grating voice piped from the back of the courtroom. "Your Honor!" the nasal voice intoned. "With your permission, I'd like to address the court."

Heads turned toward the center aisle.

The judge glowered, searching for the culprit responsible for disturbing his court's decorum. The deputies stationed near the exits stiffened as the man—stocky, wire-rimmed spectacles, gray-speckled hair swept back in a ponytail— swept up the aisle toward the front of the courtroom. He carried a soft-leather attaché.

"Oh no." Maggie groaned, recognizing the voice.

Lester Paprika had worked his way through the system. First as a public defender, then as a deputy prosecutor with the DA's office. Seven years later, he'd graduated into private practice and specialized in juvenile cases. The problem lay not in Paprika's specialty. No, as many saw it, the sour taste was due to Lester's allegedly taking most of his juvenile gang cases pro bono, then accepting illegal cash payouts from gang leaders on the side.

Maggie doubted Lester had joined the legal business for the camaraderie. As Cale had said suggested, knowing the shady shyster's clients, he was in it for" the bling."

"Mr. Paprika." Judge Hoskins appeared irritated. "You are interrupting my courtroom. I hope this is relevant to—" He glanced at his notes. "—Mr. Sanchez's case?"

"Quite so, Your Honor. Quite so."

As Lester neared the front tables, he paused a respectful fifteen feet from the bench. He kept one eye on the judge, his other on the nearby security guard, who held his hand at his hip.

"If it pleases the court," Lester announced, "as of this morning, the Sanchez family has solicited me to represent the legal affairs of Juan-Julio, here." He nodded toward the defendant, and his smile at Maggie turned shark-like.

Judge Hoskins narrowed his bushy eyebrows.

Maggie remained silent. What could she say? She watched the events unfold as if floating outside her body.

A chesty, dark-haired man lifted on his bowed legs amid the courtroom crowd. He waved his hand like a student vying for the teacher's attention.

"And who might you be, sir?" Judge Hoskins asked.

"Pepito Sanchez, Your Honor. Juan-Julio's uncle. My wife and me have paid Mr. Paprika's retainer fee."

More comedic farce, Maggie noted. Pepito Sanchez? Juan-Julio was a Latin Kings member, a gang of violent street thugs. The "uncle" looked like someone plucked from a road crew. Maggie wasn't being skeptical. But it depended, she supposed, on whose ox was being gored. At present, it was her own and on full display in a courtroom full of people.

Paprika's representing Sanchez smelled of a backroom deal. It meant Lester represented oppositional sides of the city's ongoing street gang battle. The Latin Kings versus their notable rivals—the Hombres or Satan's Apaches—both of whom Lester had previously represented.

A sweet deal as long as the bullets weren't flying at you from all sides at once. The young criminals, Maggie imagined, paid for their legal services in straight cash. Like she said, an odorous deal.

Judge Hoskins broke into her thoughts, asking Juan-Julio if a change in representation was acceptable to him.

"Sí, Your Honor." He glanced at Maggie. "*Muy* acceptable. *Bueno*."

Maggie rolled her eyes. To Juan-Julio's credit, he seemed capable of an Oscar-worthy performance.

The chorus of murmurs turned silent. "So be it." Judge Hoskins gave Maggie a meaningful stare. "It appears you've lost your client, Ms. Jeffers."

Lester jumped in. "Thank you, Your Honor." He stepped to the defense table, setting his briefcase down, and winked at Maggie from behind his wire-rim glasses. He told the court: "My client's plea stands as entered." He puffed out his chest. "Not guilty!"

Cheers and applause filled the room, accompanied by the judge's thumping gavel.

Maggie turned to Juan-Julio, whose features had taken on the smug expression of a Mafiosi's son. "Why didn't you tell me this earlier?"

"One final time, *chica*." His dangerous brown eyes dripped with sincerity. "I wanted one more look at your beauty."

Maggie glared contemptibly at his childish comment. On the other hand, hadn't she wanted off this case anyway?

"Is this really in your best interest?" she asked.

"I do what they tell me, senora." The juvenile shrugged.

Maggie began stuffing papers into her satchel. A few feet away, Paprika requested bond and was promptly denied. After a final gavel rap, Judge Hoskins swept from his chair and vanished into his chambers.

Lester Paprika turned and disappeared back up the aisle as if he'd been an apparition.

A sheriff's deputy neared their table. Sanchez leaned close to Maggie's side. "One last thing, Miss Jeffers,"—so close she could smell his hair gel—"I know about the girls."

The deputy arrived. Juan-Julio rose and stepped forward, submitting to his escort. Maggie remained frozen, however, uncertain of what he'd said. "What do you mean?" She called to him, puzzled.

He turned his shoulder and mouthed, "I know about the girls." Then he winked, and the deputy guided him from the courtroom.

"Maggie? You okay?" John Zackary's voice reached her from across the aisle. "You look pale as a ghost."

She shook her head. "Paprika."

"A major butt pain."

She wasn't listening, oblivious to the mass exodus at the courtroom's back. Juan-Julio Sanchez's perplexing message still rang in Maggie's head:

"I know about the girls."

CHAPTER 17

The vision of Lambeau Field rose in the misty gray distance as if a giant alien spaceship had landed on the city's west side. Temple-like cement steps led up to several entrances.

Cale navigated the Bronco up Lombardi Avenue, telling himself any decent investigator would pursue this angle. And though believing it wholly, a voice far back in his brain's recesses sounded unconvinced. As he neared the stadium, his stomach tightened. Born and raised in Green Bay, Cale understood the local football franchise wielded more clout than a committee of federal justices.

Nevertheless, it was a criminal investigation. It couldn't hurt to explore the local celebrity angle, could it?

He swung the Bronco into the parking lot of the franchise corporate offices, then hustled for the door while dodging raindrops. A receptionist issued him the sorry look she reserved for wet puppies. Cale flashed his ID, thankful he'd called ahead requesting an appointment with Jerry Skowing.

She tapped the extension. "Lieutenant Van Waring's here to see you," she said into her headset. Cale had his back turned, taking in the large black-and-white photos of past team glory.

She buzzed a glass door open, pointing to him: "Through those double doors down the hallway there, hon. He'll meet you in the atrium."

Slink Dooley got started on the phones. He called the families of the prior victims. Had any of them been avid sports fans? Attend Packers games? Had any mentioned hooking-up with a football player in the days, weeks, or months before her disappearance? Did any of them qualify as "jock groupies?"

Slink listened and scribbled relevant facts on his legal pad. He learned Leslie Dowd and Mary Jane Moore had attended games regularly. The other two hardly at all.

Slink noted Anton Staszak, positioned at his nearby desk, had reacted to these exchanges like a man who'd tasted spoiled fish. The "Packers angle"—as they'd decided to call it—bothered him immensely. Hell, it bothered Slink as well. A professional football player? One involved somehow in deviant kidnappings? It seemed ludicrous.

And yet, they were each dedicated homicide investigators. Despite sailing into uncomfortable waters, it was their civic duty, which they'd sworn to uphold. *No rock unturned*, Slink reminded himself.

Jerry "Scoop" Skowing was fifty-five years old with speckled hair the color of a dove's feathers. He was a former homicide detective Cale had worked with years ago when he'd first graduated from Narcotics. When Skowing retired from the force, he'd taken his current position with the local franchise as Director of Security. The job encompassed everything from stadium security to parking lot supervision to ticket scalping—along with fifty other things. These were all in addition to keeping the players safe and secure from over-zealous fans, scam artists, and autograph hounds.

Entering the massive Lambeau Field atrium with echoing footsteps, Cale spotted his former colleague as he emerged from a set of smoke-glass doors.

The men greeted like old frat brothers inside the open, seven-story structure. Cale discerned escalators and banks of elevators grouped at the far end and floors of glassed-in private offices. An elaborate restaurant occupied the lower level, and an escalator descended to the massive Pro Shop below. The open expanse beneath the towering ceilings made the place feel more like Grand Central Station than a football venue.

"What brings a homicide gumshoe to our humble abode?" Skowing asked inquisitively.

Cale remembered Scoop fondly. Like most former cops, he always cut through the BS and got straight to the chase.

Cale smiled. "Just crossing a couple of T's on a case."

Skowing's speckled eyebrows narrowed. Cale understood the man couldn't be easily snowed and was aware homicide detectives seldom stopped by for idle chitchat. The wariness in the man's gray eyes told him as much.

Scoop led them across the atrium, where they sidestepped dozens of tourists snapping phone cameras and wearing varieties of green-and-gold attire.

Entering the private, unmarked doors, the pair proceeded along an emerald-carpeted hallway. Later, a few twists and turns deposited them in Scoop's inner sanctum—the central security hub inside the stadium.

Scowing's office was modest, showing a wide desk, chairs, and seacoast prints on the walls.

Skowing must have proven his loyalty to the organization to have landed his lofty position. They seated themselves comfortably, a pair of old friends.

"You still sniffing around that pretty arm candy?" the man asked, displaying the wolfish grin Cale recalled. "The gal with you at Rodzinski's funeral?"

"Maggie Jeffers," Cale nodded. "She's an attorney with the PD's office."

"Beauty and brains to boot." Scoop fell into the folksy bumpkin act he'd perfected years ago.

"She's great," Cale said sincerely. He wasn't there to reveal details of his personal life.

Skowing's eyes twinkled. "Question is, what's she see in a Cro-Magnon like you?"

"I ask myself the same thing every day."

The security man cut back to the chase. "So, what's on your mind, Cale? I know you didn't drive out here to chew the fat with my scraggly old butt."

"Some of us were talking," he eased in, "wondering how close you keep tabs on your players?" Cale crossed one casual knee. "Mostly off-the-field stuff. You know?"

Skowing's eyebrows narrowed. "We steer clear of their private affairs. But no denying it, we keep sharp eyes and ears out."

Scoop had a long chin and narrow chest, which lifted as he exhaled. "Unfortunately, there's potential litigation lurking around every corner. Phone cams, videos, social media stuff. All this Twitter and twatter crap."

The security man leaned forward, his expression turning more serious. "Is one of our guys in trouble, Cale?"

Cale shook his head. "We've got a nasty kidnapping case we're working on. You might've read about it."

Skowing nodded, and a sad expression tightened his face.

"A new theory evolved. But it's pure conjecture."

"Involving a player. Why else would you be here?"

Cale understood the delicacy of the man's position. His old friend could not ignore a heads-up if the cops gave him one. Some player involved in unsavory business? Darn right, the director of security would want to know about it.

"Do your personnel guys keep individual psych profiles?" Cale asked. He understood the information was considered part of private HIPPA medical records.

"We run a Matrix test—a mini psych eval." Scoop further revealed players all signed medical waivers indicating any preexisting conditions, a necessary part of receiving a team's contract offer. "Modern times, eh?" he smiled humorlessly.

"But someone could omit the spicy details, couldn't they?"

"It's difficult to cover much up these days—even the old college stuff."

"Still." Cale sat forward. "It could happen, couldn't it?"

Skowing leaned back with a cop-like stare. "I see where you're headed with this, Cale. But..." He shook his head, his words fading.

Both men agreed the odds seemed astronomical. Despite this, Cale wasn't surprised when his former colleague offered to reveal any "possibles"—of which there were none, he assured. In exchange, the investigators would provide Scoop with details relevant to the team's involvement ahead of time. It was a fair deal on both sides, they agreed.

The security head escorted him across the cavernous atrium to the glassed front doors, where Cale moved into the misty drizzle and descended the concrete steps.

Behind him, Skowing held the door ajar. "Keep your little sugar cube out of this rain!" he called out. "Wouldn't want her melting, would we?"

Hitching his collar up, Cale shouted, "I'll pass along your concern."

CHAPTER 18

Traffic swept along the highway, each vehicle spraying the one behind it with a muddy wash. Cale ratcheted up the Bronco's wipers and phoned Staszak.

"I met with Skowing," he informed, getting to the point. "He agreed to help us with any pertinent info."

"You want me to do a cartwheel?" Staszak was less than enthused.

"Only if I'm around to watch." Cale pictured him hunched at his desk like a grumpy bear.

"Message from Cap." Staszak shifted topics. "He wants to meet. Chief's on him for an update."

Cale had hoped to delay disclosing his visit with Skowing. The longshot would fizzle fast. The city's brass would view it as a massive waste of time.

"Tell him I'm working on the missing cars. Don't mention the Lambeau visit."

Stasz remained disheartened. "I'm with you. No point in giving Cap a heart attack." They ended the call.

The Interstate beltline choked the city like a noose of concrete. Cale accelerated the Bronco through the drizzle. As his wipers slapped, he recalled his discussion with Chloe last evening. Did they want a psychic involved? Things were desperate enough, but the press reaction would be scalding.

Solving crimes, however, was a bottom-line business. Regardless of angry opinions, only results mattered. Perhaps seeking Chloe's expertise made some sense after all.

The sky revealed a soiled parade of clouds in the north. Temperatures had dropped, and it felt more like February than April. Old Man Winter thumbed his nose at any promise of spring.

Cale shifted lanes, cutting off a red BMW sports car while spraying it with gritty slush. The insulted driver honked, roaring temperamentally past him on the right. The dark-haired man flipped him the bird. Cale noted the car's license plate: CLSTYU. Mr. Sports Car apparently enjoyed being close but not too close.

His phone chirped. STASZAK the read-out displayed, Cale switched to speaker, figuring he'd best pay attention to the road. He asked Stasz, "Slink still out on the field search?"

"The only thing he'll catch is pneumonia."

"Did Cap set the meeting time?"

Staszak ignored him and grumbled, "Millions of people work seasonally. It doesn't mean our perp's a pro football player."

"You're right on both counts."

Staszak huffed derisively. "It's your necks on the line, Cale. I'm not dicking up my pension over Dooley's crazy theory."

"I hear you, Pontius Pilate."

A beat of silence. "And that means what again?"

"You're washing your hands of the case."

Staszak's chuckle was low. "Now you're a Bible reader?"

Cale's stomach was knotted over the case. He said, "If we don't catch a break soon, I might take it up."

Cindy Hulbreth's apartment was easy enough to locate. Cale eased the Bronco up the lane and checked the numbers above the units until he found the proper address. He parked in front of the non-descript building, then punched Slink's number.

Slink answered, parroting a stadium announcer's voice. "Live from the frozen tundra of Lambeau Field; it's Cale Van Waring!"

Cale said, "I'm outside Hulbreth's apartment."

"You disappoint me."

"Likewise. How's the search going?"

"Goose egg, so far," Slink admitted. "Sheriff deputies are handling it. The dogs look wet, tired, and pissed. Give them credit, though—they even had a search chopper combing those old woods along the tracks."

If nothing else, Cale allowed, at least they were thorough. "I'm taking a look at Hulbreth's apartment. Call the old auto body place. Culbertson's."

"The chop shop?"

"Feel them out on any missing vehicle activity."

Before hanging up, Slink shifted topics. "Hope you at least got me Aaron Rodgers' autograph."

"How about Scoop Skowing's?"

"Like I said."

Cale stood outside the door marked 202. He used the spare key Mrs. Hulbreth had provided them.

Inside, the boxy layout retained a lingering feminine scent: candles, potpourri, and a few potted plants lining one wall of the compact living room. The walls showed floral prints, and the chairs were poufy.

Snapping on gloves, Cale began a slow and thorough review of the vacant premises. Who was the person Cynthia Hulbreth? He understood that without any ransom demand, the average time abducted victims lived clocked in between three and five days via the FBI's national crime statistics.

He offered a silent prayer that Cindy was still alive.

The place was filled with knickknacks. Framed pictures on the shelves stood like lonely soldiers on the dresser top—Cindy with her grinning girlfriends and devoted family. Glimpses of a bright life interrupted.

Cale once again pictured last year's previous victims. Slink had been correct: they were all attractive young women in the same age range, possessing light-colored hair. It was significant, Cale understood, for both their abduction profiles and any potential future victims.

The thought made his stomach churn.

Inside the bedroom, Cindy's parents' smiling faces stared back from the dresser photos. Next came a framed picture of nerdy Angela—he guessed a younger, less cynical version. This Angela wore a backward baseball cap and sprayed someone unseen with a garden hose. There were no photos of her boyfriend, Ronnie Dereene. Significant? Probably not. She had already told him she was breaking off her romance.

Cale next examined inside the walk-in closet and opened bureau drawers, which all revealed nothing of substance—no signs of a hasty departure—and no girl crush photos of professional football players tacked to the walls. Of course, he had expected to find nothing of the sort. Yet the search alone doused him with the reality of how quickly our lives came and went.

Striding from the apartment building, he emerged back into the persistent mist. A northerly breeze had plastered pieces of soggy debris against the Bronco's windshield. Cale wondered how his own life would appear to an outsider looking in. Likely as empty and desolate as Cynthia Hulbreth's now did.

He still had a chance to turn it around, didn't he?

The Fourth of July weekend was coming at him fast. Cale's existence, post-Maggie, wasn't yet etched in stone. However, the same word *desolate* lingered darkly in his mind—especially if he failed to repair their relationship difficulties. After all, wasn't solving puzzles what he did for a living? Intricate and often clueless ones? How could solving a typical puzzle of love and romance be that much different?

CHAPTER 19

The room was coffin black. Cindy Hulbreth's wrists and ankles were secured, and she lay trapped inside a crypt of dead silence. A sound fluttered her way, floating as soft and downy as a baby's sigh.

Shadowman.

The tape stretched across her mouth, muting any attempt to shout or scream. She wasn't sure how long she'd been asleep and vaguely wondered how she was being drugged. Did he enter while she slept; or sneak up in her nightmares?

Cindy lay on her stomach. Twisting her head, she peered into the surrounding blackness while exhaling deep, calming breaths through her nose. Unable to focus, tears seeping from her eyes, she felt the obscene presence lurking across the room.

Shadowman.

An overwhelming sense of dread caused Cindy's skin to prickle. Her heart galloped. He was here with her once more, watching, breathing, listening. And yet, he remained encased in the onyx layers painting the place.

The music came softly, the opening few notes rising above barely a whisper. A reedy, off-key male singing voice, asking, "Why do birds *da-da-da* appear...?"

Cindy's mind shrieked like screeching violins, and her arms and legs thrashed against the taught bindings. The thin, whispery voice was suddenly beside her ear with a drawn-out chorus line: "da-da-dadely-da...close to you."

Everyone understood Green Bay Police Chief Donald Harris was prone to indigestion. And it was triggered right now, just after he'd received a blistering phone call from His Honor, the mayor.

"Remember Scoop Skowing?" Harris now inquired after storming into Captain Leo McBride's office.

His boss's presence caused McBride's guts to clench. He thought to himself: Now what?

"Jerry Skowing? Former Homicide detective?" McBride kept his tone steady.

"He works for the Packers these days. Security Head." Chief Harris said this without sitting.

"Yeah. I heard."

McBride wasn't sure where this crazy train wreck might be headed. He kept his eyes wary. The chief wasn't prone to popping in to "chew the fat," as McBride imagined they called it back in the Lone Star state, where the chief had previously worked.

"Seems one of your detectives paid Skowing a visit this morning," Chief Harris explained. "Lieutenant Van Waring all but accused a team player—for God's sake, Leo!—of being involved in this abduction mess."

McBride's eyes widened. "Did he say which player?"

Harris scowled. "Skowing didn't name any names."

The wheels inside the captain's head were spinning, and his silence rendered a sense of solemnity to the angry chief's accusatory tone.

"Skowing decided it best to report the visit to the team's president Gene Bartell." Harris added, "Bartell called the mayor, fuming and cussing a blue streak."

Chief Harris, at last, took a seat in one of the room's vacant chairs. He did not comment on the amateur artwork gracing the walls. "I'm assuming Van Waring's acting on your authority?"

Leo McBride hadn't risen through the ranks by being naïve. He was savvy enough to recognize a departmental squeeze play when one hit him between the eyes. His boss was suggesting he, Leo, fall on the sword. Take personal responsibility for the actions of his apparent rogue squad of investigators.

"Special Crimes is in charge of the abduction case," McBride said. "Van Waring's got the full go-ahead. For him to visit Skowing—well, he must've had good reason."

The Mona Lisa clock on McBride's desk ticked away the seconds.

"I hope I don't have to spell it out for you, Leo." The chief's twang was acerbic. "This thing could quickly turn into a real crap-howler."

McBride understood the Packers were a mere notch below God Almighty in a city christened "Titletown." On crisp autumn afternoons, those standings were often reversed.

"Cale's on the way here now. I'll get this mess cleaned up."

"You do that, Captain." The chief rose. He paused before opening the office door. "And Leo, keep your dogs on a short leash from here on out. You hear?"

Watching his boss depart, McBride took a cursory glance out his window. The afternoon had turned bleak, washed by the drizzle and chill of a bustling wind. The ill spring weather, he understood, was about to follow Cale Van Waring and his partners indoors.

"Already? How did it happen?" Cale asked.

While navigating the city streets, Staszak called again, describing the uproar among the department's upper brass.

"Wear your hard hat when you get here."

Thanking him for the heads-up, Cale cursed after hanging up. He should have done a better job of calculating the fallout. Before he could ream himself out too much, his phone buzzed.

Maggie's voice sounded jittery, distant from her usual confident self. Cale's neck hairs bristled. It was rare when she phoned during the day.

"Mags? You okay?"

"I suppose," she offered gamely. But after a few seconds' pause, the dam burst. "Okay, not so much. I lost the Sanchez case."

"I thought it was an arraignment hearing?"

She sounded caught between anger and tears. He pictured her standing in the kitchen, refrigerator open, contemplating a wine bottle if she were back at the house.

"I *lost* it to Lester Paprika!"

"What? How—"

"He waltzed in like a vulture, that's how!"

At least she was angry, Cale decided. He merged with the downtown traffic. Like most men, he preferred anger to tears if given a choice. Cale could deal with anger. They'd already had their share of tears over the past few weeks.

Cale imagined hearing the refrigerator door open. "Where are you, hon? Right now, I mean."

"I took the afternoon off."

He pictured her peering into the open refrigerator door, a bottle of Piesporter winking back—the image of her working a corkscrew. Cale stopped at an intersection, watching his wipers swat at the drizzle.

"When are you coming home?" she asked distantly. "There's something I've got to tell you."

His stomach knotted again, his mind flashing through multiple worst-case scenarios. "You want to tell me now?"

"No. When I see you."

Cale imagined hearing wine glugging from the bottle, sloshing into the tulip glass with the black stem he knew she favored.

"Maggie?"

"It's something my client—correction, *former* client—Juan-Julio Sanchez told me. Before they led him from the courtroom."

Cale accelerated through the intersection. The stoplights and other vehicles seemed to swim in and out of focus. "Mags? You still there?"

She spoke just above a whisper. "Yeah. Where else would I be?"

Standing barefoot in the kitchen, Maggie held her phone to her ear. She had to tell Cale what had happened. He was under heavy pressure with the kidnapping case. Maggie's inner voice cautioned that he didn't need a drama queen right now, although she genuinely desired to be one.

Maggie took a soft sip of wine. "Sanchez told me he knows something about your missing girls."

"Seriously?" Cale sounded alert. "Did he mean *our* missing girls?"

Maggie sighed. "He wasn't specific. His exact comment was: 'I know about the girls.'"

A shiver climbed her spine as she recalled Juan-Julio's dark, malevolent eyes. Stooping now, she used her free hand to scoop up Hank, who wouldn't leave her ankles alone. He wriggled onto the countertop, and she moved the wine bottle to avoid his swishing tail.

"He said that?" Cale's voice was low and steady.

"I figured you'd want to know." Then she added, "See you when you get home."

Cale pulled into the station lot and parked. He sat in silence with a dozen different questions shuffling through his brain. What circumstances might connect a gangbanger like Sanchez to a lunatic kidnapper? The abductor who may have beheaded one of his victims?

But first things first. He understood a giant crapstorm awaited him in the captain's office. Nonetheless, all he could think of were Maggie's words echoing in his head:

"I know about the girls."

CHAPTER 20

Maggie traced one fingertip along the rim of her wine glass, gazing out the living room window. The late morning was dreary and windswept. And here she was on her third glass of wine, finally starting to relax. The anger, jitters, and tension were diminishing with each swallow.

It could have been worse, Maggie decided, grasping, perhaps, at whatever tiny consolation she could manage.

Her mind flashed back to the courtroom. She'd cringed at the grating voice of Lester Paprika, and the back of her neck had warmed when Judge Hoskins announced: "It appears you've lost your client, Ms. Jeffers."

How embarrassing.

Yet despite what had transpired, Maggie decided things weren't as disastrous as they'd first seemed. Instead of slinking from the courtroom with her tail tucked—as she'd wanted—Juan-Julio had bestowed her with his obtuse message that might be helpful. Thus in fairness to her wounded psyche, she concluded the entire morning hadn't been a total waste.

Especially if the obtuse revelation helped Cale in his case.

Maggie climbed the steps leading up to the family room. Hank spotted her from the windowsill and stopped grooming long enough to grace her with a stare. She took another sip from her wine glass and gazed through the French doors overlooking the outer patio deck. The drizzle continued like angels weeping, and the budding, waterlogged leaves bowed their heads as if in communal prayer.

Maggie's reflection stared back at her in the window glass. It was a workday, and she held a private pity party in leggings and an old sweatshirt. She had half a dozen other cases she could be working on, clients, unlike Juan-Julio Sanchez, who were good and honest people who appreciated her efforts toward helping them.

"No more gangbangers ever, please," she whispered to the reflection. Let the Lester Paprika's of the world handle their situations.

Yes, it could have been worse, Maggie concluded. Cale would arrive home in a few hours. They could laugh together and perhaps find humor in her humbling experience. Isn't it what couples do? Help one another through life's ups and downs.

If only Cale would open his heart to her and wasn't so aloof and unemotional half the time. They could be so happy together.

Maggie admitted she loved Cale more than she'd let him know. Despite this admission, however, she understood it didn't change things. Empty boxes had been gathered, and her July departure plan was chugging along like an old steam locomotive. It's what hurt the most. Her love—their love—didn't hold enough depth to salvage their relationship.

In her years before meeting Cale, Maggie had accepted loneliness as a curse. Growing up in a Milwaukee suburb, she and her sister—Chloe was older by two years—had lost their parents in a tragic automobile accident. Maggie was ten years old at the time. Looking back, it had been a horrendous ordeal for two young girls.

After the funeral, the sisters were taken away together to reside with Aunt Fay. She lived in a small rural town in the heart of the state—far away from urban Milwaukee. It was the place they'd needed to patch their emotional wounds and move forward with their budding young lives. Childless and unmarried herself, Aunt Fay was pleased to come to the aid of the orphaned girls. And she had vowed to raise them as her own.

Being the eldest sister, Chloe was the more resilient of the pair. Chloe possessed a unique outlook on how the world functioned, believing in karma, fate, and the more spiritual aspects of things. In Chloe's mind, the world appeared governed by mysterious forces. People stepped in a puppet dance, manipulated by invisible dictates and suspicious, unseen forces.

This type of thinking, which she'd partially learned from Aunt Fay, allowed Chloe to open her psyche to the unseen forces hidden within us all.

As for the occasional second-sight visions her sister had displayed, Maggie could vouch for one which stood out above the rest.

"I saw dreadful images last night," Chloe had informed her one morning at breakfast, the day their parents had departed on their fateful trip.

"What kind? What did you see?"

"It was like a dream at first." Chloe's distraught tone had colored her voice, summoning deep apprehension in young Maggie. "Mom and Dad were crying. And the car was on fire."

At such a tender age back then, Maggie barely managed a reply. Chloe had to be playing a joke, frightening her for amusement. Sisters, she knew, often pulled pranks on one another.

"It's one of the crazy dreams you get, Chlo," Maggie had said dismissively. "You've had them before."

"It was *more* than a dream this time." Chloe held out both her hands. "See? I'm still shaking."

Reality had proven grim for the sisters. To their grave misfortune, their parents had pulled the family Buick off to the side of the road with a smoking radiator. A semi-truck, roaring over a blind hill, had crashed into them from behind and demolished their car on impact. Both innocent occupants of the Buick, trapped fatally inside, had perished on the spot in a blazing fireball.

The family later learned the truck driver was on the final leg of an eight-day haul and weary to the point of exhaustion. The sad revelation made the disaster even more heart-wrenching.

As for Chloe's dire vision of crying and screaming and bodies aflame? It continued to haunt Maggie all through her youth. And the eeriest part—as they'd learned much later—was Chloe had revealed her vision to Maggie hours before the coroner's "time of expiration" had been recorded on the death certificates.

CHAPTER 21

The detectives marched into Captain McBride's office like a trio of errant schoolboys. Cale followed Staszak, with Slink bringing up the rear. They closed the door behind them.

It was early afternoon, and they'd each consumed delivered sandwiches at their desks.

Cale settled into his customary chair and eyed the captain, who appeared in no mood for idle chitchat. A phony Picasso stared at Cale on the far wall, its single unblinking eye an accusatory omen of things to come.

"The Chief stormed in here earlier, gentlemen." McBride's voice turned soft, reminding Cale of a preacher warming to a fire-and-brimstone sermon. "He's not a happy camper."

"It's never an exact science," Slink said. He crossed an ankle over his knee. "Theories. Scenarios. You throw stuff against the wall and see what sticks."

The captain remained silent.

Cale sensed their boss might explode at any second. "Look, it's all my fault." He sat forward in his chair. "Scoop Skowing was my idea."

"Mine first," Slink volunteered.

"Shut up, Dooley."

Cale added soberly, "I figured why not talk to Skowing? He's a former detective?"

"Sure. Why not?" McBride oozed sarcasm. "Chief Harris gets the mayor's call ten minutes after you left Lambeau. And manure runs downhill, gentlemen—manure runs downhill."

Wind rattled the exterior windows. Cale pictured Maggie alone at home drinking wine. He could be beside her in less than twenty minutes if they suspended him on the spot now.

McBride sighed and gathered himself. "All right. Done is done. We move on from here." He studied them all. "What's our investigation status right now?"

Relief washed over Cale. "We've got a related suspicious drug death. A gas station owner named Ray Tolver. Maybe tied to the kidnapping."

Slink added, "We interviewed Hulbreth's boyfriend. We don't think he's involved."

Silence as the rain slapped the windowpanes.

"Blum's handling the Tolver drug OD—" Cale spoke fast, glancing at them all. "It went down last Saturday, Forensics says. We're waiting on the autopsy results."

McBride set down his pen. "You can run down every slime ball in this city." He glared at them. "But stay away from 1265 Lombardi Avenue. *Comprende?*"

The detectives rose and filed from the room.

Cale felt pity for their boss. The big dogs had kicked, and McBride needed his troops back in line. Cale understood it wasn't personal. And yet, one fact remained unchanged:

They needed to start making headway in the case.

A handful of post-it messages were stuck to Cale's PC screen. Mostly questions from other investigators who had taken up his caseload. He noted the numbers and extensions. He'd get to them later. Right now, more urgent matters demanded his attention.

"You believe this crap?" Slink sat on the edge of his desk, checking for phone messages.

Cale shrugged. "Manure runs downhill—he got that part right. Right now, McBride's the dump truck driver."

"Zilch from the auto body shop," Slink reported. "Said they'll call if they get anything remotely close."

Staszak swiveled in his chair to face them. "I'm glad we're off this football player thing."

"It was an idea. End of story." Cale rose and moved for the exit. Grabbing his jacket from the rack, his thoughts were already shifting to Maggie. "If you hear from Blum, have him call me."

With a lull in the afternoon bustle, they watched him exit the room.

Cale navigated the Bronco along the lower road, which ran like a funnel beneath the tall oak and elm trees while twisting a path along the murky Fox River. In the distance, exhaust plumes from papermill stacks soiled the gray April sky.

He flicked the radio to local sports and heard the Packers were holding a mini-camp in three weeks.

Cale pictured his mugshot on the team's corporate office wall like a Wild West poster: WANTED. DEAD OR ALIVE. CALE VAN WARING. He might as well be John Dillinger.

He flicked the radio off as he turned into his driveway.

Maggie's gray Mazda stood outside the soaked garages, camouflaged by the rain. Leaving it exposed was not typical Maggie-like behavior. Then again, this day felt anything but routine.

He eased the Bronco into the shadowed maw, entered the inner door, and strode up the quiet, dimly lit hallway. Cale discovered her sitting on the family room sofa, staring out the quarter-paned windows at the blurry drizzle. Her legs were curled beneath her, displaying white socks under an afghan. A half-empty wine bottle stood on the coffee table like a chess piece.

"I was beginning to wonder about you," she said.

"Had to put out a few fires before I left."

Maggie nodded, and he studied her silhouette in the faint light. The room held a lingering scent of pine. It summoned Cale's memories of the holiday nights they'd shared mere months ago, listening to corny carols, glugging wine, and laughing together.

A loving couple sharing a perfect Christmas.

"I didn't know I was cohabiting with a fireman." Maggie ghosted a smile. She rubbed at a smudge on the rim of her wine glass as if doing so might summon a genie to grant them eternal happiness.

Cale shooed Hank to the floor and slipped beside her on the couch. Hank scowled at him before walking away with a dismissive swish tail.

"Still beating yourself up over Sanchez?" He arched an eyebrow.

"Nothing another bottle of wine won't cure."

He smiled, tiny creases forming at the corner of his eyes. Cale couldn't help but admire Maggie's continence, despite the alcohol. The firm set of her jaw indicated her internal strength would win the battle against her current crisis of confidence.

"On a mission, are we?"

"Depends on we. Are you joining me?"

"I'm a sucker for self-pity." He leaned in and kissed her lips, tasting wine. "We going to talk about it? Or has your bottle of therapy done the trick?"

She set her glass carefully on the coaster atop the wooden coffee table, then laced her fingers around his neck, pulling him close.

"Talking wasn't what I had in mind."

Upstairs in the bedroom, they made love and barely spoke—just the touching and reaction to sharing physical warmth. There was desperation in their neediness, a joining of fear and sadness, which softened the shadows in the room's far corners. When it was over, they clung to one another. They both feared letting go might mean they'd never be this close together again.

After a while, Maggie pulled herself up and sat against the headboard. She drew her knees up, covered with the quilt, and reached for the wine glass she'd set on the nightstand.

Cale propped up on an elbow. He fixed her with a stare in the half-light. Her skin appeared olive-toned, like an Italian Renaissance painting. Or an Egyptian princess. He couldn't decide.

With a soft voice, she said, "Thanks for saving my day." She swallowed a sip of wine.

"It's what knights in shining armor do."

"I thought you were a fireman. Make up your mind."

"Now I'm a knight. It's situational."

He watched her grin in the gauzy light.

"A knight is pretty good," Maggie admitted. "Makes me the damsel in distress, doesn't it?"

"If the glass slipper fits."

She was silent, and then her voice hitched when she spoke. "Maybe I'm a better damsel than an attorney?"

Cale shifted beneath the blankets. "You're a fine lawyer, Maggie May. I want to get my hands on anyone who says different."

"You'd defend my honor, Sir Knight?"

"Your honor doesn't need defending."

Maggie let her head loll back against the headboard. She ran the cool wine glass across her forehead. "So what happened at work? McBride read you guys the riot act?"

Her question evaporated Cale's visions of noble knights, damsels, and stone-gray castle walls. Back in the real world, he exhaled. "Everybody's got to cover their butts. But let's say the higher-ups didn't like our investigation's direction. They yanked McBride's chain, so he yanked ours."

Maggie scoffed. "Why are there always higher-ups around to mess with the world?"

"Piss flows down a ladder," Cale said colorfully.

"Now you're a poet? I'm impressed."

"There once was a girl from Nantucket—"

"Don't! Please!" She slugged his bare shoulder. "I'm wallowing in self-pity here."

Cale reached for the glass in her hand, took a sip, and returned it. Deep inside the house, he heard the furnace rumble. So much for spring.

"I've got to interview your client, Sanchez." He paused. "You know that, don't you?"

Maggie rubbed her chin against the blanket. "I shouldn't have told you. Lawyer-client privilege."

"Thought you weren't his lawyer anymore?"

She hitched her shoulder, her expression indifferent.

"These juveniles are *always* screwing with us," Cale said. "Mind games. It's my guess what he's doing."

He pictured Juan-Julio Sanchez from a mug shot on his arrest report. Surly, cocksure. Hooded reptilian eyes.

The Latin Kings were far from the wayward adolescents Maggie imagined. They were hardened street criminals who had their fingers on the pulse of crime throughout three-quarters of the state. It was not inconceivable Sanchez possessed factual information on the abduction case. Even if only street rumors he had overheard in his detention cell. At this point, anything— gossip, hearsay, or innuendo—might help their investigation.

"Either way, I need to talk to him." Cale sighed tiredly. "You know? *Proud to Serve and Protect* the honest citizens of Titletown?"

"There's the old team spirit."

She slid back down beside him, blankets and all, their bodies touching, warm and comfortable. Cale reached over and tipped her chin with two fingers. He steered her mouth toward his. They held the kiss until Hank jumped up on the bed, signaling it was time for his dinner.

Cale remained in the bedroom after Maggie, with Hank shadowing her, had departed. He reminded himself it didn't matter if his superiors had reprimanded them. Once they received the autopsy results on Ray Tolver's death, they'd be off in a new direction.

In the meantime, thanks to Maggie, at least he had a new lead. First thing in the morning, he'd arrange an interview with Sanchez. He'd find out if the kid knew anything or was jerking them around for amusement.

Cale rose and got dressed. With the gloomy weather outside, a stark image of where Cindy Hulbreth might be rushed at him. He fought it off, not wanting to envision her nightmare more than he already had. Instead, he pictured the gangbanger, Juan-Julio Sanchez, sitting in his bare and cold detention cell.

From the image, at least, he felt a glimmer of hope.

CHAPTER 22

Thursday morning arrived with a splash of sunlight. Cale cruised the Bronco through the neighborhood. The April air smelled of lilacs the way he remembered the spring of his boyhood. He credited Maggie for his buoyant mood and made a mental note to thank her as he pressed Slink's number on his phone.

His partner's voice sounded tinny through the speaker. "You figure out a Plan B yet?" Slink asked.

"I'm already on Plans C, D, and F."

"Sounds like your high school report card."

"Nice of you to remind me."

Cale informed his partner he'd phoned the DA's office earlier and had an appointment before lunch with John Zackary, the deputy DA, to iron out the protocol of a jail visit with Juan-Julio Sanchez.

"The guy who used to date Maggie?" Slink asked.

"Sanchez is a gangbanger."

"I'm talking the Deputy Dog. Our assistant DA?"

"They had drinks once," Cale reluctantly admitted.

"I keep telling you. You're messing up, partner." Slink's eyes were soulful. "Gals like Maggie stay single for, oh, about thirty minutes. The courtship flowers begin arriving before your butt is a hundred yards out the door."

"I'll try and remember that."

"You think Lester Paprika will let you exchange illuminating discourse with his young banger client?" Slink was doubtful.

"He'll want something in return," Cale admitted. "But if the kid wants to talk, his attorney will cooperate."

"Glad you don't hold grudges." Slink understood that the feisty lawyer and Cale disliked one another. It stemmed from clashing years back when Paprika had mishandled (in Cale's mind) a handful of criminal cases as a deputy prosecutor.

Cale recited, "'A thirst for revenge is the surest sign of a diminished IQ.'"

"Confucius?"

"Yogi Berra, I think."

"Figures."

Twenty-seven minutes. Cale timed precisely how long the detectives had been holed-up in the morning conference room, watching a televised news conference.

Live from the county courthouse steps: the Mothers of Missing Daughters group, accompanied by their pair of attorneys. They were begging for help from the community, casting dispersions on the investigators' case handling. They were, consequently, upping the reward.

The thing was, Cale couldn't blame them. In their position, he'd be doing the same thing.

As he stepped free of the room, he was met by Detective Harry Blum. The silver-haired man motioned him aside, informing him they'd received the autopsy results on Ray Tolver.

"Doc Mocarek was pretty clear," Blum said, handing Cale a copy of the report. "Enough methamphetamine to 'knock out a hockey team.' His words, not mine."

"Sounds definitive."

Cale's phone trilled, and he checked the message. John Zackary, the DA's office calling. Pocketing his phone, he asked Blum, "No surprises then?"

The older detective shook his head. "Full tox report won't be out for another week or two. Forensics is still compiling data. Logging all the prints inside the home."

"And Mocarek thinks what? Suicide? Homicide?"

"Thinks our guy was offed. Meth was *injected*. Not inhaled via the glass pipe we found near the body."

Cale widened his eyes. "Tolver was injecting?"

"No track marks on his forearms, toes, or thighs." Blum shook his head. "A single needle site way up the inner thigh. Doc says he almost missed it."

Cale gave a low whistle. "So it still could be related to the gas station stop? Like we're thinking?"

Blum reported that Ray Tolver had hosted a weekly Friday night poker game. Six to eight "booze buddies" attended with regularity. As it stood, the detectives had multiple interviews to process. They were already taking statements from the gang of participants.

"Forensics says there are enough prints to fill a bowling alley." Blum's expression appeared morose.

Cale was equally frustrated. It meant the odds were slim they'd get anything resembling a clean print from their perpetrator. He also understood how time-consuming the process would be.

"I know I'm right on this—it's a homicide," Cale insisted. "More cut-and-dried than Jeffrey Epstein's jail cell."

Blum shrugged and stepped away with a promise to keep Cale in the loop.

Withdrawing his phone, Cale listened to the message from the DA's office. John Zackary was postponing their morning meeting. Some tricky hurdles had been thrown up involving Sanchez's demands for a plea deal. He couldn't elaborate on the phone.

Cale shut off the message, cursing out loud in the hallway. His outburst caused a passing secretary to look away. With his fingers pinching the bridge of his nose, he pictured the sad eyes of the victims' mothers as they stood on the courthouse steps.

Another delay. It was not what anyone needed.

Cale reminded himself Sanchez was not a suspect. Based on his cryptic message to Maggie, he was merely a lead in their case. It could quickly turn out to be just another massive load of BS.

With a headshake, he returned to his cluttered desk. Reports, messages, and emails had piled up, and he still wasn't caught up in his logbook.

CHAPTER 23

The trans-Atlantic flight from his homeland had been lengthy, and the dark-skinned man with the trim goatee was fatigued. From Liberia, on the western coast of Africa, to Boston, then to Toronto. Afterward, a private charter flight swooped across Lake Michigan and landed at Green Bay's Austin Straubel Airport.

Tazeki "Taz" Mabutu paid the charter pilot in cash. Crisp American Ben Franklins. His manner was polished, and he thanked the man profusely. He added a generous tip for the pillow-soft landing.

Watching the lean, diminutive African carry his pair of nylon travel bags across the tarmac, the pilot would never have guessed Mabutu was a member of royalty back in his native country—yet alone a cousin to the exiled crown prince.

"Hope you have a nice visit with your relatives." The pilot issued him a cheery wave.

"May good fortune bless you and yours," Mabutu replied, offering the hint of a bow.

It was Thursday night, and Mabutu parked his rental car in the hotel lot. He proceeded to check-in at an all-suite hotel catering to international business travelers. He again paid with cash up front, remaining anonymous, receiving no complaints from the receptionist, who hardly batted an eye.

The three-room suite looked first-class all the way. New carpeting and enclosed gas fireplace, full Internet access. All the amenities. Mabutu was most pleased.

After freshening from the tedious journey, he sat on the edge of the king-size bed. He familiarized himself with a city map, then GPS'd the least conspicuous route to his destination. An hour after landing, he removed a fifteen-inch, bronze-colored ceramic statue from one of his travel bags after changing clothes. Mabutu unbundled the thick oilskin cloth, which shielded the precious object from accidental bumps or turbulence during the journey.

He lit a small bowl of incense. He placed the statue of Pazuzu atop the walnut bureau. Kneeling on the plush carpet, head bowed, Mabutu recited the first of a string of well-practiced incantations.

When finished, before departing the room, he turned the idol statue toward the open-draped window. This would allow Pazuzu to gaze at the sparkle of city lights below.

The moon stayed hidden behind a thick stack of clouds. Standing at the edge of the backyard tree line, Mabutu's ebony skin and matching clothes served him well on this night. He paused and listened in the shadows, hearing the wind match his breath's steady rhythm. The ranch-style home stood a short distance away, silent and dark as a moored yacht.

Convinced no one was about, quiet as a shadow, he slipped across the backyards, moving toward his destination. Ten minutes later, Tazeki Mabutu stood in the lightless basement. He paused at the threshold of the bedroom door, which he had allowed to swing soundlessly open.

He took two silent steps into the room and froze.

On the double bed, the girl appeared content in her slumber. Positioned on her side, head turned toward one far corner, her arms were pinioned behind her back. The thin metallic cord, tight around one ankle—impossible for even a circus artist to slip from—showed ample length to allow the prisoner access to the small adjacent bathroom. Food and water dishes of unbreakable plastic were set casually upon a dresser bureau. Her sustenance ensured.

The comforts of home, he noted. Better than she'd enjoy in his country.

The wind. A creak. Subtle as the predawn sigh of a sailboat mast. Yet Cindy sensed the sound and understood someone was lurking in the bedroom watching her.

Shadowman?

No. This man seemed different. Was her imagination playing tricks again? She wasn't sure how she knew, but whoever stood in the room's doorway wasn't who usually came. His aura felt unknown, how he stirred the air. Almost foreign.

She forced herself to remain frozen. Despite this, Cindy could not prevent her soul from shivering. Was this man her executioner? Was he here to kill her?

Had her time come?

She wondered if she wouldn't welcome death's final icy embrace. Everlasting peace versus another visit from her captor? Which one would she choose?

Life? Or death?

A shudder ran through Cindy in the dark. She was at the mercy of whatever fate had chosen for her. Soft and soundless tears slid down her cheeks like rain trails on a windowpane.

Employing his luminous penlight like a cat burglar, Mabutu examined the pair of first-floor bedrooms. Each possessed an adjacent private bathroom, which was an excellent set-up. Both bedrooms stood empty now, encased in the night's thick darkness. The windows were shuttered and sound-proofed the way long-ago castles had prepared for sieges.

No light could enter the bedrooms, and no sound could escape. Very efficient, he decided, giving the design once again his approval.

Including the basement room—where the current listless victim resided—there were three bedrooms. Each had been designed to confine a solitary prisoner. Each was its own private crypt.

Mabutu smiled. His partner had done an excellent job this time. Much better than last year.

Noiseless as an assassin, he stepped back down the hallway.

Opening the refrigerator door, he examined the sparse array of contents. A bottle of milk, a half-filled bag of apples, and two boxes of cold cereal. The bare minimum required for survival. All were stored for feeding the prisoners and maintaining their sustenance.

Inside the inner door-rack, he spied three identical, clear-plastic bottles. Withdrawing one, he examined it in the thin light of the cracked door. Smelled it. Odorless. The label read *Compact Disc Cleaner*.

He had spotted a small CD player stationed on the living room floor. His partner enjoyed the accompaniment of music as he entertained his guests. Whatever trips your trigger, Mabutu conceded, snickering. Replacing the bottle, he allowed the refrigerator door to whisper closed.

Turning, he caught his reflection in a hallway mirror. A ghost in black. He could feel Pazuzu's presence guiding him on this nighttime excursion. Pazuzu was his guardian, his protector.

Pazuzu—King of the Wind Demons.

Everything appeared in proper order, Mabutu decided. The young woman was secure, isolated, and well-nourished. Two more captures, and he would accept delivery of all three females. The contract with his partner, Tobias Crenshaw, would be fulfilled. The shipment was destined back for his homeland. Like soft leaves blown to sea, three healthy females would vanish from their once-enjoyed lives.

The same as the two had last year—less the third, of course, the unfortunate headless one.

This was the plan as it stood. Elegant in its simplicity.

Mabutu slipped out the backdoor of the house, securing it behind him. A few heartbeats later, he was one with the chilled April night.

The murky clouds again shaded the moon's pale stare in the distant sky. And he could almost feel Pazuzu's enigmatic smile.

CHAPTER 24

Cale arrived at his desk to discover someone had gifted him a copy of the Friday morning newspaper. It was folded so he couldn't miss the headline on the lower half of the front page:

NO CLUES FOUND IN MISSING WOMAN SEARCH
Reward Increased

Cale thought morosely: *How many times do they have to remind us?* As he reached for his phone, it chirped.

It had been quite a while since he'd heard Lester Paprika's voice. The attorney's grating tone sounded more nasal than he remembered.

"The answer is no!" Paprika said at once.

Cale frowned. "I don't recall asking the question."

"I'm a lawyer, Van Waring. It's my job to anticipate the questions."

Just as it was Cale's job to recognize pretentious twits when he saw them. He kept the thought to himself.

All his previous dealings with the cantankerous attorney over the years rolled back into his memory. Paprika—then an assistant DA—had sandbagged more than a few of his cases when Cale had worked Narcotics. And it hadn't been him alone. Lester's reputation for being soft on crime had garnished him few friends among the law enforcement fraternity.

Neither man liked the other. Both of them knew it, and it simplified matters between them.

"I understand you want to speak with one of my clients," Paprika said.

"I thought it was the other way around?"

"I doubt it's the case."

"So, what's the harm?" Cale kept his tone light. "Ten minutes with Sanchez, you're there the whole time. Hold his hand if you like."

"Like I asked ADA Zackary, what's in it for us?"

Was it Lester's grating voice singeing his nerves? Cale wondered. Or ten other things?

Cale wasn't the first to conclude attorneys were a selfish species. Always favor for a favor. Quid pro quo was their term for it. In reality, it was nothing more than old-fashioned blackmail.

"Maybe you get a clear conscience, Lester? Especially if Sanchez helps save some people's lives?"

Paprika made a clucking sound, then put forth his terms of reducing Sanchez's charges.

"Zackary makes the deals, Lester. It's not up to me."

"If we agree to my terms, you can talk to Sanchez till the cows come home." He paused. "If it's *your* thing."

"Like I said—"

"Then the answer is no!" Click.

In the ensuing silence, Cale cursed how dickheads had become a thriving species. They seemed to grow in number by the day, multiplying like gophers.

Deputy District Attorney John Zackary had always been a decent enough guy. Cale had decided this while collaborating with the man on several cases. Although they'd never broached the subject, Cale also suspected that the prosecutor had an unrequited crush on Maggie.

When Cale had brought it up one day, she'd informed him the attraction was not reciprocated. He believed her. Why wouldn't he? It's what couples did. Believed and trusted one another. As far as Cale was concerned, end of story.

Jealousy—the emerald-eyed monster—was a form of insecurity. It afflicted both guys and ladies in equal measure. Cale knew his faults, but jealousy wasn't one of them.

The detectives had entered the DA's office a little before noon. They waited for five minutes in the small waiting room before John Zackary emerged to greet them. His manner was folksy as he ushered the investigators into his private office. He possessed blond, Scandinavian good looks. His hair was straight and swept to his left in a sharp part. He moved around his desk and sat in a swivel chair. "About the Sanchez kid, right?"

Cale and Slink sat before the cluttered desk, where they'd been many times before.

"It's a statement he gave Maggie in court," Cale said, "Before they hauled him back to lockup."

"I was there. I don't remember anything unusual."

"He claims to know something about the abductions— 'about the girls'—is what he told her."

Zackary gave it thought. "Have you talked to Paprika yet?"

"This morning. Says we can't meet with his client until he's got a plea deal."

The lawyer snickered. "Why am I not surprised?" He toyed with his Montblanc pen, tapping on a yellow legal pad. "He blindsided Maggie. It was a complete grandstand."

"She's a big girl. She'll get over it."

"A simple phone call," Zackary said, "would've saved her a lot of embarrassment."

Cale gazed out the window at the brown Fox River flowing past. "So what's with Paprika scooping up all these juvie cases, from what we hear?"

Zackary swiveled in his chair. "Nicer brand of suits these days. Not to mention the maroon Escalade he tools around town in."

Slink's eyes glimmered. "That's him? Really? I figured it for a Packer player's ride." When Zackary smirked, he added, "Word we get is he's taking these gangbanger cases pro bono?"

"The problem is, it's not illegal."

The detectives nodded resignedly.

Zackary continued toying with his pen. "Does Maggie trust Sanchez knows something?"

"Until we talk to him," Cale allowed, "it's all just BS."

They watched John Zackary mull over the options. After a minute, Cale said, "We've got a girl's life hanging by a thread, John."

Zackary wrote on his legal pad. "I doubt we'll get a single witness to flip if it goes to trial. So all right. I'll see what I can do."

"It's all we're asking."

The investigators rose. At the door, moving behind them, Zackary added, "There's a good chance Sanchez is playing you guys."

"A chance we've got to take," Cale admitted. "Backs against the wall and the rest."

Ronnie Dereene looked much better the second time around. He showed up for his interview with Cale; at least he'd been prompt.

Having already decided he was an unlikely suspect, Cale didn't spend much time grilling the young man. Even with the rat poison and bottles of acetone in his basement. The kid didn't appear to be a criminal mastermind.

"Concerning your assault," Cale said, receiving an anxious stare from Dereene. "How come you weren't suspicious when your condo reeked of dog crap."

The young man massaged his bandaged shoulder. He confessed, "I did smell it. I'd tracked the dog's crap into my place before. I was looking down at my shoes when Angela whacked me."

No, Cale decided—hardly a criminal mastermind.

CHAPTER 25

The Mexican restaurant was five blocks from the station. Well past the noon-hour rush, the detectives had the place to themselves, choosing a corner table near the wide front widow.

Slink ate quietly, sensing Cale's frustration at learning nothing new from Cynthia Hulbreth's boyfriend. Dereene lacked the criminal chops to pull off a successful kidnapping. Yet alone a string of them.

The waitress, a redhead with dainty ankles, offered coffee refills. She topped off Slink's cup while Cale waved her off, his nose buried in a file report. Slink gazed out the window. Vehicles slid along the street, fresh sunlight glinting off their windshields.

Looking up from the file, Cale said, "There's something about the drug connection. It's an angle we're overlooking."

"Maybe overlooking a lot of things. Otherwise, we'd have the perp in cuffs by now."

Cale closed the file and sat back. "We've confirmed the use of date rape drugs from the Vanderkellen girl's body. And now this Tolver character comes up a crystal meth OD." He frowned. "Could be our perp's in the drug business? Enough to get his hands on some heavy stuff?"

"Or else he'd be using rat poison, right?"

"You believe in coincidences. I don't."

Slink mulled the idea over as Cale sipped coffee. "We've got Sanchez, a Latin King," Cale continued. "They control a majority of our narcotics traffic."

"You're suggesting the Kings are responsible for kidnapping twenty-year-old women?" Slink laced his fingers behind his head. "It doesn't seem like a MO for street gangs."

"Maybe it's what Sanchez wants to tell us?"

"Either way, you've got to talk to him, or we'll never know."

When the silence grew, Slink shifted topics. "Speaking of talking? Are you and Maggie okay?"

"We've got a killer to find." Cale shook his head. "Not much time for personal chit-chat."

Slink frowned. "How can you not want a herd of little Van Waring's running around?"

"Because one would turn out an obnoxious smartass."

They both smiled smugly, and Slink turned serious again. "There's a difference between your job and life, amigo. In case you haven't figured it out."

"How about the Mothers of Missing Daughters group? Think they give a rip about my home life?" Cale stared at his partner. "All they want is their daughters back."

Slink signed the credit card receipt. "In another month or so, she's gone, Kemosabe. Vamoose."

"Your Spanish and Indian both suck."

"Not as much as your future."

"Touché."

They moved outside, walking toward the Bronco. "I'm heading to Tolver's house," Cale informed. "I want you to try to locate Kevin the-K. Remember him?"

"The hop-head? One we used to get tips from back in Narco?"

"If Tolver had buying connections in the drug trade, The-K would know about it." Cale popped the Bronco's door locks. "Also, ask if he's heard word on the street of the King's involvement in any abductions."

Slink nodded and entered the SUV.

It had been a while since Cale had talked with Special Agent Eddie Redtail of the FBI's Wisconsin Bureau. Last autumn. The agent had assisted them in establishing an initial profile on their unknown abductor—right after the headless body of Kimmy Vanderkellen had been extracted from the choppy waters of Lake Michigan.

Agent Redtail believed the individual responsible for the abductions would be a calculating loner. Perhaps married, maybe divorced. Likely Caucasian, age twenty-to-forty. Void of empathy, emotionally repressed. Good chance he's a control freak. Meticulous. Unassuming, even.

"Think functional sociopath," the agent advised.

"Got it."

"Women are like props to him. Objects he can threaten and control. These types of guys all run the same pattern."

In Agent Redtail's opinion, the degree of violence required to accomplish an act of human decapitation indicated not only rage but a reckless disregard for humanity. And this monster was walking the streets of their city. What kind of rock might he be hiding under?

Now six months had passed, and they had another missing female. Easing the Bronco south, the Friday afternoon traffic moved around him. Cale's phone buzzed, and he recognized Agent Redtail's Milwaukee exchange on the readout.

On speaker, Cale said, "I read your quote in our local paper. 'Monitoring the situation'? Sounds pretty vague."

"You know the routine." The FBI man chuckled. "Let me guess: missing vehicle, no clues, no crime scene."

"You're a regular Kreskin."

Cale made a lane change, accelerating down an entrance ramp. He was headed to Ray Tolver's house. He added, "Except for one difference: we may have a witness this time."

"Get me a composite blowup of the art sketch. We'll run it through the national database."

"Tiny problem there," Cale admitted. "Our witness can't provide a physical description."

"Redefines the term *witness*, doesn't it?"

Cale went on to outline the scenario with the gas station kid. He described how the station owner had perished the following day. A drug OD, which remained shrouded in mystery. Most likely a homicide.

"And no surveillance videos? From the gas station?"

"Nada."

"The owner's death," Redtail paused. "Sounds hinky, all right. So does the five-buck stop for gas."

Cale exhaled. "Blows up our previous profile. How our guy's some clever criminal?" He merged the Bronco into traffic.

"Perhaps. Perhaps not."

"Thanks for the astute analysis."

"Think about it for a minute." Eddie Retail's tone was even. "The headless body last year? Now a no sense stop for gas?"

"Trust me, I've thought about it."

"Makes us think maybe our guy's not the brightest crayon in the pack."

No argument from Cale.

"I'm thinking about the 'ruse' angle," the agent said. "It might all be deliberate. Designed to throw us off his trail."

"Like purposely taking another direction." *Maybe dumb like a fox?* He hadn't considered it, and he played with the ramifications. "You're suggesting our guy's clever enough to dummy his profile."

"It's a possibility," Redtail allowed. "The cat-and-mouse aspect. Not only the crime itself but the side-game."

"My partner thinks there's a chance he needed gas. He couldn't fly away like Superman, could he?"

"Now, *that* would alter the profile."

They ended the conversation.

Minutes later, Cale located Tolver's street. He prayed John Zackary and the DA's office would come through for them and get him an interview with Juan-Julio Sanchez. Whether their abductor was some sharp criminal or perhaps the luckiest dumbass on the planet, the gangbanger remained the first semblance of a lead they had.

Cale spotted the yellow crime scene tape a quarter block away. It stretched across the front porch steps and ran around the attached garage doors. It twisted in the breeze, teased by muted sunlight.

Ray Tolver's house was a modest two-story eggbeater that had seen better days. Cale wanted to see it for himself. He eased the Bronco to the curb, exited, and moved up the cracked sidewalk. The puzzle Agent Redtail had presented rolled in his head—how their perp might already be four or five steps ahead of them.

Not very comforting.

Climbing the porch steps, Cale eased open the front door. He fought the sinking feeling he was back at a too-familiar place.

Square One.

CHAPTER 26

"I talked with your old boyfriend today," Cale commented to Maggie over the hum of the Friday after-work crowd.

"Aaron Rodgers or Ryan Reynolds?"

"Try Door Number Three: John Zackary."

They sat together in a downtown sports bar at a high-rounded table in one corner. Green-and-gold Packers paraphernalia, Milwaukee Brewers and Bucks banners and pennants, and scarlet Wisconsin Badgers game jerseys decorated the walls like mismatched wallpaper. Ceiling-high windows allowed a view of the steady downtown traffic.

Maggie had messaged him while he'd been touring the Tolver house. *Drinks? After work?* Why not, Cale had replied, disgusted by his lack of progress in the case.

The place was half-filled, and music played along with the buzz of conversations. "What about?" Maggie asked. "Is Zackary accusing me of deserting my client?"

"Feels awful how Paprika bird-dogged you."

Maggie hoisted her beer bottle in a mock salute. "Here's to Lester, the Molester!" Her frown seemed gloomy.

The tour of Tolver's house hadn't helped Cale's mood any. Every iota of evidence had already been bagged, everything indicating Tolver was into meth manufacturing—chemicals, glass beakers, vials, the stash of hidden cash. The only thing remaining was the chalk outline on the basement floor.

Despite this, the puzzle burned in Cale's stomach. He'd worked Narcotics long before his promotion to Homicide and seen enough crack houses and homemade meth labs to dream about them. Ray Tolver's home felt like neither. It lacked a dealer house's dangerous vibe.

Maggie picked at her beer label. "Sexual frustration," he informed, giving her a wink.

"Now you're a shrink on top of it all?"

"Scientific fact. Somebody won a Nobel Prize for the study."

"Some virgin Ph.D., no doubt." She gazed across the crowd at the happy smiles—people released from work week tedium, letting their hair down.

"Why do you think Sanchez confessed it to me?" she asked earnestly. "About the missing girls?"

"We'll have to ask him. It's why I met with Zackary."

Maggie shivered as if a chill had descended. She set her bottle on the table, reaching for her purse. "Let's go home. I need a hot bath more than alcohol."

They departed the tavern, settling on Chinese delivery for dinner. Maggie suggested he phone order while she bathed.

"Takee outee?" His joke was lame, yet she rolled her eyes and giggled. At least he could still make her laugh.

It must be worth something.

As Maggie filled the upstairs bathtub, Cale oversaw the food order. He filled a large bowl of dry cat food for Hank, who enthusiastically tucked into his meal.

Thirty minutes before the food arrived, Cale decided he had put the call off long enough. The number sat in his phone roster in case of emergencies. This might be one. When her voice answered, Cale said, "Hey, Chloe. I figured I'd tell you we're progressing in the case."

"And you don't need my help, right?"

"Not this time. But thanks for the offer. I appreciate it."

The investigation was too hot, Cale understood. Too much politics were involved, with the press turning more hostile by the day. And now McBride and the chief were on the warpath. Not to mention the debacle over the "football player angle." No way could the investigators call in a psychic. Imagine the fallout. Besides, wouldn't it make them look like amateurs grasping at straws?

After hanging up, he studied Hank's gaze at him. The plump feline was issuing him a doubtful look.

"How about it, Hankster? Cats are also supposed to be psychic. Think you could help us out here?"

Hank blinked and turned back to his dinner.

"Just what I thought."

The delivery kid rang the doorbell. Feeling guilty about rejecting Chloe, Cale double-tipped the food gal and decided to pay close attention to his fortune cookie.

Maggie relaxed in the upstairs bathtub. The stress of the day seeped from her steam-filled pores. The beers she had consumed blessed her with a pleasant buzz. Smiling and laughing with Cale had given her a sense of normalcy again, like back when they had started dating, and every little thing they did together had a spark.

Now the odd feeling of emptiness had returned. She sighed and squeezed the loofah sponge, feeling the steamy water seep over her neck and shoulders.

Cale, she decided, appeared emotionally unfazed by it all. In his case, little on an emotional level seemed to affect him. Typical male. He possessed an on-off switch masking his true feelings. Psychologists termed it "compartmentalization." Every law enforcement officer must master it to survive. That Cale could function as an automaton didn't surprise her. How could she blame him? Especially when facing murder and mayhem on the streets each day?

And yet?

Did he need her? Maggie wondered. Would he care much if he lost her? Like actual "hurting" care if she decided to end their relationship? She honestly didn't want to leave. She truly loved Cale. Still, a gal had to do what she must, she reminded herself. Sometimes it felt harsh. But no one ever said love was simple.

The first week of July. It felt time-stamped on her brain. Her thoughts rounded back to the primary question: Was he at least going to try to prevent her departure? Keep them together as a couple?

Actions spoke louder than words.

Maggie now heard footsteps thump up the hallway stairs and stopped outside the bathroom door. In some romance movie, wouldn't he burst shirtless through the door and lift her into his arms, carrying her off to make love beneath star-filled skies and cypress trees? Somewhere exotic? Of course, they'd live happily ever after in a limestone manor house on a high cliff overlooking rolling seas and crashing waves.

"Food's here, Maggie May!" Cale called, giving the door a rap.

"Out in a minute." She eased her shoulders and neck deeper into the sudsy water. "Let's do the family room?"

"Your wish, my command."

His footsteps faded. Maggie squeezed the loofah for a final cascade over her now-pink cheeks. Melancholy washed over her.

Actions. Not words.

PART TWO
OLD COLLEGE ROOMMATES

CHAPTER 27

The Fox River runs through the heart of Green Bay, splitting the city in half like a giant ax wound. A parade of fine homes stands a few miles south, beyond coal factories and paper mills, estates dotting the riverbank landscape like a string of elegant pearls.

Quarried red brick, high castle-like turrets. Twenty-foot-tall windows comprised half the entire back wall of the house. From a distance, the multi-million-dollar Crenshaw estate appeared more castle than home. It sat nestled among green meadows and farmlands and overlooked the twisting, auburn-colored river.

The barbecue on Saturday was in celebration of Marla Crenshaw's thirty-fifth birthday. The crowd, some twenty-plus friends, were gathered in the backyard. The guests confined themselves to the low-walled patio outside or the adjacent sunroom connected to the rear of the house. A few optimistic souls had erected a volleyball net, but the ground proved too spongy to allow proper footing.

However, the same turf failed to inhibit the handful of kids gathered around the small koi pond located a short distance from the house. They attempted to catch the darting fish with a long stick and a seining net.

"Kendal! Bucky!" Marla called from the terrace. "You be careful near the water."

She glanced around, searching for her husband, and saw Tobias among a quartet of men. They discussed politics, the stock market, or whatever tales men shared inside their secretive little bands at gatherings.

"Toby! Check on what the children are up to!" Marla called in his direction.

She flipped her head toward the grassy pond in a field thirty yards away when he looked over at her.

Tobias nodded. He waved at Marla as his friends laughed at a joke-teller's punch line, one he didn't hear. The sound was covered by music wafting from the wireless speakers concealed in the shrubbery at the patio borders.

Tobias noted how Marla looked particularly fetching this pleasant spring afternoon. She wore a shimmering jade blouse and dark slacks. At the

117

moment, she conversed with a trio of women, including Jen Clayton and Dot Robicheaux. Attempting, he guessed, at convincing Dot to upgrade to a six-bedroom colonial, new to the market.

Tobias could hear her sales pitch cantering on the wind without much effort. Real estate was still the best investment; his wife preached it like a charismatic lecturing her flock.

The kids had captured one twisting fish at the koi pond, which flopped about on the brownish turf. Then the pack shifted its attention to a frog beneath the shallow surface.

"You kids, watch yourselves!" Tobias called to them in a parental voice.

"We will, Dad!" called back Bucky, not glancing up from the task. The rest of the gremlins failed to look up, focusing intently on their project.

Having done his duty, Tobias drifted away from the pond. He made his way around the periphery of the gathering. Minutes later, he found himself alone near the boathouse, content to observe the gathering from a modest distance.

"I hear a sick pervert is on the loose," said a voice near his shoulder. "Preying on innocent young women."

Tobias wheeled around to find he was staring at the last face he expected to see. An apparition? For a weird and indecisive moment, he couldn't be sure.

"Tazeki?" he said, at last, his voice unsteady. Tobias waved his beer bottle like a wand. "What on—is it honestly you?"

Tazeki Mabutu was garbed in pressed charcoal summer-weight slacks and a gray turtleneck. Fifth Avenue cocktail chic. His voice lowered, and he asked, "Who were you expecting? Nelson Mandela?"

Tobias stared into the coffee-brown eyes of his old friend. "It's just how things—"

"Stop staring, please," Mabutu interrupted, grabbing him by the elbow and steadying the wavering bottle. "You're acting as if I'm a ghost."

"What are you doing here?" Tobias narrowed his eyes. "Showing up like this?" A wild thought grabbed him: If Mabutu were here, there must be trouble. Something he didn't know about, something undoubtedly wrong.

Dots of perspiration popped across Tobias's brow.

"Relax." Mabutu's voice felt like a calm breeze. "I was in the neighborhood. Thought I'd pay a visit to my old college roommate."

Trapped between anger and fright, Tobias could manage no pithy comeback.

Mabutu glanced across the patio at the gathering of people. Who was this slick foreign visitor? They must be wondering. A visiting celebrity? A new Packers coach? Was he someone famous they should know?

He smiled back at their curious faces, giving off a Buddha-like grin and displaying ivory teeth. He whispered to Tobias, "Perhaps they think I'm your gardener?"

"Doubtful." Tobias remained taken aback by his old friend's sudden presence.

These guests, of course, could not possibly know Tazeki Mabutu was royalty in his own country. Cousin to the crown prince and head of an elite government security force. A powerful figure. What these simpleton party attendees could never imagine was how, with a single phone call, and despite the great distance from his homeland, he could have five armed warriors here within an hour. Capable of shattering bones, severing heads and limbs, and splaying torsos open wide. They would remove the steaming organs and feed them to the yard dogs.

Upon Mabutu's orders, simple as a finger snap.

Such existed the power of the voodoo witch doctor Tazeki Mabutu. And topping it off, he possessed diplomatic immunity because he was a high official of his sovereign nation. Although traveling incognito, knowing that his status commanded respect was gratifying.

"I'm uncomfortable with your showing up like this," Tobias admitted in a low voice. "Unannounced."

"You are not my chaperone, old friend. I come and go as I please."

Mabutu flashed his high-wattage smile at the crowd, nodding with feigned earnestness. Little did these provincials understand they were gazing like unwitting chickens into the eyes of a cunning wolf.

He watched as Marla Crenshaw glided across the patio to where they stood. Her blond hair was stylishly coiffed, with bangs in front and earrings dangling. Mabutu noted her confident air and the undercurrent of sensuality. A splendid catch for Tobias, he decided.

In her role as a gracious hostess, Marla extended a slender hand. Mabutu accepted, adding the gallant bow of a practiced diplomat.

Tobias introduced them with some reluctance.

"A pleasure to finally meet you, Mr. Mabutu," Marla said, playing the gracious hostess. "Toby's told me much about your college days together." Appraising the visitor, she added, "You two sounded like quite the daring duo!"

Mabutu's grin was unrelenting. "Ah, yes. Good old Madison. Madtown. Those were the days, weren't they, Toby?"

Tobias grinned the way a mongoose does at a cobra.

CHAPTER 28

Another pair of couples joined the group. Introductions all around. As Tazeki Mabutu shook hands, fractured memories of his college years shimmied across his consciousness.

He'd met Tobias Crenshaw on his first day on-campus—roommates for the next four years. Mabutu's major was political philosophy. Quite the opposite, Tobias was destined for a degree in organic chemistry. However, despite their academic differences, the roommates discovered they shared many similar interests—a love of sports and an equal penchant for anarchistic ideology. And also, no doubt, there were the women. Madison, Wisconsin, was a bastion of liberal thought in those days. The campus had been teeming with nubile young coeds whose sole desire was to prove their blossoming independence.

Friendship had formed fast for the new roommates. And out of this, camaraderie spawned along with growing trust. Each soon discovered he could share his dreams, longings, and darkest secret fantasies. And share they had, regardless of how disturbing those passions proved to be.

Yes, college. Those were the days.

"Go, Badgers!" Mabutu offered now, pumping a rah-rah fist in the air. "Go, Big Red!"

Those around them grinned and laughed as if to say: "No worries—this fine man is one of us!"

Everyone except Tobias, however, who, if Mabutu wasn't mistaken, appeared to be experiencing difficulty preventing his upper left eyelid from spasming with an annoying tic.

"What kind of game are you playing here?" Tobias asked tersely. His eyes were narrow now, his dark hair tousled as if set upon by some invisible wind.

The two men stood inside the spacious library room of the opulent home.

Mabutu surveyed the room at his leisure—three glazed oak tables, tall mahogany bookshelves ripe with leather-bound tomes—all the classics. A wall display of medieval artifacts seemed oh so nuevo-contemporary. Sets of double-height, beveled French windows rendered a magnificent view across the outer lawns. There the trees stood like tall sentries along the western flank.

Mabutu, in his tasseled loafers, stepped across the room to a large globe in one corner. His eyes sought out Africa's southernmost coast, then around the horn up to tiny Liberia, war-torn land of the proud and free.

"Liberia, Oh Liberia." Mabutu pointed to the globe, marking the spot with his forefinger. "My homeland."

"What of it? asked Tobias grumpily. "Or should I call you Colonel?"

Long seconds passed before Mabutu swung his attention back around to face him. "I'm in town checking your progress, my friend." The man's voice sounded flat. "Making certain our little business arrangement is, how shall we say, secure?"

"You failed to add *this* time."

"Yes. *This* time."

Tobias removed his glasses, pinching the bridge of his nose with two fingers. His left eyelid continued to spasm, and he stood near a window as if unable to sit while Mabutu was here.

"Necessary, I'm sure?" he asked. "In your view?"

Mabutu's smile appeared feathery. "You are not a natural criminal, my friend. Who knows better than me? And after the incident last year?"

Tobias stayed silent.

"I deemed it prudent," his old friend continued, "to ensure there be no repeat of such unfortunate business."

Tobias glared at him. Mabutu was referring, of course, to the sorry situation with last year's third victim. What was her name again? Ahh, the Vanderkellen girl, he reminded himself.

As if I could ever forget.

After drugging and capturing her, escaping in his vehicle, Tobias had secured the woman in the basement bedroom of the cul-de-sac house. All went according to plan until the victim awakened. The girl had then behaved in the most erratic fashion imaginable: screeching, screaming, shrieking, acting insane! Threatening to scratch her eyes out!

Lunacy. There was no other way to describe it other than a "psychotic break." An adverse reaction to the drug mix, perhaps? He'd imagined every possibility. People responded in unusual ways to sedation. Or she may have had some underlying, serious, previously undiagnosed mental condition triggered by the overload of narcotics in her system.

Whatever the cause, she'd become a raving lunatic.

Not that Tobias blamed himself. Why should he? The abductions of the first two girls had gone without a hitch. But the third? An unmitigated disaster. In captivity, Kimberly Vanderkellen, suffice it to say, had become unhinged.

By the fourth day, he'd been forced to administer round-the-clock sedation. Tobias pumped her full of a controlled mix of fentanyl and Ketamine—both animal tranquilizers—combined with intravenous injections of midazolam.

And on this count, Mabutu was right. By nature, Tobias had little stomach for indiscriminate violence. It wasn't in his core DNA. He was foremost a scientist—a *chemist*. Therefore, with pressure mounting, he'd decided on his best available option. He contacted his partner, Col. Tazeki Mabutu, a man far more capable of dealing with extraordinary situations.

"We've got a problem," Tobias had said, a frenetic hitch in his voice. He'd placed the call from an anonymous pay phone at the Green Bay airport. Person-to-person international, employing an untraceable phone card he'd purchased at a convenience store.

"What sort?" Mabutu's tone was stiff.

Tobias had explained the disaster and how their mission might be severely compromised. He'd suggested to Mabutu—thousands of miles away—that his assistance was required.

"Have you tried slapping her around?" Mabutu had asked emotionlessly. "Many of them prefer it. Helps overcome their guilt of being cooperative."

"It's not something—"

"It's all about respect," Mabutu persisted. "Ask any pimp worth his bling."

Tobias's displeasure increased. He had decided he was the primary talent between them both. Mabutu, despite more abundant resources, was little beyond a glorified "heavy."

A sex trafficker; a voodoo priest; a human slave trader; a military flunky—albeit a high-ranking one. But so what? Liberia was a country the size of Arizona.

Tobias had felt the partnership with his former college roommate crumbling. Their arrangement had been symbiotic early on—his capturing victims and Mabutu's making them disappear—had been *muy simpatico*. But it seemed to be unraveling these days. Tobias could feel himself drifting dangerously outside his comfort zone.

"What do you want me to do?" Exasperation had shaded Mabutu's voice.

"Send your goons," Tobias demanded. "The sooner, the better."

And it was done. Simple as a finger snap.

The following day, a trio of Liberian rogues appeared at the prearranged time. They loaded the sedated young woman into a dark SUV inside the garage and drove away.

Tobias had watched the vehicle disappear from behind a window curtain. He'd felt instantly relieved. The nutcase girl would end up in an African or Middle East harem. Halfway around the world and out of his hair forever.

Mabutu would be content with their agreed-upon three-victim contract going forward. Yet of greater importance—at least for Tobias back then—was how easily the lunatic Vanderkellen girl had been removed from his sight forever.

Simple as a finger snap.

Maggie lay in bed in the dark room, a lump of shadow beneath the blankets. Her eyes closed, and she listened to Cale's breathing beside her. It wasn't the rhythmic sound of restful slumber; instead, he seemed almost awake.

"Are we losing this battle, Cale?" she whispered. "Us, I mean?"

His voice sounded from miles away. "Things are...I can't tell what's normal or isn't anymore."

"This isn't. Two persons alone in the dark. It's almost like two strangers beside one another."

"I'm not a stranger, Mags. I love you with all my heart."

Then show me, she almost screamed: *Actions, not words!*

She felt him turn her way in the shadows. He brushed his fingertips against the smooth skin of her cheek. If only he would let her into his heart, she thought.

The night wind whistled against the outside window glass, playing a haunting lament. Far from the laughing winds of poets, Maggie decided. No. This wind brought with it a cry of aguish. Her thoughts drifted to the missing young woman, Cynthia Hulbreth. Where was she right now? Could she be listening to the same wind as it pushed the clouds along on this sad and lonesome night?

Maggie guessed Cale's fingertips would feel the moisture of her tears. Yet he still appeared incapable of revealing what she needed to hear. Cale had trouble opening up and showing honest emotions. Could he ever? It was the million-dollar question.

"Do you think we're a good fit?" she asked, her voice soft.

"Of course we are." He turned again toward her. "I've told you a hundred times."

Maggie reminded herself the Fourth of July weekend was arriving soon.

Cale stood staring out the window in the quiet of their bedroom. Maggie had fallen asleep, and his guts felt sewn in knots. He wanted to open up and be more vulnerable, yet a hundred thoughts paraded through his mind simultaneously. Things appeared broken between them like a clay pot had shattered on a floor.

Rubbing a hand over his course, sunken cheeks, a thought struck him. It wasn't some vision of clarity regarding Maggie. Instead, it involved the kidnapping case. It came first as a germ of an idea, but as it solidified, it began to expand.

By the time he crawled back beneath the blankets, where Cale doubted he'd fall asleep any time soon, the seed had taken root and germinated into a plan inside his mind. And though it wasn't perfect, if his idea worked, at least it might give him the one thing the investigation needed most of all:

Hope.

CHAPTER 29

Early Monday morning, the investigators learned their case had taken a turn for the worse. John Zackary of the DA's office informed them Lester Paprika was playing hardball. He refused to allow an interview with his client.

Zackary clarified to Cale on the phone that the DA's hands were tied. They couldn't reduce charges against Juan-Julio Sanchez. Gang violence was a political hot potato. And a drive-by shooting, no less, where lives had been at risk? The mayor sent a strong message: No leniency for violent street gangs.

"I'll keep on it for you," Zackary promised.

Cale told him he appreciated the effort—exasperating, yet not unexpected.

At his desk, he buzzed through emails as Slink sauntered up. He informed his partner of the new plan of action he had dreamed up the night before. Slink thought it could work.

They shared the idea with Staszak, who likewise agreed it was worthwhile. The three investigators would work in shifts, gathering intel, surveilling, and preparing for action.

With Slink departing to begin their initial shift, Cale's attention returned to his emails. Minutes later, he was browsing local news articles regarding their case.

The column inches were decreasing. Television coverage had died. Blog sites had moved on. Citizens wanted new bodies with their morning cornflakes, sex scandals over lunch, and exploding terrorist bombs while relaxing on the evening couch. The police Tips Hotline was down to a couple of calls per day, down from the twenty-five they'd had last week. Other murders and mayhem, local and national, were overtaking the unresolved case of the missing females.

Who could blame them? The police still didn't even have a crime scene yet. They were still chasing a ghost.

In the face of this growing public laxity, it was reported that the Mothers of Missing Daughters group was planning a nighttime candlelight vigil in a downtown park. The event garnished a mild media bump, though nothing of substance.

As for public sentiment, consensus harshly judged the investigator's seeming impotence in solving the case. Many felt anger and even more embarrassment.

Swift clouds swept overhead, light to dark, as time accelerates in a movie. By Tuesday afternoon, the traffic had turned brisk. The gray unmarked Taurus cruised across the bridge and headed east toward downtown. At the wheel, Slink glanced at Cale beside him. His partner gazed out the window with a grim expression.

Slink decided to broach the sensitive topic. "So you and Maggie talk things over? Anything new?"

"We talked."

"She's not still moving out on July fourth, right?"

"We're working on things."

Slink changed lanes, thinking: Leave it to a woman to screw up a holiday weekend. He asked Cale, "All these years together, how did I miss your insanity?"

"You're no Sigmund Freud."

"If you let Maggie leave, you best change your name to A-S-S-H—"

"I get the point." Cale scowled.

Neither man spoke, and the radio cackled. Dispatch was moving cruisers and uniforms around the city like chess pieces. Slink reminded himself of how long they'd been partners. Back patrolling the streets together in uniform, then making detective at almost the same point in their careers. They had worked Narcotics together and been through beer-drinking, joke-telling, and softball on the department squad, not to mention the skirt-chasing back when they'd both been single.

Things were different now, Slink conceded. He had found Janet, the woman he loved. His boys, ages two and four, were additions to the Dooley household that entrenched him in the role of fatherhood.

Since he'd found his life's soul mate, didn't it make sense to wish the same thing for his best friend?

Of course, it did.

Standing by and watching Cale make the biggest blunder of his life was frustrating. They'd had this discussion before, with Slink being one of the few who knew about Cale's tormented past. How his first love, Mary, had been murdered in a botched armed robbery attempt back when they'd been college students in Chicago, both twenty years old at the time. Slink understood how his friend had blamed himself for the tragedy to this day.

The shrinks had all kinds of terms: emotional impairment, cognitive displacement, attachment avoidance, and PTSD. All cookie-cutter jargon for how people dealt with internal pain and conflict.

Slink, on the other hand, was more pragmatic. To him, the past was the past. You buried it and accepted your losses, then soldiered forward. Life was about adapting to setbacks.

Still, everyone was different, Slink conceded. Some people were plain stubborn and refused to move forward. They wouldn't take advice if you offered it on a silver platter.

Cale Van Waring fit this latter category like a champ. The guy's primary talent seemed to be finding things out the hard way. Example: Maggie. Losing her would be the worst mistake his best friend would ever make. At least in Slink's opinion.

"The early July holiday," Slink commented again, flipping a gaze at Cale's stoic profile. "Little over two months."

"Like I told you, I don't function well in captivity."

"I almost forgot—you're King Kong's cousin."

Slink watched Cale gaze out the passenger window as if imagining the scenery was fascinating. "Just wonderful." he sighed, frustrated.

The sunlight splashed off the windshields of passing vehicles and glistened off the river's auburn surface.

"Spend your life alone, Kemosabe. If it's what you want so bad."

"Badly," corrected Cale.

The detectives kept their lips tight, paying little attention to the dispatcher's persistent cackle.

While his partner had prattled on, Cale forced his mind away from Maggie. Instead, he focused on the sick serial kidnapper case—a man capable of chopping off a victim's head.

After hatching his idea late Sunday night, they'd put the plan's preliminaries into action. Cale's logic went as such: if the DA wasn't assisting them with Lester Paprika, they'd take matters into their own hands.

Cale understood he needed his partners' involvement. He couldn't execute the idea on his own. They had to work as a unit and toss out the rule book. They had to get creative.

He sorted through his mound of paperwork on his desk late Tuesday afternoon. His brain continued to debate the wisdom of the idea. They had been surveilling in shifts, and though the plan was somewhat unwieldy, at least they were doing *something* and being proactive.

Cale watched Slink saunter in now, and he flicked off his PC. "Any update from the DA?" his partner asked.

Cale shook his head.

"You sometimes wonder whose side they're on?"

"Simple," Cale said. "The side playing politics."

It was time for Cale's turn at the surveillance. He grabbed his jacket without saying much more and headed out the door.

Cale arrived at his desk by Wednesday morning, frustration mounting with each passing day while Anton Staszak lumbered past. Staszak flipped him a copy of the local *Green Bay Press-Gazette*.

The below-the-fold headline leaped off the page:

HOPES FADE FOR MISSING CITY WOMAN

The article rendered a pessimistic view concerning the physical welfare of Cynthia Hulbreth. Investigators, the story implied, appeared miffed by the absence of clues in the case.

Cale's thoughts were dark. At least they'd gotten the "clueless" part correct.

In the article, Captain Leo McBride (acting spokesperson) said the police investigation's scope had shifted from a Missing Person case toward more profound and alarming concerns about Miss Hulbreth's welfare."

The article further outlined the department's frustrations. McBride added, "Thus far, we haven't issued any warrants. Without a solid lead, our hands are tied."

Staszak stood beside Cale's desk, sipping black coffee, blocking the light from the nearby bank of windows.

"Captain's right about that," Staszak said dejectedly. Cale handed him the newspaper back. "He's called a meeting," Staszak added. "His office in ten."

"Slink's out on surveillance."

"I texted him. He's on the way back now."

Having been handling the early morning stakeout of their target, Slink was running late. He joined the group in the captain's inner office.

"Nice of you to grace us with your presence, Dooley." Captain McBride's voice, if possible, sounded more irritated than usual. Minutes past nine a.m. now. Cale figured the tension was getting to the captain the same as them all.

Slink reported he'd successfully run down an old narcotics informant named Kevin "The K." The snitch had helped in the past, and they had no reason to doubt him when he revealed there was nothing on the local drug scene involving one Ray Tolver. No one knew him; no one had even heard of him. "The K" doubted he'd been dealing under any alias.

Cale suggested moving outside their standard paradigm, taking matters into their own hands while they had the opportunity. The captain leaned back in his chair, swiveling like a charter skipper. "Anybody got anything else?"

The detectives shared a look, but no one spoke.

McBride then put the capper on it. Rising, he said, "Our case backlog is piling up." He stared at them. "It means we've got to move forward to other cases."

"And the Hulbreth girl?" Cale asked. He listened to the wall clock tick away the seconds like a metronome.

They all stared at Captain McBride. After a long beat, he said, "Until we have something solid, all we can do now is wait."

CHAPTER 30

Wait?

If Cale understood one thing about himself, patience wasn't his strong suit. Once a crime had been committed and the investigation in motion, he was like most cops—he wanted a no-hassle arrest, a solid confession, and a hasty resolution—a slam dunk, hopefully, in less than a day.

However, these types of cases were a rarity in the real world. His frustration revealed how the longer you waited—calculating, deliberating, getting your legal ducks in a row—the more time a lawbreaker had to escape justice.

After meeting with the captain, Cale was even more confident about his course of action.

Wait? Ridiculous.

Back at his desk now, Cale felt his mood souring by the minute. He and his team were tired of sitting on the sidelines. There was a time for strategic deliberation, he allowed, and the time had now passed.

On Monday, two days ago, when he'd presented his idea to his partners, they had climbed on board immediately. Both Staszak and Slink agreed their best bet was to try something radical. Cale's plan was chancy; they'd be on thin procedural ice. Internal Affairs would have a field day if the thing blew up in their faces.

Cale wanted one thing made clear to his partners: their careers were on the line here. Especially if Murphy's Law prevailed and things went sideways. Salary, pensions, insurance, future job security—they'd all fly out the window. They all had families. Negative fallout, if it happened, would be a concern.

"Desperate times," Slink had admitted.

"You're in, then?"

"When's Tonto ever said *nada* to the Lone Ranger?"

Anton Staszak, in turn, had also jumped aboard. He gave Cale the approving nod of his oversized head.

"Just so we're clear on the negatives?" Cale arched his eyebrows.

"Screw it," Staszak had growled. "I can always find a job as a consultant."

"Consulting at the door outside some strip club," Slink joked.

Staszak flipped him the bird.

For his part, Cale had decided there were times when you had to bend the law to enforce it. With lives hanging in the balance, this was one of those times.

Slink had raised a mock French cutlass above his head. "The Three Musketeers ride again!"

Cindy Hulbreth stood beneath a cascading waterfall, her honey-toned hair swept back, soaked by iridescent waters. Nothing in the world could trouble her here, and nothing ever would again. That is until she began to cough up the water, suddenly invading her nose and throat.

She awoke to find herself sitting naked on the shower floor, head propped against the tiles. Warm water sprayed down on her. Cindy couldn't recall moving from the bed to here.

Another drug-induced haze.CH

A bar of soap sat between her legs, and her hands moved on their own. She washed, lathering her stomach, her breasts, and thighs. Wash off the sweat and filth.

Wash away the Shadowman.

How had she gotten here? Cindy fought to remember any details—nothing but twisted memory fragments, all jumbled.

She rose, turned off the faucet, and swept aside the shower curtain with effort. A dry towel hung from the rack, and she stepped gingerly from the tub. She fought off the desire to scrub herself raw to prove she remained alive.

The room's light was dim, the only window boarded from outside. The sink mirror showed a girl-creature with sunken cheeks and dark eye smudges. A carnival mirror? She couldn't look this awful and still be upright, could she?

The handle was wet and slimy. Cindy shuffled from the bathroom into the dimness of the adjacent bedroom.

Something seemed different.

Had the bed been moved? Was that it? The metallic cord tethered around her ankle trailed from a different direction than she recalled. However, Cindy's mind was too clouded to be sure of anything.

The carpet beneath her bare feet? Hadn't it been a wooden floor before? Then reality—or what was left of it—slammed her like a fist. She was in a different bedroom!

This was not a funhouse! It was a *madhouse!*

Cindy pitched forward, falling, her cheek scraping against the rough Berber carpet. "It smells new," was her final thought as she dropped into the embrace of blackness.

After lunch, the detectives sat in the unmarked Taurus in the station parking lot. Slink remained at the wheel—jittery, anticipation mounting. His left leg twitched.

Cale asked, "Sure you're good with this?"

Slink cast a furtive glance out the driver-side window. Cale's Bronco was parked four slots away. "Like angel food."

"Meaning what, again?"

"The job. It's a piece of cake."

Cale snickered. "Remember Murphy's Law."

"Screw it. How about 'Dooley's Law'? Says we've got to get something on the puke."

Staring beyond the parked automobiles, back at the rear exit doors, Cale said, "If this helps us break the thing, it'll be worth the risk."

"Like I said—angel food."

The Chemist

What's the greatest hoax ever perpetrated on humanity? The answer is as simple as it is obvious: it's convincing people that their lives are somehow meaningful. How they have relevance or possess so-called "purpose."

On the other hand, you recognize this falsehood for what it is: utter BS. All human lives—including yours—are as insignificant as ants on an anthill. People, with their grandiose sense of self-importance, languish in this fantasy. They cling to the false hope of being on earth for some "higher purpose." And how they alone are the progeny of some omnipotent design.

Misguided ignorance, at best.

You, on the other hand, harbor no such delusions. You operate instead on pure logic. You have long ago concluded that the undeniable truth is there is no point in *any* of our lives.

Put to the test, this theorem stands. No contrary debate holds water. As for the theological angle? Ask yourself why God—assuming such an entity exists (you hopefully pray He does!)—created dinosaurs and allowed them to be wiped out in a single stroke.

What would be the point? The logical purpose?

The Bible fails to address this evolutionary fact other than (one supposes): "He giveth and taketh away." Nevertheless, one man's immortal soul becomes another's wishful thinking.

Employing logic acknowledges this fundamental truism: human life, identical to the rest of biological life, is utterly meaningless.

Further debate is little other than repetitive logorrhea—pointless drivel because no one knows with certainty.

End of story.

Tobias Crenshaw's (aka the Chemist) brain felt bruised. The contusion (if indeed such) grew almost daily. He decided, however, he could ill-afford to waste precious time dwelling on the matter. He was a hunter, after all, and the hunt was on.

Victim Number Five. One to go after this, and his quota with Colonel Tazeki Mabutu would be filled.

He sat in the blue windowless utility van. A Miles Davis CD filled the air with haunting refrains. The mood was set as he considered his chosen prey.

A different parking lot this time. A shopping mall in the heart of suburbia. He'd decided to change things; the girl was a new variety. This one was taller and more ethnic than the previous victims—slender, with lengthy dark hair, and possibly Native American, if he were to guess.

Not a blonde.

The victim change was positive, Tobias told himself. Wasn't a pattern-break a clever gambit? Doing so would muddy the profile the FBI had formulated on him. Tobias snickered. Keep them guessing and off-balance. You are the artist, he reminded himself. And great artists never paint themselves into corners.

Perched inside the van now like a hunter in a blind, he couldn't help wondering how Mabutu might react to the selection of his newest victim. His partner had been specific in his demands. Blondes, always blondes! Like a broken record. The guy had some fetish.

"Pale skin is better for business," Mabutu had insisted, his smile enigmatic inside his tight goatee. "And that's what matters most, my friend."

Tobias, however, decided he was done kowtowing to the diminutive African's prepubescent fantasies. While no expert in human trafficking, he asked himself: What could it matter? Girls were girls, boys usually boys. Flesh was flesh.

So, screw Mabutu. And screw his obsession with fair-haired Aryan Heidi-heads.

And yet, the unfortunate incident with last year's Victim Number Two remained etched in Tobias's mind. The girl had turned animal, uncontrollable. The reaction was likely to the fentanyl or the entire cocktail mix. Deciding she was more trouble than she was worth, he had called on Mabutu for assistance. His old roommate came to the rescue and remedied the situation.

To Tobias's dismay, the clean-up job had given Mabutu leverage in their business relationship—more power than Tobias wanted to concede.

"Your men chopped off her head! For chrissakes!" He had complained feverishly at the time.

"My men are warriors. Not sentimentalists."

The Liberian had allowed the statement to linger like a noxious odor. With a smirk, he'd added, "We left sentimental theory back in college, Tobias. Along with beer-chugging and mindless frat songs."

Afterward, akin to a festering sore, the incident remained a point of contention between the two partners. Their recent conversations had done little to defuse things. And when his former roommate had shown up unannounced at his wife's birthday party? Well, enough was enough. Later, in the quiet of the library, Mabutu pointed out: "You had a problem, so you called. Did I not resolve the matter?"

"Your men didn't have to be so *animal!*" Tobias protested.

Silence gripped the room. The muted music and outdoor revelers were heard through the heavy walls, just beyond earshot.

"I expect three girls this time," Mabutu had stated, blunt as a dictator. "Three. Properly cared for and in good health."

Tobias had held his tongue, seething inside. He would not submit to being lectured like some schoolboy. Was he not the "mastermind" behind the kidnappings? The infamous Chemist? (A handle he'd bestowed on himself.) Was it not he, Tobias, who had the Keystone Cops running around like befuddled amateurs?

Mabutu, on the other hand, was little more than a clean-up man. A garbage man, if one allowed for crudity. The idea of using the girls—auctioning *his* girls in the human trafficking slave market—nearly made Tobias ill.

And yet, he needed Tazeki Mabutu to take the victims off his hands and make them disappear without a trace. They were partners, after all. Whether he approved of how his old friend did business or not, he nevertheless required the unique services that an experienced human trafficker could provide

At least, he did at the start of their partnership.

"I understand," Tobias had cordially conceded. In his mind, however, he'd been formulating his exit strategy.

After his final agreed-upon abduction, the ties of their unsavory business relationship could be severed. He would retreat into obscurity, secure in the knowledge that he (the infamous Chemist) had foisted on a degenerating society the "perfect crime."

"Well, screw yourself, Mabutu," Tobias whispered, sitting alone in his van. His words blended with the sassy piano and solo trumpet playing in his earbuds. Mabutu, along with his blood-thirsty henchmen: "*C'est la vie.*"

He had made his selection now—his own new choice. The young woman was excellent. And quite the opposite of the "blondes" his partner so desired. Mabutu would have to deal with it. What could he do otherwise? Sever the hand feeding him?

This thought added to his mounting rebellious sentiment, and it caused Tobias to sneer. Staring out the van's window, he waited for his newest prize to emerge.

CHAPTER 31

Cale exited the beltline and headed south along the shaded river road, away from the city's heart. As he drove, his phone sounded.

"Our pigeon is tucked away." Staszak was on the line. "His fancy Cadillac's parked outside the courthouse."

"Let me know when he moves."

"Copy that."

Cale hit the speed dial for Slink's phone. Slink picked up, and Cale asked, "We all clear?"

"Place is empty. I'm a go from this end."

Slink sat inside a white panel van on loan from Impound. It had been confiscated in a drug bust. The scrubbed vehicle sat across the street from Lester Paprika's two-story home. Slink wore navy pants and a sky-blue uniform shirt saying "Culligan" across the back. Embroidered above one shirt pocket was "Steve." Blending in was the point.

They had surveilled the house for the past three days. Lester Paprika lived alone in a four-bedroom Colonial. Six years divorced, and his daughter was away at college. No pets. A Puerto Rican girlfriend (a gossipy neighbor had winked). A cleaning lady appeared on Monday afternoon and stayed three hours. Otherwise, the house stood empty during the day.

"Green light," Cale said evenly. "Your phone's on vibrate. I call the minute he moves. No surprises."

"Roger that." Slink muted his phone.

"Steve" exited the van at the curb and crossed the quiet street. The suburban neighborhood was well-tended, with mature trees with leaves already thickening. Middle-class coziness.

The earlier sunshine had dissipated, and the afternoon was cloudy and warm. A starling chirped from a high tree. A gray squirrel scampered across the driveway, working its way along the side of the three-stall garage.

Slink carried a workman's toolbox. It held clever lock picks, standard hand tools, and a variety of anti-encryption software drives he required to hack computer systems. These, along with his .38 Colt revolver as a backup.

No surprises.

Nicky's Lionhead Ale House was a landmark establishment on the main drag in De Pere, a southern suburb. Dark hand-carved woodwork, lofty ceilings, and an elegant brass-railed bar created an atmosphere of homey, pub-style comfort.

Jellybear Nick was the round-shouldered proprietor of the tavern. Business was light, customary for a weekday mid-afternoon. A few stragglers sat in the high-backed booths along the far wall, catching a late lunch.

Cale slid onto a barstool near the rear entrance and ordered a club soda. Lemon-wedge. He slipped the bartender a five, telling her to bank the change. He asked if she could hunt down her boss for him.

She smiled, showing dimples. "Jellybear? He's in the kitchen." College kid, Cale decided, watching her glide away in khaki shorts and crisp white trainers.

Highlights from last night's baseball and basketball games spun muted on the TV screens behind the bar. Despite the pleasant atmosphere, Cale felt antsy. The "action" was going down across town, yet he was sitting alone in a dim tavern. A stiff drink would quell his butterflies, but now was not the time.

He considered calling Maggie but needed to keep his phone clear. Instead, he cracked his knuckles, reached for the peanut bowl, and gazed out the wide window at a handful of pedestrians strolling the sidewalk.

An oversized man in a cook's apron emerged from the kitchen's swinging doors a minute later. Jellybear Nick was unable to conceal his wide grin.

"Detective Van Waring!" his gruff voice called. "Here for the grub or the view?" Arching his eyebrows, the tavern owner flipped his head at a trio of females in a far booth.

Cale smiled. "Dance card's full, J-bear. Of which you are fully aware."

The tavern owner's eyes sparkled, creases forming at the corners. He possessed the hook nose of a boxer, maybe not a good one. "I would have married your little turtledove myself if you hadn't bird-dogged her from me."

Cale grinned, watching his old friend shake his head. "Still the sharpest bartender I ever had." Jellybear crowed.

Maggie Jeffers had tended bar at the tavern part-time during her undergrad college years. She had excelled at pouring drinks for members of the Lonely-Hearts Club and once informed Cale how she'd cherished the job. While it was nowhere listed on her lawyerly resume, she still considered her apprenticeship with the jovial tavern owner a learning experience in the intricacies of human foibles.

Cale didn't doubt it for a minute.

"How's our little darlin' doing?" the barman asked. Then turning serious, he added, "You better get a ring on her finger, Cale. Before she wises up and comes back to me."

"In your dreams."

Jellybear signaled a refill for Cale, who shook his head. He didn't need a full bladder if he had to move fast.

"Not merely a social visit, then?"

"Wondering about an old friend of ours. Lester Paprika?"

The mention of the name caused Jellybear to frown. "The fat prick"—his voice rumbled—"still owes me four large. Last year's Super Bowl, if you can believe it."

Cale's eyes narrowed. "Should be good for it, shouldn't he? He's tooling around town in an oversized pimpmobile."

"Screw his prissy Escalade," Jellybear whined, unable to conceal his contempt for the portly barrister. "Let's just say we had a little conflict of opinion."

Cale listened as his old friend relayed his Lester Paprika story. It stemmed from last season's Super Bowl wager, where the total points bet had tied. Jellybear claimed Lester owed him four Gs, while Paprika claimed it was a push.

"Stuff happens," Cale said philosophically. "When's the last time you talked to him?"

"Not since."

Cale stared at the refurbished bar, the beveled windows stretching to cathedral-like ceilings. "The bank doesn't look too broke."

"I should've cracked both his kneecaps. I still might."

It was the principal, Cale understood, and seldom about the money. It was about being honorable, stand-up. Real men didn't walk out on bar tabs, and real men didn't hustle a friend's girl or welsh on bets.

A matter of honor.

Jellybear swiped the wooden surface with a bar rag. Cale watched the clouds dissipate over the man's shaved head like a dark storm had passed.

"He gambling anywhere else, of late?" Cale asked. "With Cowens? Or Ginny Reese?"

They were names he had picked up back when he'd worked Narcotics, which often went hand in hand with illicit gambling operations. The idea was to discover dirt on the obstinate lawyer, something they could use as leverage. They wanted to force Paprika to cooperate with their investigation. Cale had to find a way to interview Juan-Julio Sanchez.

"You asking as a cop? Or Maggie's boyfriend?"

"No record. Friends. You and me."

For Jellybear Nick, it was good enough. He informed Cale he'd heard the lawyer was placing action with a pair of Puerto Rican hustlers for what the rumor was worth.

Cale's phone buzzed. "Paprika just left the courthouse," Staszak said, talking fast. "He might be heading across the river."

Cale glanced at the time. Slink already had twenty minutes inside the house.

"Keep the tail. Let me know where he's headed."

Keeping his phone ready, Cale noted the tavern owner's mirthful eyes. "New job with the CIA working out?"

"Yeah. Russia collusion."

"So you're the one who dicked that up? I shoulda known."

Speed-dialing Slink, Cale swiveled again, speaking a notch above a whisper. "Pigeon's moving. Better close up shop."

Jellybear laughed and recited, "Rubber Ducky calling Boris Badenov." He chortled.

Cale set a twenty on the bar. "Don't pocket the nice girl's tip." He moved toward the door.

"Whatever you say, Bill Gates."

CHAPTER 32

Slink Dooley had always been a whiz with his hands. Things mechanical or electronic came as naturally as goof balling in class or catching passes for the football team. As a teenager, along with playing sports and mastering the writing of computer code, Slink could often be found tinkering in his Uncle Jerry's garage. He'd learned the art of splicing wires together or setting fuse-timers there. Anything that sparked or exploded was fair game. His uncle had been a munitions expert in the Navy, so Slink came by his talents through a fine pedigree.

The entry into Lester Paprika's residence went as smooth as satin on a starlet's thighs. Amazingly, no signs of a home security system. Slink had jimmied the rear door slide-lock and entered, standing frozen. All quiet. And he'd spied no warning signs on the outer doors or windows. No dog dishes were on the floor labeled "Lurch" or "Cujo."

Slink waited for two minutes before allowing his mind to relax. Was Paprika arrogant enough to think he couldn't fall victim to a simple home burglary? Certain people in society consider themselves to be above the law. Imagined they were immune to crime—the sin of perceived invincibility.

In latex gloves and rubber soles, Slink moved into the kitchen. Soundlessly, he proceeded to the dining room, then the living room of the comfortable home, always listening.

No sounds came.

Slink climbed the stairs and moved down a second-floor hallway to the empty bedrooms. The beds appeared tidy and unrumpled. At least the pigeon-chested lawyer wasn't a slob.

He entered the den off the master bedroom and beelined for the Dell, which sat atop a cherry wood desk. He eased into the high-backed leather chair. Taking a moment to survey the setup, he searched for signs of a hidden password. Finding nothing obvious, he pressed the power button and booted the PC.

The flash drive would enable him to bypass standard encryption codes. Inserting the thumb device, the familiar churn of the electronic configurations commenced. He could rapidly navigate where he pleased on Lester's system.

Outside the window, the sun remained cloistered behind gray clouds. Despite the overcast afternoon, enough light seeped through the curtains to see without squinting.

"Hello," Slink whispered as the information unfolded on the screen. "My, Lester, you've been a busy boy."

Latex fingers clacking across the keyboard, Slink slipped along the hidden electronic channels like a ghost through dark castle corridors. Lester, he soon discovered, possessed an unsurprising attribute. He was lazy.

The attorney had his favorite "book-marked" sites open to access with four simple mouse clicks. These sites, in turn, had memorized his account numbers and passwords.

"Security, Lester," Slink whispered in the quiet room to no one. "Your computer is the window to your soul."

Humans are creatures of habit, designing their login codes for the easiest memorization. Once he'd uncovered Paprika's information, Slink had access to checking, savings accounts, online brokerage accounts, and IRAs if he chose.

Everything appeared kosher until he tapped into a series of ancillary accounts, which Lester had placed in a folder titled "GRANDMA." Bingo! Slink hit the gold mine at last. He stared at a series of offshore gambling sites. Tapping the keys, he opened the first site.

He whistled. "Lester, Lester..."

The site's account balance read $40,347. Another four offshore gambling sites showed similar credits, running in a surplus of $150,000 combined.

Paprika, it appeared, was avoiding the tight scrutiny of traditional bank accounts, squirreling away cash beneath the Internal Revenue Service's radar.

It was a clever tax dodge.

Slink downloaded the data to his thumb drive, copying the transaction histories from all five sites.

"Gotcha, Lester," he whispered to himself.

Tobias stared through the van's windows at the overcast sky and decided the rain would hold off. At least until it no longer mattered.

Exiting his van, he moved casually, employing the pretense of examining the air pressure in his tires. A moment later, with practiced nonchalance, he slipped away between the rows of parked cars. While stepping past, he doused a Toyota Camry's door handle with clear, mildly viscous fluid.

Strolling back to his van, collar up and ballcap pulled low, he re-entered the vehicle.

Invisible.

The wait was under fifteen minutes. The young woman wore blue jeans and a lightweight white sweater. She carried a pair of plastic shopping bags and was chatting on her phone as she emerged from the mall's exit. She moved up the lane of parked cars.

Preoccupied with her conversation, she paid scant attention to the blue van sitting six slots down from her Toyota.

Slink withdrew the flash drive and tucked it in a velvet pouch, slipping it inside his toolbox. Before he could leave, however, he had one bit of business left.

Slink's phone buzzed. Cale informed him their target was on the move. He acknowledged the warning, agreeing to vacate the premises at once.

But yet, Slink remained on the final offshore gambling site he'd visited. He whispered aloud, "You think you're a player, Lester. Let's see. How about the Kansas City Royals tonight?"

A minute later, flicking off the computer, he departed the workstation as he'd found it.

Cale closed the Bronco's door on the street outside the tavern, and his phone chirped in his hand.

"Paprika's crossing the bridge west," Staszak reported.

"We should have an all-clear on the house by now."

"Want me to keep the tail?"

"Yeah. Let's stay on the safe side."

Cale hit speed dial for Slink's number and received no answer. He pressed it again. No response.

"Ah, jeez," he groaned, starting up the Bronco.

Slink was at the bottom of the stairs when he noticed a shadow slip across the closed front curtains of the living room's bay window. Security? Had he tripped a silent alarm? Would the first responders be city patrol? County? Private security guards?

Stop spooking yourself, his brain warned. The shadow was likely a mail carrier or delivery drop. Besides, Culligan workers were not unusual at private residences. His phone vibrated, and Slink muted it. His objective was to extract himself safely from the premises.

He balled the latex gloves inside his pocket and exited the backdoor. He listened for footsteps or voices. All was quiet, save for the chirping birds and the hum of far-off traffic.

The back lawns stood empty, and Slink eyed the homes on either side. He stepped beneath the arch leading to the driveway, where he spotted his van parked at the curb.

He decided not to press his luck by whistling. He was now free of the house, toolbox in hand, and strode down the concrete driveway. Without warning, a male figure in a long leather jacket emerged around the home's front corner, and both men froze like gunfighters.

Slink had worked undercover narcotics for over a decade before Homicide and understood that remaining in character was crucial. With a pleasant smile, he called out, "Culligan, man!"

The stranger responded by pulling a 9mm automatic from one pocket, and a thunderous pair of gunshots shattered the serene afternoon. A swarm of starlings swept from the high trees, careening west against the gray sky.

Slink was spun around by a slug's impact ripping through his left shoulder. The second round went wide, and the toolbox crashed into the concrete. Slink staggered sideways, feeling his knees buckle, as he collapsed to the loamy dirt along the driveway's edge.

His last image was the assailant's booted ankles vanishing around the house's front corner, followed by the snap of long black coattails.

Cale sped north through the city's heart, praying their plan wouldn't be blown apart. His phone chirped. His left hand gripped the steering wheel while he grabbed it.

"Got your radio on?" Staszak sounded harried.

"I'm in the Bronco."

"Dispatch reported gunshots fired," Staszak's voice was steady. "West side. 947 Century Lane."

Cale's mind reeled. "Jesus. That's Paprika's address!"

"Said a civilian down. Rescue's on the way."

"Any ID?"

"Male. Blue workman's uniform."

Cale slammed his phone hard against the steering wheel and flipped on the Bronco's grill flashers.

CHAPTER 33

"Three thousand dollars."

The offer had been given Wednesday morning, thrown at Sid Draymus like a winning lottery ticket. Did he want the money or not? The decision was his to make—and fast—as he sat in the security monitor room at the Juvenile county lockup. Juan-Julio Sanchez, Inmate J7459, stood at the side window, offering him the payola if Sid performed a simple request, *por favor*.

"We're talking legal, right?" Sid had asked, narrowing his eyes.

Juan-Julio shrugged in his baby-blue jumpsuit, telling him it was a thousand dollars up front—another two-Gs after Sid handed over the DVD copy of the meeting with his attorney.

"A good deal. Take it or leave it."

The county jailhouse had installed state-of-the-art security cameras over a year ago. Multi-angle digital units with clean focus and zoom capability. Like the casinos used. The cameras gave the duty guards in the monitor room total control. The operator could alter the angles of the occupants being observed. They could perform sweeps, freezes, and zooms, all with the slide of a mouse.

The cameras, Sid understood, were installed to detect contraband exchanges between prisoners and visitors. The images were recorded, and hard-copy backups were stored as potential evidence in disciplinary hearings. Or in court, if needed to provide proof of nefarious activities.

"That's all? Run the camera?" Sid was wary of being set up. "It sounds too easy."

Intrigued by the gang banger's oily proposition, Sid was assured that he must keep the cameras focused on a private meeting between the inmate and his regular attorney, Ms. Maggie Jeffers, occurring later that afternoon. Sid knew who she was. He had watched her visit Juan-Julio and other clients she represented. Because the lady lawyer was an attractive brunette, Sid was further granted (a lewd wink from Sanchez) the liberty of taking tight shots. Be creative, he was told, like an amateur Steven Spielberg.

"Copy it to a disc. Then swap it for my runner's envelope," said Juan-Julio, selling the idea. "Easiest money you'll ever make, amigo."

The guard schedules had been posted for the day, and Sid knew Deputy Grace Weatherby would oversee the meeting. Sid figured all he had to do was zoom the camera in a couple of times. The recorder would do the rest. Who would care about some boring meeting between Sanchez and his lady lawyer? Especially with no sound?

"My friend will stop by after the meeting," Juan-Julio informed.

Sid pictured the jet-black Chevy Avalanche on which he'd had his eye for months. He'd been unable to come up with the down payment. What was he even hesitating about? Three thousand dollars!

The easiest money he'd ever make.

Maggie had her own plan. She stood before the bathroom mirror and brushed her flowing chestnut hair. It was early Wednesday afternoon, and she had changed from a business suit to dress-slacks and a sweater. Readying herself for a visit to the County Juvenile Detention Center.

Maggie had called and spoken to the prison's assistant administrator that morning. It's how the protocol worked. She was apprehensive about her strategy but held out hope. What was there to lose? Cale wasn't getting anywhere in his efforts to speak with Juan-Julio Sanchez through the DA's office. She might as well give it a shot on her own. After all, wasn't she whom the prisoner had confided in the first place?

After clearing her visit with the administrator, Maggie was patched directly to her former client. She'd wasted no time and got straight to the point. Would Sanchez agree to meet her? If so, she had only one demand. The meeting could only take place without his new attorney present.

"How about this afternoon, Ms. Jeffers?" Sanchez had suggested.

Maggie had already cleared her schedule. "Fine," she agreed. "Two o'clock. I'll be there."

She set aside the hairbrush and studied her reflection in the bathroom mirror. She'd always had an attractive face. Males had told her this since she'd been twelve years old. Maggie also understood that Sanchez had a crush on her. His courtroom antics were proof enough.

She might as well use a weapon if she possessed one, right? Especially if it helped Cale with his case. Juan-Julio's dramatic utterance from the courtroom echoed in her mind. *I know about the girls.* But knew what? Why had he said it? And why to her, of all people?

Only one way to find out, Maggie decided. Capping her lipstick tube, she stepped into a pair of heeled pumps. Then she exited the bathroom, prepared to take on her mission.

Thirty minutes later, Maggie sat in a good-sized room with high meshed windows and six wooden tables with 4-chairs each. She'd been in the visitation room at the County Juvenile Center countless times before, meeting with various clients over her past seven years as a public defender. Today, they'd been allowed the room for twenty minutes per Maggie's legal request.

Opposite her now, wearing the standard blue jumpsuit, with white socks and prison sandals, was Juan-Julio Sanchez. A middle-aged female security guard sat across the room—the only occupant—at a far-off table near the windows. A Styrofoam coffee cup stood before her. The badge above her ample bosom read Deputy Grace Weatherby.

Maggie noted the security cameras in two of the room's high corners, which focused down on them. She forced herself to

relax. The security, she understood, was first-rate at the facility.

She couldn't help wondering if the weeks in lockup were taking their toll on Juan-Julio. Hardening him. Turning him into an even more adult version of himself. However, the juvenile appeared upbeat, no different from how he'd been in court. He seemed pleased to see her again.

"How are you holding up?" Maggie asked, watching her former client sit opposite her at the table. He maintained his cat-like slouch, familiar to every inmate she'd ever conversed with.

He sniggered. "Got my music, TV. Xbox. Hard times, huh?"

Maggie's smile was controlled. Theirs had never been a comfortable relationship, and it had been some time since they'd talked one-on-one. Her desire, this time, was to limit the small talk while remaining polite and professional. She asked how his new attorney was working out.

The inmate's dark eyes remained flat. "Lester gets his cash," Sanchez said. "You know how he rolls."

"Sounds cold."

"Cold world out there, *señora.*" He stared tightly at her before looking away.

"I suppose it is."

She thought the youth appeared more antsy than usual, watching as he rolled his fingers together, hands uncuffed, cracking his knuckles. He glanced over his shoulder at the lady guard before returning to her.

"Paprika gets me probation—it's all I care about."

Maggie had decided against debate. Juan-Julio had been on probation prior to his arrest. Now he was facing a felony count. Even if Paprika worked it down to a misdemeanor, he faced significant jail time.

She reminded herself why she was here. Get to the point. "Why did you say that in court? About the missing girls?"

Sanchez looked her in the eyes. "Maybe I don't remember, you know? What I said?"

She glanced up at a camera and back. "Don't play games, Juan-Julio. You know what I'm talking about."

"I thought you came to ask me for a date, *chica*. You know? Pleasure before business?"

"Don't be—"

"One of those con-*jungle* visits?"

Maggie's face reddened. He was trying to rattle her. She needed to stay calm. "About the girls, then? Was it total BS?"

Juan-Julio rocked back in his chair. He flicked another glance toward the guard, and Maggie followed his eyes. The broad-hipped woman at a table sipped her coffee. She stared out the window, uninterested in their conversation.

"Paprika says we should go to trial."

"He's playing poker with your life. Are you comfortable with his advice?"

Juan-Julio leaned forward. "How 'bout we make a deal? You and me, *puta*?"

"I know what *puta* means."

Sanchez grinned. "My apologies. Miss Police Detective's *senora*. There. Better? More respect?"

He had brought up her relationship with Cale during one of their initial interviews. Sanchez had seemed to know more about her personal life than was comfortable, and this latest reference to Cale, Maggie imagined, was part of his cat-and-mouse game. She felt like she was holding a lousy hand in a poker game.

"What kind of deal?"

Another glance across the room, his third at the security guard, she noted. Maggie glanced at the cameras aimed down at them.

"Here's my offer." Sanchez leaned closer to her and said, "Ask our guard for fifteen minutes alone as my attorney." His eyes displayed the malevolent twinkle she recalled from the courtroom. "You give me your best blow job, and I'll tell you about your missing *chicas*."

Maggie's face flushed. Her initial impulse was to draw back in her chair, but instead, she placed both palms on the table and leaned forward.

"Here's *my* plan," she whispered. "Go screw yourself."

Sanchez caught her by the wrists, yanking Maggie toward him. She struggled with his vice-like grip. Before she realized what was happening, he pulled her onto the wooden surface.

"Hey! What in the—" The guard shouted at the sudden commotion, but as she rose (Maggie watched in disbelief), her shoulders pitched forward. Her drooping face slumped, and one floppy arm knocked over the coffee cup.

The dark liquid spread across the table like blood from a wound as she dropped to the floor.

Drugged? The word slapped Maggie hard, and a clawing fright took hold. She struggled with Sanchez, trying to pull herself free. She slashed her fingernails at his hand, then his wrist, shouting, "Let go of me—"

Instead, the inmate grabbed her hair. Rising and stepping around, he pinned Maggie's right arm roughly behind her while twisting her. She was suddenly bent over the table, helpless, with Juan-Julio's weight against her hips. His breath was hot in her ear.

"Ahh, *chica*. I knew you'd be a fighter."

Maggie was outweighed by sixty pounds. "You're making this worse for yourself," she panted. "The guards will be here any second."

"This is what you've wanted all along," he rasped.

One of her shoes had fallen off. Maggie tried kicking his shins with her heel, but he blocked it with his knee, and she squirmed futilely.

"The cameras are watching!"

Sanchez leaned close to her cheek. "No help, puta. The guards are well paid."

Maggie's mind reeled. He was lying, of course. She twisted her shoulders and tried kicking him again.

"The more you fight, the more I hurt you."

He spun her around to face him. His free hand gripped her throat, cutting off her air. Maggie's eyes bulged. She flailed her fists at his chest, but his elbows blocked them.

Sanchez pressed his mouth to hers, keeping his hand on her throat. Maggie gasped for breath, her strength ebbing, limbs numb and useless. He released her suddenly. She fell to the floor and slumped on one hip. Dazed and disoriented, she struggled to remain lucid. Her brain shrieked: *Fight him! Don't let him do this.*

Spotting her shoe beneath the table—*the sharp heel!*—she reached for the pump, but Sanchez rudely kicked it away. He withdrew a homemade toothbrush handle from his jumpsuit pocket. Its razor edge gleamed in the room's pale light.

Maggie gazed into his malevolent eyes. "Please, don't," she pleaded. Ragged breaths choked her words, and thin mascara trails soiled her cheeks.

Where are the guards? What's taking them so long?

Her eyes lifted from the blade to the room's high cameras, their wide lenses watching horrified as Juan-Julio unbuttoned the fly of his jumpsuit.

"Please, God. No!"

"You be a good *chica*, now," Sanchez demanded, throaty with lust. "And I'll tell you where to find your missing *putas*."

CHAPTER 34

What could seem more out of place than gunshots in a peaceful suburban neighborhood? Two of Lester Paprika's neighbors had called 911 within minutes of the cracking sounds, which startled awake the drowsy afternoon.

"A man's been shot!" one caller stammered.

The emergency operator remained calm. "Shot with a weapon, sir? Is that correct?"

"Yes! I think so. I don't know."

"Can you give me a description of the victim?"

"On the ground. He's, uh, some workman."

A pair of police cruisers were first on the scene. One of the rushing officers recognized Detective James "Slink" Dooley lying on the ground. His partner called in a "Ten 33." Officer down. All units respond.

Four minutes later, an ambulance arrived. The EMTs rushed to assist the officers attending to the injured victim, who lay semi-conscious in the driveway—losing blood by the second.

Over the following five minutes, chaos grabbed hold. Another dozen squad cars swooped in. Street traffic was closed as witnesses officered descriptions of the gunman: a Hispanic-looking male, wearing a long leather jacket, fled on foot through the backyards. They were almost certain of it.

An All-Points Bulletin was issued. A six-block radius from the shooting site was demarcated, cruisers blocking as many access streets as they could manage. Two dozen uniforms were now involved in a blind foot pursuit, sifting through the neighborhood yards, over fences, through hedges, inside tool sheds, and garages. K-9 units had been summoned and were on the way.

A police helicopter, Eagle One, radioed in. She was lifting off now, ten minutes away from the action.

Cale angled the Bronco to the curb as the emergency personnel wheeled Slink's gurney toward the back of the ambulance. He rushed to his partner's side.

The EMTs had worked feverishly to staunch the bleeding from entry and exit wounds and monitored vital signs. They'd placed an oxygen mask over the patient's face. Cale took a breath, finally, when Slink shot him a clumsy thumbs-up with his free hand.

"You're going to be okay, man." Cale stared into his best- friend's glazed eyes while moving along with the gurney. "Hang tight!"

Slink managed to pull the oxygen mask aside. His voice rasped: "Tool...box." His eyes stared up at Cale. "Copy..."

Cale gave his partner an understanding nod. Then he watched as Slink was hoisted into the rescue vehicle, where the slam of heavy doors signaled his world had disappeared.

Despite his protests about living nearby, Lester Paprika couldn't drive through the police barricade. His was the house with the ambulance in the driveway! he fumed to no avail. With mounting frustration, Lester confined his rage to the recalcitrant patrolman who stood at the window of his Escalade.

Cursing, he finally swung the SUV to the curb and parked. Lester exited, clomped up the sidewalk in his loafers, and headed toward his driveway. The patrolman called for him to halt.

"Let the A-hole go!" Staszak shouted, rolling to a stop in his car. The officer turned to his open window. "They'll want to talk to him, anyway."

Lester pounded his bulk up the sidewalk—half waddle, half turkey trot. What was going on at his house? Why an ambulance? Why were cops milling about in his front yard? Chances were, this was not something positive, and within moments, he'd be right in the thick of it.

Lester recognized Lt. Cale Van Waring. The detective was stooped down inside the bright yellow crime scene tape now stretched around his home's driveway. The detective wore latex gloves and sifted through a toolbox before sliding something unseen into his jacket pocket.

The toolbox, at least, did not appear familiar to Lester. Not one of his possessions. He stopped short of the yellow crime tape. Although it was his home, as a member of the legal profession, Lester knew better than to venture into what appeared to be an active crime scene.

The lights of a dozen cruisers and county squads flickered on the street. Neighbors had gathered on lawns and formed groups in driveways and doorsteps. Spotting Lester's uncertain intentions, a female officer warned against his approach, telling him to freeze and maintain a safe distance back.

Rising from his catcher's squat, Cale called, "It's okay, Officer. He's the homeowner."

Lester Paprika seized the opening to advance. "What's all this about, Van Waring?" he demanded. "You're on private property." His eyes were daggers.

"A police officer was shot in your driveway. About fifteen minutes ago," Cale explained.

"Why would a—"

"APB's out on the perpetrator. A twenty-man foot pursuit across the blocks."

Lester's eyes bulged. He looked around the yard, then back at the lieutenant. "Why would any officer be here? At my house?"

"Good question, Lester. Have you been up to any off-color dealings?"

Lester blanched. "My business is no concern of—was he inside my house?"

"Shot on the driveway over there—"

"On my property? Let me see the warrant!"

"Lester, why would there be a warrant for an attempted murder?" Cale sneered, causing Lester to ball his fists.

"Enough!" boomed a voice coming from behind them. "Let's everybody take a deep breath, shall we?"

Lester turned at the approach of Capt. Leo McBride. Lester understood that the fact of a shooting victim allowed the officers imminent control of the situation.

"I'm lodging an official complaint—"

"Did you not hear me right, Counselor?" asked McBride, placing his bulk between the attorney and his detective. "What part of 'officer down' do you not understand?"

The captain's angry presence caused Lester to take two steps back, his polished, burgundy loafers contrasting against the brown turf. He fumed and glared at both men.

McBride's radio cackled. He spoke into it, listening, then stepped back onto the driveway again. He was still listening.

"Something suspicious is going on here," Lester stated, eyeing Cale venomously. He crossed his arms and studied his house. "When I find out what you're up to, there's going to be hell to pay."

Cale stepped outside the yellow crime tape, moving down the driveway slope. The evidence tech van had arrived, and the technicians were invading the scene in their Hazmat suits.

Cale watched Staszak approach the Bronco, still angled at the curb twenty feet away. Cale joined him at the closed passenger door. They heard the captain say, "Let's go inside, Lester. I'll answer your questions better in private."

Paprika brushed away the captain's hand on his elbow. "Don't patronize me, McBride." Shifting his eyes to where the detectives stood, he added, "I'm not the criminal here."

Cale watched them disappear inside the house. Staszak asked, "Any word on Slink?"

"Pale. Clammy." Cale spoke solemnly. "Looked like two quarts of blood loss."

Staszak's hooded eyes searched down the block before rounding back to Cale.

"Surprised a burglar, maybe?" Cale offered. "It's the only thing that makes any sense."

Staszak looked at him narrowly. "It seems a little too...ah, geez...I don't know what it seems."

"Not random?"

The sturdy detective nodded his agreement. Standing on the street, they wondered how such a simple plan could have gone so far sideways. Cale stared at Paprika's now-active house, the afternoon shadows beginning to reflect the cruiser lights off the siding.

Staszak broke the silence at last. "Anyway, no matter how we slice it, we're all now residents of Screwsville."

Without saying so, Cale couldn't agree more.

Time had slowed. Maggie felt trapped in a breathless bubble, the rush of blood coursing hotly against her eardrums. Salty tears burned her vision.

There were rules—she reminded herself—for situations like this. Every female was taught them or learned them somehow. The lessons came from locker room chatter after sweaty 7th-grade gym classes or cluttery basement sleep-over parties. Or even more crudely, from the streets.

Rules of survival included attempted reasoning, frantic warning, scream-shrieks, arm-waving, fleeing, blowing shrill whistles, and, last but not least, wild and desperate yells for help. These were followed next by shin-kicking and punching and cat-scratching with your fingernails. You employed any weapon available to ward off your assailant.

Yet all of these survival methods were negated by one elementary rule: If the aggressor wielded a gun, knife, or any weapon that could end your life in seconds, then your response boiled down to the existential question:

Do I want to live or die?

Like it or not, logic trumped emotion. You did what you must, no matter how uncomfortable the compromise was.

You survived.

It was the dilemma Maggie now faced, trapped inside her bubble of silence. The hot tears stung her eyes. She pictured herself in her white First Communion dress. Her father, mimicking his own father's Irish brogue, had called her his "wee little angel." She remembered, darkly, the one fact she knew about angels. They were all *dead*.

How eager was she to join their ranks?

Live or die—her choice. The blade was inches away. With an executioner's slash, he could grant her wish if it's what she preferred.

CHAPTER 35

It took twenty-seven minutes to locate the driveway shooter. Uniformed officers discovered the leather duster and 9mm Glock pressed inside a trash barrel near a storage shed.

Less than ten minutes later, they discovered the suspect curled in the backseat of a rusted Pontiac. Its starter was broken, and the vehicle lodged in a residential three-stall garage. By the time the runaway suspect was tasered, cuffed, and deposited into the backseat of a police SUV, he'd suffered a broken nose and three cracked ribs. These injuries transpired in what the written report described as an "apprehension and detention" scuffle.

With the suspect conscious and upright, who would question the authenticity of such trivial details?

"Holy son of a—" Sid Draymus cursed under his breath. "I am so not believing this!"

Inside the surveillance monitoring room of the County Juvenile Detention Center, his eyes were locked on the split-screen monitor, showing two different camera angles of the Visitation room. He stared in astonished disbelief.

Three thousand dollars. Was it too late to back out of the deal?

Sid stared at both screen images, which showed inmate Juan-Julio Sanchez grabbing his female attorney by the hair.

Where was Guard Weatherby? he wondered.

Sid looked around the surveillance room, thankfully alone, then back at the monitor. He shifted the second camera into focus along the windows. The hefty female officer was slumped across a table, face down in a spreading puddle of fluid. A Styrofoam cup was tipped on its side.

"My God!" Sid blubbered, guessing she had been drugged.

Before the attack, he'd been moving the joystick in and out, zooming in on the woman's attractive face, chestnut hair, and the snugness of her sweater. He'd wondered about a future as an amateur film producer. It had to pay more than his current eighteen bucks an hour.

It was all fun and amusement until Sanchez reached out and grabbed the lady's arms, then a clump of her hair.

"Holy crap—" Sid muttered.

A sense of duty flashed through his mind. He should sound the alarm, summoning guards to her aid. But this idea was at once trumped by self-preservation. Sid was part of this conspiracy, wasn't he? Any investigation would reveal he'd accepted a cash bribe.

Sid eyed the monitor's digital recorder, watching the seconds click away like the steady drip of Guard Weatherby's spilled coffee. He whispered: "Please don't let it be blood."

Sid would remove the recording disc and secure it inside the envelope when this was over. Hand it to Sanchez's pick-up man. Then he'd erase the primary hard drive and blame it on a machine malfunction. If necessary, he'd "accidentally" discharge a riot shotgun into the device. No visual record of Sanchez and his attorney's encounter could exist.

Back on the screen, Sid watched Sanchez pin his weight against the woman's back. *Oh, Geez...* He swiped his palms on his uniform pants and averted his eyes, unable to watch anymore.

"This isn't tampering, is it?" Anton Staszak asked.

Later that afternoon, they huddled at Cale's desk computer. Staszak expressed his concern.

"It can't be." Cale inserted the small flash drive into his computer. "It's not an actual case yet."

Once the drive was activated, Cale tapped at his keyboard. "Besides, it's got nothing to do with Slink's shooting. It's between Paprika and us."

Staszak said bitterly, "I'd still like to get my fingers around the prick's fat neck,"

Cale stabbed the enter key, and images now leaped across the screen. Animated hula girls pranced beneath a dazzle of lights and palm trees. A giant pair of orange dice froze mid-roll to the sound of hearty cheering.

Staszak snorted as Cale hit another key. The hula girls disappeared, and a login screen blinked on. They digested what they were witnessing.

"An online gambling site," Cale announced. The account and password boxes had been auto-set. He clicked into the account controls and noted a surprising figure amount. He screenshot the account numbers he was viewing.

"This is the copy Slink downloaded. We only grabbed the account and history balances." Cale pointed at the main box.

Staszak gave a low whistle. "This is where the puke's been stashing his dirty gang cash."

"I think we hit paydirt."

"I prefer a bank vault, myself." Staszak shook his head.

Cale jiggled the mouse, and a second casino site scrolled into view. Another crazy balance figure. Then a second, third, and fourth offshore site.

"Not if you don't want the IRS snooping in."

Staszak watched Cale scroll through the multiple account history logs. Hundreds of transactions were revealed, each confirming dates and dollar amounts in the thousands.

"Geez," Staszak sighed. "I could pay my girls' way through Harvard and live on the interest."

Cale continued clacking until, at last, he smiled. "Here's our Slink Dooley touch."

"What's funny about getting shot?"

"How about forty-Gs of Lester's on the KC Royals tonight?"

"If I bet our house mortgage on a baseball game," the larger man scowled, "Gloria'd chase me down the block with a meat cleaver."

"And she's faster than you."

"Don't remind me."

Cale watched Captain McBride swallow a hypertension pill. He chased it with three glugs of Diet Coke. He understood the captain was more pissed-off than usual. Still, everything was a matter of degree.

"Paprika whined for the past hour like a hooker paid in singles," McBride groused. "It means you guys have one chance to explain what he's whining about."

Staszak shifted in the chair alongside Cale. They would sink or swim with Cale's explanation.

"We had probable cause to search his residence," Cale locked eyes with the captain. "For the record, both Stasz and Slink followed my authorization."

"How very noble."

Cale didn't back down. "Paprika's obstructing an ongoing murder investigation—"

"In your opinion."

"—by shielding his client from us, one who might have witnessed a known victim's murder."

"Might? Possibly?" Captain McBride scowled. "Neither are great legal terms."

Silence swelled between them. The captain seemed close to snapping his pen. "Attorney-client privilege? Does it ring any bell in your brains?"

Cale exhaled and withdrew the small red flash drive. He set it atop the captain's desk.

McBride eyed the object like a hemophiliac does a needle.

"It's the reason Slink's in surgery right now."

The captain listened as Cale described IRS tax dodges and illegitimate cash payouts for inflated attorney fees. McBride also learned about laundered narcotics payolas disguised as entertainment accounts, then flushed into offshore gambling sites via quasi-legitimate investment funds. Enough to make most people's head spin.

Outside his office window, late-afternoon shadows were slowly creeping in. The captain held up the diminutive flash drive. "And you got all this from Dooley?"

"Before they ambulanced him away."

"Obtained how?"

"He whispered that he'd found it curbside. Where Paprika sets out his trash bins." Cale smoothed his pants leg.

Captain McBride mulled the entire story over. Evidence of a crime trumped all else. Despite this, Cale understood they weren't out of the woods. But at least they'd survived the bull's initial charge.

The room air hung heavy.

McBride took the flash drive and eyed it carefully. "Does Paprika know we've got this?" he asked.

Cale shook his head. "His computer history is the first thing he'd check." He shrugged. "He can't prove his account information might've been copied." However, Cale held back that Slink's baseball wager would no doubt show up on the site's history.

"The DA can't use stolen info," McBride stated.

"It's a bargaining chip."

Cale suggested how they might leverage Paprica's data to interview Sanchez. Sign a legal promissory agreement not to reveal his computer data. No harm, no foul.

The captain contemplated the idea with his lips pressed.

"Paprika's fear isn't of prosecution," Cale insisted. "It's the IRS."

McBride weighed the idea despite his earlier misgivings.

A rap on the door interrupted them. A young officer stuck his head in and reported, "Shooter's in lockup, Cap. Prelim forensics say the weapon and bullet match."

"We got an ID?"

"DL says, Jorge Latessa. Narcotics priors. A bagman for the Diablo Hombres. Tats confirm it."

"Not a Latin King?" Cale asked.

"Apparently not, sir."

They pondered what this new twist might mean. A Latin King rival had gunned down Slink. Perhaps due to the ongoing turf battle between them.

"No way the prick sniffs bail," McBride growled.

The officer added, "They also discovered hi-grade smack in the perp's jacket. And ten Gs in an envelope."

Staszak shook his head disgustedly. "So Slink interrupted a drug drop?"

"At the home of a prominent attorney," Cale smirked.

The officer in the doorway said, "Also, Detective Dooley's out of surgery. In Bellin Hospital ICU."

Both Cale and Staszak rose together, not waiting for the captain's dismissal. They barreled past the officer. Cale heard McBride's shout from the hallway: "I'll talk to Chief Harris."

Cale could feel Staszak's labored breathing behind him as they sped through the maze of hallways. They were inside the Bronco minutes later, headed for the trauma center with the flashers flickering.

CHAPTER 36

Maggie shook inside her Mazda, with tears sliding down her flushed cheeks. She was parked in the Juvenile Detention parking lot. She withdrew a handkerchief from her purse as her phone chirped. She prayed it was Cale, then prayed it wasn't. She couldn't talk to him right now. She felt bruised and battered as if she'd fallen down a flight of stairs.

The number revealed it was Janet Dooley, Slink's wife. She answered tentatively, then was shocked at the sound of her friend's desperate voice: "Maggie! It's Jimmy!" Janet sounded hysterical. "He's been shot!"

No utterance could have stunned Maggie more. "What do you mean? Who?"

"An hour ago, a shooting," Janet reported. "They've taken him to the ICU trauma center." She choked out the words.

Jolted from her despair, Maggie agreed to meet Janet at the place. She hung up and swiped the tears from her eyes. "Get yourself together, Mags," her inner voice demanded. The voice was correct: she was alive and had survived the ordeal with Juan-Julio Sanchez. The image of the young prisoner's deadly blade flashed in her mind.

Yes, it could have been worse. Unlike Slink, she wasn't lying in surgery fighting for her life.

Maggie wanted to call Cale and scream about what had happened. He would want to know. But with the missing females and a killer on the loose, the stress he was under—and now Slink being shot—Cale was under too much pressure already without her piling on more.

She decided to keep the secret to herself, wait a few days, and compose her thoughts until she could process things more clearly. Besides, weren't some dark secrets better left staying buried?

Maggie examined herself in the visor mirror. Her eyes were puffy. The angled mirror revealed finger-compression marks on her neck. The rest of her body would be bruised, as well.

Just deal with it for now, she told herself. Unlike Slink Dooley, she was not lying on an operating table with a bullet lodged in her, fighting for her life.

Maggie withdrew a purple scarf from the glove box and fastened it around her neck. *Hide the bruises.* It would have to do for now. She could deal with the rest of it later—the mental side.

Summoning an inner fortitude she barely recognized, she turned the ignition, pleased to be doing something at least. Driving forward, she headed off to the ICU.

"Yo, El Sid! How's it hangin'?"

The greeting was called from another guard named Torrence as he entered the security monitoring room.

Sid Draymus was extracting the backup disc from the digital recorder. He placed it in a plastic cover, slipped it into a manila envelope, and sealed it.

"Same old." Sid barked like a yodel, nervously balling his fists. "Watching paint dry, for the most part."

"I hear you." Torrence was busy with the log-in sheet.

Moving across the room, Sid said, "Gotta drain the lizard." As his coworker shrugged, he added, "A heads-up—might have a glitch with seven, there. Been acting weird."

"The ghost in the machine." Torrence waggled his fingers.

"Yeah. A ghost." Sid closed the door behind him as he left.

Cale and Staszak arrived together at Bellin Hospital's third-floor ICU. Maggie was already present, sitting in a molded plastic waiting room chair with one arm draped around Janet Dooley's shoulder. The women appeared distraught and bleary-eyed, and Cale envisioned the worst. Especially with Janet looking pale and holding a crumpled handkerchief as women did at funerals.

Seeing their approach, Janet rose and hugged Staszak.

"Have we got any status?" Cale asked, searching Maggie's watery eyes.

"Out of surgery forty minutes ago," she reported, touching her neck scarf with her fingertips. "He's in a recovery room now. They're saying the worst is over."

"The bullet went clean through his shoulder," Janet added like it might be the best news of the day.

Staszak moved to the door and peered through the small window. He asked, "Can we go in?"

The door swung open before anyone could comment, and Staszak stepped back in surprise. A red-haired nurse with freckles issued them a tight look. She blocked the door with a less-than-inviting expression. Cale displayed his credentials. With a cursory nod, she agreed to let them all inside together. But only for a minute.

With the door open, the nurse warned, "He's weak." She handed them all blue facemasks as they filed into the room.

Janet moved like a specter to Slink's side. She considered leaning down and kissing his cheek through her mask but received an admonishing glare from the nurse. Instead, Janet knuckled the tears from her eyes.

A moment later, Slink's eyes blinked open. He studied them like an amnesia victim gathering his bearings.

"Hey, bucko, how you doing?" Staszak said, his voice a bare whisper.

Slink's rasp was sandpaper. "They tag the shooter?"

Typical cop, Cale thought, guessing it's what he'd likely ask if their situations were reversed.

"Captured hiding in a garage some blocks away," Staszak reported.

"My disguise didn't fool him, huh?" Slink attempted a sheepish smile.

"World's gone insane," commented Staszak, glancing at them all. "I mean, who shoots a Culligan Man?"

Cale noted Slink's drooping eyelids. He calculated the effort his partner was employing. "Our hunch is Paprika's bag-man," he said. "Dropping a payoff. We pulled ten-Gs from his jacket pocket."

"Along with a dime of smack." Staszak frowned. "Wrong place, wrong time, amigo."

"Story of my life."

Janet sniffled and swiped her eyes. Cale glanced at Maggie. She stood inside the room like a shadow, not close to her cheery self. When he caught her eye, she looked away.

The nurse coughed. She again cautioned Janet to stay clear of the bed with her eyes. Slink focused his gaze on Cale. "You find it?" he asked.

Cale understood he meant the flash drive. He nodded. "We got Lester's fat butt nailed to the wall."

The nurse frowned. Her patience thinning, she motioned them all toward the door. Slink called gravelly as they departed, "You like my Royals bet?"

Cale winked. "Sure loser if I ever saw one."

Slink's eyes closed, and Cale watched him fall into a sleep any infant would envy.

While driving home, Maggie's jittery thoughts continued sliding from Slink to Cale to Janet before returning to her miserable situation. Thoughts of the deviant Sanchez, the visitation room, the threatening blade at her throat. Her stomach lurched, and she considered pulling the Mazda to the side of the road.

Instead, she soldiered on, working through empty despair beyond anything she had ever experienced. Even worse than when her parents had died years ago.

The incident with Sanchez was like a raw wound. She imagined her recovery would come in steps, like people's grief stages. Denial, first, then the other six or seven. All one day at a time, like a toddler learning to walk.

She needed some food, a hot bath, and sleep. Maggie told herself she would make it through the night and sort her emotions out in the morning. A pity party could wait, couldn't it?

Maggie's survival instinct had allowed her to make one crucial decision. She would keep what had happened with Sanchez to herself—at least for now. She was intact and had suffered a few surface scrapes and bruises, which would heal in days. Her inner desire, above all else, was to put the ordeal behind her. Lock it in a box. Move on.

And yet, understanding that the physical part of the assault would fade, there remained the mental aspect of her trauma. It was the most challenging part—the lingering memories. Maggie wondered if she was strong enough to work through it independently. Time would tell, she supposed.

"Inner strength, Mags," the voice in her head advised. "The pain will lessen and fade and eventually disappear. Out of sight, out of mind."

After dropping Staszak back at the station, Cale wheeled the Bronco around and headed home. He muted his phone. They'd experienced enough fireworks for one day. He couldn't recall a more stress-filled afternoon, topped off by Slink's shooting. He was bone tired. He desired to be home with Maggie—open a beer, light the fireplace—and put this nightmare day behind them.

Maggie had arrived before him, and the house lights were on. Cale left the Bronco on the driveway apron in case he needed to get someplace fast. He prayed to God he wouldn't. Not on this crazy night.

Changing into jeans and a sweatshirt, Cale grabbed a bottle of Michelob and joined Maggie in the family room, where she had dished both of them plates of cold pasta salad. Hank was curled at her feet on the couch, and she picked him up and put him in her lap.

Cale noted that Maggie had changed clothes, donning gray sweatpants and a turtleneck. He sat beside her on the couch, and they ate in companionable silence, with each seemingly lost in private thought. Likely about Slink's shooting.

"Chloe called," Maggie said neutrally. "She's sorry that she couldn't have been more helpful."

It took a second for Cale to guess what she meant—it was the idea of a psychic helping the cops solve crimes.

Maggie pushed the pasta around on her plate, appearing disinterested in eating. "She can't turn it on at will, you know," she said. "Her visions aren't like some water faucet."

Cale sipped his beer and set it back on the table. "Slink's tough as nails," he said, glancing at her. "Are you doing okay?"

"It's only, you know—this day." She stared out across the room as if at some invisible sound.

Cale leaned over and kissed her temple. Maggie covered her reaction by reaching for his bottle and taking a drink.

"Want your own? I'll get you one."

She shook her head and set the bottle back down.

Cale considered commenting on her jumpiness but let it pass. His mind felt like a hamster running a wheel. Slink's shooting had been his fault. His idea. His brilliant plan! It had nearly gotten his partner killed.

"An inch here or there," he said remorsefully. "The bullet could have gone right through his heart."

"Don't even say that."

"Life's a game of inches, right?" Cale's inner voice added darkly: *And then you die.*

Maggie rose, shooing Hank off her, and gathered their empty plates. Cale imagined she needed to keep their routine and maintain normalcy with the day's crazy events.

He clicked the TV remote, guessing the afternoon's shooting was on every local channel. The shyster attorney Paprika, Cale knew, would threaten charges of police brutality, harassment, and anything else he could think. Of course, he'd cast himself as the unwitting victim.

"Go back two clicks." Maggie paused in mid-step. "Channel Seven. Renee Douglas."

Cale flipped back and spotted the severe face of the blond reporter at her news desk. Behind her, a bold caption read: "**Another abducted woman.**"

Cale exhaled. "You've got to be kidding!"

Maggie shushed him.

Douglas was reporting: "...feared today yet another young woman has been abducted in the Green Bay metro area. The family of twenty-three-year-old Shirley Koon has decided to go public instead of waiting for local authorities to...."

Cale's eyes were fixed on the screen. The TV feed revealed the downtown police headquarters, where Captain McBride moved through a gauntlet of reporters holding cameras and microphones at him. He was headed for the back exit.

Renee Douglas spoke over the bizarre scene: "Captain Leo McBride, head of Investigations, had little to say concerning this latest disappearance. It is feared that the crime may be linked to the string of missing young women, which have plagued the area since last spring."

Cale watched in disbelief. Douglas continued:

"The Captain indicated that an official statement will be issued tomorrow morning after investigators have compiled more facts and information."

Cale flicked off the TV and tossed the remote toward the loveseat across the room. It bounced and banged into an end table leg. Hank scowled up at him.

"Do you think it's the same kidnapper?" Maggie asked.

Before he could respond, Cale's phone chirped from the coffee table. He listened to the voice, then said thoughtfully, "Got it. I'm on the way."

He rose. "Gotta run," he told Maggie. Cale's mood was tense as he strode from the room with her trailing. He grabbed his jacket from the hall closet and his holstered sidearm.

He knew Maggie didn't want to spend the night alone—especially tonight. He also accepted that duty called on this foggy evening.

At the door, she told him: "Please be careful, Cale."

They embraced, and he stroked her hair. "You'll be fine, Mags. Forget it all and get some rest."

Stepping back, he stared into her glistening eyes.

Maggie smiled gamely. "Nothing a hot bath and some sleep won't fix."

With Hank's stare fixed on them, Cale stepped into the cool April night. What he couldn't see after the door closed was Maggie's back pressed hard against it. Tears leaked in rivulets down her cheeks, and she silently told herself:

Learning to walk again.

CHAPTER 37

Cale awoke Thursday morning, unable to remember ever feeling more exhausted. In his dream, he'd been climbing a cliff of craggy rocks, each crest steeper than the last, each handhold more precarious. He'd crawled into bed sometime after 3 a.m. Upon waking, it felt like he hadn't slept more than an hour.

Victim Number Five.

"Sorry." Maggie stood at the window across the room, where she'd been looking through the blinds. "I didn't mean to wake you."

Cale's voice was dry. "Got to get up anyway."

Maggie was dressed in jeans and a high-necked sweater. She told him she had canceled her morning appointments and was headed to the hospital to sit with Janet. To Cale, her demeanor was cordial, like you'd speak to an aunt you hadn't seen in years. She also told him she was fine when he asked, giving him a half-smile

"Anything new last night?" she asked. She glanced out the window at the trees again as he studied her.

"Same story. Nothing relevant."

He didn't want to reveal how another target had disappeared without a trace. They both already knew the percentages. They agreed to meet later at the hospital. Cale wasn't sure how his schedule might unfold with another missing victim.

He watched Maggie drift from the room, silent as a spirit. As he closed the door, he decided something about her wasn't right.

Cale's arrival at the station revealed ramped-up chaos. The day commander barked at the uniformed street cops and other subordinates up and down the food chain. Tempers were short, stress dripping from the walls and saturating the electrified air. It felt as if they were preparing for a hurricane while the higher-ups decided how to manage the negative publicity headed their way.

Victim Number Five.

Cale had spent most of the night at the suburban shopping mall. A credit card transaction was traced to an Old Navy store inside. The last place the missing Kuhn woman had been spotted. Other than this meager lead, the night's remainder had proved fruitless. The vanished female's vehicle was nowhere to be found, with no signs in the parking lot of anything amiss. No crime scene, no witnesses, and no clues. An all too familiar refrain.

"This BS is getting old," Staszak had growled, tossing an empty coffee container into the backseat of his boat-sized Buick. He'd slammed the door and driven off into the dark.

No argument from Cale. Without any sign of a missing victim, there was nothing else for them to do. Following his partner's lead, he slid inside the Bronco and headed home.

Moving along a hallway, Cale paused outside the door of a solitary interview room. He peered in through the small observation window.

Anton Staszak, freshly showered and dressed, conversed with a tall, handsome woman. She possessed dark hair, pinned back, streaked with wisps of silver. The woman sat at the table with her hands in the lap of her flowered peasant dress, staring at the detective through tinted eyeglasses.

Cale rapped on the doorframe and entered, carrying his Starbucks cup. He sat in an empty chair. Staszak introduced him to Samantha Koon, mother of the newest victim, Shirley Koon. He brought Cale up to speed on what they'd gone over regarding her missing daughter.

Shirley Koon was a blackjack dealer at the local Native American casino. Yesterday had been her day off. She'd had plans to visit the shopping mall and meet her mother for a late lunch. She had failed to show—unusual for an otherwise dependable young woman.

Mrs. Koon was forthright with her answers, and the detectives found her solid and credible. Her daughter didn't do drugs or alcohol and had no emotional problems. No violent boyfriends, ex-husbands, tapped-out bank accounts, or recent erratic behavior patterns existed.

"Have any of her friends heard from her?" Cale asked, his voice echoing off the room's bare walls. These days, he felt like some parrot. The same repeated questions were made doubly annoying by the identical weary responses.

Mrs. Koon reported, "I called them. They all said nothing unusual was going on."

Samantha Koon's large chestnut eyes were glazed, but she steeled them at the detectives.

Cale considered what the latest abduction location might reveal about the perpetrator. The shopping mall was on the city's west side. The previous abductee—Cindy Hulbreth—had been taken on the east side, near the Speedway station. Either way, it amounted to the same thing—a random geographical profile of no particular sort.

Staszak's notebook was filled with information, and Cale assumed Samantha Koon would be tired of the questions. Still, he had one question he couldn't resist asking:

"Why did you contact the press, Mrs. Koon? Instead of calling us directly?"

A determined look gripped the woman's eyes. "I figured you'd put me off." After a beat, she added, "Wait forty-eight hours, you know? Then file a report?"

"Not in this case," Staszak said. "Any new victims receive priority-one status."

"Detective Staszak's correct," Cale seconded, uncertain if she believed him, but it was true.

Samantha Koon appeared disheartened. "I watch those crime shows, where the first hours are crucial when someone disappears."

The detectives stayed silent.

"I don't want my daughter to be a statistic, Detectives. Not if I can help it."

"You did the right thing," Cale agreed diplomatically.

Samantha Koon wiped tears from her eyes and nodded. Cale imagined his comment made them all feel better, whether true or not.

After Mrs. Koon's departure—Staszak escorting her from the building—minutes later, Cale sat down at the heap of clutter Detective Harry Blum called a desk.

"We've got final forensics and autopsy reports on Ray Tolver," the detective said without emotion. He handed Cale a folder. "Let's just say problems persist."

"There's a news flash for you." Cale didn't smile.

As the prelim autopsy had suggested, no prior indicators of narcotic use by Tolver were showing up. Just hypertension and a fatty liver from years of alcohol and junk food.

"And they say marriage will kill you," Cale sighed.

"Nah," retorted Blum, "it only numbs you to death." He'd been married for over twenty years himself.

Cale didn't press the topic.

"Needle entered the femoral thigh vein," Blum continued, "and the meth blast caused the heart to seize." He paused. "The puncture needle mark—believe it or not—was hidden beneath the guy's scrotum. Doc almost missed it."

Cale grimaced. "It means the Brickner kid's statement checks out. It's unlikely drugs were being dealt from the gas station by Mr. Tolver."

Blum nodded.

"And the meth pipe near Tolver's body?"

"Looks like a plant," Blum allowed. "The old red herring bit."

A premeditated homicide, just as Cale had suspected while viewing the sight. It meant the murderer not only had access to enough methamphetamine—on short notice—to heart-stop a mule but was also clever enough to attempt disguising the injection site.

And he almost got away with it.

It meant their solitary lead trailed into the ether like the others. Cale doubted they'd uncover anything suspicious from Tolver's poker pals. It left the investigators in the same space they'd been in since Day One.

Blum promised information of any new developments, and Cale returned to his note-filled desk, stepping no quicker than a man approaching a gallows.

What did it all have to do with their mystery kidnapper? The unknown man who had stopped for a measly five bucks worth of gas? Cale's gut instinct told him the man was their killer. His motivation lay in imagining Tolver possessed recordings revealing his identity as an abductor and murderer.

A recording that had now disappeared.

Their perpetrator was clever enough to erase his tracks. Capable of incapacitating a grown man inside his residence and educated enough to disguise an injection site where an expert medical examiner had almost missed it.

Statistics weren't in their favor. Cale had guessed the kidnapper to be a luckier-than-average lowlife, yet the truth now suggested the opposite. They were dealing with a skilled, deviant offender—as their original profile had theorized.

Stringing together what they thought they understood, the Ray Tolver autopsy results established one undeniable fact: their kidnapper-slash-killer was willing to stop at nothing to accomplish his goals.

How many more victims did he plan on abducting? And to what end? Torture? Murder? Societal mayhem? What was his ultimate goal in creating the carnage?

The answer remained conjecture. No one had the slightest idea. And this, Cale realized, was the absolute definition of a sociopath.

CHAPTER 38

From his desk, Cale watched Captain McBride approach. He looked as if he'd aged a decade overnight. Cale doubted that he looked any better, with stress taking its toll on them all.

"The fliers out yet?" McBride asked Staszak, who was sitting across from Cale.

"Should be ready in fifteen."

"Take as many uniforms as you need," McBride ordered. "Canvass the mall neighborhoods and security cams within a half-mile radius. Maybe we pick up the Koon girl's vehicle?"

Staszak walked away. "I'll check the printing."

McBride turned to Cale. "You'll need handouts for the piranhas this afternoon." His usual unflattering reference to the media. "Chief wants you out front from now on."

McBride didn't add how it meant one less headache for him. "Also, Agent Redtail says he'll be here tomorrow."

To Cale, it came as no surprise. The agent had advised them months ago of the Fed's involvement if it appeared their case was spinning out of control.

Had it ever been in control, Cale wondered, in the first place?

It was one of those clear Wisconsin spring days where the sun was high in a cradle-blue sky. It helped folks forget the past three months of winter weather. Cale hoped it remained clear. The sun trumped April showers any day.

Bulleting the Bronco through the city beneath arches of budding elm and ash trees, Cale parked in the St. Vincent's Hospital lot. Before returning to the station for the afternoon press conference, he wanted to check Slink's condition.

Driving the shaded streets, Cale pondered the past twenty-four hours: the latest victim, identical MO, the dearth of clues, the ME's autopsy report. None of it helped in ID-ing the killer. They needed an actual break.

Slink had spent the night in ICU, then was transferred to a private room on the fifth floor. Cale tapped the doorframe, easing into the small confines.

Janet was in a bedside chair, looking like she'd been there all night. Having taken a leave day, Maggie sat a short distance away, scanning the morning paper. She still appeared pale. Hearing him enter, both their heads turned.

"He's asleep," Janet informed. "Fades in and out."

Cale scootched a chair between them, giving Maggie a peck on the cheek. She squeezed his hand. He informed them they'd interviewed the latest victim's mother and how the MO matched the previous abductions. He knew he sounded frustrated.

"Maybe he's not a stranger?" Maggie arched an eyebrow. "To simply allow him into their cars?"

Cale didn't elaborate on how they'd already worked the angle of local celebrities and pro athletes. The dressing down they'd received still stung, yet the idea continued to nag at him.

"Hey, honey. Welcome back."

Janet's voice jarred Cale from his reverie. He looked at Slink on the bed. His partner appeared dazed, a man coming around from a three-day bender.

"News flash! Rip Van Winkle returns!"

"Wonderful," Slink groaned. "I died and woke up at the comedy club." Dark smudges showed beneath his eyes. "If this is heaven, I'm going back to sleep."

They conversed for ten minutes, Cale giving his partner an update on where the case stood and the autopsy results on Ray Tolver. He didn't mention the newest missing victim. Janet moved bedside and positioned a cup with a corded straw to Slink's lips.

After a few long sips, Slink eyed Cale expectantly. "Don't keep me in suspense," he grumbled. "How'd the Royals do?"

"They lost. You nailed it."

Slink raised a victory fist, smiling for the first time since he'd been shot. His bandaged shoulder protested, and he winced. Janet scowled and scolded, "You're in a hospital, Jimmy. Not a tavern."

Slink winked at Cale. "Paprika dropped forty-Gs." He sounded like a giddy school kid.

The women appeared puzzled until Maggie computed they were talking about gambling. She frowned at Cale.

He protested, "I had nothing to do with it."

Captain Leo McBride sat in Chief Harris's office and glanced at his wristwatch. It was after 1 p.m. Thursday, and he had fifty better things to do. The chief, however, was on the phone, and McBride drummed his fingers on his knee.

The minutes ticked by.

McBride knew the meeting concerning Lester Paprika was necessary. The thoroughly pissed-off attorney demanded legal action against the city for invading his residence without a warrant. Though Paprika lacked proof, it was beside the point. The captain hoped the powwow would be brief. He had a squadron of detectives waiting and cases to resolve. Not to mention a serial kidnapper running loose and the press bearing down on his detectives with increasing scrutiny.

The chief ended his call. A rap on the door brought a second pair of suited men inside.

City Attorney Ned Kronforst was followed by John Zackary, representing the District Attorney's office. Kronforst wore his salt-and-pepper hair swept back like some character actor. Like the others, he knew of Lester Paprika's claim that officers had raided his domicile and private computer files without cause. Having already read the legal document in his hands, he waved it in the air and announced to ADA Zackary:

"You understand everything on this is inadmissible in court. It's been obtained without a warrant."

Zackary nodded. He sat in a chair with his legs crossed.

"We're aware of the details, Ned," Chief Harris said. "The idea is to leverage Mr. Paprika toward our interviewing his client—a kid named Sanchez."

Kronforst eyed them. "In other words, you're threatening him into cooperating with you."

"Leveraging," John Zackary corrected.

"That's the general idea," the chief agreed.

"And his client is currently in juvenile lockup?" Kronforst glanced again from the printout back to Zackary. "This is kosher with your office?"

Zackary sat forward. "Paprika can threaten to sue us, and we counter-sue him. He can whine to the press. But he's going down hard if we file charges for drugs, money laundering, illegal gambling, and obstruction."

"It couldn't happen," McBride added colorfully, "to a nicer dickwad."

Kronforst nodded. "And Paprika, I take it, is aware of all this?"

"Howled like a cat beneath a rocking chair," Chief Harris said in his Texas twang.

McBride glanced at his watch again. Kronforst relaxed at last and stated: "As you said, it couldn't happen to a nicer—"

"Dickwad," McBride repeated.

The agreement would be drafted at once. Lester Paprika could maintain his freedom in exchange for allowing the detectives access to Juan-Julio Sanchez. All the necessary legalese would be added to the document, which absolved the City from any liability concerns.

"Where's the flash drive now?"

John Zackary held up the device before slipping it back inside his suit jacket.

"Copies?" Kronforst surveyed the room, ensuring no surprises might come back to bite them.

"What flash drive?" Zackary asked cryptically.

Satisfied, Ned Kronforst rose to his feet. To the great relief of Captain McBride, the meeting was adjourned.

CHAPTER 39

Microphones and camera lights filled the media conference room, which the GBPD employed for public service announcements and press releases. Media members filled the place like a Hollywood premier, and their inflated sense of self-importance hung fog-like in the air.

To Cale, the macabre theater was challenging to digest. Conversely, he understood the relevance of positive press. Reporters didn't need to be adversarial to cops or vice versa.

A pair of uniforms moved through the crowd distributing fliers of the newest missing victim: Shirley Marie Koon, single, age twenty-four.

Cale recognized several media figures, along with family members of the abducted victims. Also, the Mothers of Missing Daughters group sat in jury-like attendance nearby. Additional supporters, he knew, were parading outside the building carrying picket signs. Cale hated acknowledging the investigators were sliding down a greasy slope, from bad to worse, and how it wouldn't change until they arrested a suspect in the kidnappings.

June Sammers from Public Relations introduced Cale. She was a petite forty-something with sand-colored hair, and she stepped aside like a quarterback handing the ball to a running back.

Cale stood stiffly at the podium and delivered the PR lady's prepared statement. It assured the victims' friends, relatives, and family members—along with the entire city, county, and state—that the investigation was progressing steadily.

He followed this by revealing the "essential facts" of the case, and then questions were finally allowed. Hands shot up as if electrified, and shouts came in a staccato barrage. Cale acknowledged them as best he could.

"Do you have any suspects yet, Lieutenant?"

"We have several promising leads."

"What's the likely status of the missing women?"

"We're hoping they hold on until we can bring them safely home."

"What about the kidnapper's capture method? How's he selecting and abducting his victims?"

"Sorry. That's privy to our investigators. We don't want to tip our hand."

"Why wasn't the FBI called in sooner?"

"Agent Eddie Redtail arrives today from Milwaukee. He's a profiler with expertise in serial cases."

There was a long pause before TV reporter Renee Douglas asked from the front row: "Detective Van Waring. Has your team given the kidnapper a name yet? What you're calling him?"

Cale stared at the terse faces, extended phones, and digital recorders. "Off the record, we've referred to this offender by several names."

Silence. Like a comedian's joke falling flat.

Cale studied Ms. Douglas's blue pantsuit, sitting with her legs demurely crossed—a canary-cat smirk on her lips.

"Lieutenant," she countered evenly, "as of today's six p.m. broadcast, our producers have decided this abductor is the 'Nowhere Man.'"

The loud racket of simultaneous voices swept through the media room. Cale grimaced. Over the boisterous clamor, Renee Douglas loudly added: "Because he seems to vanish without a trace."

Half the reporters exited as if a bomb threat were shouted, intent on making their deadlines. When Cale turned to June Sammers, she widened her eyes. It was out of their control. Leaning toward the microphone, Cale said, "We have no further comments."

With a polite nod, he departed from the room.

Back at his desk, feeling as if he'd narrowly escaped the Spanish Inquisition, Cale twisted in his chair. He felt drained but decided he'd emerged unscathed.

Now, one way or another, they'd deal with the fallout.

"Nowhere Man?" he muttered to himself.

It didn't conjure images of terror or bloodletting, at least. So by some measure, they should be grateful. In any case, he prayed the moniker would be short-lived.

He turned his attention to the messages attached to his computer screen. One, in particular, caught his eye. It was a note to return a call to Jerry Skowing. The listing was a private number.

Pocketing the message, Cale surveyed the detectives' bullpen. Uniforms were moving about, and everyone was active. He knew many officers were off with Staszak, assisting in the canvass around the shopping mall.

A waste of time, in his opinion. Their perpetrator was too clever to have left any clues. He hadn't thus far, so why start now? Yet it was a necessary task. Families and politicians had to be appeased. Not to mention an uneasy public.

Grabbing his jacket, Cale stepped down the hallway. Chief Harris's office door was closed. He hoped they were clearing the path for his meeting with Juan-Julio Sanchez.

As far as Cale was concerned, Sanchez remained the key to the investigation. His cryptic comment to Maggie: "*I know about the girls,*" continued to haunt them. Hopefully, Sanchez had some information they could use. It would vindicate their search of Lester Paprika's domicile. Even more important, it meant Slink had taken a slug for nothing.

A dark thought flashed across Cale's mind as he moved down the hallway. What if Chief Harris wasn't discussing the Sanchez issue? What if, instead, he was meeting with Internal Affairs? IA investigators were like a pack of vampires (in Cale's opinion) on an endless quest for cops' blood. Almost as if to justify their existence. Their decision—*his decision*—to invade the home of a local attorney had placed them all in IA's crosshairs.

It boiled down to one thing, Cale decided. They had to get in and interview Sanchez. The entire case, along with their careers, now hung in the balance.

CHAPTER 40

Splashes of sauterne sunlight glinted off the windows and hoods of vehicles as they cruised along the wide inner-city boulevard. It was late afternoon, and the sky was a delicate shade of lavender in the east.

On a tree-shaded side street a bare half-mile from the shadows of the station, Cale swung the Bronco to the curb. He'd decided to place the call from his mobile phone. Thoughts of Internal Affairs still crept through his head like NSA spies.

Scoop Skowing answered after two rings like he'd been awaiting the call. "I caught the news last night," the Packers' security director said.

"Like I told you, we've got a sick bastard working here."

"Sure seems like it." After a pause, the former detective continued, his tone subdued, "First, I've got to apologize, Cale. After we talked, I got the heebie-jeebies."

"You're in a sensitive position."

"I got to thinking." Scoop's voice stayed hesitant. "Thing is, this has got to stay between us."

"You know me, Jerry—"

"Seriously. I'm out of a job if I'm found even talking to you."

Works both ways, Cale thought darkly. With the crazy events of the past week, his visit with Skowing seemed distant. Now the guy had phoned back unexpectedly. Could the "celebrity angle" be back in play? How the victims recognized their abductor and allowed him into their cars? The theory still felt like a long shot.

Cale decided it was best to listen to a former investigator.

In his ear, Scoop said, "I went through our records, players on the current roster. Especially guys who might've been around town last spring."

Cale pictured his old mentor hidden somewhere in the city. Nervous as a squirrel. The spy image returned, and it summoned thoughts of paranoia.

A local sports talk show had reported how players were in town for a three-day minicamp. It meant a bluster of activity at 1265 Lombardi Avenue. With people coming and going, it further meant Skowing had plenty of cover. Any personal business he conducted would be unencumbered by scrutiny.

"And?"

"And I matched players' names who were in town last month, cross-referenced them with the dates you gave me." Skowing exhaled. "Whittled it down to twelve active players."

Reality slapped Cale. Twelve was too cumbersome for their timeframe. Plus, there was little chance he could run down the intel before doors began slamming in his face.

Scoop continued, "I also eyeballed their med-records to see if any had a history of, you know, incidents? That sort of thing?"

"And?"

"List narrowed further. Down to three possibles."

Cale's heart raced. Three was a workable number.

Skowing indicated he'd explored the trio's medical and psychological profiles, and it eliminated another player from his list.

Cale felt his guts tighten. Two players, two suspects. He would now have to at least look at Skowing's information. But what of the fallout? Captain McBride's response to this angle of pursuit would be predictable—it rang in his head like a funeral knell: "There is no Packer's angle!"

Cale doubted he could live with himself without pursuing every possible tip. Besides, this was the same Detective Lt. Scoop Skowing who had advised him years ago to "Always trust your gut first and last."

"Two players," Cale said softly. Two professional athletes. Could one of them be a cold-blooded killer?

"Listen," Skowing interjected, "you realize we're still talking Powerball odds here?"

"I'm not holding my breath."

"You know I couldn't sit on it, Cale. Not with you guys having a serial kidnapper out there."

"You're a cop at heart, Scoop," Cale admitted. "Trust me. It's a good thing. Want to meet me in private?" Cale gave him the address.

After the call, he drove the Bronco down the tree-lined street. Ribbons of afternoon sunlight illuminated his path. As much as he fought it, the cloak-and-dagger imagery worked into Cale's thoughts, causing him to feel uncomfortable.

Lester Paprika did not need an attorney for his afternoon meeting with city attorney Ned Kronforst. He was his own damn attorney, thank you very much.

He sat across from the man's large desk of polished maple. Lester didn't remember the colorful harness racing prints on the wall, but it had been a while since he'd been here. He'd been a fresh-faced deputy DA at the time.

Now he found himself on the opposite side of the track. He glared at the two-page document in his hands, hating how it said so little yet managed to make him perspire.

"You'll find the city's position well laid out," Kronforst said without emotion.

"In other words, I can't sue the city for breaking into my house without a warrant." He scowled.

"In exchange for this." Kronforst held the small thumb drive up. "You're free to examine it. But our detectives get a sit-down with your client, Juan-Julio Sanchez."

"Nothing on that is admissible in court."

"The IRS rarely bothers with courtrooms."

Paprika huffed his indignation. "What about my forty grand? The wager you pricks made on my behalf? Where's the mention of that in here?"

"I'm not sure I—"

"Don't piss me around, Kronforst."

The city attorney shrugged. "It sounds like more money the IRS would seize."

Paprika's lips were purple, and his gray ponytail slapped sideways while shaking his head with disgust. He angrily scribbled his signature and flung the document on the desk.

"Lousy crooks!"

The door shook behind his slamming exit.

The magenta carpet absorbed the sound. Ned Kronforst eyed the legal agreement the angry attorney had Hancocked, ensuring that Paprika had signed his actual name.

"Takes one to know one, Lester," Kronforst whispered to the empty room.

CHAPTER 41

The girl with the raven hair made frightened, whimpering sounds despite the duct tape over her mouth. Animal sounds, Tobias decided. He cringed, wishing she'd shut the hell up.

She lay on her stomach, head positioned to the left. Her legs were splayed out, stretched, and anchored to the stumps of the bed. Her arms were behind her back, cuffed at the wrist with plastic zip-ties, and secured to a stiff rubber binder. A ball-gag prevented any noise but failed to stop the incessant whimpering, which annoyed Tobias greatly.

Her captor stood near the bed. Flickering candles danced. His eerie, Nosferatu-esque shadow appeared bent and wolf-like, lurking high on one wall and ceiling.

Still, the timing of things mattered most in his plan. Tobias Crenshaw remained silent, choosing to observe rather than advance. In this fashion, as the minutes passed, he felt infused with a rush of dark energy.

He waited until the moment was perfect.

In an upstairs bedroom, a different section of the house, Cindy Hulbreth was on her back on another bed. She felt dizzy and nauseous most of the time since her capture. Was he drugging her water cup? Using hallucinogens? Barbiturates? Something that created disorientation? Strong enough that she couldn't remember what week, day, or even hour it was?

Was it in the food? The dry cereal in the bowl? The way caged animals are fed or medicated at a zoo. However her tormentor was drugging her, it was working. Cindy felt the familiar wave sweep through her, dragging her deeply into the inky depths of nothingness.

Tobias pressed the Play button on the CD player in the wide basement bedroom. It was situated in the darkest corner. Music filled the air, causing the desktop candles to flicker, and shadows shimmied across the walls and ceiling.

"Why do birds...da-de-da-de-da..." crooned the ethereal, feminine voice.

In the flickering light, the dark-haired girl thrashed on the bed. She whipped her head about, attempting to locate the sound's source.

Tobias breathed in her panicky confusion. He smelled the adrenaline escaping from her pores. Matching the song's measure in a whispery falsetto, he sang: "Da-de-da... close to me."

He placed his knee on the mattress and crept forward.

The Green Bay Packers Security Director Scoop Skowing wanted to lock himself in a closet and hide for the next three weeks. Or however long it took until the cops caught the monster responsible for terrorizing the city.

His dilemma, however, was he had discovered information relevant to the investigation. As a retired law enforcement agent, it ran contrary to Scoop's nature to sit on it. Doing so, he imagined, would chip away at his soul. He would end up living the existence of a bitter man who had swallowed a secret. One that could have saved lives.

It was Friday, mid-morning now. Scoop exited his blue Chrysler Sebring after parking it beneath the budding elm trees at the Van Waring driveway's edge. He could not have appeared more nervous, he imagined, than if he were casing the place for a heist.

He approached the house. Casting his gaze about the yard, he peered at the tall trees and bushes that shaded the place from prying eyes.

Scoop gave the door a rap with one bony knuckle.

Alone at home, having heard the car pull up, Cale advanced through the kitchen. Hearing the soft rap, he opened the backdoor as Skowing darted in like a man pursued by ghosts.

"Jeez! Take it easy." Cale stepped aside.

The man glanced around them. "Like I said, I can't be seen near you. No offense."

"Maybe we should drive across the state line?" Cale joked. He added, watching his old friend's reaction, "I'm kidding."

Skowing held a folded newspaper. The corner of a manila folder peeked out from its pages.

"I doubt you were tailed."

"NFL franchises define paranoia."

Skowing's guard dropped at last, and he shadowed Cale through the dining room and into the multi-windowed living room.

Signs of Maggie's touch defined the place: knickknacks, soft photos, colorful wall hangings, and healthy plants. Sunshine beamed in through the open vertical blinds.

"She's gone all morning," Cale said. He knew Maggie would remain at the hospital with Janet and Gloria Staszak for most of the day.

Skowing nodded. He chose a spot on the sofa's edge, a polite distance from where Cale sat. He withdrew the hidden folder, opened it, and spread the contents across the coffee table.

"The stuff I mentioned. Names of both players. It was as much as I could find on short notice."

"You're sure on this?" Cale stared at the ream of papers, surprised by the names revealed before him.

"As I said, they both fit your profile. Each guy was in town last spring. Along with the recent camp."

Skowing sifted through the contents, separating the pages he deemed relevant. "They each have a couple of priors."

"Anything serious?"

"No felony counts if that's what you mean." The former detective crinkled his eyes. "They fit the mental profile. Couple screws loose if you ask me."

Cale grabbed one of the pages. He studied the names. Both players were familiar to him, just as they were to a few million other Packers fans: Tealy "Mongo" Weathers; and Kenny "the Whistler" O'Hern.

Skowing had compiled a printed file of both players' past indiscretions, current addresses, times, and dates. Over the past two seasons, their presence in the area included games, camps, physicals, and workouts—even local radio gigs.

"Are they in town now?" Cale asked, perusing a medical report on Tealy Weathers. "These past few days, I mean?" He couldn't erase the image of Shirley Koon's face in the news.

"Mini-camp. Both." Skowing issued him a furtive nod. "Neither's practicing, though. But yeah, they're both around."

Weathers had a gimpy knee he was rehabbing, Skowing informed. O'Hern had a dinged shoulder. He scoffed, adding, "He's got a knack for malingering. So the trainers tell me."

Scanning the dates, Cale confirmed each player had been in town at the time of the kidnappings. It qualified them as persons of interest. He wouldn't go as far as calling them "suspects."

Cale wondered if they were famous enough. Would the victims recognize either as Packers players? Were they so familiar that victims would allow them inside their vehicles when approached?

Skowing rose to his feet.

"Nothing against your hospitality, Cale, but I better hit it." His eyes narrowed. "This stays between you and me, right?"

"My word on it."

Scoop's nod was sharp, and he exited the room. He moved back through the dining room area with Cale trailing.

From the windowsill, Hank turned his head, watching them. Skowing paused to study the photos of Cale and Maggie around the place—a happy couple, judging by their smiles.

"A beauty, all right." Skowing gave Cale a knowing look. "It'd take a real bonehead to mess things up with her."

Cale caught Hank's stare before turning back to his friend. "That seems to be a common sentiment."

They shook hands at the door. Cale added, "Thanks again, hombre. I owe you one."

"Chalk it up to my civic duty," Skowing said brusquely. He stepped out into the morning sunshine, the twittering birds, and the buzz of traffic only blocks away.

Cale watched the Chrysler disappear, moving down the street and sliding away into the pleasant afternoon.

He hoped Scoop Skowing's heart was unburdened and whatever guilt gnawed at him was appeased. Standing in silence, Cale understood one thing. In his heart, the man was still a good cop.

Moving slowly back through the house, Cale's heart clutched. Skowing had remarked on the photos of the happy couple that filled the home. Many included Hank. Cale tried not to dwell on it, but those pictures would soon vanish if he didn't play his cards right. Maggie would pack up boxes and take away most of them. The human touch would disappear, and the house would become desolate, bare, and pockmarked with the empty wall spots of happier times.

However, Cale reminded himself to stay focused; there was new information. He sat on the couch in the living room and studied Scowing's material.

Tealy Weathers, he learned, tipped the scales at over three hundred pounds. He bore the moniker "Mongo" with pride. He was an offensive lineman, a six-year Packers veteran. According to Skowing's file history, Weathers had received probation in Oklahoma during his college playing days. He was accused of misdemeanor sexual battery. The victim was listed as a nameless "Sooner coed."

It hadn't been his first offense.

Cale scribbled in cursive on a saffron-tinted legal pad—*Tealy Weathers: suspect Numero Uno.*

CHAPTER 42

The second man on Skowing's list, Kenny O'Hern, was a different matter. His psych profile was nearly off the charts, revealing a penchant for raging physical violence. A private team therapist had verified the diagnosis before the Packers drafted him.

Kenny, Cale learned, came from Drake University in Iowa. An unheralded, twelfth-round draft pick. A two-hundred-thirty-pound free safety with a nose for the football and an intense desire to dislodge pass-catchers' helmets from their heads when making bone-crunching contact. O'Hern could come from anywhere on the field like a heat-seeking missile. The lore around the league suggested that the only warning a receiver might have of his looming presence was a faint whistling heard an instant before the collision.

Cale guessed it was more of a psychological ploy than anything. Yet who could argue with the results? The Whistler had a reputation as someone not to be messed with. Confront him at your peril.

According to Skowing's notes, O'Hern's path of youthful aggression followed him to college. A series of run-ins with school officials and local law enforcement had been recorded. The most notable incident occurred during the lad's senior year when he was the primary suspect in the aggravated beating of a male Norwegian Literature student. The incident had been settled privately out of court.

It was the type of transgression, Cale guessed—especially years back—often overlooked by professional scouts and draft advisors.

But one fact contradicted expectations: Kenny O'Hern had been a chemistry major in college. Perception didn't jive with reality on this point. Cale couldn't have been more surprised if he'd learned the guy played concert-level Mozart.

Nonetheless, Whistler's penchant for serious violence confirmed him as a person of interest. On his legal pad, Cale scribbled—*suspect Numero Dos*.

Setting aside the manila folder, he took a few minutes to ponder the information. Skowing had been right: the chances of either player being involved in the abductions appeared remote.

If forced to decide between the two, the obvious choice was O'Hern. Tealy Weathers was too large to skulk around shopping malls or parking lots unnoticed. At the very least, he'd have been recognized by the Brickner kid at the gas station.

Staring at the coffee table, Kenny O'Hern's team publicity photo gazed back at him. In uniform, posing, the eight-by-ten glossy showed him with surfer-boy good looks. The blondish, two-toned hair was shaved close on the sides, highlighting his lantern jaw. No question about it, O'Hern was the all-American jock.

Or maybe all-American psycho, Cale reminded himself. Was he a guy who would chop the head off an innocent young woman? Dump her body in Lake Michigan? Or murder a stranger with a syringe filled with liquid meth?

Cale supposed it remained to be seen.

Imagining O'Hern whistling while he worked was cause enough for Cale to shudder. "All right, Kenny," he said aloud to the photo. "Lets you and I have a little chat."

The Chemist

It's a passion play. Midnight in your soul and an orchestra of ghosts play a hollow refrain.

The bound woman lies before you in the shadowed basement bedroom, her lord and master. Her moans ascend the scale of sorrow—cadaveric screams absent of passion. Your role is the Vanquisher, so you freeze your mind to her torment.

Desperation reigns. Limbs trapped by bindings, a sweet, savage love. Her cries are warped inside the pleasant music like absinthe poured over ice, an elixir of demons. The rhythmic beat—the slap, slap, slap of flesh—summons the vile undertones of your lust.

Her birdlike sobs grow quiet, dry despair, her sadness captured within her quavering heart. A possession now—*your possession*—she is complete, and her soul absorbed within your matrix. Despite the tumescence of momentary pleasure, you understand that yours is a cross lesser humans could not bear.

Special Agent Eddie Redtail arrived on Friday afternoon at the Green Bay PD's downtown station. He was escorted to the awaiting conference room with little fanfare.

Cale and Staszak were inside the room, reviewing details with Sergeant Richie Gastone, who headed the department's Juvenile Gang Unit. They sat at a large table. Gastone held a file jacket in one hand, briefing them on Latin King member Juan-Julio Sanchez.

The street gang officers worked closely with Narcotics and Homicide units. Many of their cases overlapped. All three teams were involved in the murder investigation of Ray Tolver—due to the involvement of methamphetamine as a suspected murder weapon. And with the FBI soon advising on the confounding case, Cale understood they were close to formally organizing a task force.

Like it or not, he remained the team's quarterback.

Hearing a soft knock, their heads turned as Agent Redtail entered the room. Cale was well acquainted with the man. Redtail had assisted them on several cases over the past five years. The agent shook hands with Sergeant Gastone as they were introduced.

"First off," Agent Redtail said to them, "I'm sorry to hear about Detective Dooley. How's he doing?"

"He's fine," Cale said. "Hide like leather."

"And head like Stonehenge," Staszak added.

Agent Redtail smiled at them. He remained standing.

"So the Bureau's finally jumping in here?" Gastone asked. "Ready to assist?"

"Not with both feet." The agent gave them a cautioning eye. "Look. You've got one headless body and four other potential abduction victims. But no hard evidence connecting them."

"They're connected," Staszak said, not flinching.

"Not to mention," Redtail continued, "these are *presumed* abductions."

Cale pierced the long beat of silence. "Assuming they are related, we've likely got more headless bodies out there."

Agent Redtail removed his navy FBI windbreaker and placed it over an empty chair. He sat down at last. "That's only an assumption."

Cale understood how none of them could disguise their frustration.

"The bureau wants me here in a liaison capacity," the agent continued. "Mostly in profiling your offender."

Staszak leaned his bulk back. "Press stirs the pot, and your bosses send you up here. No offense. But they're hoping it'll douse the negative publicity. We get it."

Though over forty-five now, Eddie Redtail possessed the unlined face of a college undergraduate. He lifted his narrow shoulders. "Not fully accurate, Sergeant. But until you ID a viable suspect, the Fed is reluctant to pump resources into a local situation."

Staszak smirked. "But if our victims were seven-year-olds, you'd have more agents here than drunks at an Irish wake."

"Modern times." Agent Redtail added, "And thanks for not saying 'Injun wake.'"

Staszak laughed. He was of Polish descent and had always been amused by ethnic jokes.

Eddie Redtail rose and strode to the table's front, where the evidence board stood. He studied it with his back to them. The photos of the missing victims stared out at them.

"You're still thinking the Tolver death was a planned cover-up?" the agent asked without turning.

"Bet my pension on it." Cale's voice was tight.

"Ballsy move."

Staszak frowned. "Seems more bonehead if you ask me."

Sergeant Gastone's phone buzzed. Reading a text, he excused himself from the room. After the door closed, Agent Redtail turned and gripped the back of a chair, facing them.

"Your report suggests he murdered the station owner to recover a surveillance disc that IDs him."

"It's the only thing making sense," Cale confessed.

Agent Redtail returned to his chair as if resigned to staying longer than planned. Ten minutes later, the detectives had him fully briefed, sharing what little evidence they possessed. The newest victim, Shirley Koon, altered the light-hair profile; the snatch locations revealed no discernable pattern, and there was no consistency about where or how the abductions occurred. Topping it off, there's too much randomness to establish any prediction algorithm.

Cale sat in contemplative quiet as the FBI man re-read his notes. When Redtail finally spoke, his voice sounded static:

"The meth injection into Tolver's femoral vein." His dark eyes revealed little. "Could reveal a working knowledge of anatomy."

"Or he got lucky," Staszak groused. "Stick a nail in an apple, and you might hit the core."

Redtail shrugged. "Regardless, let's assume your guy knows his drugs. Which implies a certain familiarity with physiology."

"So he's a doctor along with being a scumbag?"

"It could indicate some medical background." The agent recited: "Dentist, EMT, RN, mortician."

"Or a vet or pharmacist," Cale added.

"Even a taxidermist."

"Or he's just some dickhead," Staszak suggested, "who enjoys forensics shows on cable." His disgust was evident. "Great. We've narrowed it down to fifty-thousand possibles."

The FBI man glanced at his notes like a man stumped by a crossword puzzle. "By attempting to hide the injection site beneath the victim's scrotum, my guess is your guy knows his business."

Staszak didn't smile. "Or he's a perv getting jollies from messing with guys' sacks."

Cale rolled his eyes. Agent Redtail brushed aside the comment and pressed on. "Pervert or expert, you're still clueless about his ID."

Staszak peered at the room's far corner.

"Or where he strikes next. Or how to stop him."

"Touche, Agent," Staszak admitted.

Nowhere Man, Cale thought to himself. They were in pursuit of a ghost, one clever enough to vanish while laughing at their ineptitude.

Eddie Redtail's voice reached Cale through a haze. "You've got a sociopathic serial kidnapper without hesitation for violence." He sighed. "With no idea of what comes next."

"And he's David Copperfield, besides." Staszak's grumble echoed the agent's pointed summation.

Cale looked at Agent Redtail. "Any chance our guy's locally recognized? A minor celebrity in TV ads, say?" Staszak's glare at him was glacial.

"He's somehow getting inside your victims' cars," Redtail allowed.

The room was quiet.

Staszak shook his head, stating boldly, "No way a pro athlete is involved."

"Remember a guy named O.J. Simpson?" Cale asked.

Eddie Redtail's eyes widened for the first time since he'd entered the room.

CHAPTER 43

Maggie stared silently out the Bronco's passenger window. The twilight had thickened, the purple gloaming swallowing the fading daylight. Sitting rigid, the sick scenario with Juan Julio Sanchez kept looping through her mind.

They were driving to the hospital again, the traffic sparse, and Cale, thankfully, was listening to his phone messages. With his phone at his ear, he turned to her. "Message from Cap," he informed. "Paprika signed the consent form."

"Means you get your interview." Maggie was unenthused.

"I'd like to get in there tomorrow." Cale cruised through an intersection, hastening past a Volvo. "Jeez. I pray it's not some game Sanchez is playing."

It's a game, all right, Maggie thought—a *sick one.* Without Cale's knowing it, he sat beside the world's newest loser. She stared out the window as buildings and houses swept past. Their shadows whizzed by like dissolving smoke. She had decided against revealing the Sanchez incident to Cale, knowing it would destroy him and torpedo his case.

"You feeling all right, Maggie May?"

She enjoyed his curious look, but it still annoyed her at times. The "detective look" where everyone was guilty until proven otherwise.

"I'm fine." She forced a smile.

The spring night had cooled, explaining away Maggie's reason for wearing a turtleneck. It disguised the bruised flesh-prints (her definition) that refused to hide behind her concealer.

Her smile felt fragile, like people's false grins at funerals. Not gone forever but chipped at the edges for a while. Who knew when her natural smile would return?

Cale's eyes stayed steady on the street ahead, and he said, "You don't seem too excited about my talking with Sanchez?"

"I was thinking about Slink and Janet. What they're going through."

She pressed the dashboard CD player button. Airy jazz enveloped the inner space, discouraging conversation. Act natural—Maggie told herself—normal enough to make it through the evening.

She had spent over twenty-four hours locked in a chaotic internal debate. Should she report what had happened? Was revealing it worth the trouble? The wringer she'd go through, her world instantly turned upside-down. And the time for reporting the incident was running out.

As a defense lawyer, her thoughts focused on the only legal details that mattered: how much had the assault damaged her? How significant was her trauma? Would a jury believe her story? Likely yes, but then what? She'd undoubtedly reap no damages from a juvenile gangbanger. Perhaps an insincere apology.

Any sane jury would decide in her favor, but then what?

Maggie admitted she had physically suffered little. Bruises spotted her arms and neck, but no more than if she'd tumbled down a stairway. Yet every fiber in her soul screamed: *Report the sick bastard. Lock him away for two dozen years.* Sanchez couldn't walk away without being punished. Reporting the assault, after all, was the right thing to do.

And yet.

The gangbanger was already incarcerated, wasn't he? His boast about how no guards would respond to her assault (and none had) meant, in retrospect, that the cameras had been somehow disabled—a severe breech of security.

On the other hand, it also meant no recorded evidence of any crime being committed—i.e., no absolute proof.

Furthermore, Maggie reasoned that no witness had seen anything if the guard inside the room had been drugged (she pictured Deputy Weatherby slumping face-down on a table). It became her word versus Sanchez's.

The infamous "He said, she said."

Juan-Julio understood the system, first arrested when he was age eleven. He was adept at playing the "Game." He would swear, blinking puppy dog eyes, how the lady attorney made the story up for vengeful reasons.

"Ms. Jeffers hated me when I replaced her as my attorney," he would likely claim. "She swore she'd get even."

Other than the fading bruises, Maggie had no actual proof anything improper had transpired. And understanding the hoops she'd have to jump through, was it worth it in the long run? Afterward, there'd be the crude jokes behind her back, the snide remarks about the victim being at fault in these cases. It turned Maggie's stomach. There'd be no chance she could return to her job after the public humiliation. The behind-the-back snickers alone would be much worse than any physical damage. She could already hear voices hushing whenever she entered a room.

Besides, hadn't she initiated the contact between Juan-Julio Sanchez in the first place? Arranged the meeting? In Maggie's tormented conscience, didn't that prove she was at least partly to blame?

Out the SUV's window now, she watched the hospital district emerge around them, tall buildings, parking ramps, and the slow, congested traffic.

Cale lowered the CD's volume. "You look pale, Mags." Concern narrowed his eyes.

"I was thinking of Slink's gunshot. How your entire life changes instantly through no fault of your own."

He stayed silent as if thinking the same thing.

Maggie stared out the window as they pulled into the parking ramp. Her brain, however, continued wrestling with the conundrum—Cale's case involving the abducted young women. He'd worked on it for over a year, and Juan-Julio Sanchez was their first break. If she revealed what had happened, Cale and Sanchez would never speak about what he'd said in the courtroom: *about the girls.*

Maggie understood Cale's nature. If he ever found out, he'd be unable to maintain his composure. He'd seethe inside until he finally exploded, likely pounding the kid to a pulp.

Or worse.

Her revelations would destroy Cale's case along with his law enforcement career. All because she, in her naiveté, had blundered stupidly into a trap.

Maggie's biggest quandary now was internal. Was she strong enough to bury the incident inside her? Hide it forever? Erase the memory the same way people discarded their childhood nightmares—the ones everyone eventually outgrew.

Strong people healed over time, Maggie told herself. Others weren't so lucky. She wondered how deep her inner strength ran. Her fortitude. All the old clichés assembled before her like eager suitors:

Time heals all wounds; what Cale doesn't know can't hurt him; take everything one day at a time.

She reminded herself that she must appear unchanged on the surface. Act naturally. Don't worry, be happy, or "fake it 'til you make it." Maggie understood the bruises and physical pain would vanish in days. The hard part was convincing her memory to fade as well.

CHAPTER 44

Purple shadows ruled the night. Slink was awake in his hospital bed when the visitors arrived. His smile widened, and Janet waved Cale and Maggie into the room beside them.

"When are we busting you out of this joint, Dillinger?" Cale joked.

"How about yesterday?"

"What's the hurry? Hot date?" Cale winked at Janet when she rolled her eyes.

"Yeah, with your girlfriend," Slink countered. He grinned at Maggie's half-hearted smile, watching as she hugged Janet. Cale dragged two chairs closer to them.

Slink's wife proceeded to recite the medical updates. What the doctors had soberly conveyed and what the nurses opined. Cale imagined she also understood the night cleaning crew's prognosis.

"Nowadays," Janet said, "they release you if you can walk three steps without falling."

"There's insurance for you," Cale agreed.

They groused about health coverage rates for the next five minutes before Cale quipped: "There's a shortage of traffic cops out there. A bright guy like Slink here can always find honest work."

Slink flipped him the bird with his working hand. Then he asked, "You get anywhere with Lester Paprika?"

Cale conveyed the situation about the shady attorney and his illicit gambling accounts, of how he'd caved, allowing Cale access to a Sanchez interview after the city's lawyers threatened to inform the IRS of Paprika's shadowy offshore dealings.

"I'm hoping to see Sanchez tomorrow," Cale said. "If the chips fall right."

"I'll believe it when I see it." Slink's expression hardened.

Maggie maintained a far-off stare, and when Janet touched her arm, she jumped. Janet asked, "Hey! You doing all right?"

Maggie gave a sheepish nod and stayed silent.

A clumsy sound fumbled outside the door. Their heads turned as Anton Staszak lumbered into the room. He looked like a bull easing into a pen too small for him.

"Parked a frigging mile away," Stasz reported in a huff. "Walked through a maze just to find this place."

"You'd gripe if you were hung with a new rope," Cale said, giving Slink a wink. He skootched his chair aside to make room for the new addition.

"No kidding. Give me a used rope any day."

"So what? I'm not worth visiting?" Slink feigned a hurt expression. It highlighted the smudgy shadows beneath his eyes.

"You're an everyday pain in my butt, Dooley." Staszak feigned discomfort.

"Big target."

Cale's phone buzzed. He rose and spoke quietly while drifting toward the hallway. The others remained silent while pretending not to listen. Ending the call, Cale turned back. "Cap confirmed it now. I'm meeting Sanchez at ten a.m. tomorrow."

"*We're* meeting with him," Staszak corrected.

Cale shook his head. "Me alone. Sanchez claims he'd feel intimidated by the two of us. Like we're ganging up."

"Another crock—"

"His game, his rules."

Staszak rotated his bull-sized head, frustrated but unable to press further.

A new sense of hope infected them all. Talking to Juan-Julio Sanchez might finally break the case open and point the investigators toward uncovering the kidnapper's identity. In the process, they'd also locate the missing young women.

It was the first step at returning their lives to normal.

In addition, Cale theorized that any gang-related information Sanchez provided would further confirm Slink's heroics. Perhaps he'd be issued a citation instead of a reprimand.

Janet reached over and tenderly squeezed her husband's hand, hearing good news for the first time in a while.

Rising, Cale pecked Maggie on the cheek and handed her the Bronco keys. "I'll catch a ride home with Stasz," he told her, stepping toward the door. He arched an eyebrow at the bulky detective. "Ready?"

Staszak rose and joined him.

Maggie gave them both a questioning stare yet didn't ask what their task at this hour might be.

To them all, Cale said, "A couple of loose ends we've got to run down."

"They're probably headed to the casino." Slink grinned.

Staszak countered, "Couldn't do worse than your bet on the Kansas City Royals."

Cale winked at Slink, who gave him a knowing nod.

"You boys stay out of trouble," Janet said, sounding like the mother she was. "One of you in here's bad enough."

Tobias Crenshaw navigated the blue windowless van through the maze of city streets. He was headed north along roads fringed with warehouses and factory lots, moving toward his storage garage facility. The van's headlights cut the night like light sabers, washing bare trees beneath the inky sky.

When he'd left the cul-de-sac house, the dark-haired girl had been unconscious in the basement bedroom. He knew she'd be dreaming for hours, judging by the number of barbiturates he'd administered. The other girl would be equally indisposed. Neither would awake until morning.

After securing the van, Tobias would return home. He needed time to reconnect with Marla and the kids. Relax. Enjoy a quiet meal. He thought about them as he drove, calculating his next move in the grand chess match.

Tobias pressed his phone's speed dial. The Liberian henchman's voice answered on the second ring.

"It's time to move the cars," Tobias voiced authoritatively. "Two of them. I don't want to wait any longer."

"I'll check with Colonel Mabutu."

"Tonight. Tomorrow night at the latest."

The giant Liberian on the line went by the name of Kinsella. Few people knew if it was his first name or last. Even fewer cared. For his part, Tobias could not care less what the man called himself. Kinsella was Tazeki Mabutu's right-hand man, and it mattered even less these days. Though his former college roommate was unaware, in truth, Tobias had decided their partnership would terminate after his delivery of three more females.

When the time arrived—*very soon*—Tobias understood his old friend would not be pleased. Well, screw Mabutu. They'd had a decent crime run together, but it was time they went their separate ways.

Still, Tobias wondered what Kinsella had done with the crazy girl's missing head last year. It still caused his bones to shudder. Was it in an unmarked grave? Or burned in some incinerator? Or maybe they'd boiled it in a cauldron like some African delicacy? These Liberians were all still cannibals at heart, weren't they?

Tobias decided none of it mattered. The girl's head was no longer his concern.

He spoke into his phone: "You'll need a pair of semis." When the comment was met with silence, his neck warmed. "I hope that's not a problem?"

"Not a lot of notice, but it's no problem. I'll take care of it," Kinsella's husky baritone confirmed.

"Three or four a.m. then? While it's still dark. I'll leave the same garage and car keys as last time." Tobias ended the call.

Later tonight, after Marla and the kids were asleep, he would return to the cul-de-sac house. The cloak of darkness would conceal him as he navigated the dark-haired girl's vehicle to the rental garages. He would hide the keys beneath a loose rock at the row's far end, knowing it was a blind spot for security cameras. Kinsella and his partners would arrive in rented transport trucks at the rendezvous time and load the vehicles aboard. The two-truck caravan would then ease back into the quiet night. They'd return to Chicago, their drive time three-and-a-half hours.

By tomorrow, Tobias understood that both vehicles would be stripped of usable parts and compacted into box-sized squares of scrap metal.

Like the crazy girl's missing head: *Into dust, ye shall return.*

CHAPTER 45

Anton Staszak hadn't been kidding about his hike from his car to Slink's hospital room. To Cale, tired from last night's lack of sleep, it seemed like they'd walked a half-mile before arriving at Stasz's gray Buick 4-door. The left front fender was dented, and he informed Cale his daughter had nicknamed the vehicle "The Beast."

"Teaching her to drive straight," was Staszak's unneeded explanation for the bashed fender. He huffed like a bowlegged rodeo rider as he popped the door locks.

Cale nodded. "Teenagers."

He asked Staszak how the shopping mall canvass had gone. "Nada. Our phantom strikes again." Stasz slid inside the Buick.

"You mean Nowhere Man?" Cale didn't hide his sarcasm as he relaxed in the roomy passenger seat. The interior was a blessing for Staszak's arthritic knees.

"Call him Count Dickwad, for all I care," Staszak snarled. "Same as the rest—no witnesses, no nothing. Zilch."

The bulky detective aimed the hearse-sized Buick south, and they swept through the star-crested night. A hunter's moon above became their beacon.

Cale phoned Nicky's Lionhead Tavern as they drove, and a female answered, speaking over the thrum of background noise. Sure, Jellybear was around. She placed Cale on hold until the tavern owner picked-up. Cale said, "Van Waring again. Quick question—do the Packers' players still hang out at your place?"

Jellybear chuckled. "You got ESP? There's nearly a dozen here right now."

Cale thanked him and hung up.

There wasn't much secret that professional athletes were habitual creatures. When in town for camps or off-season workouts, they only frequented establishments where they felt comfortable. Nicky's Lionhead was one of those. When out together in public, the players adopted a herd mentality. They drank, conversed, and joked casually. Generally, they did not want to (a) talk about football or (b) get nagged for autographs. Their needs were simple—to relax and forget the grind of practice and mini-camp.

Their desire was to be left alone.

Jellybear Nick, a seasoned veteran of the tavern business, was cognizant of this attitude. He made sure his bar regulars were duly informed. Yet ever-so-often, some knuckleheads had to be reminded—like morons near a tiger's cage—to maintain a polite distance from the players.

Exceptions, of course, were ladies sporting slender legs and ample bosoms. "Tits on sticks," as these females were often described. Cale assumed an IQ hovering around a hundred was frosting on the cake.

When the detectives entered the tavern via the rear door, heads on the bar seats swiveled. With his considerable bulk, receding hairline notwithstanding, patrons assumed Anton Staszak must be a Packers player. Or an assistant coach of some sort, at least. Cale, in comparison, appeared more like a member of the equipment staff.

As maestro behind the polished mahogany-and-brass bar, Jellybear spotted their arrival. He lumbered around and ushered the detectives to a vacant, high-stooled table.

"Twice in a week, Van Waring? You sniffing around for a job here?"

"Yeah, yours," Cale quipped.

Above their heads, baseball and NBA playoff games spun on a dozen TV screens. Soft rock thumped in the background, and the place appeared a quarter-filled, not bad for eight p.m. on a Friday night.

"Hope you fellas didn't bring Mr. Trouble along," Jellybear joked, though maybe not. He arched bushy eyebrows.

"Left him back at the station," Staszak said. "His time of the month."

"Just innocent observers." Cale hoped his tone sounded reassuring.

"Don't try and BS a BS'er." The tavern-keep turned somber. "Sorry about Dooley. How's he doing?"

Jellybear was aware of the shooting, Cale understood, and astute enough to know they wouldn't be here if their friend weren't out of the woods.

"He's a tough skunk," Cale stated.

"Guns and gangbangers—never a good mix."

The detectives nodded soberly.

"Are you guys working or drinking?"

Staszak shrugged and ordered them pints of Porter Ale, the house tap.

Jellybear called the order to his bartender before fixing his eyes across the long tavern toward the street entrance. He indicated the oversized males gathered around a trio of pulled-together tables, like a makeshift bunker. They were primarily dressed in board shorts and casual polos, appearing relaxed.

Cale noted a pair of cute twenty-somethings—one blonde, the other with moussed Irish hair—who stood as if posing at the jukebox. Their game plan appeared obvious: draw the attention of the footballers the way a salt lick attracts deer in a forest.

The athletes seemed content to savor the sudsy content of their watered-down pitchers of beer. Cale watched as they ignored the apparent nearby honeytrap.

"Can you believe it?" Staszak grumbled. "Young dollies acting like they're on the dinner menu?"

Cale decided not to remind him his two teenage daughters weren't far from tavern age. Staszak's eyes warned him off.

"I thought about enrolling my girls in a convent," Staszak added. "Now, I'm sending them a check tomorrow."

"Why not military school?" Cale offered amicably. "Teach them to kick young horndog's rear ends?"

Jellybear arrived with their pints, and Staszak appeared glad to end the conversation. Grabbing one glass with his oversized mitt, he downed half the contents in a trio of sudsy swallows.

The jukebox continued a thumping noise between metal and hip-hop. Cale chose to study the solidly built behemoths grouped at the far end of the establishment.

"Tealy Weathers, I recognize," he informed Jellybear after a beat. "Which one's O'Hern?"

"The Whistler?" The tavern keeper locked into Cale's sight line. "Surfer-hair dude. Black T-shirt a size too small."

Cale noted the player. O'Hern gave off an air of smug self-confidence with a hint of aggression below the surface. The same way a hungry crocodile lurks in a pond. Having read his psych profile, Cale pegged him as a lifelong bully. Guys like O'Hern, generally speaking, were always overcompensating for something or another. He probably considered himself a ladies' man, and scoring with numerous females was how he defined his manhood.

"Big-feet-little-dick syndrome." Stasz summarized Cale's thoughts succinctly. It was a reference cops used to describe guys who didn't measure-up to most women's expectations.

Cale's attention shifted to the rest of the beefy young men, imagining how wildlife biologists must feel when studying primates in their natural habitat. As if sensing their stares, Kenny O'Hern returned the detectives' inspection. He offered them a bemused expression before turning away.

"God's gift thinks he's clever."

"Or maybe he thinks you're cute?" Cale offered.

"He ain't *that* clever."

Cale sipped his beer. When he glanced back at the players again, he noticed O'Hern had sidled up to the young lovelies at the juke box. He offered a comment, which caused them to giggle like schoolgirls.

Jellybear ambled back behind his bar rail. He had paying customers he couldn't neglect.

"You dragged me out here." Staszak peered over his glass. "We got a game plan, Coach Lombardi?"

Cale didn't reply, intent on watching for new development in the romantic scenario. A lean, dark-haired young man had risen from his barstool and sauntered toward the jukebox, wedging between the girls and Kenny O'Hern. The football player commented, and the younger man retorted with a smirk. Then, as if in slow motion, O'Hern head-butted the intruder in the face.

An audible gasp lifted from those watching the drama unfold, followed by a chorus of high-pitched screams and shrieks of disbelief.

Then craziness unleashed itself like a busted dam.

"Oh boy," Cale muttered. "Here we go!"

CHAPTER 46

Three of the injured young man's companions charged from their seats at the bar. They were met by a handful of rising football players, who moved into the fray as if rehearsed. Music throbbed to screams and shouts and shattering glass.

Those uninvolved at the bar held their phones extended, recording the action.

The bouncer on duty proved no match for the swelling melee. He was suddenly on the floor applying a headlock to one feisty combatant. Punches flew, and bodies wrestled in the free-for-all.

"We've got to do something," Cale offered gallantly.

Staszak was already headed across the tavern toward the fray. Jellybear pushed past them both like a corner man rushing the ring. He entered the brawl by bear-hugging one man around the chest, hoisting him like lugging a half-barrel from a cooler.

Tealy Weathers, all three-hundred pounds, fired a jab that sent a combatant sailing. A barstool toppled, and Tealy danced on his toes, looking for the next chump to pulverize. The approach of Anton Staszak caused a grin to stretch his pumpkin face. At last, a worthy opponent.

"Come and get it, sucker." Tealy waggled a fat forefinger. "You want some-a-dis?"

Regardless of his advancing years, Staszak lived for moments like this. Cale knew "Young Anton" had earned his stripes stamping out testosterone-fueled brushfires in his father's old tavern—*Lech's Polish Pickle*—in his adolescence. Despite Tealy being half his age and the approximate size of the first car he'd owned, Staszak moved forward like a freight train. He dipped his head, avoiding the larger man's roundhouse, coming up with a perfect angle on the player's exposed chin.

Not many barroom brawlers have faced a professional uppercut, and Staszak had a good one. Cale, undoubtedly, was alone in knowing Anton Staszak had been a Golden Gloves boxer in his youth. Once upon a time.

Eyeing his partner's face, he imagined Stasz thinking, "No, I shouldn't," followed just as fast by, "Yeah. I should," before letting the uppercut fly.

A tree branch cracked. Tealy's eyes rolled up, and his knees buckled while wobbling two steps back. His hands flew to his face from the pain of a shattered jaw, and crimson gushed from his mouth.

"Fuuwg bwastad!" The mammoth man mewled through sausage-sized fingers. "Ahh bwit my tug!"

Cale, however, was not as fortunate as Staszak. Locating the brawl's epicenter, he searched for Kenny O'Hern's black T-shirt. Instead, a faint whistling sound emitted from behind him. He turned, catching a severe blow to his cheekbone. He staggered and tripped over a pair of grapplers on the floor.

Between Jellybear and the bouncer—and players turned peacemakers—combatants were separated or bearhugged until they accepted their futility.

The young gals who had started it all had unsurprisingly skipped away from the skirmish

Cale touched his face, and it burned like kerosene. He couldn't spot Kenny O'Hern, and sped back to their prior table, waving his shield. He shouted at the regulars: "Police! Where did he go?"

A dozen fingers pointed toward the rear exit.

Cale swept from the tavern. He whipped his head left and right, searching the low-lit parking lot. Red taillights glowed in the distance, and he sprinted toward a bronze Corvette backing from a row of parked vehicles.

Cale slapped the driver's window before the muscle car could accelerate away. "Police! Freeze!" He pressed his shield against the glass.

In the dark inner space, Kenny O'Hern glared out at Cale. He was prepared to roar away, right hand gripping the smooth knob of the gearshift.

"At least fifty phone vids in there, Kenny!" Cale shouted through the glass. "You run, and you're toast."

The threat worked. With his career in the balance, O'Hern shoved the shifter into park and slammed the heel of his hand against the steering wheel.

The station house was quiet between shifts on a Friday night. Even the phones were subdued. Cale sat at his desk, holding an ice pack to the left side of his face.

A young officer named Truax called from a short distance, "Hey, Lieutenant, you're gonna love this!"

Cale glanced at her with a blank face.

A sweep of O'Hern's Corvette had unveiled a stash of intriguing items. Truax reported: a two-foot-long piece of phone cord; an eight-inch hunting knife—a serrated blade. Both were discovered tucked inside the trunk's wheel-well. And lodged beneath the driver's seat, they'd found a .38 caliber S&W revolver.

Though the cord and knife were most interesting, the handgun's presence didn't hurt matters. Together they provided the detectives with enough substance to detain and interrogate the suspect.

Staszak spent the first ten minutes alone with O'Hern in the interview room. They'd decided Cale needed time to cool down and continue icing his injured cheek. Staszak informed the football player of the seriousness of the charges he could be facing.

O'Hern, true to his nature, was too arrogant to lawyer up immediately. He accused Cale, that "dickhead cop," whose intent seemed to be in "coming at him." Staszak replied that the blow his partner received to his upper cheekbone had "sucker punch" written all over it.

With a rap on the door, Cale now entered the room. He sat across the table from his assailant while Staszak leaned near the door with his arms crossed, looking like the heavy in every Mafia movie ever made.

"My bad on the punch," O'Hern said apologetically as Cale sat down. "Bar fights. Reminds me of college."

"In lots of them?"

"Broke up more than I started."

O'Hern was trying the innocent act, Cale decided. Likely calculating that if he autographed a few jerseys for these bozos, they'd let him skate home within the hour.

"Chemistry major in college, Kenny? Impressive."

"Researching me?" O'Hern slouched. "You guys ought to be home with your families."

"Chemistry," Cale pressed. "An interesting major for an athlete."

Staszak added, "You must know a lot about sedatives. Some poor girl doesn't know what planet she's on, so you tell her your name's Bill Cosby?"

O'Hern snorted. "Ladies give *me* their phone numbers. Twenty a night. I don't need pills or flowers to get laid."

Cale studied the young man's demeanor. "Gun in your car? Knife? Cord? You're right. Why would you need pills?"

O'Hern's stare was hard. "Like I told Frankenstein over there, I got a CC permit. For protection."

"From whom?"

"Crazy-ass fans—who do you think?"

Cale then read aloud from a written report: "Assault on a bar patron. Aggravated assault on a law officer. Multiple weapons in vehicle consistent with possible kidnappings."

O'Hern rolled his eyes, staring at them. In a tight voice, he announced, "Two words."

"You're innocent. We get it," growled Staszak.

"My lawyer."

Maggie was asleep with Hank curled at her feet when Cale returned home. She heard his footsteps trudge up the stairs. After undressing and brushing his teeth, he dropped beside her into a bum's sleep, too tired to explain or worry about nightmares.

It was Saturday morning when she rolled onto her left side and gazed at the discolored face beside her. She managed to swallow a cry.

After climbing the basement stairs with a laundry basket, Maggie discovered Cale standing at the kitchen sink an hour later. He was sipping a glass of orange juice. She studied the purple swelling spreading across his upper cheek. The lids of his left eye were puffed, almost closed.

"Quasimodo got a better greeting," Cale joked, perhaps only halfway kidding.

"He wasn't as scary looking as you."

Maggie set down her laundry basket and moved in for a closer inspection. Cale rolled both eyes upward, blinking birdlike while she examined the swelling. She touched the edematous skin with her fingertips. It caused him to wince.

"You've got a way's to go, Florence Nightingale."

Maggie pulled her fingers away. In a serious tone, she said, "I've got the cure you need."

"The winning Powerball ticket?"

"Even better. Estée Lauder."

CHAPTER 47

The Saturday morning drive to the station allowed Cale to replay last night's dealings with Whistler O'Hern. The local pro-football team had an attorney on permanent retainer, and the players had been instructed to phone the number night or day if they ran afoul of the law.

Cale couldn't blame the player for lawyering up. In his situation, he'd have done the same thing.

Easing the Bronco to a stoplight, more questions buzzed through his mind. Kenny O'Hern was a violent athlete on the field, no doubt. But was he a sociopath? A serial abductor? The murderer of innocent women?

Cale's gut gave him an answer. It was one his brain didn't want to hear. He pulled the visor mirror down and examined his tender eye. A car honked behind him. Cale accelerated through the intersection, but his mind replayed last night's interview.

There was little doubt the popular Packer player was a self-absorbed narcissist. He recalled Staszak's right-on description: Big-feet-little-dick syndrome. Still, it didn't mean O'Hern had taken the next step up the pathological ladder—physically injuring women.

As he'd driven home from the station late last night, Cale's uncertainty about their suspect grew. Now in the clear light of day, his gut rendered a verdict on the Whistler.

O'Hern might be unpleasant, but it was doubtful he was the sadistic, cat-and-mouse mastermind behind the abductions.

He was not the man they were searching for. He was not the *Nowhere Man.*

"You guys want to hear a good one?"

Captain McBride's voice was grumpy. That was saying something. Behind his desk, the captain studied the pair of detectives before him. He took an extra second to linger on Cale's discolored upper cheek.

"Two young boys get sent to the principal's office for goofing off," McBride's story began. "The principal asks for their parents' phone numbers. The first kid gives his number. She calls the kid's mom at her office. Wham-bam, he gets sent home to face the music."

Staszak cast a sideways glance at Cale.

"The second kid's more a smartass." McBride continued. "He glances at the land phone she's using, the number on the readout. The young twerp rattles off that same number. The principal dials it several times and gets all busy signals."

The room was silent.

"And the point, Cap?" Staszak asked.

"The point"—McBride scowled—"is that second kid. He thought he was getting away with something. Thought he was *cleverer* than everyone else."

The captain stared at Cale, continuing, "Turns out he was only fooling himself."

The detectives remained quiet. Cale's thoughts drifted back to last night, to Kenny O'Hern. He wondered what the moral of the captain's story was.

While O'Hern's attorney had been en route to the station, the registry confirmed his weapon was legally registered. Due to the team's relationship with the City and O'Hern's blood alcohol level under the .08 legal limit, the assault charges were being set aside for the time being.

The attorney signed for the player's release and drove his client home.

By eight a.m. the following day, the excrement hit the fan. Cale imagined a shampoo commercial he'd watched on TV as a kid. One girl excitedly calls two friends, then the others call another two friends, and so on.

Kenny O'Hern's attorney had contacted Gene Bartell, the team president. Bartell had phoned the mayor, rousting him from bed at 6 a.m. His Honor, in turn, had reached Police Chief Harris. Like molten lava bubbling down a mountainside, the results of these events had landed Cale and Anton Staszak where they now sat, in Captain McBride's office, listening to his "Delinquent Kid" story.

"By right, I ought to blacken your other eye," McBride barked. He studied his coffee cup—cold and bitter.

"We tried breaking it up," Staszak confessed. "Things got out of hand."

The captain snorted. "Out of hand? They're telling me half the team's in the training room this morning."

"It could've been—"

"Shut up." McBride's stare was harsh.

"What surprises me most," the captain confessed, "is you didn't pull out your sidearms and start shooting up the place like Wyatt Earp!"

Cale glanced at the room's newest Jackson Pollock-like abstract on the wall—Pollock's best work from perhaps third grade.

"And nothing gave you the right to roust Mr. O'Hern."

Roust? Cale recognized now how fortunate they'd been to discover the weapon inside O'Hern's vehicle. Without that evidence, they'd be issued desk confinement or disciplinary hearings with Internal Affairs. At the very least, they'd yank him from his interview with Sanchez.

"Have you got some unresolved issues, Cale?" McBride's tone oozed sarcasm. "Cut from your high school team? Or maybe some football stud stole your girlfriend at the prom?"

Cale met the captain's gaze.

"The puzzle to me is," McBride continued, "what vendetta do you have against our local team?"

"Finding a kidnapper is my only vendetta."

"Well, you'd better check under some other rock." The Mona Lisa desk clock ticked, the solitary sound in the room. "Now listen very carefully," McBride continued, "There is *zero* Packers angle in this investigation. Got it?"

A beat of silence.

"Loud and clear, Cap."

Cale repeated, "No pro-athletes angle."

The detectives were dismissed with McBride's promise to smooth things over with Chief Harris.

From the doorway, Staszak gave the captain a backward glance. "So what happened, Cap? You know? To the young kid with the phone trick?"

"He got his ass kicked. That's what happened!"

"My guess," Cale said when the detectives were back in the bullpen, "is the smartass kid was little Leo McBride. Way back when."

"No way."

"Just saying."

Staszak's eyes widened with a newfound respect for their captain.

Cale noted his desk's growing mound of notes, messages, and paperwork. It seemed to be reproducing. He phoned John Zackary at the DA's office and was transferred to his mobile. Then he touched base with Detective Blum. Most importantly, his meeting with Sanchez remained a "Go." Thirty minutes later, he flicked off his PC. He accepted a steaming cup of coffee from Staszak's outstretched paw.

"I didn't ask before." Staszak studied Cale, his expression earnest. "You heard it, didn't you?"

"Heard what?"

"Right before he clocked you? The *whistle?*"

Cale flipped him the bird.

CHAPTER 48

Cale drove the four blocks from the station to the County Juvenile Detention Center. He had declined a painkiller for his bruised eye, desiring a clear head. Though he'd slept last night, his slumber had been anything but fitful. He wasn't complaining. The meeting with Juan-Julio Sanchez was their most significant break in the case.

I know about the girls.

After the usual entry rigmarole for law enforcement agents, Cale grabbed a chair in the sparse waiting area. A few outdated magazines, a pair of fake ferns in phony mulch. So much for ambiance.

He watched a pair of guards chatting through a wire-mesh safety window down the corridor beyond the electronically secured doors. Social workers were making their morning rounds—nothing interesting on a Saturday.

After a modest wait, Cale was ushered into a private visitation room with a desk and three chairs. No surveillance cameras. Adequate security.

A male guard with a pear-shaped body escorted Juan-Julio Sanchez into the room. The prisoner wore the mandatory blue jumpsuit, socks, slip-on sandals, and cuffs securing his wrists in front. With his jet-black hair and surly sneer, Cale noted that the juvenile appeared every bit the young felon he was. The guard stood a yard inside the room's door.

Seated at a narrow table, Cale greeted the prisoner with a nod. The younger man eyed him carefully before slumping into a wooden chair across from the detective.

"Hear you got a hard-on to see me," Sanchez said without prompting.

Cale had decided to keep the visit professional. "You have information on a case. I'm here to assess if it's credible or not."

Sanchez's dark eyes stayed suspicious. "Maybe I don't remember what you're talking about, *Señor* Detective."

Cale reminded himself this wasn't some pissing contest. Sanchez's rotten opinion of cops wasn't about to change. Besides, he had no beef with the kid. He could even help him if he kept the BS to a minimum.

"In court," Cale said patiently, "you told Ms. Jeffers you had information regarding the abducted females. The ones from the papers?"

The prisoner shrugged, then he brightened. "No offense, but your girlfriend's smokin', homes."

Cale's neck warmed. "This has nothing to do with her. And I'm not your homey."

Sanchez leaned back in his chair, shackled wrists in his lap. "Why's your eye black? Looks nasty."

The guard barked from the doorway. "Hands on the table. Don't get cutesy."

Sanchez waggled his fingers at the guard and complied.

The interview wasn't going the way Cale had envisioned. A change of tactics was needed. "Fell off my barstool." He added a hapless shrug.

The gang banger's smile was crooked. Better than a scowl. Cale didn't have time to tap dance with the guy. He wondered if Lester Paprika had revealed to his client why he'd greenlighted talking with the detectives. Cale doubted there was any mention of felony tax evasion.

"So, Detective. What's in it for me? Why should I tell you any secrets?"

"Your lawyer should have gone over it."

"I need to hear it from you, homes. Personally."

Cale motioned the guard to exit the room. He turned back to Sanchez.

"The DA's considering dropping your weapons charge to a misdemeanor. The condition being you give us something worth my trip here."

Criminal justice, Cale thought bitterly. An oxymoron right up there with "honest politician."

Juan-Julio stared at the detective, his expression sarcastic.

"Your girlfriend's got perfect lips," Sanchez said. "I'm a Latino lover. We don't kiss and tell."

Cale's blood pressure elevated. "If I walk out right now, any deal is off the table. You're stuck in this crap-hole for another six months. Then it's up to the Big House."

"Relax. I'm yanking your chain. I like Miss Jeffers. She's been good to me."

Cale reminded himself how many hoops he'd jumped through to get here today. Too many to blow it now. The kid was baiting him. It was typical gang BS. Measuring the size of his *cojones*.

"When I get out, I'm going to look her up. Miss Maggie Jeffers." Sanchez began to sing off-key: "We got a thing...going on...."

"Ouch, my ears," Cale protested humorously. "Your singing sucks." His voice was flat. "Better stay away from the talent shows in here."

"You're insulting me?"

"You've been insulting me since we sat down."

Sanchez said nothing, but he blinked his dark eyes. Cale slid his chair back as if to rise.

The prisoner glanced across at the room's door as if picturing a lifetime behind bars. It was enough to make Cale hesitate, and Sanchez said, "When you leave here, Detective, you ought to buy yourself a lottery ticket."

"Why's that?"

"Because today's your lucky day."

Tobias had a ritual. He always took photographs right after captures while his victims remained in a drug stupor. He snapped pictures with a Canon digital. It allowed his partner, Mabutu, to preview the "merchandise" he'd receive.

Tobias understood that Colonel Mabutu—an elite human trafficker—considered himself a flesh connoisseur. Via their arrangement, his partner could view the "product" images on the VPN-secure site Tobias had set up. Complete anonymity was guaranteed, ensuring there was zero chance whatsoever of traceability.

Driving the thirty miles south of Green Bay to the bustling college city of Appleton, Tobias used an anonymous public computer at the downtown library. He enjoyed blending into the busier Saturday crowd, no one paying attention.

Locating a booth computer in one far-off corner, he first disabled the system's adult-site filters. Then he code-entered onto his "Model Hopefuls" website. Next, he performed a login history check of his previous activity before activating an ID tracer, ensuring that no previous site visits had been viewed or his data compromised.

Only then did he download his latest content.

Tobias waited ninety seconds more until he found himself gazing at the dozen digital images he had snapped the day before. They showed the attractive dark-haired girl—the face and naked body of Shirley Koon.

"Superb," he whispered to himself. He knew Mabutu would be annoyed she wasn't a blonde. Tobias ghosted any trail of his presence with a sophisticated digital "eraser" and closed down the computer.

Rising, he double-sanitized the keyboard of fingerprints, then departed from the library with his ballcap lowered.

CHAPTER 49

Since Leslie Ann Dowd—the initial victim—had disappeared over a year ago, for the first time, Cale allowed himself a glimmer of hope at resolving the most confounding case of his career. However, despite newly discovered information, time seemed to slip away even faster.

Cale navigated the Bronco over the central Walnut Street Bridge headed west. Minutes later, he drove slowly into a rundown section of the city. Two-story tenement homes, dilapidated duplexes, converted single-family start-ups. He imagined he stuck out like a bricklayer in a ballet troupe. The erstwhile residents of this neighborhood could smell a cop the way seals smelled raw fish.

It was an older section close to the freight yards, railroads, and warehouses. Cale noted cars on blocks, sparse brown lawns, and gravel driveways as the Bronco crept up the pocked asphalt street. An alley dog barked. Faces of children peered from grimy windows or screened-in porches.

The neighborhood was a melting pot: Hmong families, trailer-trash whites, Latinos, blacks, and whatnot. A blend of Native Americans was added in for good measure. It was a cauldron of human gumbo. Cale decided bringing Staszak along would have been a more secure play. It was rough territory indeed for a solo cop. But stopping to pick his partner up would've slowed him, and he was buzzed with momentum after his interview with Sanchez.

The Bronco eased along the charred street. New spring potholes served as speed bumps. Cale could smell motor oil instead of flowers, and a crow on a phone wire peered down at him with coal-button eyes. The bird looked ballsy. In this neighborhood, he probably imagined himself an eagle.

The address Sanchez gave him ran in vertical numbers down the pillar of a gray-shingle front porch. 945 Augusta Street. Cale swung the Bronco to the curb, parking near an overturned child's wagon with chipped red paint the color of dried blood. Not much was happening on an early Saturday afternoon. He spotted some teens throwing stones at birds down the street.

He approached the house cautiously, climbing the steps, and gave the front doorframe's aluminum border a rap.

An elderly lady with raisin-colored hair appeared, wearing a dress similar to his grandmother's. Violets with splashes of pansies were painted on the synthetic fabric. Cale flashed his ID, and the woman responded with a quizzical stare.

She didn't comment on his purple shiner.

Wishing he knew better Spanish, he said, "Juan-Julio sent me. *Por favor?* Juan-Julio Sanchez?"

"Ah." Her nod was slight.

Without a smile, she opened the door and pointed him to narrow stairs running up the left side of the entranceway. Cale was expected. He ascended the creaking stairs covered with aging linoleum.

He stopped on the second-floor landing.

The door opened before he could knock, and he found himself gazing into the dark-chocolate eyes of a Latino man of indiscernible age—early-to-late thirties. The man wore Dockers and a golf shirt. Not exactly gangbanger chic. He possessed a sharp goatee and gelled hair fashioned in a ponytail. The small diamond in his left ear was no doubt real.

The man greeted him. "Detective Van Waring."

Cale had been expecting an accent, but his host sounded like he'd been beamed in from a physics class at Columbia. "I was informed," he added casually, "of your imminent arrival."

"You don't say." Cale peered ahead beyond his muscular shoulder. His suspicion projected three yards ahead, cop-like, scouting like a watchdog.

"I'm Carlos. Juan-Julio's cousin."

Carlos stepped aside like a matador, ushering Cale into the front room of the upstairs apartment. He was thankful he had carried a weapon for the first time in weeks.

The shooter who had wounded Slink in Lester Paprika's driveway had not been a Latin King but a rival gang member. Not surprising since Lester Paprika had his money-grubbing hands in almost every competing drug group.

Knowing this didn't make Cale feel any better. His partner was still in a hospital bed. But at least it allowed him to deal with Sanchez's cronies without revenge whispering in his ear, urging him toward some John Wick number.

What Cale had learned from Sanchez confirmed much of what the detectives already knew. The Kings controlled most illegal narcotics distribution in the central and northern half of the state. Green Bay fell within their domain. The gang was organized tighter than IBM's director's board and provided whatever substances buyers desired to send them on fantasy trips to the moon.

All things natural and unnatural, as long as it made a profit. Cale understood that the Latin Kings, first and foremost, were savvy businessmen.

As he entered the apartment, he noticed stacks of tightly wrapped packages in the second room off the living room. They filled two entire walls, floor to ceiling. Enough to make Fed Ex blush.

Cale's math went fuzzy as he imagined beyond kilos and into tonnage. And yet, he wasn't here for any narco bust. He was here because he needed their help.

A pair of tough-looking hombres sat on a long leather sofa in the living room. A third man was positioned on a lounger. As Cale had moved inside, he'd observed the men watching a 65-inch TV, which stood against one far wall. He guessed some porno tape, as they'd cut the picture on his arrival. He'd been unable to determine anything from his obtuse angle.

"My insurance agents," Carlos said cryptically, nodding toward the trio of underlings.

"Not Mutual of Omaha, I take it."

Carlos smiled and spoke something in rapid Spanish. One of the hombres rose and exited the apartment, leaving the remaining pair on the couch. Cale decided it was a lineup Charles Bronson would have fit into comfortably.

"Juan-Julio tells me you're searching for someone?" Carlos grabbed a seat on the vacated lounger.

"Help me find him, and I'll have your homeboy out by lunch tomorrow. Day or two, at the most."

"Have a seat, Detective." Carlos motioned to a vacant wingback chair. His back was to the wall, for which Cale was thankful. "My guess is you'll find this story interesting."

Carlos began with an intro about the monotonous flow of drugs from Mexico into the United States. Nothing unfamiliar about the tale.

"Huge amounts of drugs are sold to 'tourists' through the Mexican *pharmacias*," Carlos spoke matter-of-factly. "Up-front cash. Dollars. Not pesos."

Cale understood how certain synthetic substances were shipped into the country via standard U.S. mail using phony origination addresses. DEA sniffer dogs or harried U.S. postal inspectors admitted that many odorless chemicals were undetectable. The inept politicians' so-called War on Drugs remained a disaster. Millions of guns, human traffic victims, and illegal narcotics invaded the country weekly and would continue if the borders remained porous. The cartels were pitching a winning, near-half-century shutout.

"I have two pharmacist uncles who live in Mexico," Carlos said pridefully. "My Uncle Tuco. He works in a pleasant suburb outside Vera Cruz."

Through a splintered window, Cale heard a car rumble on the street. Pounding salsa music thumped from its speakers. The same alley dog barked again.

"So this uncle of yours," Cale prodded the man. "He ships in the product via the United States mail?"

"Sí. *Producto*—all over this splendid country of yours." Carlos smiled and explained. "Hallucinogens, barbiturates, opioids, and fentanyl by the tons."

Cale recalled Kimberly Vanderkellen's autopsy results, her headless body. And also the dead gas station owner, Ray Tolver. An apparent drug OD. *Enough meth to heart-stop a mule.*

"One of my uncle's clients. He resides south of our fine city here. Not far," Carlos said. "A Mr. Powell."

It wasn't much of a leap to assume "Powell" for an alias, Cale guessed. He'd likely pay with cash up front, avoiding any paper trail. It was standard business these days. But who was Powell? A supplier? A middleman? Addict? Or a murderer?

"Is there any chance," Cale asked, "Mr. Powell is connected to our string of missing young women?"

A mirthless shrug from Carlos. He'd read about the local, mysterious kidnappings—a tragedy, but it was hardly any of concern. What alarmed him was the idea of some new enemy invading their local trafficking business.

"It's my responsibility to know all this," Carlos explained. "This enigmatic Mr. Powell. What might he be up to around here? In our neck of the woods, eh?"

"So you called your Uncle Tuco? In Valdez?"

"Vera Cruz."

The gang leader steepled his fingertips. "My uncle had met this man twice. The gringo knows his drugs. Might even be a scientist." Carlos shrugged. "He pays in cash ahead of time while on vacation. No questions asked. So my uncle tells me."

Cale reminded himself that Carlos was in the commodity business. Keeping track of the competition made sense. Like Burger King keeping an eye on McDonald's.

The Latin King chief elaborated on how his uncle had informed them about this client's next shipment. And how he, Carlos, had sent his nephew Eduardo—one of the hombres sitting on the couch now—to stakeout the post office in nearby Appleton, where the shipments were mailed. And how Eduardo had waited for their quarry to show.

"Like Miami Vice," Eduardo said, flashing a gold grill of teeth at Cale. He appeared enthusiastic, suddenly revealed as a live character in the script.

The wheels spun in Cale's head. He'd already had over a year of frustration on this case and finally had his first decent clue. Carlos wouldn't have allowed him into their private lair only to tell fairytales. It would do little to help his cousin, Juan-Julio Sanchez.

Cale stared at the capo and his rough band of amigos. "So you had this man followed? This Mr. Powell?"

"*Si*, Detective." The drug leader's face was ruddy and calm. "Right to the front door of his *casa muy grande*."

Carlos escorted his guest back down the narrow stairway and out the front door of the nondescript house. They moved into the haze of afternoon light.

Cale was relieved to find the Bronco still parked at the curb. All four tires were present, and his vehicle was not resting on concrete blocks.

Thanking the gang leader for help, Cale did his best to conceal his excitement. A hound with a new scent, he moved across the sparse lawn headed toward the Bronco.

Carlos shouted from the house's front steps, "Some friendly advice, Detective Van Waring?"

Cale stopped and looked back.

"One former street boxer to another?" The impishness in the man's expression was hard to miss as he pointed to his left cheek.

"I'm listening."

"Next time, duck."

CHAPTER 50

The sun's fiery skull rose from behind the horizon, chasing away the final vestiges of predawn gray. Daybreak painted violet brush strokes above the African continent of Liberia. Monrovia is the nation's capital, where one person lives comfortably for every five thousand in squalor. A gated military compound sporting four white stucco buildings stands eight miles south of the urban city, perched along the sandy, rock-crusted coastline. High stone walls surround the place. The central structure is more home than a palace but close enough to merit comparison.

Colonel Tazeki Mabutu moved from the kitchen into the private study of the main house. He carried a chilled glass of mango juice in one hand. The spacious beachfront compound belonged to his uncle, the crown prince. Foreboding fourteen-foot-high whitewashed walls, armed guards, cameras, and dogs surrounded it. Security remained a constant in a land of ever-present political turmoil.

Beyond the outer walls, the bleached sand stretched past the guard house, which met the rolling, white-capped ocean waves. On the opposite side of the compound—the high-tree, jungle side—a thick, leafy overgrowth of massive vegetation threatened to swallow the back wall whole.

Mabutu wore pressed linen slacks and a burgundy shirt. He took his seat behind the hand-carved mahogany desk, highlighting the room. The fifteen-inch, carved figure of the wind god Pazuzu stood watch atop the desk as he flicked on his computer.

"Now we shall see, won't we, Pazuzu?" Mabutu's voice was a dry whisper. "See what our friend Tobias has accomplished in our absence?"

Pazuzu, of course, chose not to reply. He gazed across the room at the fireplace mantle, where a shrunken head the size of a furry coconut—once the skull of a living blond-haired, foreign female—stared emptily back at them.

A minute later, the clickity-clack of the keyboard grew silent. Mabutu's fingers came to rest, and what he saw on his monitor gave him pause.

"I do not believe this." His voice rose an octave. "No! No! No! This is unacceptable!"

Pazuzu, likewise, seemed to frown.

Mabutu withdrew a burner phone from his lower desk drawer and powered it, glancing at his watch as he punched the international number. He fumed in silence as he waited for the call to connect.

The steady flow of weekend traffic moved south, away from the city. Cale followed an F-150 pickup, whose color matched the cherry of many famous Wisconsin cocktails.

Though he remained invigorated by the latest events, he tempered his enthusiasm. They'd hit too many dead ends already. Keeping the Bronco steady, he wondered about the man he was now tracking—the enigmatic "Mr. Powell." Could he be the invisible monster they sought? The man behind the abductions? The deaths, even, of five innocent young women?

Was Mr. Powell the Nowhere Man?

On the other hand, maybe the press had it wrong from the get-go like they usually do. From what Carlos had revealed, perhaps they should begin calling this guy what he indeed was: "The Chemist."

Hope was a double-edged sword, Cale reminded himself as he drove. It sliced with both disappointment and success. But at least he was now in the ballgame, following a lead with an actual identity.

They were moving along the beltway, skirting the city. In fifteen minutes, they'd arrive at their destination. Keeping the radio silent, Cale's brief conversation with Carlos rolled through his mind like a looping soundtrack.

"Let me get this straight," Cale had said. "Eduardo, here, he followed Mr. Powell back from Appleton? After he made his pickup at their post office?"

"*Sí*. To a magnificent riverfront home. A mansion." Carlos had massaged his goatee. "If this house belongs to the man you seek, he must be someone of importance."

Time would tell, Cale guessed. "Okay. Then what?" he had asked.

The rest of Carlos' story lacked compelling drama. Once they had confirmed the man's identity, the gang members uncovered no evidence of his dealing "product." He wasn't some wealthy, neophyte drug lord moving in on their turf. He was no suburban Walter White.

Mr. Powell, it was decided, posed no threat to the status quo.

"Live and let live. That sums it up?" Cale had asked.

Carlos shrugged without concern.

Cale learned that this covert surveillance of the stranger had occurred approximately six weeks ago. Soon after the prolonged winter hibernation, the kidnappings started again. First, Cynthia Hulbreth, followed now by Shirley Koon. As the investigators had confirmed, the perpetrator was employing a cocktail of date rape drugs in the abductions.

As a businessman himself, Carlos understood the value of pertinent information. An info trade would benefit both the authorities and the local ethnic narcotics group—the Kings, his tribe. Carlos' plan? Exchange what he knew to purchase the freedom of a favorite youthful gang member, his cousin, Juan-Julio Sanchez.

The gang leader had smugly added, "A *diablo* deal."

It made sense to Cale.

"I don't suppose you'll testify about his fine character?"

"My apologies *por favor*, Detective." Regret had darkened Carlos' soot-colored eyes. "I'm afraid I'll be visiting relatives that day."

A bank of bruise-colored clouds had formed in the western sky. The F-150, shadowed by the Bronco, slid past farms, flat meadows, hills, grazing cattle, and culverts. Hugging the river, the road continued southbound. It wasn't long before the spatial separation between the ritzy million-dollar homes increased exponentially.

One side of the road sported hundreds of acres of flat farmlands. Brown fields had not yet recovered from winter's blanketing frost. The bordering trees showed signs of budding leaves. A large blackbird peered down at them from a high tree limb. Was the same bird following him? Not an omen, Cale hoped, and he shook away the superstitious sensation.

A minute later, the pickup slowed and drifted to the soft gravel shoulder of the road. It came to a halt opposite a pair of sand-colored fieldstone pillars. Beyond the posts ran a curling driveway, which wound its way to a magnificent mansion-like home. Bronze, stone, and beveled glass glittered in the fading light of the overcast afternoon.

Cale pulled the Bronco alongside the gangbangers' ride, engine running. The country road stretched in both directions, an empty black ribbon of asphalt. Eduardo and his partner gave nods and gestures. Yes, this was the hacienda of the mysterious Mr. Powell. The gringo they had followed up from Appleton that day.

The F-150 executed a Y-turn and accelerated away in the direction from which it had come. Task complete. The men could go back to streaming porn flicks, Cale imagined.

He studied the picturesque country estate for the next few minutes through the Bronco's window. The broad Fox River flowed behind the property, and although he couldn't see it from here, he imagined the murky water would appear gray in the fading light, with errant weeds poking up along the grassy shoreline.

Cale asked himself how anyone living in such splendor could be involved in the unsavory business of narcotics and kidnappings—not to mention murder. It made little sense. Still, his experience warned that evil hid in many different wrappings. Grabbing his mobile, he phoned Dispatch.

"Run an address for me?"

"Certainly, Lieutenant. Only take a minute."

"Fine. I'll wait."

Cale angled the rearview mirror and examined his upper cheek. The purple bruise was no longer a boxer's mouse. It had spread to the size of a cue ball, red and angry, looking like he'd survived six rounds with Mike Tyson.

Survived barely.

He quashed a surge of anger at Kenny O'Hern. It was his own fault. *Dammit.* As Staszak and Carlos had advised, he should have ducked when he heard the whistle.

CHAPTER 51

"Got it for you, Lieutenant." The dispatcher's voice broke into his thoughts.

"I'm ready. Shoot."

The home was registered to a married couple. Tobias and Marla Crenshaw. Cale didn't recognize the names among the city's newsmakers or elite charitable benefactors. He'd been crossing his fingers, praying the estate didn't belong to some mucky-muck on the Packers Board of Directors. Or a high-salaried player. It would have been just his luck.

Captain McBride's warning still burned in his ears.

Next, he called Records to search the county tax levies. Tobias Crenshaw's occupation was listed as "Corporate executive, semi-retired." His wife's separate filing reported as: "Real estate agent. Part-time."

No outstanding warrants. Neither had ever been arrested or possessed a criminal record—a couple of speeding tickets for the husband. The last one was seven years ago.

Cale stared off in the afternoon light at the spacious three-story home. An *Architectural Digest* dreams of pillars, high windows, and modern, sharp-angled cornices.

In his head, he could hear the tick of seconds passing. Cale wheeled the Bronco across the road and drove between the low stone pillars bordering the driveway entrance.

After navigating the winding drive that placed him in front of the dwelling, Cale parked the Bronco. He exited, slamming the door loud enough to announce his presence.

Making his way up the steps past a pair of granite-carved griffins, he arrived at the double-front doors of solid maple. He half-expected a butler or manservant to greet him. The door, instead, was answered by a flaxen-haired little girl, cute as a cartoon doll. Behind her and sounding a dozen rooms away, a female voice called, "Who's at the door, hon?"

The young girl stared into Cale's eyes. Over her shoulder, she shouted, "A man with a scary face!"

A moment later, she stepped back, giving way to her mother's presence at the door. Marla was dressed in cream-colored sweats and pristine athletic shoes. A soccer mom lifted from the pages of *Vanity Fair*. The inquisitive smile faded from the mother's face. Her daughter hadn't been kidding. A monster lurked before them. Marla adjusted her expression, keeping the girl within the cradle of her left arm, prepared to whisk her away at the first behavioral flaw from the stranger.

Cale flipped his wallet open, badge, and picture ID. He was a detective, he informed her—not indicating Homicide—hoping she might spare a few free minutes. Marla Crenshaw, though puzzled, allowed him entrance.

A mini-crystal ballroom chandelier graced the high front foyer. Cool Italian marble floors caused their footsteps to echo as if walking through a museum.

"Nice cottage," Cale said lightly, taking in the opulent surroundings as Marla led them into a generous front sitting room. She suggested her daughter—Kendal—busy herself up in her room. The young girl traipsed away without argument, happy to escape the monster's presence.

Cale stood before a fireplace mantle with his eyes fixed on the row of photographs. Family vacations, holidays, birthdays, and Christmases past. Four members in most of the shots. Dark-haired father, pretty wife, and two grinning kids. In several photos, the children were hugging a friendly yellow Labrador.

Cale smiled at Marla, nodding at the photographs. The Crenshaws. What a lovely family.

"How can I help you, Detective, uh, Van —"

"Van Waring. Yes. Mind if I sit down?"

She motioned him toward his pick of three chairs, and he chose a Queen Ann's, positioned with its back to the wide window with open drapes.

"Routine visit," Cale added, reassuring her nothing was amiss.

He informed her there had been reports of break-ins around the rural area. Had she or her husband noticed anything suspicious over the past months? Strangers wandering the road? Stray animals?

"What sort of animals?"

"DNR thinks it might be coyotes."

This appeared to distress Marla Crenshaw more than the idea of strangers lurking about. "Good God. In our part of the state?"

She wasn't questioning why a Green Bay detective—not a sheriff's deputy or DNR officer—was exploring a situation involving wildlife. Cale tried his best to appear sincere. "They hibernate most of the winter. Hunt for small animals, birds, chickens."

"Seriously?"

"Even attack cattle now and then if they get hungry enough." Cale decided his embellishment sounded plausible.

Marla turned pale, and he guessed her thoughts might concern a dip in property values if rumors of a "coyote problem" began circulating.

Cale paused to take in the room, getting a feel for the place. How many more hidden rooms were beyond this? A house this size? Although the home wasn't some old Victorian mansion, images of swinging bookcases, secret staircases, and shadowy compartments flashed through his mind.

He reined in his imagination.

"Your husband must be successful, Mrs. Crenshaw," Cale said, kicking himself as master of the obvious.

He glanced at the room's furnishings, then out the opened double doors and across the foyer, where a polished grand piano peeked beyond an arch. It was a separate music room.

"Call me Marla. Please."

Marla Crenshaw possessed bleached white teeth. Dressed down now, Cale couldn't miss how attractive she was.

"Tobias owns several small businesses. He inherited multiple assets from his father's estate. Stocks. Bonds. Paper industry holdings."

"Lucky guy."

"He dabbles in real estate these days. His own company. Commercial, mostly."

"Like yourself?" She looked surprised, and he added, "Saw your phone book listings. Besides, you don't exactly paint the image of a stay-at-home mom."

Marla beamed. "I try to stay active. With the kids in school all day." Her eyes twinkled. "Do you have children of your own, Detective?"

Cale's neck warmed. Hank didn't count, so he replied, "Hoping to. Someday."

"Still haven't found Ms. Right?"

He offered a lopsided smile. Cale couldn't help picturing him and Maggie during the dreaded Fourth of July weekend, her scheduled departure date. He shook away the image.

Marla surprised him by agreeing to his request for a ten-dollar residence tour. After quick peeks into the inner rooms, they proceeded to the kitchen. He decided it would make most midsize restaurants proud.

"Mrs. Beckwell comes each day. Helps with dinner and the kids for a few hours."

Cale declined her refreshment offer. Marla led them through the back sunroom and outside. They toured the low-walled outer patio. The landscaping was first-rate. The back lawns sloped gently toward the broad, auburn-colored Fox River, flowing languidly past.

They strolled down the stone patio steps, moving toward the two-story boathouse. It was not far away from a bank of five connected garages. As he surveyed the yard, Cale realized something was missing. Then it came to him. Why were there no signs of the dog? The yellow Lab he'd seen in the family photos? No doghouse, no matted grass, no chew toys strewn about. Nothing which indicated a canine's presence.

Cale kept his tone even. "The gorgeous yellow Lab? In your pictures? She looked like an excellent watchdog."

Marla's expression turned wistful. "Her name was Candy. God, the children loved that goofy dog."

"Loved?"

"Doggie heaven. Two Christmases ago," Marla said sadly. "The vet said heart attack. It happens to large dogs, I guess." Tears glistened in her eye.

"A shame."

Marla sighed. "She was only four." She added, "Seemed in perfect health. Dr. Burgess was surprised when it happened."

Cale made no reply.

They neared the two-floored boathouse, the size of many people's second homes. "Got a yacht inside?" he asked, adding a grin.

"We're not boaters. Toby uses it for storage. Or tinkers around in his workshop on the upper floor. Keeps it locked tight."

Cale thought he detected a note of unease in her voice. "The kids, you know?" she added. "They'll get into anything."

Leaning forward, Cale cupped his hand and peered into one of the lower windows. Gardening tools hung on racks. Bags of mulch and soil fertilizer. A riding mower, snow blower, a John Deere quad-runner, chemical bags, and other maintenance supplies. A railed stairway led up to the second level that he couldn't see.

A sudden voice called out from the back of the house. "Anything I can help you find?"

Cale turned from the window. He watched the approach of Tobias Crenshaw. The man was lean, with bushy dark hair and a narrow face. His stylish tortoise shell eyeglasses enhanced his angular features. He wore a navy turtleneck, charcoal slacks, and an auburn windbreaker.

"This is Detective Van Waring!" Marla called back. "He's checking the yard for animal tracks."

Tobias frowned, continuing his advance. "What sort of animals?"

"Coyotes, I guess," Marla said. She announced to Cale, "This is my husband, Detective. Tobias Crenshaw."

Not Mr. Powell.

Cale sensed a hint of unease in her voice, a tightness to her smile. He'd seen those same eyes in battered women hiding dark inner secrets—the kind no one ever imagined—secretive family sorts of things.

Crenshaw possessed an athletic gait. Cale noted this as he reacted to the man's extended hand. His handshake was firm, business-like.

"Coyotes, Detective?" Crenshaw's voice held puzzlement.

"It's what the DNR tells us."

"There's a new one." Tobias scratched the smooth skin of his cheek. "Didn't even know we had them in Wisconsin."

CHAPTER 52

"Thanks again. Sorry to bother you." Cale said this with a grateful hand salute.

Tobias Crenshaw had walked him along the curl of the front driveway to where his Bronco remained parked. Crenshaw's red BMW sports car was parked fifteen feet away.

At the house, Marla and Kendal stood smiling on the front steps. They waved like he was old Uncle Henry departing from a holiday visit.

"Anytime, Detective," Tobias said.

Cale opened the Bronco's door and glanced back at the lean and handsome man. "By the way, Marla told me you own a few properties. Anything down around the Appleton area?" he asked.

"Couple of buildings. Keep them as write-offs. Why?"

"Oh, nothing." Cale slid inside the Bronco with the door open. "One of those faces, I guess. Thought I might've seen you down there once or twice."

"Months ago, might've been. Maybe before the holidays?"

Cale closed the SUV door with a shrug. Tobias strode back to the house. Cale keyed the ignition and waved as he eased back down the driveway. As he spun the Bronco onto the county road, he thought to himself:

The Crenshaws. What a lovely family.

The return back to the city was nerve-wracking. Cale could barely manage his mental drumbeat of marching thoughts. The Crenshaw house held at least thirty rooms, he guessed. Marla didn't seem the domestic type, so it made sense there'd be hired staff for cleaning, yard maintenance, garden care, cooking, and child-care. More workers beyond Mrs. Beckwell would be needed to maintain the household functions.

Thirty rooms. Easily enough space to hide four missing, undetected girls for months.

An even more perplexing thought was: What did Tobias Crenshaw have to do with the mysterious Mr. Powell? Were they the same person?

Cale understood men (and ladies) sometimes employed aliases for various reasons—carrying on illicit extra-marital affairs or keeping secret bank accounts. Was it possible that Crenshaw received smoochy love letters? Were they sent to the Appleton PO address instead of his business or home?

Guesswork at best, he chided himself.

On the other hand, might Carlos and his compadres have gotten the man's identity wrong? Uncertain how much he trusted his newfound informants, Cale remained open to the possibility. Were they messing with him for amusement? To what end, he couldn't guess.

He navigated the twisting river road until the City of De Pere materialized ahead. Crossing the wide river bridge, he glimpsed flashes of the Interstate far beyond the banks and treetops. Further above, the pewter-hued sky contained a hint of rain.

Cale compared Crenshaw's mansion to the cozy space he and Maggie enjoyed. His old family home was inherited from his parents when they moved to Arizona six years ago. How empty would it feel after Maggie moved out? The reality of the July Fourth weekend depressed him.

Slink had only days ago reminded him, "In eight weeks, she'll be gone, amigo." According to his best friend and self-anointed prophet, it was the biggest mistake of his life. Marla Crenshaw's innocuous comment about searching for "Ms. Right" still felt like a knife in Cale's chest.

He eased the Bronco through a roundabout, thinking how strange it seemed. His first break in a year-long kidnapping case, and his mind kept pulling him back to Maggie.

Cale promised he could repair things before her timeline. Still, just the other day, he'd noticed empty boxes grouped in the basement. Was it already too far gone to stop?

Besides, hadn't Maggie seemed distant the past few days? Her eyes weren't lighting up when she smiled at him. Was she already severing their emotional ties?

My God, Cale cursed himself now. Was he so caught up in this kidnapping case to even notice?

Handling homicides over the years, Cale understood that people pressed forward, soldiering on through hurt and pain, despite great tragedies. Was Maggie doing the equivalent? Preparing to move on with her life?

Ten minutes later, he made a left turn back into the city. Cale needed to stop dwelling on personal issues and focus on the investigation. Kidnappings, murders, headless bodies. Families destroyed. Drug dealers were making *diablo* deals. A cunning sociopath was terrorizing their city—perhaps one living in a brick-and-glass mansion.

Despite it all, a dark voice in his head asked: "Am I really going to let Maggie walk out of my life?"

As if in panic, he grabbed his phone from the cup holder. He could ask her to marry him right now. This minute. They could fly to Las Vegas tonight or next weekend. Or as soon as he caught the killer and freed the missing victims.

Cale dialed Staszak's number instead.

"You disappeared quicker than Houdini with the trots," Staszak joked from his desk phone.

"Didn't think you noticed."

"That little weasel Sanchez give us anything?"

"Maybe a lead. If things pan out."

A pause for silence. "Do I have to play twenty questions?"

"Listen," Cale said, "find me everything you can on one Tobias Crenshaw." His tone was clipped.

"The interview tip? For real?"

"Real as Al Capone's funeral."

The Chemist

Don't we all have a dark twin lurking inside of us? Just ask Siggy Freud, Jung, or Fedor Dostoyevsky—our own personal Mr. Hyde, imminently capable of snapping at any moment. Your version, undoubtedly, has managed to worm itself free. By doing so, you've evolved into the quintessential conscienceless sociopath, a superior blend of cleverness and audacity. Years from now, your exploits will stand as a measuring stick by which crimes of rare intelligence will be compared.

And best of all? Like Jack the Ripper himself, for decades and beyond, future criminologists will debate the mystery of your identity.

And forever they will be left...

Uncertain.

Tobias Crenshaw sat in his tan calfskin Lay-Z-Boy. From his spot in the study, he heard activity at the front door. Bucky, his son, was home from his soccer match. In some distant part of the house, he could hear Marla puttering around, the soles of her Reeboks squeaking as she moved across the polished floor. Readying dinner, he imagined. Mrs. Beckwell had the weekend off. It was not his concern.

Black and ominous thoughts, instead, kept returning him to the inquisitive police investigator who had mysteriously visited. Something about the man had disturbed Tobias. Was it the predatory glaze in his gray eyes? And why the inquiry about visiting Appleton? It was hardly a mistake. No, it had been a deliberate attempt to rattle him.

This detective—Van Waring—knew far more than he'd let on. Why else would he visit the house? Sniffing around the property? Warning of wild animals? Coyotes! How much more BS could the man shovel?

Tobias gazed out the window now at the gray afternoon light.

Might the gas station owner, Ray Tolver, have been lying? Did any surveillance tape truly exist, revealing the shadowy image of a kidnapper stopping for gas?

Tobias stared now at the black leather medical bag atop his desk. Inside were driving gloves and the plastic bottle containing his chemical tincture, tucked alongside duct tape, a Taser, and a hypodermic syringe. Contents that may have sent him swinging from some gallows in years past.

He set these bleak thoughts aside and let his mind work the puzzle. The answer, when it arrived, proved quite simple: the cops knew nothing. The investigator, likely acting on some vague hunch, was on a fishing expedition—nothing more.

Poor Mr. Tolver was not lying as he'd struggled for his life. There was no surveillance tape, Tobias had made sure of it, and he was seldom wrong about even the most minor details.

"Honey? Why do you think that policeman was here?" Marla asked.

He hadn't heard his wife approach the open doorframe. Her sudden voice startled him, causing clammy dampness to warm his forehead. Why did the woman wear noiseless shoes?

"As he said," Tobias' voice was clipped. "Public safety. Eye out for dangerous animals."

Shaking her head, Marla departed as quietly as she had appeared.

Returning to his private thoughts, Tobias debated with the voice inside his head: *The gumshoe—this Van Waring—he knows something.* The stern, inner head voice further scolded: *"If you imagine he's stupid, you're the one wearing the dunce hat. Why else would he show up here poking around?"*

"Shut up!" Tobias whispered to the quiet air.

"He knows about the girls."

CHAPTER 53

Sliding the Bronco into a slot in the station parking lot, Cale logged in and entered the building's back entrance. The place was quiet, a few uniforms coming off ten-hour weekend shifts. A handful of officers filled reports, with others sliding in and out.

Cale's conversation with drug capo Carlos, followed by the afternoon's visit at the Crenshaw residence, had created more questions than answers. Yet one thread linked the two—if Tobias Crenshaw was "Mr. Powell," he certainly possessed a working knowledge of narcotics.

This was the angle Cale decided to pursue.

Grabbing his desk phone, he called the morgue. These days, they often worked Saturdays on backlogged cases and paperwork. He read the assistant the requested case number and waited. In the background, he heard whining saw noises, loud enough to make your blood curdle. Then they stopped, and Dr. Heinz Mocarek came on the line seconds later.

"Kimberly Vanderkellen," the ME announced. "You find her missing head for me yet?"

"Maybe by next Christmas, the way this is going."

"She can wait," he joked darkly, his droll humor.

Cale stared at his file copy. "Doc, the tox report indicates high levels of GHB and fentanyl."

"Excessive sedation toxicity. Yes." Mocarek reported this without emotion.

"There's another drug listed. Something called mid-zo—"

"Midazolam. Trade name Versed. It's a common surgical sedative." Mocarek paused before adding, "It was my call. I had the lab check on it myself."

"It's not on the routine tox-screen list?"

"No. It's given intravenously," the ME said. "Very fast-acting. Sedation kicks butt in a minute or less."

"Why check for it? If you don't mind my asking?"

"A liquid narcotic like Versed would be consistent with your perpetrator's MO."

241

"How so?"

"Speed, right? He aims to knock them out lickety-split and minimize the witness risk."

Cale held his breath.

"Besides, under the influence of midazolam," the doctor expounded, "a person has almost total amnesia afterward. If you want to create yourself a zombie, Detective, use Versed."

Great, Cale thought sarcastically, just what the scumbags out there need—a new zombie drug.

"Everything else on the report seems kosher to you?" Cale asked, politely probing.

The silence grew as the pathologist surveyed the file. Seconds later, Mocarek said, "Standard fare, except for the mix. Most date rapists use one thing or another. They seldom take the time to put a cocktail together."

They ended the call, and Cale pondered the new reveal. Versed equals "zombie drug." He now had a new demon to keep him awake at night.

Staszak's shadow loomed above his desk.

"Found everything I could on your Crenshaw fellow." He waved a sheaf of printouts while plunking into his desk chair. "A silver spoon rich dude, from all appearances."

"You're right. His riverfront digs make my place look like a doghouse."

They spent the next hour pouring over the life and times of Tobias Crenshaw. Income tax returns from the past seven years, personal, partnership, or corporate group real estate holdings; employment history; who and where his relatives lived. At last, they added up his business assets and stock investments.

"Guy's got a master's degree from UW." Staszak sounded impressed. "Biochemistry, believe it or not."

Cale considered the information. The man's mansion alone suggested that Crenshaw came from old family money. Like his wife had said: "Inherited wealth." The detectives surmised that not many actual chemists lived in riverfront estates.

"All the chemists I know," Staszak confessed, "cook meth in trailers in the backwoods somewhere."

Cale let the exaggeration slide, studying a printout as the idea marinated deep inside his brain. The chemistry angle was beginning to feel like a pebble lodged in his shoe—first Kenny O'Hern, with a chemistry degree, now Crenshaw. Even Chloe's husband—Ed Ravelle—was a pharmacist. Might he be a suspect, as well? Add in the Latin Kings with their drug knowledge, and they both pictured amateur chemists lurking around every corner, hiding behind every clump of bushes. Besides, selling and distributing brought in more cash than making the stuff. Couldn't they all be considered "chemists" up and down the narcotics chain?

Cale recalled the words of FBI Agent Eddie Redtail: "Even if he has a street degree, your guy knows his drugs. Along with a working knowledge of human physiology."

Cale pictured the all-American Crenshaw family waving at him like a Hallmark greeting card from their front porch. And the dad, Tobias, just so happens to hold an advanced degree in biochemistry. It must mean something. Cale was not a big fan of coincidences.

Staszak handed another printout his way. The new one indicated Crenshaw had been the local recipient of a state Humanitarian Award five years ago. He contributed multiple donations to the Kidney Foundation. A Civic Beauty Award was also issued for the restoration of a dozen condemned downtown properties. One of his companies had purchased the locales and shined them up to create affordable housing for the needy.

"Is this guy related to Mother Teresa?" Staszak asked with a groan.

"More like Charles Manson," Cale said humorlessly.

"No way we're staring at a serious criminal here."

"Un-serious ones rarely hack women's heads off." Cale thought grimly: *Mr. Crenshaw? Mr. Powell? Are they the same person?*

Even more poignantly: *Is he even our guy?*

The detectives waded through the paper maze, becoming more depressed as the clock ticked and the outside shadows emerged. After another hour, Staszak glanced his way. "On the bright side, at least your eye looks better."

Cale touched his upper cheek and smirked. "Yeah. I'll be back on the runway in no time."

Maggie and Cale retired to the family room sofa after dinner. He considered lighting the fireplace but hesitated. Earlier in the afternoon, he'd been ready to propose marriage this evening. Now, at home together, the idea felt overwhelming and almost ridiculous. After the crazy day he'd had, groggy from sleep deprivation, he decided that tomorrow would be better. Sunday was a more relaxing day. Better designed to talk about spending the rest of your lives together.

Darkness held the evening captive, and sitting up in their family room, Cale observed their ghost-like reflections in the windows, which overlooked the outside yard. Maggie held Hank in her lap, brushing him. She had kept the television off in favor of slow blues playing low on the house stereo. Cale couldn't help but notice her somewhat distant demeanor. Something was troubling her.

She'd inform him when she was ready to talk, he supposed. Like Maggie always did. At the moment, it was best to give her space and listen when she decided to speak.

"So Sanchez came through for you?" Maggie asked, her voice breaking into his thoughts. She continued brushing the contented feline on her lap.

"His friends are hardly boy scouts." Cale twisted the cap off a bottle of Pabst. "An interesting lead, though. I hope something comes of it."

Despite Hank's disappointment, she set the brush on the coffee table. "What did he say? Sanchez? I'm curious."

Cale's guts knotted. He was hesitant to reveal the juvenile had insulted them both. Also, at the moment, there seemed little point in conveying Sanchez's comment about visiting her after his release. Youthful bluster, hardly serious.

Before Cale could answer her question, his phone chirped. Saturday night? God! *Please don't let it be another victim.* He answered cautiously.

"There's a compound called dimethyl sulfoxide." Dr. Heinz Mocarek sounded like a quiz show host. "Ever hear of it?"

"This for a free trip to Hawaii?"

The ME chuckled. "Visit me first thing Monday morning. I've got something even better for you."

"Better than Hawaii?"

"Depends on your perspective, doesn't it?"

CHAPTER 54

Cale wore a dark tuxedo in his dream—rakishly dashing, a present-day version of Rhett Butler. Maggie was in a long champagne gown, and they waltzed across the polished dance floor. Orchestra music cascaded around them in a sparkling waterfall of sound.

They were dancing to "The Wedding March."

Cale yanked awake with a start. He sat halfway up in bed with the covers twisted. He didn't need Sigmund Freud to analyze the dream. The image made him shiver.

Alone. The fear of being lonely forever. A solitary life of quiet desperation. How much clearer could a dream be?

Across the ink-shadowed room, he noticed the gauzy silhouette standing in front of the window.

"Mags?" he whispered.

She drifted silently back to the bed like a ghost.

"Are you all right?" he asked.

"Not so much." Her voice faltered as if catching a sob. Cale gathered her in his arms. She said, "I love you, Cale—it can't end like this. It just can't."

He whispered his deep love for her, crushing his face into her hair. "So much it hurts." His heart pounded with the fear of isolation, a lifetime of regret. "You're so right, Maggie May." He paused. "We'll make it work. We have to."

Her body trembled, "Don't say it if"—her voice quavered—"if you don't mean it."

"I do mean it. With all my heart, Mags."

They continued the embrace as Maggie slipped beneath the blankets. They were together in the darkness, two souls adrift but no longer navigating by the moonlight of indecision.

The spring night's crescent moon sat bone-white against the velvety sky. Tobias sat alone in his study chair, watching the shadows creep and fall away like fearful suitors. The house, otherwise, was silent. Marla and the kids were asleep.

The buzz of his mobile jarred the graveyard atmosphere. Tobias noted: 1:33 a.m.

"I just got off the site." Mobutu's voice was a hissing snake in the far-away night. A continent removed. "Can I term it any stronger? It's unacceptable!"

"What are you talking—"

"The girl is wrong!" the Liberian blurted. "I told you the type I need."

"Blondes. I know." Tobias couldn't prevent his snicker yet swallowed it like a bitter pill. "It's how it worked. Nothing's written in stone, is it?"

"Don't quibble with me," spat the Colonel. "Why should I have to spell things out for you?"

Tobias rocked forward in his leather chair and exhaled. Around him, the air stirred, and he calculated the distance between his spot and the obsidian jungles of Liberia. He was weary of his partner's stubborn, nearly adolescent demands. Blondes, brunettes, redheads? What the hell did it matter? For all he knew, it would be albino twins with shaved heads and Nazi tattoos next.

"Seriously. At this point, what difference does it make?" Tobias asked.

"It makes a difference to the buyer."

"The girl is exceptional. I can vouch for her, myself."

A long beat of silence. When the Liberian spoke again, his tone was softer, more sinister. "I have a proposition for you, Tobias. One that will prove most beneficial."

"To you, I'm sure."

"To us both."

Tobias leaned back in his chair and listened.

Cale was in the county morgue at eight a.m. sharp on Monday morning. He noted how Heinz Mocarek, MD, appeared as exuberant as a ten-year-old on his first fishing trip. He motioned Cale to his workstation. There were vials of liquids, beakers, and syringes in sterile paper packets on the countertop. A large electron microscope with an attached teaching tube took up three square feet of the surface.

With a twinkle in his eye, the ME suggested: "A quick experiment. Watch." He opened a small strip of paper and dropped it into a beaker half-filled with clear, slightly viscous fluid. Stirring the mixture, it turned bright orange.

Cale almost made a "Tang" joke but checked his sarcasm.

Mocarek next employed a small eye dropper. He sucked up a tube full of the solution. Hiking up one sleeve, he held out his left forearm and squeezed a quarter-size puddle of orange liquid from the dropper onto his skin.

Cale watched the fluid disappear, absorbed through the skin of the doctor's forearm as if sucked from within.

"Whoa. There's a trick."

Mocarek did it again, a second drop. "Dimethyl sulfoxide. DMSO," he informed. The pathologist set aside the dropper and rolled his sleeve back down. He grabbed a ceramic coffee cup labeled "Kiss the Butcher!" Morgue humor. Cale winced.

The doctor continued, "I thought of it after we talked. How would I get a sedative into a stranger without injecting or inhaling it? Or taking it orally?"

Cale stayed silent.

"Later, the answer came to me. Why not right through the dermis?"

Having watched the orange liquid dissipate through the doctor's forearm, Cale didn't have to question the theory's plausibility.

"Think about it." The ME's eyes widened. "We employ skin patches all the time. For motion sickness, quitting smoking, birth control." Cale crossed his arms, giving Mocarek his full attention.

"I remembered back in med school. Good old DMSO."

"DMSO?"

"Vets use it on animals all the time. For inflammation, joint pain, and a few dozen others." He spoke with authority. "And people also take it for all kinds of ailments."

"Prescribed?"

"It's OTC. In and of itself, it's a modestly benign substance."

The pathologist explained how dimethyl sulfoxide could quickly penetrate human skin. In liquid form, the drug works as a "carrier," directly bringing substances of the correct molecular size into a person or animal's bloodstream. In years past, it was detectable due to its sulfur odor. But these days, similar to garlic tablets, it came in a no-scent variety.

Cale stood in silence, pondering it all.

"The *piece de resistance*," Mocarek continued, waving one hand like an opera tenor, "is how an unknowing individual wouldn't even know they'd been exposed."

"It's that simple? Just getting it onto someone's skin?"

"By adding strong sedatives to the mix," the ME added, "with DMSO as a carrier, it could also be very fast-acting."

"How fast?"

"Take fentanyl or Versed, as I mentioned earlier," the doctor theorized. "Depending on dosage and body weight, you'd likely feel the effects in under a minute. Like a super toxic snakebite."

Cale shook his head.

Mocarek glanced at his wristwatch. He grabbed a chubby penlight from the tabletop. Marching across the room, he motioned the detective to follow. The ME slipped into the closet-sized, lightless restroom and didn't close the door. Cale lingered in the doorway. The doctor unzipped and began urinating in the toilet bowl.

"We're not too shy here in the morgue," he quipped.

"Don't suppose so." Cale glanced behind them at the row of stainless-steel drawers awaiting future visitors.

"Remember the orange strip a few minutes ago?" Mocarek asked casually. "I combined fluorescent dye with DMSO. The black light makes for a better display."

"I'll take your word for it."

Finished, the ME zipped up. He turned his penlight on. The UV blue light cast the toilet bowl in a brilliant wash of orange hyper-fluorescence.

"Like Luminol," Cale remarked.

The doctor flushed the toilet. He brushed past Cale and moved back into the lab area. "I applied dye on my arm about four minutes ago." He nodded at the fact. "Proves how fast DMSO works."

Cale pondered the ramifications.

"So you're thinking our guy blends this stuff with the right drug mix—"

"Your victims never knew what hit them."

Cale walked briskly to the room's exit. "When we catch this sicko," he called over his shoulder, "your Penn-&-Teller act should play well in the courtroom."

"Show biz, Detective. I can hardly wait."

Cale sat in the Bronco and considered the ME's revelations in the parking lot outside the morgue. The victims quickly pass out. No struggle, no violence, no witnesses.

The DMSO is the carrier, and the drug cocktail seeps in through their skin. Once they're out cold, he gets inside their cars somehow—an essential point to Cale's thinking. Then he drives away with no witnesses to anything amiss. It was a theory, but it made sense from a practical standpoint.

Doc Mocarek's toilet bowl demonstration was impressive. The visual effect of the orange dye still swirled before Cale's eyes like a maelstrom.

Like a super toxic snakebite. The words continued ringing in his head.

The modus operandi was clean, fast, and silent but deadly. Furthermore, it fit with FBI Agent Eddie Redtail's initial profile of their offender a year ago. A clever, educated perpetrator. Precise. Detailed. In control.

One who, to this point, hadn't left them a ghost of a clue.

Cale watched the nearby morning traffic buzz along. A pair of pigeons pecked at crumbs on the nearby grass. A squad car cruised past—business as usual.

The killer was somewhere out there, relaxing, perhaps enjoying a breakfast omelet. He would find amusement in law enforcement's futile efforts to identify him.

Cale started the Bronco. "Screw the press," he told himself out loud. "This sick SOB is the *Chemist*."

PART THREE
ONE FINAL VICTIM

CHAPTER 55

Cale drove the Bronco the four blocks back to the station house and watched a parade of picketers marching in somber silence on the sidewalk outside the building. Their expressions matched the recognizable determination of professional advocates. He read their placards as he cruised past.

We Pay Taxes: Find Our Missing Daughters.
The Police: *Missing in Action!*
Find Cindy and Shirley—NOW!

Easing around the distant corner, Cale wished he could join their ranks momentarily. Whether they believed it or not, he understood their frustration.

Three minutes later, as he approached his desk, he received the morning's second major surprise. He stared in disbelief and asked, "What are you doing here?"

Det. Slink Dooley sat at his desk typing one-handed, his injured arm and shoulder cradled in a sling. His partner grinned. "Detective Lazarus, reporting for duty."

"Let me guess—you couldn't stay away from the gambling sites any longer?"

"That hospital needs better Wi-Fi."

"Wi-Fi's not a selling point when you check-in." Cale studied his partner. Slink shrugged his workable shoulder.

Cale regarded him as he stepped closer. "Does Janet know you're here?"

Slink held a finger to his lips. "You ever try resting with two young banshees running around?"

Cale well understood both Slink's dedication and stubborn nature. Leaning close, he performed a cursory check of his partner's pupils. Was he loopy on painkillers?

Slink elbowed him away. "I'm in the hospital three days, and already you're gay for me?"

"Don't flatter yourself, Liberace."

Slink's humor remained intact, but their playful discourse was interrupted by the bulldog approach of Captain McBride. "What the hell, Dooley! What the hell!"

"I can't sit on my butt at home, Cap."

McBride glared at Cale like it was his fault. To Slink, he said, "Pack it up. Union will be up my butt if they catch wind."

"Cap. We need Slink's hacker skills. Especially here and now."

McBride sharp-eyed them both. But his decision was final, and he flipped Slink the umpire's thumb. To Cale, he ordered, "My office. And bring Staszak with you. I spotted his size-fifty-rear-end loafing around here somewhere."

The captain vanished, and Cale gazed back at his partner. "Better do what he says. He's on the warpath."

Slink flicked off his PC and rose, mindful of his arm sling.

"I'll walk you out," Cale said.

The detectives moved along the narrow hallway toward the back exit, with Cale bringing Slink up to speed on the case. He explained his interview with a surly Juan-Julio Sanchez and how it had led him to the Latin Kings' drug house. He revealed the dangerous home of Carlos, the gang leader, and added how their meeting had resulted in his visit to the near-palatial home of Tobias Crenshaw.

"You think he's our guy? This Crenshaw?"

"A definite person of interest."

Cale further revealed how Dr. Mocarek's updated drug-absorption theory rendered them a plausible method of how the kidnappings might occur. The perpetrator could employ a barbiturate mixture—absorbed quickly through the skin—to incapacitate his victims.

"Does Agent Redtail have an opinion?" Slink asked.

Cale hadn't spoken with Eddie Redtail since the FBI agent returned to Milwaukee last Friday. The Bureau required his return home, not chasing phantoms around Green Bay when they had no viable suspects or evidence in their case.

Outside, the Monday morning parking lot was gray and unwelcoming. Cale understood Slink's frustration at Captain McBride's forcing him to the sidelines. Especially with the new lead possibility.

"What's our next move, amigo?" Slink asked.

"I'm proposing a stakeout to Cap." Slink widened his eyes, and Cale added, "Neither of us. I've got somebody better equipped in mind."

Slink slid his free hand inside his jacket, jiggling his keys. "Sounds like a job for a size-fifty rear end."

"Custom-made for stakeouts."

Tobias awoke Monday morning with a mixture of dread and relief. His late-night discussion with Mabutu continued to loop through his head. They were halfway home, and now Mabutu wanted to alter the rules. He desired his merchandise sooner, directing that they expedite the delivery date to appease his buyers' demands.

All because he didn't get the hair-type he desired, Tobias concluded. In his opinion, the colonel was unraveling, causing their partnership to spin off-axis.

Of course, Tobias had countered the idea, hoping to interject logic into the matter. He'd just taken a new victim, and it would be asinine to risk another capture so soon. His exposure risk would be significantly heightened.

"I've barely spent time with this new one," he'd protested over the phone, an unpleasant whine in his voice.

But Col. Mabutu was unyielding. "We agreed on three to fulfill your contract. Otherwise, those photos I possess might reach your wife."

Tobias had detected a sneer, as his partner added: "I have faith in you, Toby. You'll figure something out."

The phone call had ended on a sour note.

It was morning now, and the gray April weather matched the colorlessness of his mood.

Tobias hadn't revealed his conversation with the Green Bay police detective at his home a day earlier. How he'd been flagged and appeared to now be on law enforcement's radar. Their operation together had to end. Entirely. And he could not risk grabbing yet another victim.

Things were becoming far too warm for his liking.

Captain Leo McBride was on his fourth cup of coffee when Cale, with Anton Staszak shadowing him, entered his office. The captain spoke as the detectives seated themselves. "I just met with Chief Harris, so I'm not mincing words here."

He had their full attention.

"Kenny O'Hern's attorney called. O'Hern's got an airtight alibi for the sixth of April—the Hulbreth girl's abduction."

"Nursing his sick mother, huh?" Sarcasm dripped from Staszak's voice.

"Try the Indian casino," McBride said. "Five straight hours playing blackjack."

"He still could have—"

"Surveillance tape." McBride talked over Staszak's protest. "Six different dealers. Three pit bosses. All verify he was there in the flesh from mid-morning to afternoon."

Cale stared at the far wall, where a single-eyed Picasso figure curled a lip at him. It mattered little. They'd already dismissed O'Hern as a suspect.

"But the manure gets deeper." Lines creased the captain's forehead. "O'Hern's attorney's barking now about suing the department."

"On what grounds?"

"False arrest, false imprisonment. Lack of probable cause. He claims O'Hearn's 'Whistler' brand might be affected."

Watching their disbelief, McBride studied them humorlessly. "Any way we slice it, you two are neck-deep in the sludge."

CHAPTER 56

Cale's new plan was hastily formulated. By 2 p.m., he figured they were ready.

Reporter Renee Douglas sat to one side of television Studio B, looking her usual pert self. She scanned her notes like an actress memorizing a script, wearing cream-colored pumps and a beige pantsuit. Cale decided she was more attractive in person than on camera.

On the set's opposite side, a makeup girl dabbed concealer around Cale's high cheek bruise. When she held up a mirror, he admitted she'd done a superb job. Not quite Cary Grant, but who was?

"Everybody, countdown!" the producer called. He was stooped between a pair of large cameras on wheels, whose legs appeared like giant *Star Wars* storks. "Detective Van Waring? On set?"

Making his way center stage, Cale squeezed the shoulder of Samantha Koon, standing in the wings. He figured having at least one of the mothers present for support was a good call.

The stage had a pair of comfortable chairs behind an oval-shaped coffee table. Cale was collar-mic'd, and Ms. Douglas held a leather-bound notebook as they seated themselves.

Seconds later, the producer called, "And we're green!"

Acknowledging her cue, the reporter flashed her best Hollywood smile and began her lead-in.

"We're talking today with Lieutenant Cale Van Waring, the Green Bay Police Department's lead investigator. He's here to reveal they've narrowed down their possible suspects in the Nowhere Man Abductions—the recent string of kidnappings, which have plagued the city's metro area for over the past year."

Douglas turned to Cale, and Camera Two cut to his solo. He thanked Renee, then read aloud from the teleprompter:

"This is a direct message for the Nowhere Man—who we've renamed *The Chemist*. The noose is tightening. We know how you kidnap your victims. And we know about the dimethyl."

He paused, listening to the room's breathless silence.

"Please release Cynthia Hulbreth and Shirley Koon. Along with Leslie Dowd and Mary Jane Moore, who disappeared last year. Release them all unharmed, and our legal system will assist you in retaining the attorney of your choosing."

Cale stared directly into the camera. Into the dark eyes, he hoped, of the sadistic kidnapper.

"Turn yourself in," he continued grimly, "the clock is ticking."

The room had turned stone silent.

Renee Douglas followed with a plea of her own. "Nowhere Man? Chemist? Or whatever you want to be called? We promise you will not be harmed if you turn yourself in."

The director signaled to cut the cameras, concluding the public statement. Studio lights flashed on like a tavern at closing time.

Cale unclipped his collar mic.

Renee asked, "Think he'll consider it?"

"Slim and none."

Cale glanced over at Samantha Koon standing off in the shadows. Her eyes were misty. "But I've been wrong before," he added.

Renee arched a penciled eyebrow and said, "Remember. My exclusive, right?"

He nodded his thanks and said, "We appreciate it, Renee." Then he strode toward the exit.

Watching him depart. "Hey, Van Waring—"

He half-turned back.

"Stay out of bar fights, okay?"

Cale continued out the studio door with of friendly wave.

Two o'clock the same afternoon found Tobias Crenshaw ensconced inside his study, clicking at his laptop. Across the room, the television ran a commercial with the sound muted.

Reaching for his phone, Tobias looked up to see the chyron scroll across the screen's bottom: RENEE DOUGLAS: A SPECIAL REPORT. Wasn't she the bubblehead who'd anointed him with that ridiculous moniker?

He upped the TV volume with his remote. On the screen, the female reporter appeared constipated to Tobias. She introduced Lt. Cale Van

Waring, whom he recognized as the annoying "coyote detective." He snorted derisively.

The detective stared straight into the screen, his piercing gaze like the eyes of a mesmerist.

"The noose is tightening!" Van Waring's tone revealed confidence. "We know how you've kidnapped your victims. We know about the dimethyl."

Tobias's jaw tightened. He heard blood whooshing in his ears like a sudden discharge of steam. "

'Turn yourself in," the detective added. "The clock is ticking."

Flicking the TV off, Tobias stared at the darkened screen. His stomach muscles were tight. How could these Keystone Kops know about the DMSO? It seemed impossible.

Moving from the study into the hallway, Tobias grabbed his windbreaker from the front closet. Minutes later, he was inside the red BMW, heading for the cul-de-sac house.

Maggie had spent the entire day in her office, catching up on her backlogged cases. She was easing back into the flow of things.

The day had been productive, serving more than anything to take her mind off matters. Now it was nighttime, and she rested beside Cale on their family room couch. "I'm a little behind," she answered his question. "Nothing I can't make up in a few days."

"You'll be fine, Mags. The courts move slower than turtles on Xanax."

She curled her stocking feet beneath her. "I can't believe Slink came to the station."

"You mean Detective Lazarus?" When Maggie arched an eyebrow, he added, "Morgue humor. I'm learning from Doc Mocarek."

Hank jumped onto the couch between them and purred as Maggie scratched his neck. They'd been debating Cale's television appearance, trying to gambit the kidnapper into showing himself. It still bothered her, and she returned to the topic.

"You realize you're playing with fire, don't you? This guy's dangerous."

"I'm dangerous too. Remember?"

"But you play by rules—psychos like him don't" Maggie's eyes revealed concern.

"We've upped the stakes," he said. "Trying to stress him."

"Don't get burned, Cale. Please. Promise me?"

"I don't intend to."

The Chemist

"Nowhere Man? Chemist? Turn yourself in. We know who you are." Sob, sob. Good god! Is that the best they can come up with?

A band of eighth-graders could have contrived something cleverer. And yet, you understand the nature of the game. They're attempting to prod at you, anger you, then bait you into a mistake.

The ruse won't work. Even with the authorities changing your moniker to *The Chemist* (morons), so what? It's how you dubbed yourself, anyway. Let them bluff till their heart's content. And who cares if they've figured out about the DMSO? They've taken a wild guess and got lucky. It means nothing whatsoever. They have no evidence, no clues.

They have zilch for proof.

Still, it should never have come to this. Your attempt at invisibility has been exposed and compromised. Have you underestimated this twit detective—Van Waring? He might be a notch brighter than the average plodder, but he's light-years away from being a Mensa candidate. These amateurs fail to comprehend the intricate Chinese warfare tactics of Tsingtao. How the true artistry of battle requires fluidity, and adjustments are continuously made on both the battlefield and the Go board.

The only constant is that things change. Entropy arrives unannounced, and chaos rears its inevitable head. It's the nature of the universe at play.

Ashes to ashes, dust to dust.

The sky was dusky and overcast, the soiled clouds typical of mid-April. Anton Staszak could think of a hundred things he'd rather do on a Tuesday morning than sit in his car. He was thankful, at least, for the Buick's roominess. He could almost stretch his legs out fully if he angled them right.

Almost.

Stakeouts were an ass-pain and hardly made easier by his generous girth. If Stasz had a fin for every dull minute he'd spent on stakeouts over the years—Bingo!—he'd be living in Tahiti, surrounded by half-naked hula girls like that actor Marlon Brando. There was a guy who had it right.

Sitting alone now, Staszak had ample time to ponder Cale's strategy. On paper, it was an elementary plan. Spook the man—Crenshaw—by positioning an unmarked vehicle outside his home. Tell the slimeball they were there, not going anywhere.

Tightening the noose, as Cale had put it.

Staszak's phone chirped. He answered gruffly.

"See anything yet?" Cale asked.

"Quiet here at the Ponderosa. Red BMW sporty is parked in the driveway." Staszak sighed. "Those plates are killing me. What's C-L-S-T-U supposed to mean? Maybe claustrophobic or something?"

Cale snickered. "You were never too hot at Scrabble, were you?"

"I was good at beating the snot out of my little brother. Who said anything about Scrabble?"

"It says *Close To You*," Cale revealed. "Probably a birthday present from his wife."

"The car or the plates?"

"Likely both. They've got the dough."

Staszak grunted. His wife, Gloria, was far more pragmatic. He'd gotten a new grill starter for his birthday last year. At least she'd thrown in a sack of charcoal to go with it.

"Any signs of the wife or kids?" Cale asked. He could hear Staszak chewing before he responded.

"Got Subway to keep me company." Staszak slurped from a straw. "His kids were picked up in an aqua SUV. Wife's a negative."

"Don't drink too much soda on a stakeout, Stasz. I learned that lesson years ago."

"Right. I forgot about the whizzing. Thanks for the tip."

Parked thirty feet down the paved road from the curling driveway's front entrance, Staszak used his field glasses to study the front of the oversized home. The brownish lawn displayed the first signs of turning green. Buds were swelling in the nearby trees.

"Let me know if anything changes," Cale said.

"You got it, hoss."

CHAPTER 57

Through the window of his study, Tobias watched Bucky and Kendal climb into the back of Shelly Arrison's maroon Grand Cherokee for their ride to school. Soon they'd be free for the summer, and Tobias planned on spending more time with his kids. Perhaps even get them a new Yellow Lab puppy once his business with Mabutu was finished.

Watching the SUV drive down the curling driveway, he noticed a new wrinkle in the mundane landscape. Something disturbing.

Why was an automobile sitting not far from the driveway entrance? It was a dust-gray Buick perched along the road's shoulder. Some hard-luck driver? Maybe broke down during the night?

Tobias searched his desk drawer for his Bushnells. He stepped across the generous front foyer and into the sitting room. There he positioned himself at the far corner of the window's edge. The angle allowed him to peer out without being spotted.

The dented old Buick did not appear distressed as far as he could tell. No driver had approached the house requesting assistance or to borrow a phone. Was a tow truck en route?

When the realization dawned on him, Tobias' forehead warmed. Cops. There was likely an undercover officer inside. He'd even bet on it—either Van Waring or one of his inept henchmen. Tobias recalled the detective's pathetic message from yesterday's TV broadcast: "We know who you are. We know how you've kidnapped your victims. We know about the dimethyl."

A rictus expression tightened his face. Moving to another window ten feet away, Tobias peeked around the edge of the wispy drapes. He peered across the grounds, up the road, then at the parked vehicle from a second angle.

"Toby? What on earth are you doing?"

Marla's voice caused him to jump. He whipped his head around, his contorted face frozen. "Some motorist," Tobias stammered. "Might be stranded."

Marla frowned. "Aren't you going out to help them?"

"Yeah, sure. Of course, I will."

Tobias scuttled from the room to the foyer, where he flung open a closet door. He rummaged inside. "It's exactly what I'll do." His voice echoed in the hallway. "Just grabbing my phone in case he needs a tow."

Marla stood in the hallway, frowning while studying his odd behavior. "Are you feeling all right?"

"Tip top. Why?"

Her suspicious eyes remained on him. Deciding not to comment further, she drifted back toward the kitchen.

Returning to his study, Tobias set down the binoculars. A sardonic expression angled his narrow face. He grabbed the rolled-up morning newspaper, still wrapped in plastic, and his leather medical bag.

Up the hallway, he opened the access door to the garages.

The biggest problem with daytime stakeouts was the need to micturate. Staszak once word-searched a thesaurus during another boring surveillance. Micturate meant "to whiz, piss, drain the lizard, urinate," or—famously cheeky in the U.K.—"to shake hands with the governor." After that, he'd always kept an empty plastic jug in his trunk for such purposes.

Staszak gazed across the acres of open farmland opposite the Crenshaw estate. He'd forgotten to bring the plastic bottle this time. He was out of practice. A small stand of trees stood forty yards up the road, too far to hike. His best option was to employ his car door as a shield and hope no school bus or trotting Amish buggy came blundering along.

On the verge of opening his car door, Staszak caught a flicker of movement up near the garages. A grinding sound reached him as one garage door opened, the sound carried by the breeze off the river. A second later, the BMW's orange taillights emerged, and the vehicle wheeled around and drove away from the house.

"Son of a—" Staszak barked.

The sports car navigated down the long asphalt driveway. Staszak instinctively hunched his broad shoulders, lowering in the front seat. He wasn't trying to hide because didn't they *want* the puke to know he was being watched?

It was the game plan.

Staszak glanced at the burgundy sports car as it halted at the stone entrance pillars. Engine purring, the driver's door opened, and a man exited.

He was lean, wearing black jeans and a dark suede jacket, wore glasses, and strode confidently toward the parked Buick.

The driver—Crenshaw—carried a long object in one hand. Staszak snaked his right hand slowly inside his jacket to his holstered weapon, a reassuring gesture.

As Crenshaw neared, saying something, Staszak buzzed down his driver's-window to listen to the man's voice.

". . . sitting at my house all day," Crenshaw was saying. "You might as well at least enjoy yourself."

Staszak felt like an actor caught in bed with a key grip. Before he could speak, the man flipped the long tube-like item at the open window. "Morning paper," he called. "So you don't get bored sitting out here."

Catching the plastic-wrapped newspaper through the open window, Staszak realized it was damp and slick as if a dog had drooled on it. "What the hell!" he said out loud.

"Plastic cover," Crenshaw called back. "Protects it from the morning dew."

The man then turned and strode back to the running vehicle. Staszak stared at the newspaper in his hands. Through the window, he called, "Hey, Crenshaw!"

The man looked over his shoulder.

"We're on to you, jackass!"

Crenshaw smiled, and Staszak decided it could have been a snarl in a different light. He watched the man slip inside the BMW. The sportscar turned onto the open country road and accelerated away, heading north toward the city.

Staszak flipped the slimy newspaper onto the passenger seat. Raising the window back up, he shifted the Buick into gear. His hands were damp, and he rubbed them on the edge of his jacket.

"Scumbag," Staszak mumbled. He Y-turned on the empty road and followed the sports car at a comfortable distance. He hit his phone's speed-dial.

"Our guy's on the move," Staszak reported to Cale, feeling like some character in a spy thriller.

"Got a direction?" Cale's voice sounded tinny through the speaker.

"Toward the city. North."

"Stay on him. Loose, so he doesn't panic." Staszak noted a nervousness chipping at Cale's words. "And Anton—"

"Yeah?"

"Watch your butt. I don't need to remind you...we've got one headless victim already."

Staszak scoffed. He stared at the glowing taillights ahead. "Guy seemed friendly enough."

"You talked to him?"

"For a sec. He tossed me the morning newspaper."

Tobias navigated a roundhouse curve and downshifted the burgundy roadster. He didn't want to get too far ahead of the Buick, knowing he could run laps around the cop's tugboat if he chose. However, it was not part of his strategy.

Seconds later, he watched in his rearview mirror as the Buick caught up to him. The traffic was heavier as they neared the city outskirts.

In the distance, Tobias could see the buildings grow taller—the approaching suburbs. Smoke from a tall mill stack oozed against the blue morning sky.

A large silver Air-Stream motor home drove at him opposite, heading his way at a brisk clip. Tobias glanced in his rearview mirror at the old Buick, slowing as he came up behind an orange-colored semi-truck. Another glance behind showed the vehicle making a sudden swerve. As it corrected itself, losing ground, its tires brushed the soft dirt shoulder of the road.

Excellent, thought Tobias.

Tobias felt his smaller vehicle shimmy as the motor home rumbled by him from the opposite direction. The Airstream raked the wind like a southbound freight train.

Glancing in his rearview mirror once more, Tobias watched the Buick. He'd bought a ringside ticket to this show and planned on enjoying it.

CHAPTER 58

Cale had picked up Slink early Tuesday morning. With Maggie headed to her office to catch up on her caseload, they'd have his house to themselves—a command post in the den. Access to Cale's home PC would allow Slink to continue his Internet searches while, at the same time, they'd monitor Staszak's ongoing surveillance. Slink had also brought along his laptop. Multi-tasking. The more data they could gather on Tobias Crenshaw, the better.

They sat at the computers, Slink's arm in its sling as he typed one-handed. Cale's phone rang for the second time, and he glanced at the readout. STASZAK. Four minutes since they'd last spoken. No cause for concern. With their target on the move, updates were expected.

Cale's phone was on "speaker." Staszak's voice sounded raspy and uneven. "Fol-wing subec. Headed nor-uh..."

Cale imagined a four-martini drunk. "Stasz! Come again—I didn't copy! Repeat! Didn't copy!"

No response.

Cale glanced at Slink's worried look as he barked, "Stasz? Can you hear me?"

"Eyes not...long—"

Alarm bells sounded in their heads. Cale shouted into the phone, "Anton! Are you OK? Do you copy?" A premonition of disaster had enveloped the room. Behind the desk, Slink sat frozen, his eyes wide with alarm.

"Pull over, Stasz!" Cale yelled frantically into his phone. "Do you copy? Pull your *car* over!"

Tobias watched in his rearview mirror as the boat-sized Buick bucked across the road. The driver (cop) had over-compensated, pulling at the wheel like a charter boat captain being lashed by a typhoon. The car rocked on its suspension.

Horns blared. The older car drifted across the center line, clipping the passing Airstream's rear fender. The giant vehicle careened off the road to one side, thumping over the soft shoulder, still moving, braking, sliding. There it rumbled through the grassy culvert before coming to a halt.

The rebound force of the collision had sent the Buick screeching into a one-eighty spin. Suddenly airborne, it flipped on its side and skidded along the roadway. A shower of sparks exploded with the screaming protest of metal on asphalt.

One of the Buick's tires burst into flame, and dark smoke spewed into the air.

First, smoke, then fire. Tobias snickered to himself. In seconds, the wiring would spark, and the spewing gasoline would catch. The Buick would ignite in a glorious ball of orange-yellow flame.

"Good riddance, fatass," Tobias whispered. Shifting the Beamer into high gear, he zoomed around the orange semi like a NASCAR vet on a time-run.

Inside the den, Cale and Slink were numb. They stared at Cale's phone, listening to a thrumming silence. Moments later came a heart-gripping metallic grinding. A louder crash followed, then a whooshing sound. It reminded Cale of winds howling during a thunderstorm.

An eerie silence followed, the quiet so abrupt it sounded louder than the crash—and no doubt, more ominous.

"Staszak! Stasz!" Cale shouted at the phone. "Answer me, for God's sake!"

Slink was equally distressed. "What just happened?"

Ending the connection, re-hitting speed-dial, Cale listened to a robotic No Service voice.

"We gotta get over there," Slink suggested darkly. He was already moving toward the door.

Cale joined him, and they rushed from the house, headed for the parked Bronco in the driveway. A minute later, they were speeding street to street, grill lights flickering madly. Slink gripped the dashboard with his sling-arm hand, calling Central Dispatch with the other. He shouted into his phone: "Ten-thirty-three! Emergency! A nasty vehicular crash. Somewhere south of De Pere."

The dispatch operator requested more details, and Slink interrupted, yelling: "A police officer might be injured! Repeat. Officer down!"

The Bronco accelerated up an uncongested entry ramp and merged frantically with highway traffic. Around them, buildings and vehicles blurred past like a movie on fast-forward.

The Chemist

The stakes have been raised. You contemplate the nuances of Mabutu's latest proposal. It's the final epitaph for two former college roommates: one last victim captured, and the adventure is complete. You will disappear back into the woodwork like a specter, entrenched in the sanctity of your castle. The dark rook retired, at last, from the chess match.

You will laugh amusedly at a world of fools from your secure, relaxing perch. And you will bid a fond adieu to the Chemist.

Cindy Hulbreth awoke with a skull-stabbing headache. She listened for noises inside the house but distinguished only the hum of the furnace sending gentle currents through the vents—otherwise, nothing.

She forced herself to sit upright on the bed's edge, letting her equilibrium settle. Drugged again. But what could she do about it? Nothing. She had to eat, had to drink—had to survive.

Rising, Cindy walked zombie-legged the few feet to the dresser. Her arms were bound, and one ankle was tethered by the metallic cord attached to a bed leg. She couldn't loosen it. She'd already tried. The bed frame was bolted to the floor.

Cindy pounded her bare foot on the carpeted floor of the bedroom three times like a horse. If there were another girl downstairs, perhaps she'd hear the thumps. Maybe somehow respond.

Or was she already dead?

Cindy listened and heard nothing. With tears in her eyes, she lowered her head to the bowl atop the dresser and began to eat the dry cereal.

She had become an animal.

Tuesday morning. 11:47 by the dashboard clock. The blue windowless van sat in the parking lot of a sprawling grocery store—a different location from the previous one. Tobias was taking no chances at repeating a pattern.

He watched the flaxen-haired girl with the oval face exit her tan Kia sedan and stride toward the store. She wore a business suit beneath her raincoat, her low-heeled pumps setting off the firm shape of her calves.

A blonde for Tazeki Mabutu and his newest buyer, Tobias thought. One last *Screw you!* for old-time's sake.

He exited the van and slipped between the parked cars around him, moving steadily toward the goal. Easing past, he doused the Kia's door handle with his chemical spray.

Less than a minute later, he was back inside the van.

Cale adjusted their plan while speeding along the Interstate. Dispatch informed them the ambulance had arrived at the crash site and was already en route to the nearest trauma center, their injured victim aboard. The detectives would forego the accident scene, knowing Staszak's life might be hanging by a thread.

Ten minutes later, Cale swung the Bronco into the center's entrance and parked beneath a parking ramp overhang. Ambulance lights spun a short distance away as an efficient hospital crew unloaded Anton Staszak—an EMT and RN team working with rehearsed precision.

Cale rushed up beside the moving gurney with his badge held high. Slink kept pace like a shadow, four steps behind him.

"How's it looking?" Cale asked one of the med techs. They continued rolling forward, the stretcher aimed at the opened ER doors.

"Extensive blood loss. Shoulder's mangled." The man's voice was clinical. "BP's steady, head bash is likely a fractured skull."

"Stasz?" Cale's eyes were lasers as they continued along the sidewalk. "Can you hear me?"

Staszak's eyes rolled open at the sound of his name. He was semi-lucid, like a lizard awakened from the cold.

"News...black...off," Staszak stammered. Then his eyes closed, and he lapsed into unconsciousness.

The detectives pulled up short in their advance, standing helplessly by as their partner was wheeled through the gaping doors of the entrance.

"What's that supposed to mean?" Slink asked, bewildered. "'News? Black off?'"

Cale shook his head. No matter how he worked the phrase over in his head, he failed to decipher any sense.

CHAPTER 59

Cale phoned the dispatch operator from the street curb. He stood twenty feet away now, separated from the commotion. "Patch me through to any unit working the crash site. Yes. County Double-Q."

Thirty seconds later, a gruff voice came on the line. The man identified himself as Sergeant Mahone, Brown County Sheriff's Department.

Cale ID'd himself. Rescue had already identified Anton Staszak at the scene via his DL and police ID. Staszak was a Green Bay homicide detective. Cale informed them the man was one of his long-time partners.

"Any prelim on the accident cause?" Cale pressed.

"It's looking like your friend passed out at the wheel," MacMahon said, keeping his tone nonjudgmental. "Got three witnesses saying he swerved into an oncoming motor home."

The imagery made Cale shudder. He'd been on the phone with Staszak as he had lost control of his car.

"Gas tank split. Lucky he wasn't fried."

In the background, Cale could hear the cackle of radios and the whoosh of passing traffic along the county highway. "Did you find anything suspicious? Inside the vehicle?"

"We bagged a few small items. Nothing much." The officer paused. "Got a reason for asking, Lieutenant?"

Cale knew it wasn't time to hedge, not when each passing minute might prove crucial. "First, it wasn't an accident," he said. "Second, Detective Staszak and I are working an active homicide case. I was on the phone with him when—"

"We've got a trucker claiming—"

"Sergeant," Cale interrupted. "Can you tell me what you've found?"

A minute lapsed before the officer came back on the line. "Let's see. Service revolver, couple of ballpoints. Pair of empty Mountain Dew cans, a fast-food bag, and a single tennis shoe—female. Subway wrappers. Today's rolled newspaper is still in the wrapping. The phone's smashed nearly to bits." The sergeant paused before adding, "Pretty much covers it."

Cale remembered Staszak's statement from earlier: *"Guy seemed friendly enough. He tossed me the morning paper."*

He requested they not touch anything else and indicated that the sergeant should consider the accident an attempted homicide—part of an ongoing investigation. He was sending a forensic tech team out to the site at once.

"Four credible eyewitnesses, Detective," MacMahon spoke evenly. "Far as accidents go, this one seems pretty cut-and-dried."

"Trust me, Sergeant," Cale said with authority. "It may look like it to you, but it's anything but cut-and-dried."

Dusty Harold's real name wasn't "Dusty." It was Abraham. But since he'd begun working as a crime scene tech fifteen years ago, he'd been called "Dusty." The nickname, not surprisingly, had stuck.

Cale asked the man on the phone, "How soon can you have a team out there?"

"Fifteen minutes, Lieutenant," Dusty said. "Twenty tops."

Cale told him to drop everything else. The county road crash was now a priority. Dusty asked, "Are we searching for anything specific?"

"Pay attention to the soft drink cans or bottles. The food wrappers. And especially the newspaper."

"Newspaper?"

"Yes. Wrapped in plastic. Check for indicators of foreign substances or dried drug residue."

Cale conversed on his phone with Captain McBride in one corner of the ICU waiting room. In a somber voice, he reported, "We lost the tail."

"You mean the tail no one authorized?" McBride sounded frustrated and annoyed.

Cale stared across the room where Slink and Janet were seated. Janet held Gloria Staszak's hand as she dabbed away tears with a handkerchief.

There were times when Cale's job frustrated him. His friend was on the operating table, yet they still had to work the case. The troops marched on. "Collateral damage" was how Staszak and Slink's injuries were considered.

The captain asked, "You think this guy Crenshaw is behind the crash somehow?"

"Bet my pension on it."

McBride sighed. "So now what? We got a Plan B, here?"

"We need an APB out on Crenshaw's red BMW."

"Not without evidence." McBride was silent for a moment. "We can't risk a harassment suit. Not with the O'Hern thing still hanging out there."

The captain was right. Cale understood they could not risk even more negative fallout. Nor could they send officers to Crenshaw's home or business offices without solid proof of wrongdoing. And no judge would sign a search warrant. The haystack may have shrunk, but the needle remained elusive.

Cale recalled Marla Crenshaw giving him the tour of her magnificent residence. The family pictures on the fireplace mantle flashed through his head. The pretty little girl, the boy with green-and-gold-colored braces. The smiling Yellow Lab. Candy? Wasn't it the poor dog's name?

He wondered if he was jealous of Crenshaw's perfect family, his ideal life. What if he was wrong about the guy?

McBride's voice broke into Cale's thoughts. "Not enough for a warrant. But I'll have watch command give our street units a heads-up. BOLO his red BMW."

It was better than nothing. The entire bloody mess had been Cale's plan—Staszak and Slink were blameless—and had seemed so promising. Flush out the quail, get him on the move, see if he'd panic.

He'd panicked all right, as the results now showed. Cale said, "Slink and I are hitting the streets. I'll call if we come up with anything."

"Dooley?" McBride barked. "Dooley's inactive!"

A nurse in blue scrubs entered with what looked to be an update. Cale held his phone at arm's length. "What did you say, Cap? Sorry...losing you—"

Knowing his neck was on the chopping block, he ended the call. Cale would accept whatever sentence fate dished out. Besides, there was one thing he'd wager heavily on—that Slink wouldn't sit home on his couch. Not any more than he would if their positions were reversed.

Not with Staszak lying on the operating table.

It was a risk Cale would take as long as the monster remained trolling the city's streets.

Maggie awoke in a cheerfully pleasant mood Tuesday morning, one unfamiliar to her over the past few weeks of relationship uncertainty. A prescient idea enlightened her outlook: *Whatever happens, things will turn out all right.*

After her teary-eyed discussion with Cale the other night and his swearing he'd get them back on an upbeat track—how much he adored her and promised he was in it for the long haul—Maggie now felt an overwhelming sense of relief.

Cale had informed her they would move forward again as a devoted couple. They'd begin discussing marriage plans and Maggie's dream of starting a family together. She felt as if she could finally breathe again.

Best of all, Maggie abandoned her obstinate decision to leave the house in early July.

She almost immediately felt the stress lift from her back and vanish.

Maggie had been a miserable wreck over the past weeks—burdened, edgy, disheartened—and couldn't wait to share with Chloe the good news. Stability would return, and she and Cale were a wholesome unit again.

Not everything, however, was peaches-and-cream. Maggie couldn't predict how long it would take to cleanse the Juan-Julio Sanchez incident from her memory. But time healed all wounds. So at least, she was now headed in a positive direction.

Later at work, reading over transcripts on a drama-filled wife-beats-husband domestic case, Maggie's desk phone buzzed. She answered calmly, and her seemingly brighter outlook took seconds to shatter. Cale informed her that Anton Staszak had been injured in a vehicle accident. Hurt badly but hanging on. He knew she'd want to know.

Maggie told him that, of course, she would join her friends in this time of need.

That was twenty minutes ago. As the nurse approached, Maggie held Gloria's hand in the ICU waiting room. She shifted her eyes to Slink and Janet, two chairs away, doing the same.

At least the news was positive. Thank God.

A minute later, Cale arrived. Maggie rose from her chair, and they hugged. He pressed his cheek to her hair, remaining steady as she thumbed away her tears.

The surgery, they'd been informed, had gone well. Staszak had survived, and his vital signs were stable. The surgeons felt optimistic about the long-term outcome.

Cale nodded at Slink, and his partner walked anxiously to them. Cale hugged Maggie again and said, "Sorry. We've got to run."

"But you only just—"

"Stasz's accident involves our case. I'll call you. And see you at home later." Her smile was supportive.

Cale hugged Gloria, patting her shoulder. "Anton's a mule, so don't worry. He'll be out of here in no time."

The detectives departed through the swinging doors.

CHAPTER 60

The trench-coated woman strode from the store's sliding exit doors and headed across the parking lot. She paused, allowing a pair of boys on bicycles to pedal past. Around them, the lot was half-filled with cars. A honk caused her to look left. Then she proceeded up the parking lane.

Having swapped the BMW for his blue van again, Tobias watched her every step. The afternoon sky was clouded, and the girl's blond hair wisped in the breeze. She walked with a confident stride.

Arriving at the Kia, the woman popped the trunk remotely, inserted the packages, and closed it. She grabbed the driver's door handle and paused, staring at her hand for a second.

Tobias saw her crinkle her nose from inside the van and scan the parking area. Spotting no one suspicious, she wiped her hand on the sleeve of her coat before slipping into her car.

Tobias pulled from his parking spot. Employing his side mirrors, he backed the van down the lane, easing to a halt behind the parked Kia.

The trap was set.

Jessica Handy was in somewhat of a hurry. Her hair appointment was scheduled for four o'clock. Then she had to rush home to prepare dinner for her fiancé. Inside her car, she wondered about the dampness on her door handle.

She wiped her coat again for good measure and started up the vehicle. One foot on the brake, she shifted into reverse while at the same time glancing over her shoulder.

"Ohmygod!" she cried out, slamming her brake foot down. A blue van was parked behind her, and she hadn't even noticed it. She could have plowed right into him.

"Settle down, Jess," she said out loud. She forced calmness into her voice that she didn't feel. No harm, no foul. It could have been far worse.

Jessica placed the gearshift back in park and took several deep breaths.

It was early afternoon, and Maggie headed back to her office. Driving from the trauma center, she answered her phone on the second chirp. Chloe.

She gave her sister the rundown regarding Anton Staszak's accident and how fortunate he was to be alive.

Chloe, ever compassionate, relayed her sincerity for things turning out well for everyone.

"I guess it's in God's hands," Maggie agreed.

After thirty minutes at her office, she filled her satchel with paperwork. She'd head home, understanding she needed to stay busy to prevent her mind from thinking about Anton.

She stopped at a downtown intersection.

The sky was covered with soot-gray clouds in the north. Noticing a few windshield sprinkles, Maggie gave the wipers a swipe. Her phone chirped.

Chloe again, and she could sense hesitation in her sister's voice. "Chlo? Is everything all right?"

"I didn't tell you, Mags, but I had a . . .vision. Late last night. It was intense."

Maggie kept things light. "You're the family psychic. You're supposed to get visions, right?"

"Not like—this was the real deal."

Her voice chilled Maggie, and an iciness tingled up her spine. She paused at an intersection across a city park and watched the wind sway the high treetops.

"*Real* is good, isn't it?" she asked.

Maggie didn't know much about "visions" other than her sister had been experiencing them since they were young.

Chloe said haltingly, "The problem is you were in it, Mags. And it wasn't coming out so hot."

Tobias stared out the van's window at the Kia. He watched the girl move her head around, growing more agitated at the large vehicle blocking her backward exit.

The drugs were taking effect. He glanced at his watch. Two forty-four...two forty-three...

His attention back on the vehicle, he saw the girl's head loll onto her shoulders. She snapped it back. Close now, very close.

A car horn blasted.

Tobias checked behind himself. Saw nothing. Inside the Kia, the woman had slumped forward in her seatbelt. The horn, he now knew, had bleated the coarse note due to a butt of her forehead.

Tobias noticed a big-bellied man in a cowboy hat now approaching the vehicle. The stranger peered inside, rapped the glass, and pulled the handle. His mind racing, Tobias guessed the girl must've shifted her car into gear. She locked herself inside.

This is a bubbling cauldron, his head voice warned. *Get out of here now!*

Other pedestrians were walking opposite the lane, some rubbernecking at the Good Samaritan cowboy.

Tobias checked all his mirrors and cautiously proceeded forward, mindful of his speed. He eased past the final cars in the row. He swung across open asphalt like a boat escaping a harbor and angled toward the exit. Perspiration warmed his forehead and steamed his lower back. It had been a narrow escape, but an escape, nonetheless.

CHAPTER 61

The Bronco was parked in the alley outside the hospital's south entrance with police credentials clipped to the visor. A breeze ruffled Cale's hair as he and Slink slid inside the vehicle. He felt overwhelmed by the string of increasingly bizarre events. First, his partner gets shot; then, Shirley Koon is abducted. And here was Staszak now, bloody and battered, luckily pried from a coffin of twisted metal.

Terrible things happened in threes, didn't they? Hopefully, this was the end of it. They were due for a decent twist of good fortune. Wishful thinking, Cale decided, but so be it.

From the passenger seat, Slink broke the silence. "Have we got a next move, Kemosabe?"

"Back to the station." Cale keyed the ignition. "We need more intel on this Crenshaw. There must be something we're missing."

"Cap booted me out, remember?"

"Screw it. I'm booting you back in. We need every hand on deck."

Slink nodded gravely.

"Besides, it's personal now."

Dirty clouds churned across the sullen afternoon sky. A light mist glistened the Bronco's windshield. In the silence, Cale worked things over in his mind. If Doc Mocarek's theory was accurate, Crenshaw had likely drugged Staszak like his previous victims. The sedatives caused him to lose control of his vehicle. If the toxicology prelims proved out, they could get a warrant to search the guy's home. And if Dusty Harold uncovered anything else at the accident scene, even better.

Still, the case contained too many "ifs," and the mystery confounded the detectives.

Cale's buzzing phone broke into his thoughts. He pressed "speaker" for Slink's benefit. "It's Burke, Lieutenant," the scratchy voice said. "Dispatch patched me through to your cell."

"Yeah, Burke?"

"We've got a strange parking lot incident. Thought you might want a look-see."

Cale discerned the familiar crackle of police radios in the background. Burke continued, "Female found unconscious in her vehicle. Drugged, the EMTs confirm. Possibly an aborted two-oh-seven."

"Kidnapping? Where is she now?"

Cale felt Slink's stare.

Burke conveyed the address. It was a large shopping mall on the city's east side. They were eight minutes away. "Keep her at the scene. And get an evidence tech there ASAP."

He flipped on the Bronco's grill flashers.

Slink's features appeared chiseled in the blue afternoon light. He said, "We nail him this time, right?"

Cale's nod confirmed the sentiment.

Tobias drove his van south through the city. His heart was no longer thrumming. Each stoplight and every corner turn separated him further from the parking lot fiasco.

He needed to concentrate. Stop fleeing ghosts. No one was following, and no one knew a thing. He imagined shoppers gathered around the Kia, peering in through the windows. A young woman had passed out in her car. Nothing more.

Tobias smirked evilly, and a soft drizzle began to spot his windshield.

A blue van at the scene? He doubted anyone had noticed. Why would they? Regardless, it would make sense to switch vehicles again.

He recalled the detective's threat on TV. "We know how you've kidnapped them. We know about the dimethyl."

Tobias understood the clock was ticking, whether they found a foreign substance on the Kia's door handle or didn't. He pictured the pesky detective, Van Waring. The man was becoming his personal Inspector Javert, closing on him with each passing minute. An idea popped into his head—something worth considering.

Changing course abruptly, enough for a Volvo to bleat its horn, Tobias pulled into a gas station. He parked close to an older pay phone, positioned away from the island of pumps. His new idea played the way chess masters digest their every move—the same way he'd solved abstract chemistry calculations in his sleep for years.

The solution was simple. To extract from his partnership with Mabutu, Tobias needed three female victims delivered to the Liberian. All three healthy and alive. It was the original deal they had struck.

"Van Waring," Tobias whispered aloud. His guts clenched as he pictured the detective. How much did the man know?

Opening his phone's back casing, he removed the SIM card and tossed it out the window into a nearby weed bed. Tobias then withdrew a new burner phone from his medical bag and powered it on.

Donning his ballcap, he exited the van.

Traffic cruised on the street with a whoosh of slick tires. The drizzle had stopped, and the air smelled metallic.

With his windbreaker collar turned up and head angled away from the station's cameras, Tobias thumbed through the older phonebook pages attached to a metallic sliver cord. Seconds later, he had the address.

He ripped the page free and hopped back inside the van.

CHAPTER 62

A trio of police cruisers had joined a county sheriff's squad car. An ambulance completed the parking lot grouping along with the tan Kia. Cale was reminded of a circle of covered wagons as the Bronco joined them.

He parked near a cruiser and exited with Slink.

Approaching the officers' huddle, Cale asked if they had any witnesses. Informed there were none, they directed him to a parked cruiser twenty yards away. Sitting with the door open, Sgt. Burke tapped his report on an iPad.

Burke noticed Cale's approach and continued to tap. "Got names and addresses for you," he said while typing, "if you need them."

Looking back at the Kia, Cale saw Slink conversing with the paramedics attending to a man seated on the ground. The heavyset man held a Stetson in his lap.

"What's with the cowpoke?" Cale asked Burke.

The sergeant explained how the man was the first to spot the girl unconscious in her vehicle but had witnessed no crime. He couldn't open the locked door. "Weird thing is," Burke added, "he almost passed out afterward, himself."

Cale glanced again at the man with his Stetson. "Is he okay now?"

"EMTs say fine. He's a diabetic—maybe late with his shot."

Five minutes later, Jessica Handy sat in the passenger seat of the Bronco. To Cale, she appeared nervous, her expression like someone uncertain if they'd broken the law.

Jessica remained clueless about what had happened to her. She had consumed a minimal salad for lunch, which likely accounted for becoming lightheaded.

"You notice any strangers?" Cale asked, attempting to jog her memory. "Anyone fooling around near your car? Acting out of the ordinary?"

She shook her head.

She was attractive, he noted, examining her through the eyes of a perpetrator. Was there anything that made her stand out enough to become another victim? Like the two others, she had blond hair and seemed confident and self-assured. Otherwise, there was nothing extraordinary.

"I've got a killer headache," Jessica confessed, massaging her left temple. "Like a hammer pounding."

"You've been drugged."

"How?"

He asked, instead, "Once you were inside your car, do you remember what you did?"

Jessica relayed how she'd begun feeling dizzy within a minute of entering her Kia. The next thing she knew, she'd come-to lying in the parking lot in an oxygen mask.

"Do you recall putting your car in gear?"

"Yes. I almost backed up and hit a guy. Why?"

"In gear would have auto-locked your doors." He smiled at her gently. "It's why he couldn't get in. Do you remember what the vehicle looked like?"

She shook her head. "I don't remember much of anything."

The evidence tech's name was Trudy. She knelt inside the Kia, dusting nearly every inch for prints. Cale directed her attention, instead, to the outer door handles, and she arched her eyebrows.

"Check for any sort of residue," Cale directed. "A liquid sedative might've been applied.

"Whatever you say, Lieutenant."

Cale noticed Slink walking his way, swinging his bandaged arm like a jaunty sailor. To Trudy, he added, "Also, have the lab check for traces of a solvent called DMSO."

"Dimethyl sulfoxide?"

"Head of the class, Trudy." He winked at her.

As Slink arrived, Cale asked, "He's diabetic, right?"

Slink nodded. "Got knocked flat on his butt. Doesn't think it was a sugar level drop."

Twenty yards away, the cowboy had risen in his boots and relayed his story to a trio of senior citizens.

"Is he a real cowboy?" Cale asked.

"Are you a real detective?"

"I've got a gold badge."

"He's got a cool Stetson."

The Bronco pulled from the parking lot and merged with the afternoon traffic. Cale left Maggie a voice message, telling her he'd be home by five. He imagined she was still comforting Gloria at the hospital.

"By the way," Slink stated, "I spoke to Mags at the hospital yesterday." He glanced at Cale. "She says you guys have patched up your differences. So congrats."

"We're finished with the drama." Cale didn't bother hiding his grin.

Tobias swung the BMW to the curb. It had taken him fifteen minutes to tuck the blue van inside his storage garage and exchange vehicles. He was now parked four blocks away on a quiet, tree-lined side street.

He extracted his tablet from the medical bag and used his real estate software to access the city property logs. Ten minutes later, he had all the information he needed. He turned off the tablet and set it on the passenger seat.

Tobias flicked on the car's CD player. Springsteen blasted loudly, infusing the air about being born in the USA. It was Tobias's anthem of sorts. Shifting the Beamer into gear, he tapped out the rhythm on the steering wheel as he drove.

Her legal name was Magdalene Jeffers.

Would she mind very much if he called her Maggie?

Forty minutes later, Slink sat at his station desk, hunting and pecking at his keyboard with the fingers of both hands. Concentrating, he forgot about his shoulder until yanking at the stitches reminded him. Regardless, Slink would rather be here doing something positive than sitting at home wasting precious time.

Captain McBride stepped from his office and spotted Cale's approach down the hallway. He bobbed his head in Slink's direction. "He's not on meds, is he?"

"Negative, Cap," Cale said. "Can't blame him for wanting to help. It's personal—with the way things went with Staszak."

Outside the windows, the sky was darkening. It was mid-afternoon, and the lack of color cast a grim pallor over the city.

"I saw Stasz right after," Cale said, frowning. "Busted up pretty good."

"This Crenshaw better be our guy." McBride's expression was tight. "Things will blow sky-high otherwise."

Cale pulled his phone free, checking for messages.

"Bingo!" Slink called from his desk. He glanced their way. "Might have something here."

Cale and McBride converged on his workstation.

CHAPTER 63

Eyeing Slink's desktop screen, Cale wondered why his partner was so revved-up. McBride was equally perplexed. They were staring at multiple rows of figures highlighted in translucent green.

"Financial info on one Tobias Powell Crenshaw," Slink said. "Age thirty-eight. I pulled it off the county tax registry."

Powell. The name's mention thundered in Cale's head. The boxes were clicking into place.

Slink explained he'd discovered an Appleton PO Box listed under "Powell," a single surname, as Carlos had suggested. They could now classify it as a suspected drug drop and put an APB on Tobias Crenshaw's red BMW.

McBride knitted his brow. "Works for me."

"The tags are easy enough to spot." Cale wrote out C-L-S-T-Y-U on a notepad. He flashed it at Slink, who rolled his eyes before handing it to the captain.

"How about a narcotics warrant? Search his zillion-dollar home as well?" Cale asked hopefully.

"It'll never fly with the DA," McBride said. "We're on shaky enough ground as it is. We've got only hearsay on Crenshaw being this Powell guy."

They were silent, thinking about it. Cale addressed Slink: "Can you hack Crenshaw's medical records? Or his wife's?"

Without another word, McBride turned and strode back to his office. Cale hovered over his partner's shoulder as he typed in the search.

"It might take a while. Stuff's encrypted to the max." Slink continued to clack at his keyboard, adding his left fingers as best he could, careful of the shoulder stitches.

The intercom buzzed at Cale's desk. He stepped over to answer. It was Dusty Harold from the forensics lab.

"Struck out on Kia's door handle. Maybe the drizzle. But we picked up the residue of dimethyl sulfoxide on the wrapped newspaper in Staszak's car."

Cale requested they fax him the results. They'd need a copy to apply for a search warrant. Hanging up, he noted it was almost 4 p.m. His phone chirped. It was Maggie's sister.

"Hey, Chloe—"

Before Cale could utter another syllable, she dove headlong into describing her latest vision: Dark and dangerous, murky images involving Maggie. Her sister was in imminent peril, Chloe insisted. Not to mention Maggie had chosen to slough off her warnings.

"I'm sure she—"

Jumping his comment again, Chloe protested how it might already be too late.

"Listen. Chloe—"

"I know you think it's nonsense."

"I didn't say—"

"Cale," she interrupted again, "I *scary* believe this. You've got to make her listen."

He promised to call Maggie at once, and they ended the chat. Staring at his silent phone now felt louder than Chloe's tirade. Cale hit autodial and got Maggie's voicemail again.

"Hey. I'm still at work," he reported, glancing out the window at the dreary afternoon sky. Soft raindrops were glistening on the glass. Cale added, "Call me when you get this. Okay?"

CHAPTER 64

Arriving home that afternoon, Maggie parked her Mazda on the driveway apron. After time at the trauma center consoling her friends, then briefly back at her office, she hoped the day's stress was behind her.

Departing for home, Maggie had muted her phone, mainly to avoid speaking with Chloe about her distressing "visions" of pending doom and destruction.

With Slink in the hospital the day before, and Anton now lying in the recovery unit, she couldn't abide hearing about darkness any longer. Enough was enough.

Maggie approached the backdoor carrying her work satchel and purse. The on-off drizzle had let up, yet the clouds remained, making her surroundings feel like a gloomy harbor after a storm. Puddles dotted the driveway, and she could discern dripping from the tree branches. At least the roof's overhang had shielded the side-porch door. Maggie inserted her key in the lock and noticed the handle felt damp while turning it.

Wiping her hand on her jacket, she entered the house. She set her things on the kitchen counter and washed her hands in the sink.

Maggie spotted the tiny light blinking on the answering machine in the dining room. Before she could press the button, Hank trotted up to greet her, and she lifted him, smushing her face against his until he squirmed free and plopped back to the floor. She rewarded him by filling his food dish.

While Hank chomped his dry food, Maggie listened to the machine's message. It was Chloe again, frantically demanding she return her call. "Sorry, sis. Not right now," she whispered aloud. Then Maggie walked down the hallway, kicking her shoes off before ascending the stairs in her stocking feet.

Maggie made for the bathroom in the bedroom, pulling her sweater over her head as she walked. As she turned, her reflection in the mirror swam out of focus.

"Whoa!" She gripped the sink with both hands and waited for the sensation to pass. Looking back in the mirror, she noticed her cheeks and neck flushed.

What had she eaten today? Not much. She'd been either at the hospital or her office. Her carb count must be low. With her brain lusting for a sandwich, Maggie moved back into the bedroom and peeled off her slacks. Another wave of lightheadedness swept over her, and she steadied herself by grabbing the dresser. Maggie's reflection in the full-length closet door mirror revealed her standing in a bra and panties, looking warped around the edges. Another wave of dizziness swam through her and settled sourly in her stomach.

So much for the sandwich.

Was she coming down with a flu bug? No surprise. She'd spent most of the afternoon at the hospital and read it's where most illnesses congregated.

A new wave of dizziness assaulted her with a head rush. Glancing up, she was surprised to notice the dark silhouette standing in the doorway, backlit against the window at the hallway's end. For a weird moment, Maggie thought of Juan-Julio Sanchez. Was he released from jail already? Set loose for providing Cale with information about the kidnapping case?

Not possible, Maggie decided. No way he'd be released this soon.

"Cale? What are you—"

"Sorry, sweetie." The stranger's voice was low. "You got Door Number Two."

It wasn't a voice she recognized. Maggie's face flushed, and her mouth suddenly tasted like sandpaper. She forced herself to swallow, maintaining her composure.

"Who are you? What are you doing in my house?"

He offered her a half-smile while edging forward into the bedroom.

"Hello, Maggie," the stranger said frankly. "I was hoping you'd be a blonde."

Cale sat down heavily at his desk. The excitement of the chase, the adrenaline rush—if indeed it were coming—had failed to reach him yet.

Stationed three desks away, his computer humming, Slink glanced at him. "The APB's out on the wire. I'm checking GPS," he reported. "We should get something soon."

"The guy's making mistakes. He might be cracking."

Cale hoped it was true. Every misstep Crenshaw took brought them closer to stopping his terror spree. He pictured Staszak lying in the ICU. Then his thoughts shifted to the missing girls and their devastated families.

Too many lives hung in the balance for them to fail.

Cale grabbed his desk phone and called the FBI office in Milwaukee. ,

Special Agent Eddie Redtail answered on the third ring. Cale decided it best to update the FBI head on their case, revealing what they'd discovered and where they stood. He described the DMSO-plus-sedatives theory and how their perpetrator possibly incapacitated his victims. The kidnapper would drive away in each victim's vehicle, escaping the abduction scene.

No struggling, no witnesses, and no clues.

"It explains the disappearance of the cars," said Redtail, thinking it through. "Along with the seasonality aspect. He'd need decent weather for his compound to work outdoors."

Cale agreed. Indoors, the guy would have been spotted by security cameras; outdoors, any coldness or precipitation would likely interfere with the rapid absorption through the victim's skin.

"All you need now is a suspect."

Anticipating the response, Cale said, "We've got a primary. He missed another snatch-and-grab in a parking lot a few hours ago."

"Your guy's accelerating," said the agent clinically. "Some external stressors must be speeding up his time frame."

Cale hoped that he, himself, was the stressor. "Do you think his mental state is different than before?"

"If he's disintegrating, he'll become more desperate. And hopefully more careless."

Cale pictured Tobias Crenshaw's handsome face around the cagey eyes and insincere smile. Crenshaw's family waved at him from the front steps of their *casa muy grande*.

"Remember what I told you, Cale," Agent Redtail said. "Approach this guy with caution."

"Right. Like coming at a cornered rat with a stick."

"It's how he'll react."

After a pause, "Good," Cale said. "Cornered rats are my specialty."

With a promise to keep him updated, Cale ended the call. He stepped past Slink, who continued attempting to access Crenshaw's encrypted medical records. Cale grabbed his jacket to depart. He waved his phone at his partner, who nodded.

Cale decided that sitting around was driving him crazy. He needed some fresh air and to check in with Maggie.

Maggie took an unsteady step toward the bed. Her horror mounted with every thud of her heart, and she could barely feel her numb legs and feet. Where was Cale when she needed him?

Her phone chirped. She couldn't recall where she'd left it—the bathroom? Maggie wanted to move, but her legs were frozen in place. The shadowy stranger across the room grinned at her. Her vision had turned colorless, filtered by a smeary gray lens. She balanced one hand on the mattress. "Whoever you are, get out of here *now!*"

The intruder cocked his head, his expression thoughtful. His eyeglasses gave him an academic look. Was he a threat, or did she imagine it?

"Please leave! Or I'm calling the police."

The man appraised her in silence.

Then it dawned on Maggie what he was doing. He was waiting.

Waiting for what?

"*Get out, now!*"

Her voice echoed in her head, and dark wasps swarmed at her from the room's edges. Maggie tried swatting at them, but her arms wouldn't function. A *meow* sounded far away, and she watched Hank enter the bedroom.

Maggie lurched forward, both of her hands gripping the bedspread. "Hank! No! Run!" She attempted screaming—*enraged!*—trying to get to the doorway. Yet she only emitted rasping sounds as she toppled face-first to the mattress.

Then she watched, horrified, as the male stranger stepped sideways and kicked the small animal. She heard Hank's wail, followed by a sickening thud as he smashed hard against one sidewall. Lying on the carpet, the feline failed to move.

Maggie's eyes were tearing, and she gasped for breath.

"No worries." The man's voice was hypnotic. "You'll feel better in a minute."

The swarm of wasps closed in further, and Maggie fought desperately to keep her eyes open. She lay frozen, unable to move an inch.

With a buttery voice, the man said, "Doesn't it feel much better now?"

Then the black wasps overcame her, dragging her down into a cave of total darkness.

CHAPTER 65

Cale strode across the parking lot and was about to open the Bronco when his phone sounded. He prayed it was Maggie. Instead, it was Slink.

"Almost forgot," his partner said, "I re-checked. The auto body reports zilch on the missing vehicles. None of their sources have heard anything, either."

The after-work traffic swept along the side streets. The air felt swollen, but the misting had stopped.

"Cars don't just disappear in thin air." Cale nodded to a pair of officers coming off shift. "Nor people. Are we dealing with David Copperfield here?"

Slink didn't laugh. "I uncovered more fun facts about the Crenshaw family. You might want to get back in here."

A minute later, Cale stood over his partner's shoulder. Slink typed two-handed without flinching. Cale wondered if he might be secreting meds. He kept the idea to himself.

"Marla Crenshaw, the wife," Slink said solidly. "Sold fifteen real estate properties over the past two years. Five of them to a company called Bermuda Holdings Group."

"Doesn't ring a bell."

"That's the point." Slink sipped from a water bottle. "It's a front. Want to guess who's on their Board of Directors."

Cale only smirked.

"None other than Tobias Crenshaw," Slink answered.

Cale's insides tightened as his mind considered what it meant. "So his wife sold properties to her husband's dummy Corp? Any chance she's in on this?"

Slink leaned back in his chair. "Marla may not have a clue he's behind the purchases. She sold them to a holding group."

Cale arched an eyebrow as Slink further clarified that Bermuda Holdings had also purchased three properties in Appleton, Wisconsin. Thirty miles away. The other two were local, in Green Bay.

"The problem is," Slink continued, "I can't find the Green Bay addresses listed anywhere on the city rolls. It just says BHG. Their shorthand title."

"How about utility bills?" Cale leaned closer, studying the address listings. "Water? Electric? Can't we access them from those?"

"I tried it. They're hacked out of the system. Wiped clean, like they don't exist."

The Chemist, Cale thought gloomily. Maybe their suspect was a master magician, after all, along with being a computer geek who disguised his digital footprints. He took two steps away from Slink's paper-strewn desk to assess these new revelations. Turning, Cale announced, "I'm driving out to Crenshaw's place."

"Phones use less gas."

"I want to see Marla Crenshaw's face when she tells me she doesn't know anything about all this."

Cale zipped his windbreaker as he strode past the desks. "Besides," he called over his shoulder, "if Crenshaw's car shows, I'll arrest him on the APB."

"Do you need backup?"

Cale shook his head. "Just let Maggie know I'll be late for dinner again."

Cindy Hulbreth's breaths were soft. She couldn't feel her chest rise. Tucked beneath the covers, she listened for noises. She heard the garage door grinding, followed moments later by an opening door. Then came shuffling footsteps as if something heavy was being dragged across a floor.

Another body? Like her own?

Shadowman had returned to the house again, and an icy shiver ascended Cindy's spine. Had he kidnapped another victim? Similar to the unknown person locked in the basement where she had previously been imprisoned?

Cindy burrowed beneath the sour, crusted blankets. She listened to the scraping sounds until they stopped in the hallway outside her door.

In frozen silence, she tried not to breathe.

The night's dark hammer drops quickly in the spring. The Crenshaw estate stood quiet in the early evening shadows. The inside lights were ablaze, however, shining like some church cathedral. Down the sloping back lawns, the brackish water of the river flowed past, its surface stippled once more by the fall of raindrops.

Cale eased to a halt in the circular front drive. He cut the Bronco's ignition, catching the wiper blades in mid-sweep. He habitually checked the

Glock's ammo clip—safety on. Holstering the weapon beneath his jacket, he exited the vehicle.

The front door opened before he could knock, and he found himself staring into the attractive made-up face of Marla Crenshaw. She had ditched the soccer mom act for a pantsuit and low-heeled pumps, looking like she might be headed out to dinner somewhere.

Marla raised her eyebrows. "Detective Van Waring? What a surprise."

"Mind if I come in? I've got a few questions maybe you can help me with."

After frowning, she ushered him into the house, and Cale's senses were on high alert. Could Crenshaw be lurking around some unseen corner? He recalled Agent Redtail's cautionary warning. *"Like coming at a cornered rat with a stick . . . ."*

"Is your husband around?"

"Tobias? Not right now. I'm not sure when he'll be back. He knows I've got bridge club."

He stopped short of another appraising look, and she offered him a timid smile. Did women these days dress up to play cards? If so, it was news to Cale. But then the world was full of surprises.

He followed her through the foyer, passing at least three rooms with open double doors. Both children were present this time around. Little Kendal sat at a dining room table with blond hair twisted into French braids. She played a board game with a teenage girl, who Cale guessed was the sitter. They both laughed, ignoring him. He spotted young Bucky, feet up on a sofa in the TV room. The boy worked a Game Boy and failed to look up as the adults shadowed past.

Marla led him into a parlor room. She said, "Not more problems with coyotes, I trust?" Tiny crow's feet crinkled the corners of her eyes.

Cale sat on the edge of a wingback chair. "It's a different matter this time."

She remained standing, and an uneasy silence formed between them.

"The other day, I couldn't help noticing your husband's sports car."

"There hasn't been an accident—" Her eyes widened.

"No. Nothing of the sort."

Marla sat down gently on the edge of a loveseat.

"His license plates? Just asking for my curiosity?"

"Oh, that." Her eyes showed relief. "It's the first song we danced to—one of those silly things. We even played it at our wedding. Corny, I know." Her blush was genuine.

Cale wondered briefly what his and Maggie's song might be. Did they have one? He decided that if Marla Crenshaw were an actress, he'd nominate her for an Emmy.

Withdrawing a small notebook, he flipped it open. "Real estate? Part-time, you said?" Marla issued him a puzzled look. Cale added, "Do you recall selling any property to a company called Bermuda Holdings? Would've been a few years back."

"Of course," Marla confessed. She remembered the sales. Three were commercial office buildings outside the city limits; the other two were local single-family homes. "The singles were somewhat unusual," she volunteered.

"How so?"

"Corporations seldom purchase residential properties."

"But a sale's a sale, right?" Cale widened his eyes.

Marla shrugged. Each transaction, she revealed, had taken place via phone, fax, or email attachments. Intermediary real estate attorneys managed forms, deeds, and contracts. Even odder, she now recalled, was how she'd never had to show any of the properties in person.

"Would it surprise you," Cale asked bluntly, "that your husband is listed as the Bermuda Holdings' board chairman?"

Marla gave him an empty stare.

CHAPTER 66

"Tobias?" Marla Crenshaw's expression revealed her surprise. "I find that hard to believe."

"How about the addresses?" Cale persisted, "The single families? We can't locate them on the city tax rosters."

Marla's eyes flickered with confusion. "May I ask what this is all about, Detective? Is there something—"

"Show me the addresses, and it'll clear everything up."

She nodded, and the click of her heels echoed down the wide hallway floor.

Cale checked his phone messages. He pressed Maggie's number and received her voicemail again. She was likely at the hospital with Janet and Gloria, their phones muted. It was getting late, and her failure to respond was concerning.

Marla returned carrying a business ledger and set it on the coffee table between them. She opened it to a page she'd marked.

"Here's the first one—906 Dream Lane." Cale jotted the address in his pocket notebook. Then Marla flipped a few pages further. "The second one here, 1222 Spinnaker Court." She recited: "A pleasant little charmer on a quiet cul-de-sac. It's a new development."

She handed him a pair of spec sheets. He double-checked the locations and studied the listing photos—both were pleasant neighborhoods. He pictured tall trees, kids, romping dogs, and sturdy swing sets.

Was one of them a house of horrors?

Cale grabbed his phone and stepped to the heavy drapery covering the now-dark windows. He hit Slink's number and updated their information, then returned his focus to Marla Crenshaw.

"You're frightening me, Detective Van Waring." Her voice was tense. "What does this have to do with my husband or these home sales?"

"I'm sorry, Marla. But do you know where Tobias is right now?"

Darkness had deepened the sentinel shadows lining the far edges of the property. Cale wheeled the Bronco around the circular front drive. Looking back at the house, he saw Marla and the children staring through tall French windows. Their eyes appeared wide with concern.

"The Crenshaws," he told himself. "all-American family."

However, other than the husband's absence, a missing puzzle piece now prodded at Cale's brain. The family portrait he'd seen on the fireplace mantle felt suddenly incomplete.

Shaking away the idea, he accelerated the SUV back down the curling driveway.

Maggie awoke with a roiling sensation in her stomach. She was face down on some bed, with her arms secured behind her. Her breaths were shallow and labored. Something in her mouth impeded her intake of air. She tried spitting it out but was unable to dislodge the blockage.

Panic swept through her as she attempted to move on the oversized mattress, and she thrashed her head painfully back and forth. Her struggle proved futile, and each breath caused her nostrils to flare.

A light flashed somewhere behind her.

Maggie whipped her head sideways, seeing only the dark shadows. She noticed the faint odor of butane, she guessed, blended with a lavender scent. A candle being lit?

What on earth is happening? She tried yelling around the cloth, but only a guttural moan escaped her lips. Where was she? What in God's name was going on?

Maggie attempted piecing together the shards of blurry, incoherent memory. Her mind struggled to recall details of what had transpired. She pictured her bedroom. A stranger had stood in the shadows, talking in a hypnotic voice. The same man who kicked Hank aside like an annoying toy. *Hank! Is he...?* Tears stung her eyes. *Please, God. Let him be all right.*

Was this same monster in the room with her now? Maggie struggled frantically against her bindings, attempting futile shouts for help. The gag muted her cries, and she ceased the efforts when her breathing turned ragged.

Soft music came next, starting slow and building. Maggie angled her head, trying to locate the sound's source. Useless. The melody began to crystallize in her mind—an old song from the 1970s.

"Why do birds da-de-da-de-da...." The ethereal, feminine voice sounded rich. But more disturbing was the monotone voice singing airily along with the lyrics. A male falsetto?

On her stomach, legs splayed toward the corners of the flat mattress, Maggie's mind shrieked. Please, God! Don't let this be happening!"

A clammy hand then pressed tenderly against the small of her naked back. "Relax, darling," came a whisper close to her ear. "We've got all the time in the world."

Maggie clamped her eyes shut and screamed frantically, yet it was a scream no one could hear.

The canopy of night spread across the starless sky like a closed stage curtain. The soft, intermittent drizzle glazed the windshields of passing cars. Cale sped north, headed back to the city. His phone sounded—it was Slink—and Cale reported Tobias Crenshaw was nowhere to be found. His car was also gone. He doubted Marla Crenshaw was involved. However, she had given him the locations of the mysterious Green Bay homes.

Slink jotted down the addresses. "I'm on it," he said. "I'll GPS the locations."

"Any word on Staszak?"

A pang of guilt sliced through Cale's chest. He wondered if he shouldn't be at the hospital with Janet, Gloria, and Maggie. No. He understood Staszak would rather he be out hunting for the lunatic who'd put him there.

"I spoke to Janet five minutes ago," Slink reported. "He's stable. Doing okay for the most part."

"Is Maggie up there with her?"

"Janet says no." Slink paused. "They're also wondering where she is. They tried calling her phone."

Cale glanced at his dashboard—6:34 p.m. Something wasn't right. "She's probably with Chloe somewhere. They've got issues they need to work out."

"No surprise there."

Cale bit the wrapper off one of the protein bars he kept in the Bronco. Food was a weapon. He was no Nostradamus, but he imagined this night might be a long one.

"It even gets weirder," Slink relayed. "I hacked into Marla Crenshaw's medical records like we discussed."

Cale accepted Slink's dark talents for what they were. Right now, he didn't care about the details.

"Cliff Notes version," added Slink. "She saw a neurologist three times. About eighteen months ago."

"What for?"

"Headaches, dizzy, hot flashes. Blackouts for no apparent reason," Slink rattled it off. "They ordered CAT scans, EEG—the whole nine yards."

Cale waited.

"A healthy woman her age, they guessed migraines as a catch-all. Put her on meds, but only when she needed them."

Cale considered this as he drove. The symptoms sounded familiar, and it came to him like a bolt: Jessica Handy—the failed kidnapping victim from earlier that afternoon. Marla Crenshaw's symptoms mirrored what Jessica had described before passing out in her vehicle.

The time frame now made sense. Cale pictured how young Leslie Dowd had become the Chemist's initial known victim over a year ago and how the pattern was repeating.

"My God!" Cale steadied his voice. "Crenshaw was likely perfecting his knockout formula two years ago. Tweaking the dosage. He'd have needed a human guinea pig or two."

Slink gave a low whistle.

The Bronco reached the stoplights before the ramp to the Interstate. The light drizzle started again, and Cale flipped his wipers back on. He recalled the words of Dr. Mocarek: "Three or four minutes...like a very toxic snakebite."

"You're thinking he practiced on his wife?"

"The mixture works fast yet doesn't harm the victim."

Both men considered the mindset they were dealing with. *Evil* was the word Cale kept returning to.

"So he's a heartless sociopath?" Slink said.

Cale remembered his opening conversation with the friendly Marla Crenshaw—the fireplace mantel gaily filled with family photos, especially the happy ones with the smiling yellow lab. "Candy," wasn't it? The kids' beloved pet had abruptly passed away for no apparent medical reason.

"Christ almighty!" Cale groaned sadly. "That sicko must've also murdered their family dog. Dosed it into cardiac arrest."

Slink was quiet for a lengthy moment. "Now that's *beyond* heartless."

Cale pictured Crenshaw's smarmy grin as they'd shaken hands in the backyard. He recalled how the hackles on his neck had risen like they were doing now.

"Those addresses!" Cale ordered while he drove. "Screw the warrants—get units over to both houses immediately!"

CHAPTER 67

The Bronco sped along the beltline. The lights of the dash flashers flickered off the windshield, casting the vehicle's interior in a frenetic blue glow.

Cale phoned central dispatch.

"GPS me your fastest route to 1222 Spinnaker Court." His clipped tone conveyed his seriousness. Within moments, the operator relayed directions to the address. "We've got three units in progress ahead of you, Lieutenant. Plus Tactical. They should be arriving in minutes."

Cale lusted at being first on the scene. After all, he was the lead investigator and wanted the first crack at the deviant maniac Crenshaw. Still, with lives in the balance, it mattered little who arrived first.

He hoped Captain McBride had properly briefed his units and emphasized the danger. Crenshaw was an intelligent sociopath, capable of extreme violence to innocent victims (not to mention family pets). Do not underestimate him.

Agent Redtail's "cornered rat" depiction sprang again into Cale's mind. He prayed their men were on high alert.

Shooting beneath an underpass, the Bronco accelerated past the Saturday evening traffic. Other vehicles drifted aside as the blue lights approached. Cale honked and roared around them with his jaws clenched.

His phone buzzed. Perhaps Slink with an update? Could units have arrived at the houses already?

Cale barked into the phone's speaker. It wasn't Slink. Instead, some 1970s music was playing against an otherwise silent background. The caller ID read: UNKNOWN.

"Who is this?" he demanded, easing off his accelerator.

"Ahh. The savvy detective lieutenant," the sardonic voice oozed.

Cale's stomach knotted. "I said, identify yourself."

"One guess."

The voice had a sing-song quality, nailing Cale like a stomach punch. He raised the phone to his ear. "Crenshaw! How'd you get this number?"

A droll chuckle. "It seems we have a mutual friend."

Cale wanted to slam the phone against the dashboard, but a profound fear gripped him. *What mutual friend?* Was if Marla, his wife? Cale had given her his mobile number fifteen minutes ago.

The Bronco zoomed past a FedEx truck on the right as he vectored toward an exit ramp. "Cut the BS. You need to turn yourself in right now." He fought to maintain his composure, keeping a steady hand on the wheel.

"We're having a little soiree, Detective. I wanted to extend you the courtesy of an invitation."

Cale heard indistinct noises in the background, shuffling sounds. Then Crenshaw's measured voice softly commanded: "Say something to the nice policeman, dear."

Cale held his breath as a desperate voice cried, "Cale! He's got me—"

Click. The connection went dead.

It had sounded tinny through the speaker and, even worse, unexpected. *My God!* Cale's brain screamed desperately. Had Crenshaw returned to his opulent home? Found out about his visit? Threatened his wife? Yet it didn't make sense. It hadn't been Marla Crenshaw on the line. Instead, it was *Maggie's voice!*

Cale dialed back and received a busy signal. In the dim inner light of the Bronco, he screamed at the top of his lungs. A car horn blared, and Cale swerved back into his lane. *Calm yourself.* He was no good to anyone in a body bag. A new thought recalled Chloe's earlier vision. She had warned him of Maggie being in eminent danger, and like an idiot, he had sloughed it off.

Why didn't I listen?

Cale flipped the phone aside. It sat in silence, mocking him like an unpinned grenade. Yet it didn't matter how or why, but only that Crenshaw now had Maggie in his grip. Along with the other women— assuming they were even still alive.

Pressing the accelerator, he roared past a stream of cars on his right. Grabbing his phone again, Cale tried calming his voice when Slink answered. "What's your twenty?" he asked.

"I'm with Cap. We're closing on the Dream Lane address."

Cale pictured them inside the captain's old Crown Vic, driving across the city's opposite side. Cale kept his voice level. "I'm heading to Spinnaker

Court." He paused. "You haven't heard anything from Crenshaw, have you? No calls to the station?"

"Why would he call us?"

"The sick SOB just phoned me." Before Slink could speak, Cale uncontrollably shouted: "Maggie!" Saying her name felt like a stab to his heart. "He's got Maggie!"

In her lightless bedroom prison on the house's ground floor, Cindy Hulbreth heard odd, crashing noises through the walls. Coming from the next-door bedroom, she knew. Furniture was being moved around, scraping and scratching.

A prolonged and eerie silence came next, followed by the sickly-sweet music, which caused her stomach to retch. Cindy struggled to raise herself but had slurped water from her dog dish five minutes ago.

She fought against the wooziness suddenly seizing her, yet could not fight it off. Surrendering to the narcotics, she slumped to the mattress as the familiar darkness defeated her again.

The house stood silent in the night's black drizzle.

Police cruisers swooped in from all directions. Red-blue lights flickered in the dark. A blocky TAC unit truck slid to a stop on the damp street in front of 906 Dream Lane. Another cruiser moved up the driveway, blocking the double-door garages.

The TAC team advanced in military silence with weapons drawn, signaling via nods and hand gestures. A moment later, they barged through the front and back doors simultaneously. Another trio had already swept around the back of the two-story home, securing the perimeter after quietly emptying the pair of neighboring houses.

The dark blue Crown Vic pulled in front of the address moments later. , Slink rushed from the car with Captain McBride trailing him. They hastened to the front door with the second unit of uniformed officers. All wore Kevlar vests, with weapons drawn and pointed low as they advanced.

Inside the house, the thunder of stomping footsteps came from everywhere. "Somebody get the lights on!" the captain bellowed.

"No electric, sir!" a voice called in the dark.

Slink followed the captain into the empty dining room. The surreal pattern of crisscrossing flashlight beams swept the rooms like a laser show.

"Upstairs is clear!" An officer's boots thumped down the narrow steps. "Place is empty."

"Basement's clean!" another voice shouted.

McBride barked: "We got a bogey. It's the other address."

The officers hastened from the house, scuttling across the front lawn toward their vehicles.

CHAPTER 68

Cale noticed the cruisers' domers flickering ghostlike in the distance. They reflected off houses, trees, and the sky's low bank of clouds. Thunder rumbled in the distance.

A pair of turns later, the Bronco roared up the cul-de-sac. He pulled in behind a TAC-unit vehicle, which blockaded the driveway. From a distance, he could hear the whoop and wail of rescue vehicles headed their way.

Cale witnessed vested officers dodging about. They moved in and out of the ranch-style house like worker bees. Lights were ablaze inside, and he could discern shadows sliding behind the closed window blinds.

Entering the front door, he spotted a barefoot, stringy-haired girl huddled on the living room couch. Her face appeared haunted. Dark rings rimmed her eyes. Her head was slumped, and she reminded him of a surgical patient still under sedation. He recognized her from the photographs—Cynthia Hulbreth.

Thank God. Alive.

Officers led a second woman with darker hair and a blanket wrapped around her swami-style up the basement stairs. She emerged as gaunt as a prison survivor. Shirley Koon.

Where was Maggie?

Cale spotted Sergeant Burke down the narrow first-floor hallway. "Any sign of the perp?" he called out.

"Negative, so far, Lieutenant."

Officers milled about, the tension ever-present during any home breach, where surprises were the norm. Shots could explode from anywhere at any moment.

Cale worked his way back to the living room, then to an open kitchen door leading to the garages. He cursed while staring at Maggie's Mazda, feeling the front hood with his fingertips. The engine was cool and likely hadn't been driven for over an hour. No sign of Crenshaw's BMW in the space beside it. His phone call could have come from a disposable phone, so there'd be no chance of a trace.

Studying the garage closer, Cale spotted a parked Suzuki motorcycle. He wondered if serial criminals had hobbies. Of course, they did. It's what made them so frightening. They were your cousins, neighbors, or the average churchgoers on Sunday mornings.

Cale reentered the house. He joined officers lingering near the adjacent bedrooms down one inner hallway.

"Some crazy stuff in here," one of the men said, and Cale poked his head inside the first hallway bedroom. "Windows boarded from inside," a TAC officer explained. "Locked tight as a prison cell. The bathroom's a plus."

"We needed a laser saw," added a second officer, "to cut her ankle tether." The man shook his head grimly.

Driving up the cul-de-sac, Cale had counted a row of only four homes on the block. "Anybody check the house next door?" Cale asked Sergeant Burke.

"Two men are there now. It's vacant and listed for sale. We got the lock box combination from the real estate agent."

Cale nodded, appreciative of the unit's fast work.

"He had a third victim." Cale's tone was clipped. "Anyone see signs of another female?"

"Negative, Lieutenant," the sergeant reported, and the rest shook their head.

"Hey, Lieutenant. Check out the back bedroom here. This guy's one sick puppy." A TAC member indicated the second adjacent bedroom situated further down the hallway.

Cale steeled himself and headed his way.

The farthest ground-level bedroom appeared similar to the other one, and Cale surveyed it with desperate eyes. One window was shuttered from the inside, bolted closed, and soundproofed. However, the bedroom's second window remained closed but not fully shuttered.

Ropes, leather bindings, thin nylon cords. They remained attached to the heavy legs of the double bed. Cale squatted in a catcher's stance for closer inspection. The tie-cords had been sliced, the victim's bindings seemingly cut free.

Cale's phone buzzed.

Crenshaw again?

Instead, it was Slink. The Dream Lane house was clear. He and Captain McBride were on the way to join him. "Any sign of Maggie?" Slink asked anxiously.

"Her car's in the garage. Looks like he escaped somewhere in his vehicle." "We've got the APB out."

Cale pocketed his phone. He stepped across the bedroom to a dresser, where three dripless candles stood in their onyx holder. The black wicks were cool. He spotted a woman's bra lying near the closet door.

A small portable CD player sat on a bedside end table. Cale withdrew a pen from his jacket and employed the tip to press the eject button. The tray slid open. He freed the silver-colored disc, staring at it in the room's harsh light.

He slid the CD inside a plastic baggie and felt the player's warm casing. Still warm. Could they be closer behind Crenshaw than he'd thought? If the man had called from the house earlier, they'd probably only be twenty minutes behind him.

A sudden idea struck Cale, causing him to wheel from the room. In the outer hallway, he shouted, "Listen up! Everybody! The perp might still be on the premises. If he is, he's got a female hostage with him."

The officers froze at his remark.

"Everybody move!" shouted Sergeant Burke from nearby. It propelled the men into a frenzy of action. "Check every closet and cubbyhole," Burke ordered. "Every crack in this place!"

Cale added in a harried voice: "The entire house—basement and attic. Look for hidden rooms and sliding panels. Anyplace someone might hide."

CHAPTER 69

Officer Cam Whitten aimed his flashlight at one desolate basement corner. The place was otherwise empty, imbued with the morgue-like quiet of freshly poured concrete. The basement was uninhabited, and he hastened back up the narrow, backless stairway.

Footsteps thumped from the inner bowels of the house, and Whitten was joined in the living room by his partner, Officer Paul Splawski. "Nothing upstairs," the man reported. "Place is clean."

Officer Whitten spoke into his shoulder com unit: "Next door house is clear, Sarge. Dead empty. No signs of entry."

Burke's voice crackled back. "Lock her down. Meet us in the backyard."

The officers exited the house and secured the front door, closing the lockbox with the keys dropped back inside. They moved across the slick lawn and past the For Sale sign. In the flickering glow of the cruiser lights, they disappeared around the west side, between the houses.

Inside the bedroom, Cale stepped to the shutterless window. It was a horizontal two-pane style. Finding it unlatched, he slid it open sideways and leaned into the misting drizzle. He peered across the shadowy darkness, his eyes drawn toward the back lot lines, where a thick expanse of woods extended across the rear of the entire row of properties, bordering the vast farm fields beyond. A perfect hiding place?

Perhaps an escape route.

"Hand me your flashlight," Cale ordered to one of the officers searching a closet.

Leaning out the window again, Cale sprayed the beam across the ground near the window. He noticed rutted scrape marks denting the brown grass. Soggy footsteps lead off in multiple directions—many made by the Tac officers who'd surrounded the house earlier, Cale decided. Pulling his head back inside, he examined the edges of the frame in closer detail. Flakes of parchment-like patches and a few reddish specks were evident inside the trim. Could they be human skin or dried blood?

Had something heavy been pushed through the window? Heavy like a body?

A body like Maggie's?

Forensics could tell, but their team wouldn't arrive for a while. Cale cursed, rising from the window. The officer across the room noticed the contemplative glaze in his eyes as he rushed from the room.

Bursting out the backdoor, flashlight in hand, Cale joined the officers converging in the gloomy backyard from different directions. Standing in the cool, persistent mist, he examined the lighted bedroom window and the lawn below.

Then turning from the window, he eyed the large, two-story Cape Cod home next door. It stood silhouetted in eerie shadows, bathed by the cruiser lights bouncing off her broad facing. The inside was cleared, Cale knew. It was empty, with no signs of anything amiss.

He recalled the details of Crenshaw's phone call. Maggie's voice had shouted, then she'd been abruptly cut off. The call could have come from anywhere but was most likely from Crenshaw's vehicle. He was long gone by now.

Cale decided that everything now hinged on locating the red BMW. APBs were already out on the sportscar.

He organized his thoughts. Still, the blood-like specs on the window trim bothered him. They seemed too fresh to be flakes of rust. But if so, how had they been there? And why wasn't the window shuttered like the others? Along with the CD player still warm to the touch?

Cale wrestled with the questions.

He turned his attention to the forest stand bordering the back property. It stretched along the lengthy stretch of five decent-sized homes. What if Crenshaw had not been in his car when he'd called? Could his escape plans have dissolved with the surprise arrival of a squadron of police officers? Forcing him to improvise on the fly?

Cale contemplated the chances of escaping into the stretch of modestly dense woods while fleeing the law. He reasoned that carrying his victim like a heavy sack of wet cement would be implausible but not impossible.

Through the trees, he studied the twinkling lights of the far-off subdivision. Way too distant to reach on foot. Closer by was the neighboring farmhouse. A vast stretch of farm field stood between the farm structures and the grove of trees on this side. It was flat and nearly a quarter mile from where they were.

The forest strip comprised tall elm and ash trees, with a few firs and pines among them. If an escape into the woods had been tried, why were there no reports of anyone shouting for help?

The answer came fast. None of the Chemist's victims had struggled during their capture. As Dr. Mocarek had pointed out, the sedation solution zonked them unconscious for hours.

Nevertheless, despite it being a long shot, Cale decided he had little to lose in searching the woods.

"Come on!" he motioned to a handful of nearby officers. They immediately trailed him across the backyard toward the cluster of trees. Entering the tree line, Cale ordered, "Comb for escape tracks. One male, possibly with a victim."

The officers fanned out across the twenty-yard width of the narrow forest. Their flashlight beams exposed uneven, leafy terrain. They advanced through the airy dampness with careful steps.

Cale turned to Sergeant Burke beside him. "Let's get K-9 out here." As the makeshift troop advanced through the woods, the sergeant barked the order into his shoulder coms.

Fifteen minutes later, after progressing halfway and finding nothing of interest, Cale stopped and finger-stabbed his phone.

Ed Ravelle, Chloe's husband, answered on the third ring. "Ed, it's Cale. I need to speak to Chloe."

The man hesitated. "Is this about the nonsense earlier? Her seeing things and—"

"Please, Ed," Cale interrupted. "I need her right now."

Maggie's sister answered five seconds later. Cale nearly shouted: "Chloe. I need to know what you saw before. In your vision or dream?"

"Well, uh, I—"

"We don't have much time."

Haltingly, she reported: "Trees and clouds. Nighttime. And moist, like it's raining. No moon. The landscape was pockmarked like those dark pictures of Mercury they show."

Trying to imagine it, he prompted: "Anything else?"

"Broken glass and thunder. Or maybe cannons firing off? Explosions and cracking sounds. Loud."

Cale watched the men move across the terrain around him. They could be mistaken for dark statues stepping between the shady trees. "Okay, thanks," he said resignedly.

Chloe interjected, "Cale. I've left Mags a dozen messages. Why are you asking me this stuff?"

"I'll explain later." He ended the call.

Night, clouds, trees. Chilly rain and thunderclaps. It sounded like an old war movie or a dystopian sci-fi scene. Cale prayed Chloe's vision was somehow relevant to their search, for all their sakes.

He rejoined the patrol in their gloomy forward march. The trees provided modest shelter from the mist, and the officers stepped over gnarled roots and heavy unkempt underbrush. Flashlights bobbed like fireflies as they pressed onward.

Cale recalled his brief encounter with Tobias Crenshaw days earlier. The guy had seemed in decent shape, but how far could a man get navigating woodsy terrain in a drizzle while carrying an unconscious person?

Maybe a quarter mile, he decided. Adrenaline could take you only so far before fatigue set in. Survival mode after that. He'd dump the body aside if it meant saving his hide. Cale told himself they'd catch up with him if Crenshaw had come this way. With such a brief head start and sloppy weather, there was no way he could continue carrying his load forward.

Once the police searchers reached the end of the woods, they would have to search inside the distant cul de sac homes. If armed, Crenshaw's desperation would make him dangerous. He'd attempt any means of escape.

Not catching them was unthinkable.

It meant losing Maggie forever.

CHAPTER 70

Tobias Crenshaw's father—Hans Renier Crenshaw—was a local paper company engineer who had made a quiet fortune fifty years ago when employees had been allowed to register patents in their private names. The result of growing up without financial concerns spoiled the elder Crenshaw's only son. Consequently, Tobias had always considered Lady Luck more his personal friend than a casual acquaintance.

He wondered if his long-time mistress remained faithful to him as he lumbered through the wet forest. And yet, perhaps good fortune was merely the ability to see three moves ahead of your opponent. Tobias had always been a superlative chess player. So maybe "luck" had little to do with it after all.

Whatever the case, he was fortunate he'd had time to grab his jacket before the police had invaded his hidey house. They'd stormed inside like a Barbarian hoard. Before they'd arrived, things had been going smoothly for Tobias. His candles were lit, the feathery ethereal music playing. His newest captive—Maggie Jeffers—had squirmed delightfully on the bed. Bound and gagged, she moaned the low sounds Tobias enjoyed hearing.

Still, having three victims at once was stressful. Due to the investigators' closing in, Tobias had decided to accelerate his mission. *When opportunity knocks*, he'd reasoned and set out, hoping to surprise Van Waring's girlfriend at their home. His gamble paid off, and Tobias now had his third victim. The fact she was the detective's live-in girlfriend was the icing on the cake. And who cared that she wasn't light-haired? The Liberian flesh peddler, Mabutu, would simply have to deal with it.

Thirty minutes earlier, Tobias had decided that drawing the window blinds inside the first-floor bedroom was best. While doing so, he'd noticed the flickering blue lights approaching from nearly a mile away. Reacting swiftly, he dashed down the hallway and grabbed his peacoat, which contained an almost full bottle of his mixture. Back in the bedroom, he'd sprayed the fluid across his captive's naked back, knowing she'd be out cold in minutes. He slipped on his gloves, grabbed his folded hunting knife, and sliced the wrist and ankle cords. Pocketing the knife inside his coat, he'd flicked off the CD player and extinguished the candles.

Police cruisers were rounding the street corner, hastening toward the cul-de-sac's entrance as he slid open the bedroom's back window. The girl was heavier than she appeared, but he levered her through the window headfirst, and she tumbled to the soggy ground below.

Tobias had tossed his coat out after and scrabbled through the window as the cruisers were skidding to a halt in front of the house. Closing the window behind him, he heard car doors slamming and footsteps tramping through the misty night. He'd wrapped her in his dark coat and lifted the unconscious girl in a fireman's carry. Tobias beelined for the woods directly behind the house, not risking even the slightest glance back.

After minutes of moving through the narrow strip of the forest behind the row of homes—while jack-booted officers invaded his house like stormtroopers—he'd finally stopped to gather his bearings.

Tobias was moving again. He carried the woman deeper through the dark stretch of trees, navigating the terrain like a woodsman. Having eluded the police raid by using his wits, it was decision time once more.

Tobias set the woman on the leafy forest floor. Rain droplets dripped from the damp leaves above. He distinguished an open, undulating farm field through the trees far to his left. It stood like a flat ocean in the moonless night. A farmhouse sat perched in the shadows. Tobias could take his chances breaking in if he could navigate the muddy expanse. But the girl was becoming heavier as they fled. Besides, prolonged exposure increased her risk of hypothermia. "Damaged goods" would prove pointless.

Tobias analyzed the situation. The invaders had blown apart his plans, and his arms and legs were fatiguing. The woman—remarkable though she was—was becoming a dubious reward. A savvy gambler knew when to cut his losses and escape while he could.

On the other hand, Tobias had always considered himself a risk-taker. Hadn't he come too far to cash in his chips and surrender?

Equations flashed in his head, turning into probabilities. What was the least likely scenario the cops would imagine? At last, a sardonic smile played across his face. He hoisted the limp girl into his arms again. Doing so, Tobias heard the jingle of her Mazda keys as they slipped from his peacoat pocket. He needed her vehicle to escape, didn't he?

Perhaps. The keys to his Beamer remained in his pants- pocket. He'd left it parked across the city. He also had the motorcycle keys if worse came to worse. Tobias had no flashlight or phone. The narrow window of escape was shrinking rapidly. So yes, he decided. The dropped keys might work in his favor.

Changing directions abruptly, he cut down toward the lower part of the woods, where the back of the neighboring houses now came into view. He reminded himself that an unpredictable target was the hardest to hit.

He paused inside the tree line at the woods' edge. He studied the broad, deep backyards of the row of dwellings. Back across the lawns, he spotted a man's head and torso leaning out of the back bedroom window of his "former" house. Van Waring, he recognized, searching the ground with his flashlight.

Tobias' attention turned to the empty Cape Cod house angled not far in front of him. It sat unlit in the shadows. He noticed flashlights spraying around the inner first-floor rooms. Of course, they'd have officers inspect the empty place. Tobias had been inside the vacant house numerous times before and knew the floor plan by heart. It was about to become his spider's trap door—perhaps his most daring gambit ever.

To hide in plain sight.

The whoop of an ambulance sounded as it swept a distance away. It was likely headed to some medical facility.

After scanning the backyards of the other adjacent homes—the coast clear—Tobias sprang out from the lightless woods. He carried the girl in his arms like an infant, bolting across the shadowed back lawn toward the Cape Cod house next door to his ranch home. No voices shouted, spotting him. No startled screams of: "There he is! Freeze! Police!"

He silently executed the twenty-yard dash to the rain-slicked, darker garage side of the Cape Cod house.

Breathing heavily, cloistered within the shadows, Tobias laid the unconscious woman down on the damp grass. He kept her wrapped inside the dark peacoat, and the garment concealed her in the darkness.

A door closed somewhere. Tobias crept along the garage edge of the two-story structure and peeked around the front corner like a bandit. He watched the departure of the pair of officers who had just finished searching inside the house.

Perfect, he told himself. They would cross it off their list.

When the men had disappeared around the home's far side, Tobias slipped across the driveway apron. He moved over to the front porch, stooped low, and remained hidden beneath the roof's overhang. Seconds later, he tapped in the lockbox code he had long ago memorized and withdrew the realtor's house keys. Silently, he opened the front door and slipped inside.

CHAPTER 71

Naked and shivering, Maggie awoke to a chilly drizzle on her forehead. Where was she? Outside somewhere, lying on the cold, damp ground. A woolen coat covered her, and a nail-driving pain shot through her temples when she moved her head.

Dark images of her capture rushed back at her: of being tied face-down to some bed, gagged, drugged, helpless. But at least she was alive.

Terrified, Maggie decided it best not to move. She had no idea where she was, so keeping her eyelids closed was her best bet. How close was her captor to her now? Maybe only feet away and studying her at the moment.

Maggie's heart fluttered, and her body shivered in the chill. She slowed her breaths. *Stay calm. Stay alive. Survive.*

Tobias imagined himself a cat burglar,

He pocketed the keys. Easing the front door open again, he slipped outside and crouched while stepping along the front porch. A reasonable distance away on the circular street, a dozen police vehicles now inhabited his home's front and driveway. Officers were walking about, a forensic team no doubt on the way.

Staying low, Tobias moved opposite them and crept across the dark driveway. He dipped around the garages again to the house's shaded side. Without hesitation, he gathered the girl inside the peacoat and carried her up to the garage's front edge with her bare legs dangling free. Peeking cautiously around the corner, the coast remained clear. Staying low, he bolted across the driveway and front porch overhang to the front door.

Tobias slipped inside the vacant home again. Closing the door silently behind him, he set the bundle down on the tiled floor of the front foyer. He locked the door behind him. Humid from the mist and his perspiration, Tobias inhaled the new carpet smell of the place.

At the door again, he listened for outside sounds. He heard nothing but the blood rush in his head. In grandmaster fashion, he remained three moves ahead of the game.

The empty house felt cavernous. Tobias removed his shoes, then used the woolen coat to swipe away rain drips of soggy bits of soil and leaves.

He bundled the girl back inside the peacoat and carried her down the tiled first-floor hallway with his shoes in one hand. He'd return to wipe away traces of his footprints after they'd settled in.

Knowing the layout, Tobias opened a hallway door outside the kitchen. The open-back, wooden steps descended to the basement. Stepping carefully in pitch blackness, he used the girl's legs against the railing to guide them down. The open basement area was large and unfinished. It smelled of cement and caulking. He progressed along a far wall, away from the high ground-level outside windows.

Tobias set the girl on the concrete floor next to a water heater tank, then slid down alongside her. He breathed deeply, at last, feeling his adrenaline levels subside. He touched the captive female's forehead. Not feverish. Here they would nest together as a couple, waiting like old friends having a campout. Roughing it a bit, without food or change of clothing. Toby and Maggie.

He liked the way it sounded.

"Where is everybody?" growled Captain McBride while entering the cul-de-sac house's front door. Slink, cradling his shoulder slightly, trailed behind him. Three TAC officers in vests followed them inside.

A pair of evidence techs knelt in the living room, dusting the furniture for prints. "Foot pursuit, Captain," one tech said. "The woods out back." He flicked his head that way.

Turning to the doorway, the captain ordered his men to assist in the search. They tromped off into the night.

"Where's Lieutenant Van Waring?" Slink asked the tech.

"One guess."

"Leading the charge. I should've known."

Slink grabbed a flashlight from an end table. He followed McBride back out the front door. The captain was already advancing around the side between the houses. His footsteps were heavy on the glistening grass. Slink studied the entire cul de sac street block, whose scarcity of homes and weed-strewn vacant lots—dotted with For Sale signs—made the place appear desolate.

Officer Cam Whitten exited out through the side garage door. Slink asked him, "Anybody check the house next door?"

"Splawski and I just went through it," the officer said. "Head to toe. Nothing amiss. Keys are back in the lockbox."

Slink and McBride paused on the side lawn, staring beyond the homes at the dark, ominous woods bordering the rear of the properties. Numerous flashlights bobbed erratically between the witch-finger trees.

"I'm joining them in the search," McBride announced. "See what they're looking for."

Slink watched him stride across the slick, damp grass. He moved in the contrary direction and crossed the generous lot separating the two properties. The vacant Cape Cod home stood like a massive, dry-docked battleship. The flickering lights of a half-dozen parked cruisers reflected off the broad western wall, creating a carnival of menacing shadows.

Flashlight in hand, Slink advanced toward the front of the vacant home. Climbing steps to the porch, he shone his light across the first-floor windows. All were intact. He examined the lockbox attached to the front door handle. It was unlocked but empty. Officer Whitten had reported they'd replaced the keys. It was likely a minor oversight, and Slink would check with them later.

Slink tried the front door handle. Secure. The house was locked drum tight. A few steps further along the porch, he aimed his light in through the unshaded lower windows of the front room. He noted how the brand-new carpet and painted walls appeared unblemished.

Slink stooped and angled his light in at the front foyer. Was that a smudge of mud or grass on the carpet near the hallway? From his distance, he couldn't tell. Shadow on shadow. The dirt clump, Slink guessed, had likely been tracked in by the officers during their inspection. The city, of course, would reimburse whomever for carpet cleaning.

And yet, something about the empty lockbox disturbed him. It was a frenetic atmosphere, with lights bobbing and everyone rushing about. Victims were being rescued, med-checked, and transported. Add in the active search for a killer, and Slink supposed forgetting to return keys to an empty lockbox was a minor detail.

Nevertheless...

Aiming his flashlight through the window again, he focused on the soiled carpet smear. Slink decided to follow his gut. Besides, the city was already on the hook for cleaning the carpet.

"Here goes nothing," he whispered to himself.

Slink smashed a windowpane with the butt of his sidearm. Reaching his good arm inside, he flipped the latch. Then he slid the casement window halfway open and eased into the house.

CHAPTER 72

Cale slipped between the lightless trees and stopped at last. Something niggled inside him like a thorn stab. Ahead, where the woods ended, lay a dark stretch of open farm fields. The vast acres would be mud-caked from the recent precipitation, impossible to cross on a night like this, and made far worse if you were lugging a hundred-twenty pounds of dead weight.

Chloe's ominous warning continued sounding in his head. Trees, clouds, blackness, cannon booms, rain. Cale glanced around the woods and decided she had it mostly correct.

And the rest of it? Was Maggie in trouble? It was accurate beyond doubt. The other part was related to broken glass, cracking sounds, lightning, and cannons. Cale didn't understand the glass part, not standing here surrounded by trees. To him, "visions" didn't hold much water. It seemed just as likely that Chloe's "second sight" would lead them on a luckless hunt, wasting precious time.

Crenshaw, by all odds, was long gone by now. As Cale had earlier surmised, the psycho likely escaped with Maggie in a second vehicle.

Whether he liked it or not, it made the most sense.

These grim thoughts were interrupted by a sudden voice shouting in the dark. Cale spun around and spotted an officer hunched over twenty feet away. Her flashlight was trained on the ground. Other officers were moving toward her.

Cale peeled back and joined them all. The group parted as he elbowed in to discern better what held their attention. Gleaming in the glow of their flashlights, he spotted it.

A set of car keys with an attached plastic ID card.

Cale withdrew a clear plastic evidence bag from his jacket pocket. He knelt and used his ballpoint tip, guiding the keys into the bag. Holding the bag before his flashlight, he saw Maggie's face smiling back at him from the key-chain photo. She was holding Hank in her arms.

"Aww, geez," he groaned, his voice hitching. "It's Maggie Jeffers."

A TAC officer spoke into his shoulder com. "We've got confirmation ID on the hostage. It looks like they came this way through the woods."

Looking at them all now, Cale barked, "All eyes hyper-alert now. Everyone. This pursuit is now hot. Keep your eyes peeled for every detail."

A TAC officer loudly added, "And be on the lookout for dirt mounds. Any signs of a recent burial point!"

The officers separated off in all directions, their flashlights scanning the ground. Cale slipped the evidence bag inside his jacket, then focused his beam over leaves, dirt piles, twisted logs, and clumps of gnarled underbrush—the small forest's entire surface. He was filled with more despair than hope and stunned into silence.

The facts didn't lie. Crenshaw had Maggie.

After five minutes, Cale extinguished his flashlight. He stared beyond the trees and into the dark abyss of open farm acreage. He pondered the unlikeliness of crossing it. Did reaching the edge of the woods and venturing across a muddy field in the rain make sense? Particularly for a criminal they'd profiled as being *cunning and clever?*

It seemed neither plausible nor worth the risk.

Around them, officers plodded between the tree shadows, their flashlights penetrating the ghost-like gloom. A tempest of dark thoughts swirled inside Cale's head, and a harsh voice warned: "Screw the worst-case scenarios and concentrate on finding her. Focus on the task at hand."

Ever since the first victim had gone missing last year, their perpetrator had seemed multiple moves ahead of them. He'd been elusive, leaving behind no solid clues. His secluded horror house was surprisingly positioned in the peaceful and serene suburbs.

Hiding in plain sight.

A strange idea sprang into Cale's mind. He was almost afraid to acknowledge it, with Maggie's life now dangling by a thread.

Yet, after discovering the ID, what did he have to lose?

Cale turned and looped back through the woods, brushing aside branches and sidestepping bramble. He headed back in the direction they had come. With his neck hairs bristling, he wondered if their kidnapper hadn't somehow doubled back on them.

Lying naked on the basement floor, bundled inside the thick peacoat, Maggie forced herself to lie still. She used the slow rhythmic breathing she'd learned in yoga class to suppress her physical pain.

Her captor was no doubt the "Chemist" kidnapper. It also meant he was a killer. Nothing could prevent him from slicing her throat at any moment. He'd revealed the sharp-bladed hunting knife earlier, and Maggie accepted that she was in a deadly game of survival.

Her best option was to feign unconsciousness, guessing he might disregard her if she were asleep. Since they'd stopped moving through the freezing woods, Maggie again calculated her options. As he'd carried her down the stairs like a child, she felt a rigid weapon tucked inside the upper pocket of his coat. The one covering her now. Was it still there?

Ever so gently, Maggie trailed her fingers along the coat's inner lining like a spider moves in the dark.

Tobias had tied his soggy shoes and huffed his glasses clean. A distant noise reached him from somewhere above.

Bloody hell! He slapped one fist against the concrete wall, his ears instantly alert. It sounded like glass shattering. Was someone entering the house? But why? It made little sense. The cops had already searched the entire place.

"Keep it together, moron." (In his mind, he heard Mabutu Mabutu's sarcastic snicker.) "There's no need to panic."

Tobias guessed the mysterious invader might be Detective Van Waring. It was the most logical theory. He'd be searching in desperation for his missing bitch.

He squinted through the basement dimness, trying to spot any weapon—something beyond his serrated hunting knife. The detective would be armed. Gun versus knife? The outcome was predictable: *the gun wins every time.* Tobias squinted through the surrounding darkness but discerned no bricks or metal pipes on the concrete floor. To survive, he would have to improvise.

At least the girlfriend remained unconscious. It was one less distraction.

Tobias patted his coat pockets for the knife. Where was it? He couldn't feel it, and cold sweat popped across his forehead. Had the knife fallen out? Perhaps it had landed on the living room carpet when he'd lifted the girl?

What can go wrong next?

From another pocket, he withdrew his plastic spray bottle. The knockout fluid. It wouldn't help much in a physical battle, yet it remained a weapon.

Tobias detected soft-soled footsteps creeping above them, stepping from room to room. He transferred the bottle to his right hand. Surrounded by darkness, he held his breath and waited.

Slink paused after breaking the window and entering the home's living room. His shoulder throbbed from pulling at his stitches, and he played his flashlight over the empty walls and stepped across to the carpet's soiled edge.

He aimed the beam up the central hallway. Around him, the uncovered windows showed the reflections of flickering light from the cruisers outside. Crazy patterns jittered across the inner walls and ceiling.

The mystery of the empty lockbox still bothered him, and Slink decided another look around the inside couldn't hurt. He advanced quietly through the open house. He viewed the spacious rooms, then cautiously explored the empty double-stall garage. He scaled the stairs to the second level, studying the vacant bedrooms, baths, and open closets.

A faint noise reached him from somewhere below, maybe outside the house. He wasn't sure. Slink cautiously stepped down the staircase, listening as he descended. He paused in the central hallway and scanned his flashlight, listening for unfamiliar sounds.

Besides a few scattered secondary rooms and closets, the basement was the only place he hadn't searched.

CHAPTER 73

Each tree was a lurking scarecrow, and moisture dripped from the gnarled upper branches. Led by his flashlight, Cale sprinted back through the woods toward the houses. He hurdled broken limbs and stumps and skidded over slick patches of mushy earth. The moon remained hidden, and shadows ruled the night.

Chloe's dire warning rang in his head like a funeral knell. *You've got to warn her, Cale!*

A dark silhouette was heading his way, and his flashlight revealed Captain McBride. He lowered the beam. "What's going on?" the captain asked breathlessly. "You nearly scared the bejesus out of me."

"They came this way not long ago." Cale's chest heaved. "I'm making sure he hasn't doubled back."

"He'd be insane—"

"That's what he'd *expect* us to think."

Cale didn't have time to debate. He swept past the captain, moving through the darkness. Reaching the forest's edge a minute later, he stopped. Thirty yards away to his right, Crenshaw's house of evil remained lit inside by the forensic lights, and the jittery flashing strobes from the street cruisers rendered the night a frantic feel.

Cale focused on the vacant house next door. The two-level Cape Cod stood eerily quiet. As he moved close, he noticed a faint light from inside—a first-level hallway or perhaps the kitchen. The light made little sense. The house was already cleared and confirmed empty.

Cale scuttled across the glistening lawn to the house's back and stopped when he heard a sudden voice cry from the pitch-black basement. He dropped to one knee beside the ground-level window and peered into the inner blackness.

Maggie peeked through slitted eyelids in the basement and heard footsteps moving across the house floor above them. She lay frozen on the cold concrete, hoping her attacker would ignore her. However, he edged closer as if huddling near her body might help them remain invisible.

Maggie was covered by the peacoat and gripped the open knife, her right hand pressed beneath her thigh against the cement floor. She wasn't sure but imagined the man was armed. Maggie thought she'd seen a handgun earlier when he'd entered the bedroom of her house. Just before he'd kicked Hank aside like a child's toy?

Or had she imagined it? Her memory was clouded by the stuporous sedatives she'd been given.

The sound of footsteps continued through the floor above them. This was her chance, Maggie decided. Now or never. She jolted suddenly to life beside him, and as the man turned in surprise, she slashed the knife at his chest. The blade caught him above his left pectoral muscle; if he hadn't been twisting, it might have pierced his evil heart.

Enraged, he grabbed her wrist with both hands and bent it back as she cried out: "Down here! Help! *He's the killer!*"

The man jerked her across his body, lifting himself to one knee. He slammed Maggie's head against the water heater, and the knife skittered across the floor like a misfired arrow. Dazed, she tried rising until a fluid stream sprayed her face, and Maggie coughed, spit, and hacked before curling fetally on the floor.

Above them, Tobias heard footsteps stomping along an upstairs hallway. A solitary person, from the sound of it. He searched the darkness for the knife but couldn't spot it. Seconds escaped, and he was down to his final option. He rose and lurched gamely toward the shadows beneath the open, backless stairway, ignoring the pain in his chest.

The basement door opened. A flashlight sprayed down the steps and lit the concrete floor. The cop's weapon would be held in his opposite hand. A voice shouted: "Police! Show yourselves!" Then, without waiting, the officer's footsteps pounded down the steps above Tobias' head.

Timing it right, he reached up through the open space halfway down and grabbed the man's left ankle, tripping him. The flashlight hit the cement floor first and then his weapon, as the cop's tumbling body followed. He landed on the unforgiving cement surface at an awkward angle, slamming his shoulder and head down simultaneously. The flashlight spun crazily, and its beam pointed opposite the stairs when it stopped.

Tobias scampered from his hiding place, blood seeping from his injured upper chest. He felt the sticky, wet warmth spreading across his rib cage. His adrenaline froze the pain, and his eyes searched the dimness for the wayward gun.

The cop—*not Van Waring*—was moaning near the base of the stairs, barely conscious. The window glass now shattered across the long basement. Two bullets caromed off the wall above Tobias' head. Ducking instinctively, he heard a third gunshot.

Abandoning the weapon search, he rushed toward the stairway with his head ducked. He climbed two steps at a time as a fourth and fifth shot chipped the wood near his feet.

Cale pulled himself up from the ground outside the basement window. His shots had been errant in the dark, and an unknown officer possibly lay wounded on the basement floor. It had sounded like Maggie's desperate cry. Thank God she was alive, and saving her life mattered most now. He prayed that one of the errant shots he'd fired hadn't caromed and stuck her.

Cale sprinted around the unlit side of the shadowed house. Reinforcements would arrive in minutes from the gunshots. As he rounded the garage corner, the front door blasted open. A man flew out and leaped down the front steps like a long jumper. He made it as far as the cul-de-sac's curb.

"Freeze, Crenshaw! You're in my sights!" Cale's Glock was raised as he tossed the needless flashlight aside.

Tobias Crenshaw hesitated momentarily and stopped as if realizing he'd finally run out of options. He turned and faced Cale in the misty drizzle. The man's eyes held a glassy gleam, and the left side of his shirt was soaked with blood. Cale wondered if one of his shots had hit home. He hoped so. Any pain he inflicted on this cowardly prick was a bonus in his book.

Crenshaw glanced over his shoulder at his private house of horrors, at the garage where his motorcycle was waiting. Slowly, however, his eyes swung back to Cale.

In a bitter voice, he asked, "Detective Van Waring. Still out searching for coyotes?"

CHAPTER 74

"On your knees, scumbag. Do it now."

The man, instead, began advancing across the glistening lawn toward the detective. He held both his arms in the air. Cale noticed what looked to be a plastic bottle filled with fluid in his right hand.

"I said hit the ground!" Cale shouted. He held the Glock steady, aimed at the crimson blossom on the man's chest. Maggie's image flashed through his mind. She had better be alive.

Crenshaw stopped fifteen yards away with a lopsided grin. "C'mon, Detective. You aren't stupid enough to shoot an unarmed man."

Cale's eyes focused on the plastic bottle. Crenshaw rattled it like a man teasing his pet with treats.

"She better be all right."

The Chemist angled his chin back at the house. He cocked his head to one side as if not understanding the comment.

"The bottle." Cale's eyes were hard. "Is it acid?"

The man offered him a condescending sneer. "You'd like to shoot me, wouldn't you, Detective? You can taste it."

Cale didn't take the bait.

"I hacked into the Internal Affairs data bank," Crenshaw said cockily. "Examined your psych profile."

Cale kept his weapon steady.

"You killed a teenage boy back when you were in college." The man snickered. "Shot him face to face. Like we are now."

The painful memory swelled inside Cale. It was the thirty seconds of his life he'd been trying to forget for the past seventeen years.

"What was your girlfriend's name again? Mary. Pity she had to die that day because of you."

Cale tasted the hatred, which turned even more acidic as Crenshaw advanced another step toward him.

"Your little hero act got young Mary killed, didn't it?"

"Shut your mouth!"

Crenshaw was now twelve yards away. The cruiser lights continued to flicker behind them. Thunder rumbled in the distant sky *like cannon fire*, Cale thought.

He shifted the Glock to the center of Crenshaw's forehead.

The man said, "Go ahead. You're the real killer here, aren't you?"

Cale's finger tickled the firm trigger. The easiest thing in the world, squeeze and wipe the smirk off this slimeball's face forever.

"Don't do it, Cale!"

McBride's stern voice barked from forty yards away. He was approaching at a trot, emerging from between the houses. A dozen officers trailed the captain with their sidearms drawn.

Cale kept his weapon on Crenshaw. "You've got an officer down. And an injured hostage in the basement!" He flipped his head toward the house. "Get Rescue out here now!"

Two of the officers dashed into the Cape Cod's front door. A third hurried to one of the cruisers to radio the call.

"Lower your weapon, Cale." McBride's voice reached him through the tense humidity.

"It's Slink down in the basement."

"Shooting this man won't change a damn thing."

Cale wasn't convinced. He understood Crenshaw would have killed Maggie eventually. His intentions made him guilty, at least in Cale's mind. Crenshaw smiled, and the moisture on his eyeglasses caused his vision to appear unfocused. Cale remained fixed on his target. He called back to McBride: "You saw the headless girl's autopsy photos, Cap. You know what he's capable of."

"That's an ugly lie!" Crenshaw spat on the ground near the For Sale sign. "I didn't kill anyone!"

"He's not armed, Cale." McBride's tone remained stern.

More officers converged on the scene, easing cautiously in from different angles with their weapons drawn. Crenshaw once again shook the plastic bottle at Cale, taunting him, his sneering smile even more sinister.

"The bottle's filled with acid, Cap. He was going to use it on Maggie."

Crenshaw blanched. "What are you talking—"

"Drop the acid!" Cale's sharp voice froze McBride and the officers. Then Cale lowered his Glock an inch and discharged a single gunshot. The bullet ripped through Crenshaw's right thigh, spinning and dropping him to the ground.

The kidnapper screamed with his face twisted in pain. He pleaded to the nearby witnesses: "He shot me! The prick shot me!"

"Next one's through your forehead," Cale growled.

"Stand down!" McBride shouted, advancing toward Cale. "I mean it, Cale! This can only end bad."

"Badly," Cale corrected and flipped his weapon onto the damp lawn.

CHAPTER 75

A man fleeing Satan's minions could not have entered the house and tromped down the basement stairs faster than Cale. The officers already inside employed their flashlights to illuminate the bleakness. Cale spotted Slink propped against the rough sidewall near the bottom of the chipped steps. Bits of stone and wood lay scattered about the floor like strewn confetti.

Slink cradled his injured shoulder and said, "Always late to the party." He shot Cale a lopsided smile. "Don't worry. She's okay."

"Over here, Lieutenant!" one of the officers called. He was stooped twenty feet away, near a water heater. Cale spotted a dark-stained hunting knife on the concrete floor and recalled the crimson blossom on Crenshaw's chest.

The officer on his knees beside Maggie said, "Vitals are normal, Lieutenant. Rescue should be here any minute."

Cale dropped low and touched Maggie's face. The officers had bundled her in a dark, woolen coat, and she appeared peaceful in her repose. Then, despite the officer's protest, Cale scooped Maggie in his arms and carried her slumbering body across the debris, scattered glass bits, and up the wooden stairway.

A blocky rescue vehicle had whooped into the driveway and parked with its engine running. At least twenty cops milled around on the front yards of both houses. More forensic techs, it seemed, were arriving by the minute.

A pair of EMTs now rushed with a rolling gurney toward the front steps as Cale descended with Maggie in his arms.

"We'll take it from here, sir," one attendant offered. "Let's get her aboard."

Cale helped them lower the patient onto the wheeled cot. As they did, Maggie's eyes blinked open, and she stared up at him with a frightened look.

"I'll follow you to the hospital," he said.

"You can't, Cale." Her eyes were wide and desperate. "At the house—he's hurt!"

When Cale frowned, puzzled, she added, "Hank! He kicked him hard against the bedroom wall!"

EPILOGUE

The port of Chicago. Sunshine shimmered off the water as a seal-gray freighter slipped past the final bridge, setting out for the deeper depths of Lake Michigan. The cargo ship *Kwensana* was headed across the Great Lakes, then up the St. Lawrence Seaway, where she would emerge into the vast Atlantic.

Destination: Monrovia, Liberia.

The bulky, pock-faced African named Kinsella wore a dark suit with no tie. He stood on the sidewalk of the busy Michigan Avenue bridge. His sleeves were rolled elbow-high, his black sunglasses almost opaque. He frowned unpleasantly with his phone at his ear, watching the freighter shrink in the distance.

Five thousand miles away, Colonel Tazeki Mabutu's voice was flat. "Nothing at all?"

"No females. Cars are still sitting there. And no word from him." Kinsella's tone was void of emotion. "You want me to check into it?"

Mabutu mulled over the question, calibrating the odds like a baccarat player. Ensconced in his study, he stared at the glum-faced image of Pazuzu on his desk, then across the room at the shrunken female head adorning the fireplace mantle.

"That won't be necessary," he said at last. "All good things must come to an end."

Kinsella pocketed his mobile on the sidewalk and strode north toward the towering high-rises of the city's famous skyline. Within moments, he was swallowed by the crowd. He did not glance back at the freighter, the size of a child's toy now, as it slid through the cobalt blue waters of the lake.

The May afternoon sun was warm enough for shorts and to redden flesh turned pasty by the Midwest winter.

Cale sat on a comfy lounge chair on the deck outside his house. He had one Topsider propped on a low stool. He wore a cargo shirt and baggy board shorts, with a bottle of PBR in one hand, which completed the ensemble.

Slink relaxed on a nearby chair around the wooden spool table, garbed similarly. Off-duty cops weren't known for their range of fashion styles. Slink's left arm was free of its sling.

"I can get back to two-fisted drinking now," Slink bragged, raising his beer bottle. He took a generous swig.

Anton Staszak rounded out their threesome, sitting back in navy-colored shorts with his meaty legs extended. "A true Renaissance Man, aren't you?" Staszak pushed the sunglasses up his broad nose.

"You'd be one, too, if you could spell it."

Staszak accepted the challenge and spelled the word in one try before flashing it at them on his phone. It created hoots and other spelling challenges amid the throaty laughs and opening of fresh beer bottles.

At the lawn's edge near the tall trees, Maggie knelt at the budding flower beds thirty feet away. She wore shorts, a T-shirt, tennies, sunglasses, and protective gardening gloves. She was digging in the moist brown soil, and glancing back, she hand-shaded her eyes. "You guys behaving up there?"

"Always," Cale called back.

"It's Saturday." Slink's voice rose above the music escaping from inside the house. "You're supposed to be relaxing."

"This is relaxing."

"Great. How about changing the oil in my car when you're done?"

She saluted him with her middle finger, and they laughed.

Maggie, Cale decided, seemed to have recovered from her encounter with pure evil. The shock of her narrow escape had worn off. She accepted how close she—*they all*—had come to disastrous fates at the hands of a maniac. Tobias Crenshaw had nearly destroyed their lives.

A short while later, Maggie climbed the deck's steps. She arched an eyebrow at Staszak. "The gals?"

"On their way. Grabbing more steaks and a couple of those fancy boxes of wine."

Maggie gathered up a handful of empty bottles from the table's center and, giving them all a wink, vanished inside the house. When she was out of earshot, Staszak asked Cale, "She doing all right?"

"Tough broad." Cale nodded. "I mean that in a good way."

"To the team!" Slink offered. They clinked bottles together in closure. They could sit back now and enjoy a pleasant and relaxing afternoon.

Moments later, Hank emerged through the cracked screen door and hopped onto Cale's lap. Purring, he appeared ready to settle in, and his green eyes stared off at the high trees and chirping birds, seeing things only cats could detect.

With Staszak and Slink debating the latest football draft picks, Cale watched a cardinal swoop overhead, returning to its nest in a nearby elm. He scratched Hank's neck, feeling the plump feline's tail swish as they watched the bird zip away from its nest again.

He decided it was going to be a pleasant summer after all.

ACKNOWLEDGMENTS

Thanks to Dawn Mancheski, who, in a true motherly fashion, reminded me to finish any project I started. Special thanks to Kevin Harbick, Bob Van Drisse, Glen Berhow, Scott Browne, and John Nick, who rendered valuable insight into the foibles of being human. Thanks to Michael Drage, who shared his thoughts on the inner workings of the business mind. To Det. Lieutenant Paul Splawski (retired) of the Green Bay PD for his professional expertise in undercover work. To John Helfers, Grant Cousineau, and the rest of the local Green Bay writer's group: Keep up the excellent work. To Randy Rose, Gary Lambert (RIP), Tom Ebli, Dale Berg, and the other members of our The Corporation East High Athletic's (Alcohol) Group—a "Think Tank" for creative Life Solutions. To Patrick Olejniczak and Jamie Dooley, to whom the events presented here could have easily happened. And lastly, to Ashley Emma and Fearless Publishing, and to the countless friends and professionals who helped me navigate the turbulent waters of book re-covering and republishing, despite my (always reluctant) remarketing endeavors. You all remain in my scattered but fervent prayers.

ABOUT THE AUTHOR

Janson Mancheski is an award-winning author of six novels. The Chemist Series (*The Chemist (2010), Trail of Evil (2011), Mask of Bone (2011)*, and *Drowning a Ghost* (2021), all featuring Detective Cale Van Waring. They are set in Green Bay and other Wisconsin cities. *The Chemist* captured first place for fiction in the Sharp Writ Book Awards in 2010. Janson's screenplay version of this book (since delayed by Covid) is currently being reviewed for potentially both movie and television series options.

Janson has also authored several short stories and received awards for multiple screenplays. The movie script version of Janson's fourth novel, *Shoot For the Stars (2016)* (a historic Green Bay Packers "What If" novel), was a finalist for the 2012 *Writers Digest Creative Fiction Awards*. His autobiographical novel, *The Scrub* (a memoir featuring the ghost of Curly Lambeau), was published in December 2017.

A University of Wisconsin–Green Bay graduate and practicing optometrist (Illinois College of Optometry– Chicago, IL) from 1985 – 2005, Janson worked as the team eye doctor for the UW–Green Bay men's and women's basketball teams. He also functioned as the team eye doctor for the Green Bay Packers from 1990–to-2002.

Janson is an ardent football and Packers enthusiast, a UW-Green Bay Fighting Phoenix, and Wisconsin Badgers fan. Multiple new novels remain works in progress.

For further information on Janson's books and activities:

SEE **www.Jansonmancheski.com** (Featuring *The Chemist* movie trailer, starring Steve Golla.)

Facebook @ **Janson Mancheski author**

Want more of the Chemist Series?
Sneak Peek of Book 2: Trail of Evil

PROLOGUE

Inside a mountain cavern on a rainy African night, the drumbeat slows. The crowd of worshippers shuffles in place, swaying, a devoted maelstrom gathered in the vast central chamber.

Near the granite altar, a witch doctor—a *botono*—raises a fiery torch. Garbed in a dark robe, he touches the brand to the fire pit and sparks roar in a sizzling display. The drums increase their intensity. The participants—first twenty, then forty—dance to the sound of the shakers, whirling in place, shimmying, enraptured by the guttural throb of the skin drums.

Another burst of flame erupts from the pit. Across the room, a *mambo* eases her way to a fern-woven basket. She opens the lid and withdraws a fat, green serpent. The snake coils around her arms, its shimmery tongue flicking in the firelight. Near the center pole, the mambo begins to sway as if entranced. The celebrants form a circle around her, stepping in and out, clapping to the drumbeat.

The witch doctor raises his left hand in the air at the altar. He is summoning a *petro loa*, a dark god he hopes will grace the ceremony with its presence. The pulse of the drums continues to echo off the craggy rocks.

The village chief steps forward, leading a goat by a tether. A pair of shirtless men assist, maneuvering the animal so its neck drapes over a wooden basin. The goat offers a frightened bleat, black eyes wide with fear—and the botono steps toward the creature. After the flash of a long, gleaming knife...warm blood gushing...the animal's twitching legs...sprays of thick crimson spurting and splashing into the basin.

When drained, the men hoist the carcass above their shoulders and are swallowed by the frenzied crowd. The drumbeat lowers to a dull throb.

A silent parade of nubile young girls appears from an antechamber off the main room. Each is clad in a white tunic. Twelve in number, they march forward, lining themselves near one shadowy gray wall of the cavern. They stand barefoot, still, expressionless, and each has a "sponsor" positioned behind them.

At the altar, the botono turns to the crowd. He holds a carved wooden bowl filled with bits of "seasoned" bread. The chief and villagers watch, eyes rapt.

At the basin, with the snake adorning her, the mambo fills a chalice with the steaming blood of the goat. She joins the witch doctor, and together they face the line of virgins. The botono dips a piece of bread into the mambo's chalice. He feeds it to the first girl, who opens her mouth to receive it. He utters no holy phrase, for wherever Christ might be, He is nowhere near this mountain cavern on such a bleary, rain-sodden night.

The witch doctor progresses down the honor line, administering his "offering." Before he reaches the fifth young virgin, the first one sways and collapses into the arms of her sponsor. She is carried off to a shadowed chamber, out of sight. By the time the unholy pair reaches the end of the line, the first half-dozen girls have collapsed.

When the final virgin is eased from the cavern, the *tanbu* drums resume their more intense pounding, with the shakers rattling, all accompanied by the frenetic, jerky, wanton dancing of the near-naked celebrants. A possessed teenage girl suddenly lurches about, zombie-like. An invisible spirit has taken hold and is riding her.

Guzzling from a rum bottle, the contents seeping down her smeary cheeks, the mambo cackles. A frenzied pack of worshippers rushes to the dead goat—tearing the animal's limbs apart and waving steamy entrails in the air.

By this time, the witch doctor has vanished. The drums and twirling revelry of the voodoo celebration will continue long into the night until a fresh dawn arrives to scrub the mountainside with pure purple light.

If you enjoyed this sample, please search for Trail of Evil on online bookstores.

Printed in the USA
CPSIA information can be obtained
at www.ICGtesting.com
CBHW032006291123
2217CB00004B/22